LIGHTNING STRIKES TWICE

PUBLISHED BY:

Rayne  Publishing

Acknowledgements:

I want to say thank you to my wife for supporting me in this adventure of publishing my first book. Forty-four years of putting up with my ever-changing hobbies, and finally I think I have found one we can both live with. I also want to say a special thank you to Rose for keeping me straight about Hart County and the editing she completed in this endeavor. I hope I inspire her as she has inspired me. She has been the best Sis a man can have that is not related, but the love and encouragement will forever be cherished.

First Edition, July 2024. Cover design by Larry Burks This is a work of fiction.

Names, characters, places, and incidents either are products of the author's imagination or are used fictitiously. Any resemblance to actual persons, living or dead, events, or locales is entirely coincidental.

Table of Contents

Chapter 1

The air was stale, suffused with the scent of cigarette smoke and the undercurrent of tension that clung to the room like a second skin. Simon Wilson's heartbeat was steady—a disciplined drum in the chaos—as he leaned against the wall of the dimly lit backroom, his keen blue eyes scanning the scene from beneath a heavy brow. In his nondescript suit, he could have been any other mid-level operative in the clandestine gathering, but his mind was sharp, coiled, ready to spring into action at the slightest provocation.

"Are we certain the route will be unchanged?" a raspy voice cut through the murmurs.

"Affirmative." The speaker's tone was laced with confidence that didn't quite reach his fidgeting hands. "Dealey Plaza, during the motorcade."

Simon's muscles tensed, his focus narrowing. Every word spoken was a live wire, every gesture a potential code. He mentally cataloged the details, the plans unfolding before him dark and treacherous like the waters of an uncharted river. President Kennedy's name hung over them, a specter summoning images of Dallas streets lined with unsuspecting crowds.

"Security detail?" Simon's voice was measured, feigning casual interest. It was a dangerous dance, each step measured, each word weighed for its potential to betray his true allegiance to the CIA.

"Minimal," came the reply, followed by a smattering of cold laughter. "Our man on the inside will see to it."

The conspirators nodded in agreement, their faces a grotesque tapestry of shadows and malice. Simon felt the killer instinct within him stir, a familiar companion in his solitary existence. He resisted the urge to intervene, to break cover and end this now. Patience, he reminded himself.

As the meeting continued, Simon's mind raced, sifting through the information. His role as a loner, a ghost within the agency, had prepared him for this—his life a series of moments just like this, balancing on the knife-edge of peril. No backup, no cavalry—just his wits and the burning need to prevent a national tragedy.

"Timing is crucial," someone emphasized, drawing Simon back to the present.

"Indeed." The word left his lips like the whisper of a snake in the grass. He knew his next steps were critical, the weight of history pressing down upon him with an urgency that left no room for error.

In the darkness of the room, among the plotters of doom, Simon Wilson, the CIA spy, stood alone—but resolute. The fate of a president, and a country, rested unknowingly in his capable hands.

The urgency thrummed in Simon Wilson's veins like a siren call as he strode away from the clandestine gathering, his mind replaying every word of the assassination plot that had just unfolded before him. The Dallas skyline receded into the background as he headed towards Love Field Airport, the gravity of his mission anchoring every step.

Once aboard the aircraft bound for Hart County, Kentucky, by way of Nashville, Tennessee, Simon melded into the anonymity of his window seat. He was a shadow among the unsuspecting passengers, his muscular build folded into the confinements of the cabin. His blue eyes, usually calm pools reflecting an unwavering spirit, now flickered with a restless energy. Time was slipping through his fingers, and each tick of the clock echoed the beating of his heart—rapid and unyielding.

As the plane ascended, piercing the Texas sky, Simon delved into the chaos of hastily scribbled notes scattered before him. Scraps of paper and napkins bore the scrawls of a man desperate to document the unthinkable. With each piece he examined, Simon's trained memory pieced together the puzzle, etching details onto a legal pad retrieved from his satchel—a trove of evidence that could alter the course of history.

"Is everything alright?" The flight attendant's voice cut through his concentration, her gaze questioning the intensity etched onto his features.

"Fine," Simon replied curtly, not lifting his gaze from the papers. "Just work."

"Can I get you anything?" she persisted, sensing the palpable tension emanating from this passenger.

"Just some quiet," he said, softer this time, realizing his terse exterior belied the controlled chaos within.

"Of course." She nodded and moved along the aisle, leaving Simon to the solitude he preferred, the loner back in his element.

With each scrap of paper cataloged and then tucked away into the satchel for safekeeping, the magnitude of his solitary duty solidified. There was no room for error. No second chances. As the plane cut through the clouds, racing against

the very fabric of time, Simon knew that the fate of a man—
and indeed a nation—rested upon his shoulders.

The plane descended towards Nashville, its wheels kissing
the tarmac with a sense of finality. Simon gathered his notes,
his mind already strategizing the next move. This was more
than espionage; it was a race against destiny, one that he did
not intend to lose.

The rhythmic clack of the Underwood typewriter keys
filled the small cabin, punctuated only by the occasional shuffle
of paper as Simon Wilson transposed the scribbled notes from
his haphazard collection onto a clean white sheet. It was late,
the kind of late where the night seems to press close against
the windows, and time itself feels heavy, laden with secrets.

Simon's fingers flew over the keys, each stroke a testament
to his relentless focus. He had been at this for hours, the lamp
on the desk casting a pool of light that fought back the
surrounding darkness. His mind was a steel trap, capturing
every detail, every whispered conspiracy from the meeting in
Dallas. But even steel can become weary, and he felt the
stiffness seeping into his muscles, an unwelcome distraction
from the urgency of his task.

He paused, flexing his fingers before standing abruptly, the chair scraping against the wooden floor. The cabin groaned softly around him, the wood settling as if it too felt the weight of the secrets it harbored. Simon arched his back, stretching to relieve the tension, then decided a short walk outside might clear his head.

As he stepped off the porch, the first rumble of thunder rolled across the sky, distant but closing in fast. Dark clouds gathered above the Nolin River, swelling with the promise of a storm. The air was charged with electricity, a palpable energy that seemed to resonate with the intensity of Simon's mission. He watched as lightning snaked through the sky, illuminating the river's surface in brief, stark flashes.

The river's proximity to his land, bordered by the Green River, offered some solace in its constancy. Tonight, though, the rivers seemed to be murmuring secrets of their own, the water whispering against the banks under the cover of impending rain.

Another flash of lightning lit up the landscape, closer now, the thunder following almost immediately, a deep growl that vibrated through the ground beneath his feet. Simon gazed out toward the horizon, his blue eyes reflecting the intermittent flashes of light. Wind began to whip around him, carrying the scent of rain and earth, stirring the trees into a frenzied dance.

For a moment, his CIA training receded, replaced by the primal force of nature asserting its power. Yet, even as the storm approached, Simon's mind whirred with thoughts of the conspiracy, the assassin's plot, and the undeniable knowledge that he alone stood between chaos and order.

As the first heavy drops of rain began to fall, pelting the wooden planks of the porch, Simon turned back to the cabin. The storm was here, its arrival an echo to the tumultuous thoughts swirling within him. He would weather this tempest, both the one raging outside and the other, far more dangerous storm brewing within the hearts of men who sought to bend history to their will.

With a last glance at the darkening sky, Simon retreated to the sanctuary of his cabin, where the typewriter awaited. There was work to be done, and not even the fury of the heavens could halt the progress of a man on a mission.

Lightning split the sky, a jagged line of pure, ferocious energy that connected heaven and earth in a brief but cataclysmic moment. Simon's gaze darted up, an inexplicable chill running down his spine just as the world around him erupted in blinding white light. The force of the strike sent him hurtling through the air, his body limp as a ragdoll, before he crashed onto the damp ground.

The impact was monumental, a hammer blow delivered by the gods themselves, and it reverberated through every fiber of his being. Simon's consciousness flickered out like a snuffed candle, the storm continuing its relentless barrage overhead, indifferent to the man it had struck down.

Time passed—an hour or perhaps an eternity—before Simon's mind clawed its way back from the dark abyss. His eyelids fluttered open, heavy as lead, and he drew a sharp, ragged breath. Pain throbbed through his head, an insistent drumbeat that matched the pounding of his heart. Disoriented, he tried to move, to rise, but his limbs betrayed him, heavy and uncooperative.

As his senses gradually returned, Simon became aware of his surroundings. No longer outside, he found himself lying on the cold, uneven floor of the Hidden River Cave, the entrance from his land leading into this tributary of the vast cave system. The air was thick with the musty odor of damp earth and stagnant water, a scent that filled his nostrils and seemed to seep into his very pores.

"Where...?" The word was little more than a hoarse whisper, his voice echoing off the cavern walls and blending with the distant sound of flowing water. Confusion gripped him, yet beneath it lay a sense of profound wrongness, a certainty that the world he knew had shifted on its axis while he lay unconscious.

Simon struggled to sit up, his muscles protesting after the shock they had endured. He took stock of his surroundings, the dim light filtering in from the cave's entrance casting eerie shadows across the rock formations. He needed to piece together what had happened, to understand why he had been transported from the storm's fury to the bowels of the earth.

But for now, all he could do was draw breath after shuddering breath, each one bringing him closer to the realization that time had betrayed him, that the moment of lightning's touch had altered far more than he could have imagined.

Simon paced the uneven floor of the cave, his boots scraping against the limestone. His heart pounded a relentless rhythm that echoed the throbbing in his head. He couldn't shake the feeling that something was fundamentally amiss. The storm had been violent, but its fury paled in comparison to the turmoil within him.

He stopped, staring at his reflection in a small pool of water. The face that stared back was unmistakably his own, yet it bore no signs of aging, no new lines etched by time or worry. It was as if the lightning had seared away the years, leaving him untouched and unchanged. A surge of disorientation washed over him, and he steadied himself against the slick cave wall, grappling with the impossibility of it all.

"Keep moving, Wilson," he muttered to himself, using the voice that had commanded operations and orchestrated escapes. "Answers aren't going to find themselves."

Emerging from the cave, Simon strode toward his cabin, the familiarity of the path offering scant comfort. As he pushed open the door, a cloud of dust motes danced in the shafts of sunlight piercing the gloom. The room was exactly as he had left it, save for the layers of dust that cloaked every surface like a shroud. His military precision, the meticulously arranged tools, and maps, preserved in time, now lay under a fine powder that spoke of long years passed.

"Damn," he whispered, running a finger through the dust on the mantelpiece, his mind racing with questions he could not yet answer.

Compelled to seek out clues to this bizarre reality, Simon made his way into the town of Horse Cave. The walk there felt surreal, his feet treading familiar ground while his senses absorbed the unfamiliar. The air buzzed with sounds he couldn't place, and the skyline was altered, punctuated by structures that had no business in his memory of the place.

People bustled past in strange attire, fabrics, and cuts foreign to his trained eye. They carried devices that glinted under the sun, their fingers dancing across screens with casual ease.

On a bench near the town store, a newspaper lay abandoned, its date glaring up at him like a beacon: years beyond what should have been. **March 26, 2023**. With a shaking hand, Simon picked it up, the paper's rustle sounding unnaturally loud. As he scanned the local stories, a photograph caught his eye—a political figure he recognized, older, lined with age he himself had somehow escaped.

"Impossible," he breathed, the word lost amidst the hum of the unfamiliar world around him.

A knot tightened in his stomach as the truth pressed in on him. Time had not stopped; it was he who had stepped outside its march. The implications were staggering, the consequences unknowable. Yet here he stood, a man unstuck in time, holding a fragment of history that would lead him down a path fraught with uncertainty and peril.

Simon's breaths came in short, ragged gasps as he darted back into his cabin. The layers of dust became a mocking testament to the time that had slipped away from him. His eyes darted frantically across the room, searching for anything that could anchor him to reality, to explain the chasm between what was and what now is.

"Think, Simon, think," he muttered, throwing open drawers and rifling through cabinets. He needed evidence, a clue, something to tell him how the world had continued spinning while he remained frozen in a moment long past.

A knock at the door shattered his frenzied thoughts. Standing before him were two local law enforcement officers, their brows furrowed with curiosity and concern. They took in his outdated clothing and the wild look in his blue eyes.

"Sir, are you alright? We got reports of a man wandering around, looking confused," one officer said, his voice steady but edged with caution.

Simon steadied himself against the doorframe, trying to compose his scattered thoughts. "I... I was walking around my cabin. There was a storm, lightning. I think I was struck." The words felt hollow, unbelievable even to his ears.

"Struck by lightning?" the second officer echoed, skepticism tinging his tone.

"Yes, and I woke up in Hidden River Cave. But that's not important right now." Simon's voice grew urgent. "President

Kennedy —" His throat tightened on the name, the weight of his mission crashing down on him once more. "Is he safe? Have they caught those who were planning to—"

The officers exchanged glances, their expressions turning somber. "Sir, President Kennedy was assassinated. Years ago," the first officer said gently as if revealing an old wound the whole nation shared.

"Dead?" Simon's heart pounded against his ribcage, the implications spiraling wildly while his mind fought what he knew to be true about the time he was out. "But... but the suspects, the conspirators—were they caught?"

"Most say it was just one man. Lee Harvey Oswald. It's all history now," the second officer replied, folding his arms across his chest.

"History..." Simon's voice trailed off, haunted by the echo of his failure.

"Maybe you should sit down, sir. You seem like you need a moment," the first officer suggested, guiding Simon back inside the cabin.

"Thank you, but I need information." Simon's focus returned with sharp clarity. "I have to go to the library." At the library, Simon sat before the microfiche reader, his fingers trembling as they threaded the film through the machine. The articles flickered into view, recounting that fateful day in stark black and white. Each headline was a hammer blow to his psyche, each image of mourning, each detail of the investigation, a litany of what could have been prevented.

He scanned through the pages, absorbing every word about the assassination, the arrest, and the aftermath. But there was no mention of the plot he knew, the names he had committed to memory. History had unfolded without the truth he held, and now it lay buried beneath decades of settled dust and faded memories.

Leaving the library, Simon's mind raced with the need to set things right, to unearth the reality he had witnessed. The urgency that had driven him years ago surged within him anew, a silent vow that he would not let this knowledge die in the obscurity of a cave or the haze of lost time.

Simon's boots crunched on the gravel path as he trudged back to the cabin, his mind still whirling from the images of the microfiche. The door creaked open with a familiar groan that now sounded foreign in his ears. He stood for a moment on the threshold, a silent intruder in his own life.

As he paced the room, his hand instinctively dipped into the pocket of his worn trousers. His fingers closed around a small, hard rectangle. Pulling it out, he examined the faded CIA identification card, the edges frayed, the face younger but unmistakably his own. A relic from a past mission that had never left him, even if the world had moved on without his story.

"Time to make a call," he muttered, the words hanging oddly in the silent cabin.

He again returned to town, found a phone, and dialed the number from memory. After several rings, a voice answered, "Central Intelligence Agency."

"Agent Wilson checking in. Badge number 5173-D," Simon said, his voice steady despite the decades it had been since he last uttered those words.

"Sir, that designation... Please hold."

Minutes stretched into eons until another voice came on the line, terse and authoritative. "Wilson? We've got no active agents by that name. Who is this?"

"Ask Harlan Cross," Simon insisted, naming his former handler.

"Cross retired years ago. What is this about?"

"Tell the director I have urgent information regarding the Kennedy assassination—information that was never disclosed. I need to be debriefed."

The line went silent before a careful response. " What is your address?" Stay there! Someone will be there shortly." The party on the other end of the line told Simon after he gave the address.

Hours later, Simon sat in a nondescript office at CIA headquarters, a sterile light washing over him. Medical personnel had poked and prodded, taken vials of blood, and scanned his brain, eyes filled with cautious disbelief after verifying his identity and hearing his story.

"Your vitals are...remarkable," one of the doctors had remarked before leaving him alone once more.

Finally, the door opened again, and the director entered— a woman with sharp features and sharper eyes. Clutched in one hand was his service record, filled with pages of reports and evaluations. She scanned it intently, firing questions at him with a mix of skepticism and intrigue.

"Mr. Wilson," she began, her tone measured, "the JFK case is cold, but you claim to have actionable intelligence? Start from the beginning."

"March '63, Dallas," Simon started, his voice a low thrum of conviction. "I was undercover. A meeting... They laid it all out. The who, the how, the when."

"Names," the director pressed, leaning forward.

"Seven men. All connected, all with the means and motive." Simon leaned in too, his gaze unflinching. "They spoke of a book depository, a parade route, a rifle..."

"Go on."

"Oswald wasn't alone; he was the fall guy. I documented everything. But then..." Simon paused, the lightning strike feeling like both yesterday and a lifetime ago.

"Then?" the director prompted.

"Lightning struck, literally. When I awoke, it was all history," he finished, the weight of lost time heavy in his voice.

The director's voice trembled as she spoke. "If what you're saying is true—" she hesitated, unable to finish her sentence. "We cannot simply take your claims at face value. They will need to be thoroughly verified and investigated."

"Of course," Simon agreed, his hands resting on his files of that day on the table, steady and sure. "But we don't have much time. Those men—if they're still alive—they're dangerous. And I remember every single one." He then slid the file under his hands to the director.

Simon stood in the center of his cabin, a pair of sleek, black jeans clinging to his legs and a crisp white shirt hugging his broad shoulders. The air was filled with the scent of lemon-scented polish and fresh paint, subtle yet pervasive changes that rooted him firmly in the present. He moved across the room, his muscular frame navigating effortlessly around the now-modern furnishings—a sharp contrast to the rustic decor he remembered.

The soft hum of electronics punctuated the silence that hung in the air, an ambient reminder of time's relentless march forward. Simon glanced at the flat-screen TV he had purchased and had connected to a satellite dish, mounted on the wall as he tucked in his shirt, pausing to watch as the newscaster's voice broke through the quietude.

Footage of the Kennedy assassination played on a loop, each frame a haunting reminder of history. The anchorwoman's perfectly coiffed hair and serious expression were projected onto the flat-screen TV, her image flickering slightly in the dimly lit room. On the screen, the faces of the conspirators now revealed as traitors, flickered briefly. Years of deceit and betrayal were being exposed, vindicating Simon's long hard work. He couldn't help but feel a surge of satisfaction as he watched the downfall of those who had been the target of his work, all while keeping a stoic mask in place like a devoted sentinel.

The newscast shifted to other stories, but Simon's thoughts lingered on the implications. His gaze drifted to the window, where the last light of day seeped through the panes, casting long shadows across the clean floor. He had cleaned the cabin himself, scrubbing away years of neglect, wiping away layers of dust, erasing the physical remnants of his absence.

As darkness crept in, he flicked off the television and stepped outside, the cool night air brushing against his skin. The moon hung low over the horizon, bathing Hart County in a ghostly glow. The serenity of the countryside belied the undercurrents of danger that now threaded through the community.

Simon tilted his head, listening to nature. There was a rumor, whispers of something malevolent taking root in the fertile Kentucky soil. A dangerous gang, a cartel they called it, had slithered its way into Hart County, embedding itself within the very fibers of this otherwise peaceful place.

He clenched his jaw, feeling the familiar itch of adrenaline, the pull of intrigue, and the tacit promise of conflict. This land was his home, and the thought of it being poisoned by such ruthless ambition stoked a fire within him. Simon Wilson, the loner, the killer, the spy, might have been lost to time, but he was not forgotten—not by history, and certainly would not be by those who would threaten the peace of Hart County.

Silhouetted against the nocturnal backdrop, Simon contemplated the looming storm. Once again, he would be called upon to protect and to serve, to use the skills that had defined his past life for the sake of his future.

And as the distant rumble of trouble echoed through the calm, Simon turned back toward the warmth of his cabin, ready to face whatever challenges lay ahead.

Chapter 2

Simon Wilson leaned back in the creaking rocking chair, the aged wood of the porch groaning under the shift of his weight. His gaze was fixed on the horizon where the sun hung low, flirting with the edges of Hart County's rolling hills. Beside him, Sheriff Mark Thompson rested a boot on the railing, the two men wrapped in an easy silence that spoke of shared history and unspoken understandings.

"Remember when they finished up the sewer plant back in '63? This place sure has come a long way."

"Sure has. Cleaned up nicely. Tourists can't seem to get enough of our little slice of heaven these days."

"Never would've thought it," Simon mused, his blue eyes reflecting a time when the county was more rough-and-tumble than picturesque. It seemed a lifetime ago, another world entirely from the one he'd navigated as a CIA spy—a career that had demanded everything and given back in scars and shadows.

Mark let out a heavy sigh, shifting his gaze to meet Simon's. "Speaking of change... What's life gonna be like for you now, Simon? After your recovery?"

"Retirement." The word felt foreign on Simon's tongue, but it was his reality now. The government had been generous—or perhaps just eager to close the book on his service—with a pension and back pay. "Can't say it suits me, but I'm no longer suited for duty, apparently." He shrugged a half-hearted attempt to brush off the finality of it all.

"Retirement." The sheriff echoed; his voice tinged with something that might have been envy if it weren't for the undercurrent of concern. "Never pictured you settling down, old friend."

"Neither did I," Simon confessed. His muscular frame—a build earned through years of necessity rather than vanity—shifted as he pushed himself up to stand. "But I suppose everyone's got to hang up their hat sometime."

"Guess so." Mark's piercing blue eyes, shadowed by the weight of his own battles, lingered on Simon a moment longer. "Just promise me you'll take it easy, yeah? You've earned a bit of peace."

"Peace," Simon repeated, a ghost of a smirk on his lips as he considered the quiet life ahead. "I'll give it my best shot."

The wooden planks of the porch creaked as Simon shifted, breaking the silence that had settled between them. "Sheriff, I've been hearing some unsettling rumors since I got back. Talk about a gang, or cartel now, moving into Hart County?"

Sheriff Thompson's gaze hardened, the lines in his face deepening. He looked out over the expanse of green that stretched beyond Simon's property line. "Yeah, those aren't just rumors. People are going missing, Simon. Good folks. And drugs... They're flooding the streets faster than we can keep up."

"Cartel business, here?" Simon's brows knitted together. The idea seemed incongruous with the rolling hills and quiet life he'd envisioned for his retirement.

"Seems so," the sheriff replied. "It's like they see our little corner as ripe for the picking. I'm doing what I can, but..." His voice trailed off, leaving an unsaid plea hanging in the air.

"Understood," Simon said, though his mind was already racing with strategies and countermeasures from a past life he thought he'd left behind.

The clang of plates and chatter surrounded Simon as he sat at a window table, his favorite in Horse Cave's local eatery, Farmwald's. A steaming mug of coffee warmed his hands, and the scent of freshly baked bread filled the air, mingling with the aroma of fresh-brewed java. Across from him sat Loran Smith, her slight frame making her look even younger against the vinyl seat.

Simon and Loran discussed computers, with Simon expressing interest in learning about them. Loran agreed to teach him, and they made plans to meet at the library for a lesson after Simon purchased a computer system she recommended.

Simon strode into the library, the Best Buy bag in his hand telegraphing a mix of intent and uncertainty. Loran was already there, her slight figure hunched over a table near the back, her indigo-tinged complexion blending with the rows upon rows of books that lined the walls. She looked up as Simon approached, a small smile creasing her face. The tint of her skin, though uncommon to most folks, was familiar to people in Kentucky who knew of the Blue People, though they were rarely seen nowadays. Simon found her smart, and her tint was just part of who she was.

"Got yourself geared up, I see," she drawled, eyeing the bag.

"Sure did," Simon replied, setting the bag down and unloading his new arsenal: a sleek Microsoft Surface laptop with all the trimmings. "Hope this is what I needed."

Loran moved closer; her curiosity piqued. "You did well, Mr. Wilson. Let's get you set up." Her fingers danced across the keyboard as she flipped open the device, initiating its first boot with practiced ease.

"First things first, we need to get you on the internet. Here's where you'll be able to learn just about anything."

"Even about cartels?" Simon asked, leaning forward. His voice was low, almost hesitant.

"Especially about them." Loran opened a browser and typed 'cartel' into the search bar. The screen filled with articles, news reports, and definitions. "This is Google. It's going to be your best friend for finding things out."

She showed him how to navigate through the results, pointing out reliable sources and warning against the less credible ones. "Now let me show you something called Google Docs. It's where you can keep notes, write down your thoughts, whatever you need." She demonstrated, creating a blank document and sharing it with Simon's newly created email account.

"Alright, let's say I wanted to make a list or keep track of these cartels," Simon said, attempting to replicate her actions with a concentration that belied his former profession.

"Then we use Google Sheets." Loran opened another tab and started a spreadsheet. "Like this. Each cartel can have its own sheet. You can note down names, activities, locations... whatever info you dig up."

Simon nodded, absorbing each click and keystroke. He repeated the process himself, slowly gaining confidence. "And if I wanted to do a deep dive?"

"Same thing, just more detailed. Say you pick a name— Juan Ortiz, for example. You'd research him, find connections, build a profile."

"Sounds like building a case file," Simon mused, his past life briefly casting a shadow over his features.

"Exactly. Only difference is, you're using the web instead of field intel."

"Field intel..." Simon echoed, a wistful grin tugging at the corner of his mouth. "Well, I've traded that for this now." He gestured at the laptop, a tangible symbol of his new battleground.

"Welcome to the digital age, Mr. Wilson. Where the wars are silent but just as deadly."

Simon leaned back, the reality of his quest settling in. He watched Loran close the laptop; her lesson was complete. "Thanks, Loran. Guess it's time I started my homework."

"Anytime. Just remember, the internet's vast. But so is your determination."

As she walked away, Simon's gaze lingered on the screen's dark reflection. In it, he saw not just his own determined eyes, but the faint outline of a path leading into an uncertain future.

Simon sat at his cabin's kitchen table, the sleek surface of his new laptop reflecting the perplexity in his blue eyes. He tapped a key, then another, frustration mounting with each fruitless stroke.

"Problem is," he began, looking up as Loran took the seat opposite him, "I can't seem to get past this darn home screen at home."

"Because you need internet," Loran said, her voice carrying that slow southern drawl that seemed to stretch time itself. She reached over, her fingers gliding across the trackpad as she navigated to the network settings with ease. "Here at the library, it's all connected. Your cabin? Not so much."

"Internet, huh?" Simon mused aloud. "How do I bring that out to my little slice of solitude?"

"Let's get you set up." Loran's slight frame leaned forward, her indigo fingers typing deftly as she guided him through the digital maze of service providers. Within an hour, Simon had arranged for a technician to come out and wire his rustic retreat into the modern age.

"By next week, you'll be searching away to your heart's content," Loran assured him with a smile.

"Appreciate it, Loran," Simon replied, the corners of his mouth lifting in a grateful grin. With a tap on her watch, Loran excused herself, leaving Simon to close his laptop, a gateway to the world that felt both alien and necessary.

As dusk settled around the cabin, Simon reclined on the porch with a dog-eared William Johnstone western cradled in his hands. The warm glow from the setting sun dipped beneath the treeline, painting the sky with strokes of fiery orange and cool lavender.

A crunching noise from the gravel driveway pulled Simon's attention away from the trials of cowboys and outlaws. A silver pickup truck rolled to a stop, its engine cutting off with a soft purr. Out stepped Jack Thompson, a man whose presence seemed to command the space around him.

"Evening," Jack called out, his voice resonant as he ambled up to the porch. "Simon Wilson?"

"Depends who's asking," Simon said, his words casual but his posture subtly tensing, a remnant of instincts honed from years in the field.

"Name's Jack Thompson. Heard you might be needing some help with... a certain problem."

Simon marked his page and set the novel aside, studying Jack's face for any hint of subtext. "Heard that, have you?"

"Word gets around. Especially when the word involves cartels and missing folks."

"Seems like you're well informed," Simon observed, standing now, matching Jack's height.

"Comes with the territory." A faint smirk betrayed Jack's otherwise stoic facade. "May I?"

Simon gestured to the wooden chair beside him, and Jack took it. The two men sat in companionable silence for a moment, their gazes lingering on the darkening horizon.

"Beautiful out here," Jack finally said, breaking the quiet. "Easy to forget there's a storm brewing."

"Storms are nature's way of clearing the air," Simon replied thoughtfully. "Sometimes, they're necessary."

Jack nodded, and the conversation that followed was unspoken but understood—an alliance forming in the tranquility of a Kentucky evening, two men united by a common cause, ready to weather the tempest ahead.

Simon leaned back in his chair, the creak of weathered wood beneath him a familiar comfort. The fading light cast long shadows across the porch, painting Jack's features with an amber hue. No crickets chirped yet; it was that in-between time, not quite day, not quite night.

"Twenty years in the Air Force Security Forces," Jack began, his voice carrying a timbre of pride mixed with a hint of something else—perhaps nostalgia. "I've seen my share of action, but nothing quite like what we're up against now."

Simon nodded slowly. "CIA," he said simply as if those three letters encompassed the entirety of his life's story. He could still feel the weight of a concealed weapon at his side, phantom gunmetal pressing against his skin. "Trouble has a way of following me."

"Seems you and trouble are well acquainted. Greg Smith mentioned you're looking into some local cartel activity. Said his daughter's been helping you out."

Simon raised an eyebrow, the corners of his mouth twitching into a half-smile. "Loran's sharp knows her way around more than just computers. But I'm not about to drag her into anything dangerous."

"Good man. But about this cartel—rumor has it they're led by Juan Ortiz. Mean son of a bitch. Heard of him?"

"Ortiz," Simon repeated, rolling the name on his tongue like a bitter pill. Images flashed through his mind: reports, surveillance photos, the scar trailing down the man's face. "Yeah, I read about him. And he doesn't belong here, or anywhere in this country for that matter."

"Damn right." Jack's fist clenched momentarily. "I have some contacts that can help when needed. How about you Simon, still have any contacts in your old life?"

"I do, and planning's good," Simon agreed, his gaze drifting toward the darkening treeline. "But action's better. We need to be ready for when the storm hits, so planning will need to be done quickly."

"Agreed." Jack stood up; his silhouette framed by the twilight. "Just wanted to let you know, I'm in. Whatever you need, I've got your back."

"Appreciate it," Simon said, his voice steady despite the turmoil brewing within. The quiet of the evening belied the violence he knew was coming.

Jack leaned against the porch railing, the fading light casting long shadows that stretched across the wooden boards. "So, it's settled then. I'm with you on this. Consider me your second-in-command, or whatever military jargon suits the situation."

Simon nodded slowly, the weight of responsibility settling in his gut like a stone. He could feel the quiet determination emanating from Jack, a kindred spirit in the fight that lay ahead.

"Good to have you aboard," Simon replied. "And about those contacts..."

"The Mountain folks. They're not too fond of outsiders, especially ones stirring up trouble. But they respect me. And they'll listen when I say we need them."

"I'm sure Greg is part of that," Simon added, the corners of his mouth turning up slightly. "I'll make sure Loran stays out of the line of fire. She's a smart kid, got potential."

"Don't be fooled by his facade. Greg is a cunning predator, willing to do whatever it takes to protect his own." Jack reached for his phone, unlocking it before thrusting it at Simon. "Take my number. You'll need it when the time comes."

"Will do," Simon said as he saved the contact information. He watched Jack stride down the steps and head to his truck, the engine rumbling to life before disappearing down the road, leaving behind a cloud of dust and the scent of diesel in the cool evening air.

Simon settled back into his plush armchair, the western novel still cradled in his lap, its pages untouched since Jack's arrival. His fingers traced the embossed title, but his eyes were drawn to the river beyond, its rippling surface a canvas for the last glimmers of twilight. The sky was awash with hues of fiery oranges and soft purples, casting a warm glow over the landscape. He could hear the faint sound of rushing water and the gentle rustling of leaves as a breeze swept through the trees.

This was his favorite time of day when the world seemed to quiet down, and he could lose himself in the beauty of nature.

What had been a lifetime of secrets and shadows, a world where trust was a rare commodity, and every step could be your last. What might be ahead was uncertain—a battle on home turf, alliances with mountain folk, and a young girl with an indigo tint who reminded him of the strength found in these hills.

The night was quiet. Too quiet. Somewhere between the rustling leaves and the distant hoot of an owl, Simon felt the approaching storm in his bones. He closed the book with a soft thump and rose to his feet, eyes scanning the horizon.

"Tomorrow," he murmured to the empty air, "we start planning for war."

The night had settled over the Hawkins plantation, a sprawling estate that held memories as old as the river it overlooked. Inside the grand house, Lori Hawkins and her daughter Jennifer lay in the grip of sleep, their breaths steady in the stillness of 3 AM. But the tranquility was about to be shattered.

Without warning, shadows coalesced into figures at the edge of the treeline, creeping with predatory grace toward the home that had once been a fortress of solitude for the Hawkins family. The front door gave way with barely a sound, a testament to careful planning and even more careful execution. They moved with an eerie choreography, each step measured, each breath controlled.

Jennifer's room was first. The door eased open, a sliver of moonlight cutting across her peaceful face. One figure stepped forward, gloved hands reaching out. A small gasp escaped her lips—a startled awakening that turned into a sharp scream as she was pulled from the safety of her bed.

The scream pierced the silence of the house, jolting Lori awake. Instinct took over; years of living alone, of whispers of danger in hushed tones, had prepared her for this moment. Her hand found the cold metal of the gun in her bedside drawer as she sprang from her bed, her heart pounding against her ribs like a drum.

"Jennifer!" Her voice was raw with fear.

She entered the hallway, the gun leading her way. Moonlight filtered through the windows, casting long, twisting shadows that danced on the walls. Then she saw him, a dark silhouette framed by her bedroom doorway, one of them left behind—perhaps as a lookout, perhaps as a final threat.

"Get out!" she barked, her finger tightening on the trigger.

The figure froze, just for a second, but it was enough. The gunshot echoed through the house, a resounding declaration of a mother's defiance. The man crumpled without a sound, his purpose unfulfilled.

Outside, the night swallowed up the remaining assailants, their retreat hastened by the crack of gunfire. They vanished with Jennifer, leaving behind only the lingering scent of fear and the unanswered echoes of a mother's desperate cry.

Lori stood trembling, the smoking gun in her hand and resolve etched into her features. She had defended her home, but at what cost? Her daughter, her vibrant and outgoing Jennifer, was taken by shadows before dawn.

The night reclaimed its silence, but for Lori Hawkins, life would never be still again.

Chapter 3

Lori's hands trembled, the revolver slipping from her grasp and clattering onto the floorboards. Her breath hitched as she stumbled toward Jennifer's door, the echo of the gunshot still ringing in her ears. She pushed the door open, her heart hammering against her ribs. The room was a maelstrom of overturned furniture and scattered belongings, but it was the empty bed that clawed at her soul. "Jennifer!" she screamed, her voice tearing through the silence of the house like a physical force.

Panic wrapped its icy fingers around Lori's throat as she frantically searched the room for any sign of her daughter. Sheets were thrown aside, drawers yanked out, but there was nothing—no trace of the vibrant, outgoing girl who had been her world. Lori's knees felt weak, her mind reeling from the stark terror that gripped her. She couldn't lose Jennifer, not after everything they'd been through together.

"Think, Lori, think," she muttered to herself, trying to quell the rising chaos in her head. She needed help. Now. With shaking hands, she grabbed the landline phone from its cradle and dialed 911, the numbers a blur as tears streamed down her cheeks.

"Dispatch, what's your emergency?" The voice on the other end was calm, practiced, an anchor in the storm of Lori's despair.

"Someone's taken my daughter, Jennifer," Lori gasped out, choking back sobs. "I—I shot one of them, but she's gone!"

"Ma'am, stay calm. I need your address."

"3184 Green Mile Rd, just outside Munfordville. Please hurry!"

"Units are being dispatched immediately, ma'am. Stay on the line."

Lori could hear the dispatcher relaying information in the background, the urgency in their voice matching the pounding of her own heart. Within moments, she knew that Sheriff Mark Thompson would be roused from his sleep by the call of duty, once again facing the very danger that haunted his every step.

"Ma'am, can you tell me more about what happened? Are you injured?"

"No, no, I'm not hurt," Lori said, her gaze locked on the empty space where Jennifer's smile should have been. "But my baby girl is out there with those monsters."

"Help is on the way, ma'am. Sheriff Thompson has been notified and is en route. Try to stay calm and wait for law enforcement to arrive."

"Thank you," Lori whispered, the receiver slipping slightly as her grip faltered. She leaned against the wall for support, the coolness of the paint barely registering against her skin. All she could think of was Jennifer—her laugh, her strength, her unyielding spirit. She had to believe that somewhere out there, her daughter was fighting to come back to her.

"Please, just bring her home," Lori uttered into the phone, her plea hanging in the charged air of the room like a silent prayer.

The morning sun streamed through the windows of Farmwald's restaurant in Horse Cave, casting a warm glow on the worn vinyl. Simon Wilson sat alone at his usual spot, methodically working his way through an Amish Farmer's Breakfast of a biscuit and gravy, two slices of bacon, one sausage patty, two pancakes, a helping of hashbrowns, and scrambled eggs. His gaze occasionally flicked up to the door, a force of habit from years in the field. It was his third cup of coffee that had just been refilled by Laura when the bell above the entrance jingled, announcing a new arrival.

Jack Thompson stepped inside, scanning the room with eyes honed by decades in the Air Force Security Forces. Spotting Simon, he nodded in acknowledgment and ambled over with the confidence of a man comfortable in his own skin. Simon raised his hand slightly, motioning Jack to join him.

"Morning, Jack," Simon greeted, sliding his plate aside to make room.

"Simon," Jack replied with a nod as he slid into the booth across from him. He caught Laura's eye and held up two fingers. "Coffee and a Haystack please."

"Coming right up," she said, scribbling onto her notepad before bustling off.

A moment of silence settled between the two men, filled only by the clinking of cutlery and the low murmur of conversation from other patrons. Jack's gaze locked onto Simon's for a beat, his expression grave.

"Did you hear about the mess over at the Hawkins place?"

Simon put down his cup, the black liquid barely disturbed. "No, I haven't. What happened?"

"Jennifer's gone missing. Lori shot some scumbag last night who broke into their house. After she dealt with him, turns out Jennifer wasn't in her room."

Simon's blue eyes hardened, the muscles along his jaw tensing. A kidnap on his turf made it personal. He could feel the old instincts kicking in, the cold focus that had served him so well in his CIA days.

"Any leads on where she might be?"

"Nothing solid yet. sheriff's out there now, trying to piece it all together. But you know how these things go—time's not on our side."

Simon nodded; his breakfast forgotten. Jennifer Hawkins, bright and full of life, spirited away into the early hours of the morning. He knew Lori must be out of her mind with worry. And if the cartel was behind this, as he suspected, things could get a lot uglier before they got better.

"Keep me posted, Jack. If there's anything I can do—"

"You'll be the first to know," Jack assured him, just as the waitress returned with his order.

But Simon's appetite had vanished. All he could think about was the danger Jennifer was in and the race against time to bring her home.

The clatter of his fork against the plate echoed Simon's sudden loss of interest in the eggs and bacon that had seemed appealing just moments before. Jack's words hung heavy between them, a haze of shock and urgency settling over the diner's usual morning hum.

"Explain what all you know," Simon said, his voice steady but low, commanding the full attention of his impromptu breakfast companion.

Jack leaned forward, his broad shoulders hunching as he shared the details he had gleaned. "Well, it looks like after Lori shot that son of a bitch who broke into her house, she went straight to check on Jennifer, only to find her bed empty and the window open."

"Any signs of struggle?"

"The room looked tossed, nothin' taken, but there was this... piece of fabric caught on the window latch. sheriff thinks it might've come off the kidnapper's clothes during the abduction."

With furrowed brows, Simon's eyes lost focus as he imagined the early morning light exposing the horrifying news of the missing girl. He had known Jennifer as a bold and self-assured teenager. The mere idea of her being held against her will filled him with rage.

"Anything else?"

"Footprints outside, leading away from the house towards the woods," Jack divulged, eyes narrowing with concern. "They're looking for tire tracks or anything else that could point them in the right direction. But it's like she just vanished into thin air."

"Vanished..." Simon murmured, the word tasting bitter. His mind raced, considering every possibility, every connection that could lead to Jennifer's whereabouts. There wasn't much to go on, but it was something. And for a man with Simon's particular set of skills, sometimes something was all it took.

Simon finally said, pushing his untouched plate away. "Tell Mark if he needs an extra set of eyes, I'm here."

"Will do. We could use someone with your... expertise."

As Jack tucked into his meal, Simon's thoughts were elsewhere—on Lori, on Jennifer, and on the dark tendrils of fear that were no doubt wrapping around his neighbor's heart. He would offer that help, not just because it was the right thing to do, but because inaction was simply not in his nature.

Silence settled over the diner table, broken only by the clinking of silverware and the low hum of other patrons' conversations. Jack glanced up from his half-eaten omelet, catching Simon's gaze.

"Look, I know it's not really my place, but we can't just sit here twiddling our thumbs. Lori... she'll be riddled with worry, not knowing what's going on."

Simon nodded; his mind was already made up. "Agreed. Let's head over to her place after we're done here." He pushed aside the remnants of his breakfast, feeling the urgency build within him.

"Good. We'll take my truck," Jack said with a decisive nod, signaling for the check.

The drive to Lori's home was quiet and contemplative, the only sound being the gravel crunching beneath the tires of Jack's pickup as they wound through the tree-lined roads of rural Kentucky. The early morning mist still clung to the fields, and the sun played hide and seek behind the clouds, casting an eerie glow over the landscape.

As they pulled up to the Hawkins homestead, the sight of Lori sitting on the porch swing, her body racked with sobs, hit Simon like a punch to the gut. Sheriff Mark Thompson stood beside her, his hat in hand, exuding an aura of helplessness that seemed to darken the space around him.

"Stay strong, Lori. We're doing everything we can," Mark's voice was gentle but carried the unmistakable tremor of a man walking on shaky ground.

Lori's response was lost in the wind, her cries carving a hollow echo into the morning air. Her blond hair fell like a curtain around her face, hiding her blue eyes that Simon knew would be swimming with fear and grief.

Simon's throat tightened at the sight. He had seen despair before and had stared it down in the darkest corners of the world, but nothing quite compared to the raw pain of a mother fearing for her child. It was a silent vow to himself as much as to her— he'd move heaven and earth to bring Jennifer back.

Simon stepped out of Jack's truck, his boots crunching on the gravel driveway. The early morning light cast long shadows across the lawn, and for a moment, he hesitated, taking in the sight of Lori Hawkins, her figure small and defeated on the porch swing. Sheriff Mark Thompson straightened up as they approached, his gaze flickering between the two men.

"Jack," Mark said, his voice low and urgent. He motioned for Jack to come closer, pulling him aside for a private word. Simon watched them for a brief moment before turning his attention to Lori.

He walked over to her, his movements slow and deliberate, mindful of her fragile state. "Lori," Simon began, his blue eyes soft with concern as he reached out and gently took her hand in his. "Can you tell me what happened? It might help us find Jennifer."

Simon felt his heart drop as he saw the fear and anguish etched onto Lori's face. She spoke with a quavering voice, her Southern drawl thickened by tears. "I heard a noise last night, and I went to check it out. I saw someone standing in the hall, yelled at him to get out, he stopped then moved towards me and I shot him." A chill ran down Simon's spine as he realized that Lori had been the sole witness to Jennifer's abduction, and he couldn't imagine the weight of guilt she must be carrying.

"And Jennifer?" Simon prompted gently, crouching down to be at eye level with her.

"Her room was empty... bed and room was a mess. I called out, but there was no answer." Lori's voice cracked, and she pulled her hand away to cover her face. "Oh, Simon, why have they taken her from me? Why didn't they take me instead?" she sobbed.

"Hey, look at me," Simon said softly, reaching out again to tilt her chin up so their eyes met. "I promise you, Lori, I'm going to do everything in my power to bring your girl home safe."

Tears spilled over Lori's cheeks, and she leaned forward, her body trembling as she sought comfort. Simon wrapped his arms around her, pulling her in close. Her sobs were muffled against his shirt, each one sending a ripple of determination through him. He held her tight, the protector in him rising to the surface, vowing silently that he would not let this injustice stand.

"Thank you," she whispered, her voice barely audible. "I just want her back, Simon."

"You'll have her back," he assured her, his tone laced with conviction. "I won't rest until she's home."

As Lori clung to him, Simon felt the weight of responsibility settles firmly on his shoulders. He wasn't just a CIA agent now; he was a lifeline to a desperate mother clinging to hope. And he intended to see this through, no matter where the path might lead.

The weight of the morning's revelations hung heavily in the air as Simon and Jack left Lori's porch, stepping into the crisp Kentucky sunlight. They walked side by side in silence until the gravel driveway gave way to the smooth asphalt of the main road leading back to town.

"Can't let this thing with the cartel fester any longer. Mark told me the one Lori shot was undocumented but had ties to the Ortiz cartel for sure," Jack finally said, breaking the stillness between them. His voice was steady, but the set of his jaw betrayed his anger.

Simon pulled out his phone, thumbing through the contacts as he nodded. "Yeah, we need to cut it off at the head." He hit the call button and waited for the other line to pick up. "Loran, it's Simon. Meet us at my place in an hour please."

"Will do," came the reply, her voice slow and tinged with a deep mountain drawl that spoke of hard living and resilience.

Jack glanced over at Simon, both men now fueled by a grim determination to untangle the web spun by the Ortiz Cartel. They were warriors in their own right, bound by a shared mission to restore peace to their beleaguered community.

Pulling into the cabin's dirt lot, Simon noticed Loran's beat-up pickup parked under the shade of an old oak tree. The slight indigo tint to her complexion stood out against the lush green backdrop as she watched them approach from the porch.

"Got your computer?" Loran asked, her tone efficient despite the underlying shyness.

"Right here," Simon confirmed, handing over the laptop before settling into a worn rocking chair. They all sat down, forming a makeshift war council on the weathered wooden planks, the homely sound of the porch swing creaking a soft accompaniment to their serious undertakings.

"Let's start piecing this together," Simon suggested, leaning forward, elbows resting on his knees as he watched Loran boot up the computer.

"Alright, what we got on Ortiz?" Jack chimed in; his disciplined, military-honed mind ready to dissect the available intel.

"Ruthless, smart..." Loran began, her fingers dancing across the keys. "...spent time in U.S. and Mexican prisons, but always slips through the cracks like slick owl shit."

"Likes to think he's untouchable," Simon mused, his blue eyes narrowing in thought. "But everyone has a weak spot. We just need to find his."

"Been battling it out with the National Police down in Mexico, too. Got some serious firepower behind him," Jack added, his brow furrowed in concentration.

"Which means we're not just dealing with local thugs," Simon concluded, the stakes of their endeavor becoming increasingly clear. "It's a whole network we're looking at."

"Plus, he's got that scar," Jack pointed out, tapping his cheek in remembrance. "Knife fight?"

"Seems fitting for his type," Loran murmured, her search yielding bits and pieces of information that painted a grim portrait of their adversary.

"Let's keep digging," Simon encouraged, watching the screen as news articles, social media snippets, and various reports started to form a clearer image of Juan Ortiz and the dark empire he commanded.

"Cartel's like a hydra, though," Loran warned. "Cut off one head..."

"Two more will take its place," Simon finished the adage, but his tone held no defeat, only resolve. "Then we'll just have to be thorough, won't we?"

As the sun dipped lower in the sky, casting long shadows across the porch, the trio continued their work. Silence fell over them again, punctuated only by the occasional click of the keyboard and the murmured exchange of ideas. It was the kind of quiet that wasn't empty but filled with purpose—a shared commitment to see justice done.

Simon's fingers danced over the keys of his new phone, wishing he had one of those in his CIA days, as he dialed a number committed to memory. He leaned back against the porch railing, the wood creaking under his weight, his gaze fixed on the horizon where dusk painted the sky in strokes of orange and purple.

"Briggs," came the sharp answer after the third ring; Nathaniel Briggs' voice was always clipped, a no-nonsense tone that matched his reputation within the Agency.

"Briggs, it's Wilson. I know you have heard I have resurfaced. I hate to ask, but I need some help on a situation I have found myself in."

"Still can't keep yourself out of trouble, huh Wilson?"

"It doesn't seem I can," Simon said with a chuckle.

"What do you need, Wilson?"

"I need everything on Juan Ortiz," Simon said without preamble, the urgency knitted into his voice. "His cartel, their operations, and current whereabouts."

There was a beat of silence, the kind that spoke volumes between two men who had traversed the murkier paths of intelligence work. "That's a tall order, Simon. Ortiz isn't just a blip on our radar."

"I'm aware," Simon replied, his eyes narrowing as a cool breeze swept across the porch, sending a shiver down his spine. "But time isn't a luxury we have right now. Someone's life is hanging by a thread."

"Understood," Briggs conceded with a heaviness that suggested he grasped the gravity of the situation. "I'll see what I can do. Don't go dark on me."

"Wouldn't dream of it," Simon responded dryly before ending the call. He pocketed the phone and exhaled slowly, the tendrils of his breath barely visible in the chill evening air.

Three days crawled by at a snail's pace—a waiting game that gnawed at Simon's patience. When the shrill ring of the phone finally shattered the silence of the cabin, Simon sprang up from the old leather couch where he'd been attempting to decipher a potential pattern in Ortiz's movements.

"Wilson," he answered on the first ring, his tone bracing for news.

"Simon, it's Briggs." The voice on the other end was crackling with static, but the underlying urgency came through clearly. "Check your email. Everything unclassified has been sent. Expect more intel by courier tomorrow—stuff we can't risk on the wires."

"Got it," Simon replied, his heart rate ticking up a notch. "Anything I should be wary of immediately?"

"Let's just say Ortiz hasn't been twiddling his thumbs," Briggs hinted darkly. "And watch your six, alright? You're diving into shark-infested waters here."

"Always do," was Simon's curt reassurance, though his mind was already racing ahead to the content of that email, the secrets it might unlock.

"Good luck, Simon," Briggs added before the line went dead.

Simon stood motionless for a moment, the weight of the impending revelations pressing on him. He turned to his laptop, an unassuming piece of technology that was about to become the window into a world of danger and deceit. His fingers hovered over the keyboard, a silent prayer for Jennifer's safety lingering on his lips before he dove into the digital abyss.

Simon's eyes, tinged with fatigue and relentless determination, scanned the email one last time. The screen's glow barely illuminated Jack's living room, where the hum of a ceiling fan mixed with the occasional rustle of paper as Loran sifted through the information the courier had delivered. Jack leaned over the back of a worn leather sofa; his gaze locked on the documents spread out before him. Each page turned felt like peeling back another layer of the dark world they were about to infiltrate.

"Anything?" Jack's voice was low, almost hesitant as if he feared the answer.

"Bits and pieces," Simon muttered, closing the laptop with a soft click. "It's like trying to paint a picture with half the colors missing."

Loran looked up from her examination of a grainy photo, her tinted skin catching the light oddly, making her seem part of the shadows that filled the corners of the room. "We'll find the rest of them colors," she said, her slow southern drawl a stark contrast to the tension that hung in the air.

Before anyone could reply, the front door creaked open, and Sheriff Mark Thompson stepped inside. He paused just beyond the threshold, his tall frame casting a long shadow that merged with the darkness of the hallway. His eyes, piercing blue and shadowed with concern, swept the room before settling on the trio.

"Evening," he said, breaking the silence. The casual greeting did nothing to mask the worry lines etched deeply into his face.

"Simon," Mark acknowledged with a nod. "Wish I had better news for you."

The sheriff joined them in the center of the room, hands clasped tightly behind his back. "No leads on Jennifer." His voice was steady but betrayed an undercurrent of fear.

"Nothing here either," Simon admitted, the weight of the admission heavy in his chest. "But we've got enough to start putting together a plan. I'm headed to South Texas—see what I can shake loose down there."

"Crossing into Mexico?" Mark's question was more of a statement, an acknowledgment of the dangerous path Simon was choosing.

"Have to," Simon replied, the resolve in his tone leaving no room for argument.

Mark ran a hand through his graying hair, the action revealing a man wearied by the fight yet unwilling to surrender. "Be careful, Simon. Ortiz isn't known for his hospitality."

A grim smile tugged at the corner of Simon's mouth, but it didn't reach his eyes. "I don't plan on staying long enough for pleasantries."

"Keep us updated," Jack interjected, his military background evident in the firm set of his jaw.

"Will do," Simon assured him, turning to gather the papers that held fragments of a puzzle only he seemed to believe could be solved. As he tucked them into a nondescript folder, he felt the weight of their collective hope pressing down on him—a burden he accepted without hesitation.

"Let's get this bastard," he murmured, more to himself than to the others.

"Bring her home," Mark added quietly, the plea resonating in the stillness of the room.

Simon met the sheriff's gaze, a silent vow passing between them. Then, without another word, he turned and walked towards the kitchen, the folder clutched tightly in his hand as if it were the key to unlocking the darkness that had swallowed Jennifer Hawkins.

Simon leaned over the cluttered kitchen table; his gaze fixed on the crumpled map of South Texas. The lines and contours seemed to blur as he traced a route with his finger from McAllen to Reynosa. "The intel's solid," he muttered, almost to himself. "Ortiz's operation is rooted deep in Reynosa."

Jack, who had been leaning against the doorframe with arms crossed, straightened up. "Then you'll need backup. I've got your six, Simon. Let's do this together."

A flicker of gratitude passed through Simon's blue eyes, but it was quickly replaced by the hard glint of the loner operative who had survived countless missions. "Appreciate it, Jack, but no. It's too risky, and I move faster alone."

"Simon's right," Mark added, stepping closer. His shadow fell across the map, darkening the border towns. "You're needed here. We can't play all our cards at once."

Jack's jaw clenched, the scar along his jawline whitening as he pressed his lips into a thin line. He knew arguing with Simon was like trying to bend iron, but it didn't sit right with him—sitting back while his friend walked into the lion's den.

"Fine," Jack conceded, pushing off the frame with a sigh. "What do you need me to do?"

"Let your keen eye be our guide," Simon said, his hands moving deftly as he folded the map with practiced precision.

"Examine every inch of this area. Search for any clues that may lead us to the cartel's hiding place—restaurants, shops, and houses that seem out of place. We need any advantage we can find."

"Got it." Jack nodded, the soldier in him responding to the clear directive. "I'll document everything, keep it low-key."

"Keep out of trouble," Mark chimed in, though his tone carried an undercurrent of concern. "We don't need more missing persons."

Simon watched as Jack absorbed the instructions, his posture shifting subtly from disappointed comrade to duty-bound investigator. It was a transformation he'd seen before, a testament to Jack's ability to adapt and overcome.

"Remember, eyes and ears only. No cowboy stunts," Simon reminded him, a wry smile softening his stern demeanor for a moment.

"Hey, who do you think you're talking to?"

"An ex-Air Force Security Forces member who's itching for action," Simon retorted, the corner of his mouth twitching.

"Guilty as charged," Jack admitted, "but I'll play it smart."

"Good man." Simon clapped Jack on the shoulder, a silent acknowledgment of the trust between them.

"Keep your head down, Simon," Mark said, meeting Simon's gaze. "And your eyes open."

"Always," Simon replied, tucking the folder under his arm as he stepped towards the door, the weight of their task settling on his shoulders once more.

"Keep sharp, both of you," Mark called after them, his voice carrying the weight of command and concern as they dispersed—their paths diverging, yet united in purpose.

The sun was dipping low, casting long shadows over the Hawkins' farmhouse as Simon pulled up the gravel drive. He killed the engine of his truck and sat for a moment, collecting his thoughts. This wasn't going to be easy. Lori had been through hell already, and here he was about to tell her he'd be walking straight into the lion's den.

He stepped out onto the crunching gravel, the sound slicing through the evening stillness. The porch light flickered on, and there she stood, a silhouette framed by the doorway, her posture rigid with anticipation.

"Simon," Lori called out, her voice tinged with an anxiety that clawed at his resolve.

"Evening, Lori," he replied, forcing warmth into his greeting as he made his way up the steps.

"Any word?" Her eyes searched his face for a shred of hope.

"Nothing yet, but I'm not sitting around waiting for news." He took a deep breath. "I'm headed to Mexico. Ortiz's operation is based out of Reynosa. It's time to take the fight to him."

"Mexico?" Lori's voice quivered, her hand flying to her mouth. "But that's—"

"Risky? Yeah," Simon interjected, his gaze steady. "But it's a risk I have to take. And I need you to do something for me."

"Anything, Simon," she said, steel entering her voice as determination overtook her initial shock.

"Keep in touch with Jack. Anything you hear about Jennifer, no matter how small, let him know. He'll pass it on to me."

"Jack?" She nodded slowly. "Okay, I can do that."

"And one more thing." Simon hesitated, knowing the weight of his next words. "Look after yourself, too. This—" He gestured vaguely, encompassing the danger, the uncertainty, "—it's not just about getting Jennifer back. It's about keeping you safe as well."

Lori stepped closer, her blue eyes glistening in the fading light. "You better come back in one piece, Simon Wilson," she said, her voice firm despite the tremor that ran through it.

"Plan on it," he assured her, offering a smile that didn't quite reach his eyes.

She reached up then, wrapping her arms around his neck in a tight embrace. Her body felt small and vulnerable against his, yet there was a strength in her grip that spoke volumes. Simon returned the hug, feeling the tremble in her shoulders as she fought back tears.

"Thank you," she whispered, her breath warm against his ear.

As they parted, Lori stood on her tiptoes and planted a soft kiss on his cheek. It was a fleeting touch, but it lingered like a promise, a silent plea for his safe return.

"Take care, Lori," Simon murmured, stepping back. He turned and walked down the porch steps, the weight of her gaze heavy on his back.

"Be careful, Simon," she called after him, her voice trailing off into the twilight.

He lifted a hand in farewell without looking back, his mind already racing ahead to the dangers that awaited him. As he slid behind the wheel, the last rays of sunlight vanished, leaving the world in shades of gray. With a rumble, the truck came to life, its headlights cutting through the gathering darkness as Simon drove away from the Hawkins home, away from Lori, and toward an uncertain horizon.

Simon zipped the last compartment of his worn duffel bag with a practiced motion, the fabric strained over the tactical gear and a few personal items he'd need for the journey ahead. His cabin felt more like an outpost than a home; functional, spartan, with the bare essentials scattered about in a semblance of order.

A knock on the door pulled him from his thoughts. He glanced at the clock—Loran was punctual as ever. The door creaked open, and Loran Smith stood there, her slight frame almost lost within the heavy wooden frame. She offered a shy smile, the indigo tint of her skin muted in the dim light of the cabin.

"Got somethin' for ya," she drawled, holding up a thumb drive like it was a peace offering. "Did some extra diggin'."

"Appreciate it," Simon replied, motioning her inside. He watched as she crossed the room, her movements deliberate, a mountain woman's grace that belied her toughness.

She slipped the thumb drive into his laptop, her fingers deft despite their size. The screen came to life, illuminating the lines of concentration etching her face as she navigated through folders and files.

"Here," Loran said after a moment, pointing at a list of names and locations sprawling across the digital canvas. "These here might be what you're lookin' for. Ties to Ortiz's web deeper than we thought."

"Thanks, Loran," Simon said, scrolling through the data, absorbing information with an efficiency honed by years in the field.

"Be sure to watch your back, Simon. That's a nasty hornet's nest you're pokin' at," she warned, her voice low but firm.

"Always do," he assured her, though his eyes didn't leave the screen.

With a nod, Loran retreated towards the door, pausing only to add, "I'll keep things runnin' from this end."

"Wouldn't expect anything less." Simon's reply was distracted but sincere.

The door clicked shut behind her, leaving Simon alone with his thoughts and the glow of the computer screen. After several long minutes, he shut the laptop, his mind already racing through scenarios and strategies.

The hum of the aircraft's engines provided a white noise backdrop to Simon's reflection as he stared out of the small oval window. Below, the patchwork of the earth seemed distant and detached from the dangers he was approaching.

He settled back into the stiff airplane seat, attempting to find a comfortable position. Simon's gaze flitted over the other passengers, ordinary folks with probably ordinary destinations, unaware of the invisible threads of intrigue weaving through their world.

Larry Harlow. The name echoed in his mind. His mentor had been out of the game for a while, frail health trading cloak-and-dagger for doctors and quiet. But if anyone could help navigate the treacherous waters ahead, it would be Larry.

"Will he still have the pull needed?" Simon mused silently, his blue eyes clouding with concern. The CIA wasn't known for its loyalty to the old and the worn.

As the plane chased the sunset toward Texas, Simon leaned his head against the cool window, the drone of the engines lulling his senses. There were too many variables and too many unknowns. Yet amidst all the uncertainties, one thing remained clear: Jennifer's life depended on him.

"Let's hope Larry's still got some fight left," he whispered to the reflection in the glass, before closing his eyes and trying to snatch some rest before the storm that awaited him.

Chapter 4

The wheels of the Boeing 737 kissed the tarmac with a screech, jolting Simon Wilson from his reverie. He stretched his muscular frame as best he could in the cramped window seat before shuffling off the plane and into the humid embrace of Corpus Christi. His blue eyes scanned the airport crowd, always wary, always calculating. He made his way to baggage claim, where his duffel bag emerged with a mundane thud onto the carousel.

"Welcome to Texas," he murmured to himself, sarcasm lacing his tone like barbed wire.

The sun was dipping low on the horizon by the time Simon slid behind the wheel of a nondescript rental sedan. Kingsville lay ahead, a short drive but a world away from the kind of places a CIA operative usually finds themselves. The road unfurled before him, dusky orange and violet painting the sky as day surrendered to night.

Kingsville's lights were a beacon as Simon arrived. The La Quinta Inn & Suites stood like a sentinel at the edge of town, its neon sign buzzing gently in the twilight. He checked in under an alias, a habit as ingrained as breathing, and found his room on the second floor.

The space was standard fare—king-sized bed, flat-screen TV, and a lingering scent of industrial-strength cleaner. Simon tossed his bag on the bed and pulled out his phone. It was time to check-in.

"Hey Larry, it's Simon. I'm in town," he said, his voice even, giving nothing away.

"Simon! Good to hear from you. You find the place, okay?"

"Like clockwork," Simon replied, eyeing the bland room art as if it held state secrets.

"Great. Meet me tomorrow at El Dorado, about 1:30. You can't miss it—it's got a big old cactus painted on the sign-out front."

"Got it. El Dorado, 1:30."

"Alright, see you then. And hey, be careful, alright?"

"Always am." Simon hung up, the line dead before the words finished echoing in the room.

He sat on the edge of the bed, fingers drumming against his knee. The slow pace of Kingsville life was a stark contrast to the adrenaline that normally fueled him when he was in the field as an agent. But beneath the calm surface, he knew currents of danger swirled. He'd swim those waters tomorrow. For now, he needed rest.

Simon lay on top of the bed covers and settled in for a nap, his mind already mapping out the next day's moves. As sleep crept in, his last thought was a silent promise to Loran—he'd bring back more than just information. He'd bring back results.

Two hours later he was up and out of the room and to a nondescript dinner at a local diner, Simon Wilson found himself behind the wheel of his rental, the dashboard's glow illuminating his stoic features. Kingsville at night was quiet, almost too quiet for a man accustomed to the cacophony of danger. He drove past El Dorado, noting the neon-lit cactus Larry had mentioned, its green hue casting an eerie shadow on the deserted street. With a nod of satisfaction, Simon made a mental note of the surroundings and headed back to La Quinta.

In his room, the hum of the air conditioner filled the silence as he hunched over his laptop, the blue light from the screen washing over his focused expression. Papers littered the desk—maps, notes, profiles—all pieces of a puzzle only he could piece together. Every so often, his hand would dart out, adjusting a paper or tapping a key with precision.

The clock ticked on, and Simon rubbed his eyes, feeling the weight of the day pressing down. He reached for his phone, dialed a familiar number, and waited for the connection.

"Hey, Loran," he greeted when the call connected, his voice betraying a hint of fatigue that his posture did not.

"Simon. Anything new?"

"Nothing yet. I'm meeting Larry tomorrow. Should know more then. How are things holding up your end?"

"Quiet as the grave," Loran replied, her tone suggesting she didn't trust the calm.

"Let's hope it stays that way. I'll update you after the meet," he promised, a silent acknowledgment of the risks ahead.

"Be careful, Simon," she said—a simple plea from someone who knew the cost of carelessness.

"Always am," he repeated the mantra from earlier, as much for her as for himself, before ending the call and surrendering to sleep.

The next day, at exactly 1:20 pm, Simon's car rumbled into the parking lot of El Dorado. He sat in the driver's seat for a moment, his keen eyes scanning the area like a hawk eyeing its territory. With a satisfied nod, he stepped out of the vehicle and was immediately embraced by the hot Texas air. He took a moment to survey the near-empty lot, taking in the scattered cars and the shimmering heat waves rising from the pavement. The sound of cicadas buzzed in the background, adding to the intense summer atmosphere.

He pushed through the doors, the chime announcing his arrival to a place that seemed frozen in time. The interior was a patchwork of Mexican motifs and dim lighting, creating pockets of shadow and secrecy. His gaze flitted across the booths and tables until it landed on one where time seemed to have claimed victory over the occupant.

Larry Harlow, a man whose frailty was at odds with the reputation that preceded him, lifted his hand in a tired wave. Simon strode through the maze of chairs, the sound of his boots against the floor asserting his presence.

"Simon," Larry greeted his voice a whisper of its former strength.

"Good to see you, Larry," Simon replied, taking a seat opposite the aged operative, his posture relaxed but his mind alert. The game was about to begin, and he was ready to play.

Simon settled into the booth, his keen blue eyes briefly catching the flicker of a television screen mounted in the corner before returning to Larry. The old spy's face wore the creases of countless missions and sleepless nights, a testament to a life lived in the shadows.

"Made it without any trouble?" Larry's voice cracked slightly as he spoke, a hand reaching out to steady a trembling coffee cup.

"Smooth sailing," Simon confirmed with a nod. He rested his forearms on the table, leaning forward slightly. "I did a little recon last night—wanted to make sure I could find this place without a hitch."

"Always the professional," Larry remarked, a ghost of a smile playing on his lips.

"Old habits," Simon replied, his gaze briefly scanning the nearly empty restaurant. His attention was a laser, missing nothing, always calculating. It was the kind of focus that had kept him alive in a world where the smallest detail could be the difference between life and death.

"Place hasn't changed much since the last time I was here," Simon added, allowing himself a moment of reminiscence. "You'd think time would leave its mark."

"Time and tide wait for no man," Larry quipped, though the glint in his eye suggested a storm brewing beneath the surface.

"Except maybe for El Dorado," Simon said, a hint of dry humor in his tone.

"Indeed," Larry agreed. "We've got a lot to cover, Simon. But first, how are things back in Kentucky?"

"Moving," Simon replied succinctly. "But we'll get into that later. For now, let's focus on why we're here."

Larry nodded, a sense of urgency passing between them, unspoken but understood. As they settled into their conversation, the weight of their task loomed over them, an invisible presence at the table. They were two operatives, bound by duty and the relentless march of time, fighting a war that never seemed to end.

The El Dorado's ceiling fans hummed a lazy tune, stirring the heavy South Texas air as Simon and Larry sat across from each other in a booth upholstered with wear and nostalgia. The sun-bleached curtains fluttered occasionally as a rare breeze slipped through a crack in the window, carrying the scent of sizzling fajitas from the kitchen.

"Then, out of nowhere, this bolt from the blue slams right into the ground not ten feet from where I'm standing," Simon recounted, his hands animating the scene for emphasis.

"Damn, son," Larry murmured, his eyes wide with admiration and disbelief. "Lightning strike, you say? Close call."

"Close enough to singe the edges of my soul," Simon said, a wry smile creeping onto his face.

"Never did take you for the superstitious type," Larry chuckled, shaking his head as their server approached with a clatter of plates.

"Wouldn't say I am," Simon replied, his gaze tracking the server's movements as she laid out their orders: enchiladas verdes for him, carne asada for Larry. "But it does make you think about fate. Chance."

"Or maybe someone up there likes you," Larry suggested, grabbing a tortilla and scooping a generous helping of beans onto his plate.

"Or they're just keeping me alive for something worse," Simon countered, digging into his meal with purpose.

Silence fell between them as they ate, the clink of cutlery punctuating their thoughts.

After the last bite was savored and the dishes were cleared away, leaving behind gleaming patches on the otherwise timeworn table, the server returned, coffee pot in hand. She poured two steaming cups and vanished like a ghost, wordless and efficient.

"Alright," Larry began, his voice dropping to a conspiratorial hush as he cradled his mug. "Let's get down to brass tacks. Ortiz Cartel's been busy round these parts."

Simon leaned forward, elbows on the table, his blue eyes fixed on Larry's weathered features. "What's the play?"

"Smuggling routes have shifted. They're using some of the old cattle paths, hard to track, even harder to intercept."

"Means they've got someone with local knowledge," Simon surmised, his brain already mapping out possible leads.

Larry leaned in, his voice low and tense. "But it's even worse than that. They've infiltrated the Border Patrol. Our own comrades could be working against us, making our job a helluva lot trickier."

The weight of this revelation hung heavy in the air, settling like a thick fog over their plans. Larry's eyes darted around, searching for any sign of betrayal from those around them. The tension was palpable as they considered the dangerous reality they were facing.

"Any names?" Simon's question was a low growl, the hunter part of him rising to the surface.

"Few potentials, but nothing solid yet." Larry's frailty belied the sharpness in his eyes, the mind behind them as keen as ever.

"Anything else?" Simon prodded, patience giving way to urgency.

"Word is, there's a new player in town, someone with ties deeper than we've seen before. Goes by the name 'El Ingeniero.' They say he's bringing tech into the equation."

"Tech?" Simon's brow furrowed. "As in?"

"Surveillance. Drones, maybe more. It's all rumors at this point, but if it's true..." Larry let the implication hang in the air, heavy and foreboding.

"Changes the game," Simon finished for him, leaning back against the worn leather of the booth. His mind was racing, pieces of a larger puzzle starting to fall into place.

"Exactly." Larry took a slow sip of his coffee, the steam fogging his glasses momentarily. "We need to be smart about this, Simon. One wrong move and we're not just burned, we could very well be dead."

"Understood," Simon nodded, his expression hardening. The stakes had never been clearer, and neither had his resolve. It was time to hunt.

"El Ingeniero," Simon muttered, tapping a finger on the table's worn surface. "That's new intel." The creases deepened on his forehead as he cross-referenced the information with what he had learned before his trip. There were discrepancies—small ones, but in his line of work, they could mean life or death.

Larry watched Simon's face, reading the minute expressions like a book. "You're thinking of Loran's info, aren't you?"

Simon nodded. "And Briggs'. They never mentioned this tech angle. Drones could compromise us before we even start."

"Could be why they're staying so elusive," Larry suggested. "They might've caught wind of our prying eyes."

"Or they've got their own inside the Agency," Simon added, the idea leaving a bitter taste in his mouth. He felt a twinge of worry for Loran, back in Kentucky. She was tough, born and bred in those mountains with a resilience that came from a long line of the Fugate clan. But she was also a target if her name ever slipped into the wrong hands.

"Speaking of which," Larry said, leaning forward, "everyone back at base doing alright? Are they people you can trust? I know they are not trained for this kind of situation. Civilians hardly ever are."

"Sharp as ever," Simon smirked. "Loran's been digging up half the dark web. And before you ask, yes, she's discreet. Her family... they're survivors, have been since they settled in Troublesome Creek. You know about the Blue Fugates?"

"Can't say that I do," Larry responded, curiosity piquing his weathered face.

"Genetic quirk, methemoglobinemia. Gave 'em blue-tinged skin. Made 'em stand out like sore thumbs back then. Now, not so much—the trait's diluted over generations. But it's symbolic, isn't it? They were different, outsiders, and yet they thrived. Just like Loran." Simon spoke with a hint of admiration. "She uses that outsider perspective to see things others miss."

"Sounds like she's quite the asset," Larry complimented, nodding his approval. "And it sounds like you've got yourself a solid team in Kentucky."

"Sure do," Simon agreed. "But it's not just about survival anymore, is it? We're up against a whole new breed of cartel. Tech-savvy, ruthless, and now, apparently, with drones."

"Times change, and we adapt—that's the nature of the game," Larry said. "Your knowledge, Simon, it's going to give us an edge. Knowing the lay of the land, understanding the players on both sides of the border, that's key."

"Knowledge is only part of it, though," Simon countered, his eyes locking onto Larry's. "We need to be one step ahead, always."

"Which is why we're here, planning over stale coffee in a place that's seen better days," Larry pointed out with a dry chuckle.

"Exactly," Simon replied, a wry smile tugging at the corner of his lips. "Besides, stale coffee has fueled more covert ops than we'd care to admit."

"Can't argue with that," Larry said, raising his mug in a silent toast to their shared understanding.

The two men sat in quiet camaraderie, each lost in thought. Simon's mind whirled with strategies and contingencies, while Larry seemed to reminisce about operations past. They were agents of change in an ever-evolving battle—a battle that required both the wisdom of experience and the innovation of the new.

"Tomorrow," Simon finally broke the silence, "we put our plan into action. For now, let's enjoy the calm before the storm."

"Agreed," Larry said, his eyes meeting Simon's with a steely resolve. "To the calm, and to the storm that follows."

"Mission Texas. That's my entry point," Simon stated, leaning forward as he traced a line on the map spread across the table. It was an unremarkable diner, but it served as their war room for now. The hum of an old air conditioner provided a mundane soundtrack to their clandestine conversation.

"Reynosa's close by. If I can slip through there, get a sense of how the Ortiz Cartel operates stateside, we might just unravel their network in Kentucky," Simon continued, his gaze fixed on the geography that represented so much more than towns and roads—it was a blueprint of danger and opportunity.

Larry's wiry frame seemed to tighten, his frailty belying the sharpness in his eyes. "It's risky. Reynosa is their backyard. Trust is a luxury you can't afford, not even with those you think are on your side."

"Except for a few names you'll give me?" Simon questioned, skeptical yet hopeful.

"Exactly." Larry reached into his jacket pocket and produced a worn notebook. Flipping through pages yellowed with age and stained with coffee rings, he finally tore out a sheet and slid it across to Simon. The paper was filled with names, each accompanied by an address scrawled in hurried handwriting.

"Those are your lifelines," Larry said, his voice heavy with the gravity of what he was imparting. "Guard them with your life, because they will be guarding yours."

Simon memorized each name before tucking the paper into his pocket. This was the currency of their trade— information more valuable than gold, more dangerous than any weapon.

"Speaking of which," Simon began, shifting the subject, "I'll need more than intel to survive down there."

"Already taken care of," Larry assured him. "La Lomita Mission. There's a spot at the base of the old chapel wall, loose stones. You'll find what you need for crossing the river."

"Mexican pesos and firepower," Simon mused, the reality settling in. He'd walked this tightrope before, but no matter how many times one dances with danger, the music never gets any less haunting.

"Enough to blend in, enough to protect yourself," Larry added, locking eyes with Simon. "But remember, the less you have to rely on iron and steel, the better. Your wits have always been your best weapon."

"Point taken," Simon replied, though he couldn't help feeling reassured knowing there would be something solid and lethal waiting for him—a tangible piece of security in a world built on shadows.

"Alright then," Larry concluded, standing up, his body language signaling the end of their meeting. Simon rose as well, the two men sharing a look of mutual respect that needed no words.

"Stay sharp, Simon," Larry said, clasping Simon's shoulder briefly. It was a subtle gesture, but it conveyed a wealth of meaning—be careful, be brave, come back alive.

"Will do," Simon promised, his voice low, carrying a weight that was part determination, part resignation. He knew what lay ahead, and he welcomed it with the quiet confidence of a man who had made peace with the chaos of his calling.

The moon hung like a silent witness over the La Lomita Mission, its pale light filtering through the Spanish moss that draped from the ancient oaks. Simon Wilson's breath was steady as he approached the designated spot—a spot in the back of the mission, the loose stones he was told about. He removed the stones and reached under the mission floor. His fingers, calloused and sure, found the cache Larry had left for him: a snub-nose .357 pistol, a small box of ammunition, and a wad of Mexican pesos folded neatly inside a plastic bag.

"Old school," Simon muttered to himself, appreciating the weight of the revolver in his hand. It was a tool from another era, but it felt right—like meeting an old friend in a foreign city.

With the gear stowed securely under his loose-fitting jacket, Simon melted into the shadows, becoming just another phantom in the night. He crossed the border with nothing but silence as his companion, the Rio Grande, whispered secrets beneath him.

On the other side, the world changed. The air carried the scent of earth and struggle, the sounds of distant music weaving with the barks of street dogs. Simon's blue eyes, always watchful, scanned the surroundings as he made his way towards Reynosa.

The town seemed to be sleeping, but Simon knew better. Under the stillness was a pulse, a rhythm of life that thrived in darkness. He hitched a ride on the back of an old farm truck, the vehicle's rusted frame groaning as it navigated the dirt roads. The driver, unaware of his silent passenger, hummed along to a tune crackling from the radio.

Simon jumped off as the truck slowed near the outskirts of Reynosa, landing with a soft thud on the packed earth. The streets were narrow here, the houses huddled together like weary travelers. He navigated them with practiced ease, heading to the address Larry had given him.

It wasn't long before he stood outside a modest dwelling, where the man named Rudy Salgado lived. Rudy answered the door, his face creased with lines that spoke of hardship and too much sun. The farmer's clothes were tattered, yet his posture held a resilience that belied his appearance.

"Señor Wilson?" Rudy asked, his voice cautious but not without warmth.

"Call me Simon," he replied, offering a hand which Rudy shook firmly.

Inside, Rudy shared what he knew, speaking in hushed tones as if the walls themselves might be listening. They pored over maps, Rudy's finger tracing routes and alleyways, pointing out safe houses and dead ends. He spoke of the main players, the enforcers, and finally, the house of Juan Ortiz—a fortress among shacks, guarded like a president's residence.

"Ortiz doesn't play," Rudy said, his dark eyes serious. "He's got men with eyes sharp as eagles. And guns... they carry Uzis like farmers carry sickles."

"Gracias, amigo," Simon said, absorbing every detail. "Your help won't be forgotten."

"Be careful, Señor. Ortiz's reach is long, and his memory is longer."

"I'll tread lightly," Simon assured him, though both men knew that in this game, even the slightest misstep could be lethal.

The Salgado household was a stark contrast to the opulence of the Ortiz estate that Simon would soon infiltrate. The dinner table was modest, and the food was simple yet flavorful. Rudy's wife, Emilia, had prepared a traditional Mexican meal, which filled the small dining area with mouthwatering aromas. They sat down to eat, the ceiling fan stirring the humid air as evening settled over Reynosa.

"Since Ortiz took control, it's like the devil himself has claimed this place." Rudy pushed the beans around his plate, not really eating, just moving the food as he spoke.

Simon noticed the worry lines etched deeply into Rudy's face. "How so?" he asked, taking a bite of the warm tortilla.

"Teenage girls," Emilia cut in, her green eyes flashing with a mix of anger and fear. "They vanish. And the police—they do nothing." She set down her fork with a clatter that seemed too loud for the quiet room.

"Disappearances are just where it starts," Rudy continued. "There's been more killing than ever before. Pillaging, too. People are afraid to leave their homes after dark."

"Sounds like Ortiz runs a tight ship," Simon observed, his mind racing with the implications of what he was hearing.

"The tightest," Rudy agreed with a nod. "His house... it's like something out of an American movie about drug lords. A monster of a place with walls higher than any wave I've seen crash onto our shores."

"Armed guards?" Simon inquired, already imagining the layout from the descriptions.

"Every corner, every gate," Rudy replied. "And dogs, too. Patrols all day and night. Those Uzis aren't just for show; they mean business."

Simon mulled over this new information; his supper forgotten. Security like that wasn't just precautionary; it spoke of paranoia, of secrets buried deep within fortified walls.

"Thank you for sharing your home with me," Simon said, pushing his plate away. He'd lost his appetite but gained valuable insights into the fortress he'd soon be facing. In the silence that followed, Simon could tell that Rudy and Emilia understood the gravity of the task ahead of him. They were allies made strong by adversity; their resolve hardened by the suffering Ortiz had brought upon their community.

"Be careful, Simon," Emilia said as they cleared the dishes. "Ortiz doesn't forgive, and he certainly doesn't forget."

"Neither do I," Simon replied, his blue eyes hardening like flint. He knew the stakes, and he knew the risks. Tomorrow, he would come face to face with the stateliest house in Northern Mexico, its ten-foot fence and patrolling guards a testament to the power held within—and the fear it wielded without.

As Simon left Rudy's house, blending once more into the fabric of the night, he felt a familiar thrill coursing through his veins—the thrill of the hunt, the dance with danger. This was his element, and he was ready to play.

The neon sign of Punto del maniako buzzed like a swarm of lazy wasps, casting erratic shadows over the dusty street outside. Inside, Simon Wilson nursed his beer at a back table while picking at a plate of nachos that were soggy with too much cheese and jalapeños. The air was thick with the smell of fried food and cigarette smoke, mingling into a scent that clung to clothes long after leaving.

The bar's atmosphere was one of calculated neglect; the kind of place that thrived on its own reputation for being a little rough around the edges. A jukebox in the corner spat out a steady stream of norteño music, each accordion squeeze vying for dominance over the chatter of patrons.

Simon's eyes, blue and perceptive beneath furrowed brows, scanned the room nonchalantly from under the brim of his worn baseball cap. He had chosen the table for its strategic view of both the entrance and the dingy, mirrored wall behind the bar, which allowed him to keep an eye on everything—and everyone—without appearing to.

A group sauntered in, their laughter jarring against the backdrop of melancholic tunes. They were a rugged bunch, denim and leather-clad, with the sort of swagger that came from carrying unseen but palpable power. Simon didn't need to hear their conversation to know they were cartel; it was written in the way they moved and the energy they brought into the room.

One of them, a broad-shouldered man with a scar bisecting his left brow, glanced around before locking eyes with Simon. There was a moment of silent assessment before he strode over, his cohorts slowly fanning out in a loose semi-circle around Simon's table.

"¿Eres americano?" the man asked, his Spanish sharpened by suspicion as he leaned against the adjacent table, muscles tensed like coiled springs.

"De España," Simon's voice carried the deliberate lilt of a Castilian accent, his vowels clipped and precise. The suspicion in the cartel member's eyes lingered for a heartbeat longer before it was replaced with begrudging acceptance.

Simon kept his expression neutral, taking another sip of his beer before replying. "No, just passing through," he said, his words spoken in the Spanish of a Spaniard. One of four languages he had mastered in his days as an agent. His gaze didn't waver, even as he sensed the others closing in, their movements almost serpentine in their subtlety.

"Ah, un español. ¡Que disfrutes tu estancia!" the man said, a smirk tugging at the corner of his mouth as if he'd shared an inside joke with his comrades.

The cartel members exchanged glances, a silent conversation flowing between them. They were predators sizing up prey, deciding whether to strike or bide their time. Simon remained still, the picture of calm indifference, though every muscle in his body was ready to react at a hair's trigger.

"Gracias," Simon replied, nodding once as they backed off, their presence in the bar dissipating like a threat passing in the night.

"Enjoy your meal," the scarred man finally said, a hint of mockery in his voice as he pushed away from the table. He gave a curt nod to his companions, and together they retreated, melting back into the crowd as if they'd never been there at all.

Simon exhaled slowly, letting the tension drain from his shoulders. He picked up his fork and resumed eating, though his appetite had long since fled. His mind was abuzz with thoughts, plans weaving and reweaving themselves as he plotted his next move.

The mission was clear, but the path was fraught with peril. Simon knew he'd have to tread carefully; the stakes were far too high for anything less.

Left alone, Simon took a sip of his lukewarm beer, his blue eyes scanning over the rim of the glass. He'd bought himself some time, but this respite was nothing more than a fleeting shadow in the grand scheme of things. As the men rejoined the low hum of conversation and laughter that filled Punto del maniako, Simon tuned his ears to the cacophony, sifting through the noise for nuggets of gold.

A group at the bar spoke loudly, their words slurred by alcohol but clear enough for Simon's trained ear. They bragged about the eastward expansion, their voices tinged with excitement at the prospect of fresh territory. 'Kentucky' spilled from their lips like a promise of riches yet to come.

Simon's mind whirred into overdrive, piecing together the scraps of information, the puzzle slowly taking form. It was there, amid the din of clinking glasses and boisterous laughter, that another thread unraveled—a name that made the hairs on the back of his neck stand up: Juan Ortiz.

The boss himself was moving pieces on the board, stepping out from the shadows to oversee the next phase personally. The casual way they mentioned his travel plans to the States sent a chill down Simon's spine. If Ortiz was leaving the fortress-like safety of his Reynosa compound, it meant something big was brewing.

"¿Y quién va con él?" a woman asked, her curiosity piqued as she leaned closer to the group.

"Los de siempre, y algunos nuevos. Prepárate, porque esto va a ser grande," one of the men responded, a wolfish grin spreading across his face.

Simon committed every word to memory, the names of those accompanying Ortiz etching themselves into his consciousness. This was more than just intelligence; it was a lead, a tangible string to pull in a web that spanned borders.

Finishing his beer, Simon stood up, dropping a few pesos onto the table. He needed to get back, to relay what he'd learned. As he stepped out into the balmy night air of Reynosa, the weight of the mission pressed down on him, a constant companion whispering reminders of the danger that lay ahead. But he was ready—ready to chase the shadows until the truth was dragged into the light.

The midday sun blazed down on the coarse asphalt of the hotel parking lot as Simon dialed Loran's number. His shadow stretched long and thin across the white lines marking the empty spaces. He leaned against the rental car, the metal hot to the touch, waiting for her to pick up.

"Hey, it's Simon. I'll be landing back home tonight. I need a ride from the airstrip. And gather everyone at my place, would you?"

"Sure thing, Simon. I'll let the others know. We'll be there."

"Thanks, Loran. See you soon." He ended the call and took a moment to look out across the flat expanse of Kingsville, feeling the weight of what he had learned in Reynosa pressing on his shoulders.

By the time nightfall wrapped its cloak around the hills of Kentucky, Simon's cabin was alighted with light, and the familiar faces of his makeshift team were gathered inside. The worn wooden table groaned under the collective lean of anxious bodies as Simon recounted his findings from across the border. Mark, the sheriff, rubbed his jawline thoughtfully, his eyes clouded with worry.

"This Ortiz... he's making big moves," Simon said, locking eyes with each person around the table. "He's heading east, and he's not traveling light."

"East," Mark repeated, his voice low, the word tasting bitter. "That means us."

"Found some places of interest," Jack said, his arms folded across his chest, the scar on his jaw tight with tension. "Five houses scattered out, all of them crawling with new faces. Hispanics, mostly. Lots of run-down cars and bikes. There's also this old adult bookstore in an old strip mall. The sheriff's office shut it down a while ago. There used to be lots of fights and even a couple of people were killed there. There are lots of cars and bikes being parked in the back, mostly out of sight."

Simon nodded, taking in every detail. "Good work, Jack. We need to keep tabs on those houses and that old porn shop. Something tells me they're not just here for the scenery."

"Can't say I'm surprised," Mark added, shifting uncomfortably in his chair. "But knowing it's coming and being ready for it are two different things."

"Which is why we're going to be ready," Simon stated firmly, his gaze sweeping over the group. "We're going to dig in our heels and push back before they get the chance to sink theirs in any deeper."

The room was silent for a moment, the gravity of the situation settling over them like dusk. They were a small band, but each one carried the resolve of an army. As the night grew heavier outside, the cabin became a beacon—a place where plans were formed and the seeds of resistance were sown.

Simon leaned back in his chair, the creak of the worn wood a stark reminder of the mounting tension in the room. He rubbed at the stubble on his chin, his blue eyes hardening with each passing second as he considered their next move.

"Jack, those old revolvers and bolt-action rifles I'm used to might not cut it this time." He reached into the duffel bag at his feet, drawing out sheaves of paper thick with notes and observations. "We're up against some serious firepower."

Jack nodded, his broad shoulders tensing beneath the fabric of his flannel shirt. His piercing blue eyes met Simon's, unflinching. "I figured as much. I'm game for whatever training you've got in mind."

"Good," Simon said, sliding the papers across the table to Loran. We need to get all this into the system. Cross-reference it with what we have."

Loran gathered the papers in her slight arms, her fingers brushing over the text as if committing every word to memory. She pulled out the laptop, its screen flickering to life, the hum of its aging processor filling the silence.

"Here," Simon said, handing her a sleek black credit card from his wallet. It glinted under the overhead light, an omen of the gravity of their situation. "It's getting pretty intense. I don't know if these laptops can handle it. Go get us whatever tech you think we need to do this right."

Loran accepted the card; her usually reserved features softened with a trace of a smile. "Does this mean I'm part of the team?" Her words were slow, her deep mountain drawl wrapping around each syllable.

"Always have been, Loran," Simon replied, his tone warm but edged with the weight of responsibility. "But remember, you're the brains of our operation. Your job is to keep us one step ahead with intel. We'll keep feeding you the updates."

"Understood," she said, a new resolve firming her posture. "I'll make sure we've got the best tools for the job."

"Excellent," Simon nodded, his gaze lingering on her a moment longer before turning back to Jack. "Let's start with your weapons training first thing tomorrow. We're going to need every edge we can get."

As the night pressed in around the cabin, each person inside knew that the real battle was only just beginning.

Chapter 5

The holdup house stood like a festering sore in Poteet Valley, its infected presence hidden among the rolling hills and thickets near the Mammoth Cave National Park. Once a family home resounding with laughter, it now echoed with the groans and cries of despair from those unfortunate enough to be within its walls. The cartel had invaded this sanctum, transforming it into their personal den of vice, where up to twenty members lounged in a twisted semblance of domesticity.

In one of the bedrooms—one spared the ignominy of becoming a makeshift cell—Jennifer Hawkins lay on the bare mattress, her once vibrant spirit now shackled by terror and pain. The room reeked of sweat and fear, a pungent reminder of the unspeakable atrocities that had been committed here. The once lively green eyes, which used to mirror the vitality of the forest surrounding this cursed place, were now dulled and lifeless, filled with nothing but defiance and agony.

One of the men sneered at her, his breath hot with malice as he pinned her down forcefully. Jennifer's body was already bruised and battered from days of torture, but still, she refused to submit quietly. She fought back with every ounce of strength left in her, her soccer-toned legs thrashing against her attackers in a desperate attempt to defend herself.

But it was futile. They were too strong, too relentless in their assault. One by one, they took turns violating her body, each act more brutal than the last. Jennifer's screams echoed off the walls, mingling with grunts and laughter from her attackers.

As they finished and left her broken and bleeding on the mattress, she could only lie there in shock and disbelief. This was not the first time she had endured such brutality, but it never got easier. And yet, somehow, she found the strength to keep fighting, to never give up hope for escape or rescue.

Jennifer was not just a victim, she was a survivor. And no matter how many times they tried to break her spirit; she would always rise again.

"Enough," another voice commanded—a different timbre, cold and detached. "She's done for today." This was not mercy but calculation; they operated on a chilling schedule, rotating their prisoners to preserve their depravity.

"Let her be," the cold voice continued, and the room gradually emptied, leaving Jennifer curled on the bed, her breaths coming in shallow gasps as she fought the urge to succumb to darkness. In her battered state, thoughts of coaching her team of ten-year-old girls seemed like a distant dream, an echo from another life.

"90 days," they had said, a reprieve dictated by their twisted logic. But for Jennifer, each second in this hell was an eternity, each bruise a mark of her unyielding spirit. In the stillness of the aftermath, she whispered promises of survival to herself, her Kentucky accent barely audible amid the tears and ragged breaths.

"Jenny, keep fightin'," she murmured, her own voice a lifeline amid the sea of torment. As darkness threatened to claim her consciousness, Jennifer clung to the image of her mother's warm embrace, a beacon of hope in the relentless storm.

As the morning sun spilled through the gaps in the timber walls of Simon's cabin, he picked up his phone and dialed Lori's number. The line crackled faintly before her voice, tinged with a persistent weariness, answered.

"Morning, Lori. How about breakfast? I've got eggs and coffee waiting."

"Okay, Simon. I'll be there soon."

When Lori arrived, the cabin was filled with the aroma of freshly brewed coffee mingling with the scent of pine. The table was small and unadorned, save for two steaming mugs and a plate of scrambled eggs flanked by crispy bacon. They settled into their seats without fanfare, consuming the meal with a silence that hung heavy between them.

Finally, Simon cleared his throat, breaking the quietude as he met Lori's gaze. "Reynosa was... tough. Like hitting a wall of silence, but I've got leads to follow up on."

Lori's fork clattered against her plate, her hands trembling. She looked up, eyes brimming with tears that streaked down her cheeks, cutting through the resolve she had mustered. Her voice came out broken, the words choked with despair.

"Simon, I'm never gonna see my baby again." It wasn't just a fear; it was a conviction rooted deep within her, growing like thorny vines around her heart.

"Hey, now," Simon said softly, reaching across the table to offer a steadying hand. The muscles in his arm flexed instinctively, not from physical exertion, but from the weight of the promise he was about to make. "I'm going to find Jennifer, Lori. I swear it on everything I am."

She looked at him then, really looking, seeing the determination etched in the lines of his face. It was the same stoic expression he'd worn in countless covert operations, one that belied the turmoil churning beneath the surface. Here was a man who understood loss, who'd stared into the abyss and hadn't blinked. If anyone could bring her daughter back, it would be Simon Wilson.

"Bring her home, Simon," Lori whispered, her voice laced with a plea that resonated in the quiet cabin. "Please, bring my baby home."

Simon nodded once, solemn and resolute. "I will, Lori. That's a promise."

The hush of the cabin was broken by the creak of the front door, and in walked Loran Smith, her arms cradling a box that bore the image of a sleek computer monitor. She moved with an understated grace, her slight frame belying the strength it took to haul electronic equipment around.

"Simon, would you mind fetching the rest from my car?" Her voice, slow and melodic with a mountain drawl, cut through the lingering tension like a warm knife through butter.

"Sure thing, Loran," Simon replied, pushing back his chair with a scrape against the wooden floor. His movements were efficient, a testament to his training—no wasted energy, even in something as mundane as retrieving computer parts.

Loran set the monitor on the table with care, then started unpacking it, her fingers deftly peeling away the tape and cardboard. Each component emerged with a soft rustle, the air filling with the scent of new electronics. As she worked, the quiet click-clacking of assembly accompanied Simon's in-and-out trips as he brought in the remaining boxes.

By the time Lori Hawkins had steadied her nerves enough to pour another cup of coffee, the sound of gravel crunching announced another arrival. Jack Thompson's imposing figure filled the doorway moments later, his shadow stretching across the room as he stepped inside. There was an air of readiness about him; the kind that came from years of military discipline.

"Thought we could use these," Jack said, nodding toward the duffel bag at his feet, the outline of firearms barely concealed within its bulk.

"Thanks, Jack." Simon's eyes swept over the bag, his mind already cataloging and assessing. The weight on his shoulders seemed to ease with the knowledge of added firepower—it was one more step towards their goal.

"Ready for a little target practice?"

"Let me just give Loran a hand with this setup, and I'm all yours," Simon said as he turned back to the dining table where Loran was now connecting cables with quiet precision.

"Take your time, I'll get the coffee going," Jack replied, moving into the kitchen with the ease of someone who'd done this many times before. He didn't need to watch Loran work to know she was capable; the mountain woman had a way of handling tech that belied her rustic upbringing.

"Almost ready here," Loran announced, her voice still calm but with a hint of satisfaction at the job nearly done. "Just need to power it up and we're good to go."

"Great work," Simon said, admiring the newly assembled station. With a final glance at the technological hub that would serve as their strategic center, he clapped a hand on Loran's shoulder—a gesture of thanks that needed no words between them.

"Alright, let's see what you've got for me, Jack," Simon said, grabbing another cup of the strong black coffee and joining Jack on the worn couch. The fabric was soft beneath his hands, a stark contrast to the hard steel he'd soon be holding.

"Four handguns and an AR-15," Jack began, his voice a low rumble of contained excitement. "Once you're comfortable with these, we'll be a step closer to bringing Jennifer home."

Simon nodded, the warmth from the coffee seeping into his palms. This was more than just learning to shoot; it was preparation for a rescue, a fight for justice. And with each passing moment, he felt the promise he made to Lori growing into a plan of action—one he intended to see through to the very end.

The gravel crunched under the tires of Jack's truck as they rolled to a stop near the river, a secluded spot where the burble of water and rustle of leaves created a quiet cocoon. Simon stepped out, stretching his limbs, his gaze sweeping over the calm expanse of water before settling on the task at hand.

"Alright, let's set up," Jack said, reaching into the bed of the truck and producing a handful of dented cans. He walked over to a clear patch of dirt and spaced them out like soldiers ready for inspection.

Simon watched, feeling the weight of what these preparations meant. This wasn't some backyard plinking—each can represented a step closer to facing the vilest of humanity. A shiver ran through him, not from the crisp morning air but from the gravity of their mission.

Jack drove forward another fifteen yards, then killed the engine. The tailgate of the truck served as an impromptu bench as Jack laid out the trio of pistols: the sleek 9mm Beretta, the formidable Glock .40 cal., and lastly, the robust Ruger 10mm. Each one glinted ominously under the early sun, tools of deadly precision that Simon would need to master.

"Let's start with the Beretta," Jack suggested, picking up the 9mm with the ease of long familiarity.

Simon leaned in, watching intently as Jack deftly disassembled the weapon. "You'll want to get a good feel for each part," Jack instructed, his hands moving with practiced care. "Understand how they fit together, how they function."

"Looks simple enough," Simon remarked, though he knew there was nothing simple about it. This was a dance of metal and mechanics, where every piece had its place and purpose.

"Your turn." Jack handed him the disassembled gun.

With a nod, Simon mirrored Jack's movements, his fingers fumbling slightly as he pieced the firearm back together. It was a puzzle that required both finesse and force and after a few minor hiccups, the pistol lay whole once more on the hood.

"Good," Jack said with a brief nod of approval. "That's the first step. Now for the ammo."

He picked up a round, holding it between them. "Each bullet is your promise to protect those who can't protect themselves," Jack said, his tone solemn. "When you pull that trigger, you're making a commitment to see it through."

Simon took the round, rolling it between his fingers, the cold brass a tangible reminder of the weight behind each shot he would take. It wasn't just about firing a gun; it was about firing with intention, with the resolve to end a nightmare and bring someone home.

"Once fired, the casing ejects, and a new round slides into the chamber," Jack explained, miming the action. "Ready for the next fight, just like you will be."

"Let's hope it's that smooth in real life," Simon said, feeling a somber kinship with the semi-automatic process. One challenge down, another queued up, in an unending cycle until the job was done.

"Life's rarely smooth, but you'll be ready for the rough parts too," Jack assured him, clapping him on the shoulder. It was a reassurance Simon clung to, grounding himself in the knowledge that while the path ahead was fraught with peril, he wouldn't walk it alone.

Simon's focus narrowed as Jack's hands worked with the practiced ease of someone who had done this a thousand times before. Four sharp reports rang out across the open expanse along the riverbank as Jack expertly put rounds through the center of each can. The empties ejected with a metallic clink, punctuating the silence that followed each shot.

"Your turn," Jack said, offering the 9mm Beretta to Simon with a loaded magazine.

Taking the weapon, Simon felt its weight settle comfortably in his hand. He slammed the magazine home and with a smooth motion, he pulled back the slide, chambering a round. The click of metal on metal was satisfying—confirmation that he was locked and loaded.

He aimed down-range, holding his breath for a moment before gently squeezing the trigger. The pistol bucked slightly in his grip, but less than he anticipated. "Not as much kick as I expected," Simon admitted, lowering the gun to glance at Jack.

"9mm's are good like that," Jack said with a nod, his eyes following another round as it zipped toward an already peppered can. "Makes staying on target for follow-up shots easier."

They worked their way through two magazines each for the three pistols, the air around them filling with the smell of gunpowder and the sound of cans dancing to the rhythm of the gunfire. Once the last round was fired, they stepped back to survey their makeshift range. Cans were punctured and torn, some thrown several feet from their original places.

"Let's up the ante," Jack suggested, and they moved the pickup back another 75 yards. From the back of the truck, Jack retrieved the AR-15, its black finish absorbing the light rather than reflecting it.

Again, Jack broke down the rifle, pointing out each component to Simon. "It's just like the pistols, only bigger parts," Jack explained. Simon watched intently, committing each step to memory before repeating the process himself. His hands moved with cautious precision, guided by Jack's occasional pointers.

"Alright, let's see what you've got," Jack said once the AR-15 was reassembled.

Simon lay prone on the cool grass, the rifle nestled into his shoulder as he peered through the sights. He took a moment, allowing the world to shrink until there was nothing but the target and his breathing. The rifle cracked loudly as he squeezed the trigger, sending rounds punching through the targets downrange. He shifted to kneeling, then standing, firing with and without support, finding the rhythm of the weapon.

"Nice grouping," Jack commented after a while, checking the targets.

"Feels different from the pistols," Simon observed, setting the rifle down and rubbing his shoulder. "More power."

"More power means more responsibility," Jack replied. "But I've got a line on a couple more of these if we need them."

"Make the call," Simon said, his voice even, but his mind already calculating the funds he would allocate for their small arsenal. "We'll need every advantage we can get."

"Will do," Jack replied, already reaching for his phone.

The river flowed quietly beside them, indifferent to the sounds of preparation and the undercurrent of tension that threaded through the crisp morning air. Simon knew that every round fired was one step closer to a confrontation he could not—and would not—avoid.

The rifle's sharp rapport still echoed in Simon's ears as they made their way back to the cabin, the brisk air carrying away the remnants of gunpowder and exertion. Inside, the warmth enveloped them like a comforting shawl. Simon poured two steaming cups of coffee, handing one to Jack before sinking into the worn cushions of the couch.

"Start from the top," Simon urged, his voice low and steady. "Every detail about those places you scouted."

Jack obliged, setting his mug on the low table before him. "The adult bookstore is some type of storage. Don't know what they are keeping there," he began, his brow furrowing as he recalled the scene. "Heavy security for an empty building in the middle of nowhere, even on the Interstate. Guys with neck tats eyeballing everyone who walks by. And the houses? They're fortresses, Simon. Cameras, barred windows, guards on rotation."

Simon nodded, taking slow sips of his coffee while his eyes traced the lines of the map Loran had pinned up. Each location Jack described was marked with a red dot, forming a sinister constellation on the paper.

"Good work," Simon finally said, setting his empty cup aside. "We'll need every bit of intel we can get."

"Speaking of getting..." Lori's voice cut through the room, tinged with resolve as she stepped forward from where she'd been lingering in the doorway. "I want to learn to shoot. I'm not sitting on the sidelines while my little girl is out there with those... monsters."

Simon frowned, his protective instincts flaring. "Lori, it's not that simple—"

"Neither is sitting around waiting," she shot back.

Silence hung between them until Simon's sigh broke the tension. "Alright. Jack, take her down to the river."

"Sure thing," Jack agreed without hesitation, standing up. "Let's go, Lori."

As they left, Simon turned his attention to Loran, who was already booting up the new computer at the dining table. Its screen flickered to life, revealing a neatly organized digital fortress of information.

"Show me what you've got," Simon said, pulling up a chair beside her.

Loran scrolled through an extensive database, her fingers dancing across the keyboard with a surprising grace given her shy demeanor. Documents, photographs, and maps filled the screen, each click uncovering another layer of the cartel's network.

"Everything I could find is here," she explained in her slow, mountain drawl. "It's all connected, just gotta find the weak spots."

"Good work, Loran," Simon praised quietly, impressed by the depth of her research. The blue hue of her skin seemed almost to glow in the light of the screen, a reminder of her unique heritage and resilience.

Together, they delved into the data, piecing together the puzzle that might lead them to victory or defeat. Outside, the echo of gunfire reached them intermittently as Lori took her first steps toward becoming her daughter's avenger. In the quiet of the cabin, surrounded by the weight of impending conflict, Simon felt the gravity of their mission settle upon him, heavy and unyielding.

Simon leaned closer to the monitor, scrutinizing the images that flickered across the screen with an intensity that matched the seriousness of their situation. Loran's voice was a steady undercurrent as she provided him with a stream of information.

"Carlos Ramirez," she said, clicking on a file labeled 'El Fantasma'. "He's the one pulling the strings for the Kentucky cell." A photograph of a man with piercing black eyes and a ghost tattoo on his forearm filled the screen. "They say he can slip through the shadows like they're part of him."

"El Fantasma," Simon murmured, committing the face to memory. "And this?" He pointed to another photo.

"Miguel Alvarez. Goes by El Lobo." She clicked on the image, bringing up the profile of a dark-haired man with a predatory gaze. "A real piece of work, that one. Keeps the kidnapped girls... terrified. He uses fear like it's his own personal weapon."

"Thanks, Loran. You've done good here."

The room was silent for a moment, save for the soft hum of the computer and the distant sounds of gunfire from the riverbank where Lori was learning to shoot. It was a stark reminder of how far they had all been pulled into this fight.

The front door swung open, and Jack walked in with Lori trailing behind him. The two were dusted with the signs of their impromptu shooting lesson, and there was a faint flush on Lori's cheeks from her exertions – or perhaps her determination.

"Hope y'all are hungry," Jack announced, pulling the fixings for sandwiches out of the refrigerator. "Lettuce, tomato, onion, mayonnaise, mustard along with ham and bologna."

"Sweet tea too," Lori added, a hint of a smile tugging at the corners of her lips despite the circumstances.

"Perfect," Simon said, welcoming the brief respite. They gathered around the table, each making the sandwich of choice, grabbed some chips, and took a seat where they could find one.

"Nothing beats a good sandwich after some target practice," Jack commented as he took a big bite, crumbs falling onto his shirt.

"Or data mining," Loran added quietly, sipping her sweet tea.

Conversation waned as they ate, the weight of their mission lingering like a shadow over the cabin. Halfway through the meal, Jack's gaze drifted toward the wall where several photos were pinned next to a detailed map. His eyes narrowed as he recognized one of the faces.

"I have seen that man! He was over in Rowletts," Jack began, rising from his seat to get a closer look at the photo Loran had printed earlier.

"El Lobo," Simon confirmed. "Miguel Alvarez."

"Thought I recognized that cold stare," Jack muttered, studying the image.

"Let's just hope we can wipe that smugness off his face soon enough," Lori interjected, her voice laced with a newfound steeliness.

"Indeed," Simon agreed, glancing between his companions. They were an unlikely team, each drawn into the fray by circumstance and necessity. But as they sat there, sharing a makeshift meal and plotting against a common enemy, Simon couldn't help but feel a sense of camaraderie building among them.

"Alright," he said once they'd finished eating, standing up with a sense of purpose. "Let's get back to it. We've got a cartel to take down."

Loran nodded, her fingers already poised over the keyboard, ready to dive back into the depths of their digital arsenal. And for a moment, in that small cabin, they were more than just individuals; they were a united front against the darkness encroaching upon their lives.

Loran leaned back in her chair. Her indigo-tinged skin gave her a ghostly aura in the dim light. "Alvarez has been with the Ortiz cartel for nearly a decade," she said, her slow southern drawl stretching each syllable. "He's risen fast, all due to his... methods.

"Lori's hands clutched the edges of the table, her knuckles going white. "What kind of methods?"

"Let's just say he doesn't hold back," Simon answered grimly. "And he enjoys his work a little too much.

"The conversation was cut short by a firm knock at the door. Simon stood and strode over, opening it to reveal Mark standing on the porch, his posture tense with urgency.

"Got a minute?" Mark asked, stepping inside without waiting for an invitation.

"Of course," Simon replied, closing the door behind him.

Mark began, his eyes scanning the room before settling on Jack. "Heard you're looking to stock up on some firepower."

Jack nodded, crossing his arms. "A couple of AR-15s to start with."

"Good choice," Mark said. "But if you need a little extra punch, I've got an officer who's handy with hardware. He can modify those ARs from semi to full auto.

"Simon raised an eyebrow, the implications of such an action hanging heavily in the air. "Isn't that..."

"Against the law? Yeah." Mark shrugged. "But sometimes the book needs a rewrite. Especially when it comes to dealing with scum like the Ortiz cartel."

"Sometimes you gotta fight fire with fire," Jack said, his voice resolute.

"Exactly." Mark's jaw set firmly. "I'll have him come by, off the books. We're not playing games here."

"Appreciated," Simon said, his gaze returning to the map and photos on the wall. The stakes were high, and the path ahead was fraught with peril. But as he looked around at the faces of those gathered—each marked by the resolve to see this through—he knew they were ready to do what needed to be done.

Simon flicked through drone footage on the laptop, squinting as the grainy images jumped across the screen. Around him, the cabin was silent except for the soft whirring of the computer and an occasional sip of coffee from Lori, her hands wrapped tight around the mug like it could anchor her to this moment of calm before the storm.

"Cartel's been usin' these things for surveillance?" Jack muttered, leaning over Simon's shoulder. "Gives them eyes everywhere without riskin' a single one of 'em."

"Should we be doing the same then?" Simon asked, finally looking up from the screen, his blue eyes searching the room for answers.

"Could keep us from walking into a trap," Mark added, his thumbs hooked into his belt loops, weight shifting from one foot to another.

"Problem is, none of us have the chops to fly these things." Jack's gaze was fixed on the screen, his brow furrowed as if he could solve the problem by sheer force of will.

"Actually," Loran's voice cut through, soft but steady, "my brothers are pretty damn good with drones." She tucked a stray lock of hair behind her ear, her slight indigo tint more pronounced under the cabin's lighting.

Simon turned toward her, an eyebrow raised in surprise. "Your brothers?"

"Yep, they can fly 'em like they got wings themselves," Loran said. "Might be worth bringin' 'em into this."

"Sounds like a plan." Simon closed the laptop with a snap. "But we should talk to Greg first, make sure he's okay with it."

"Let me give Pa a call," Loran said, pulling out her phone and stepping outside for privacy, the screen casting a blue glow on her face as she dialed.

The group watched through the window as she spoke, her gestures minimal but her posture resolute. When she returned, there was a resolve in her step that hadn't been there before.

"Pa says come on over," she announced, pocketing the phone. "He'll let the boys show you what they can do."

"Alright then, let's roll out," Simon declared, collecting his jacket from the back of a chair.

They stepped outside, the cool air of the Kentucky morning nipping at their skin. The world seemed oblivious to the gravity of their mission, birds chirping carelessly in the trees surrounding Simon's pick-up truck. Lori slid into the middle of the bench seat, Loran slid in next to her, the vinyl cold against her jeans, while Jack opted to ride with Mark, the two of them sharing a nod that spoke volumes of their shared history.

"Everyone buckled in?" Simon asked as he turned the key in the ignition, the truck rumbling to life beneath them.

"Ready as we'll ever be," Lori replied, her voice steadier than Simon expected.

"Then let's get moving," he said, glancing in the rearview mirror before easing the truck onto the dirt road, gravel crunching under its tires.

"Feels like we're assembling an army," Simon said through the open window as they followed behind Mark, a wry smile touching his lips.

"More like a family," Loran corrected quietly, gazing out the window at the passing scenery, her reflection mingling with the blur of trees.

And with that simple truth hanging between them, they drove on, leaving trails of dust and determination in their wake.

Simon's pickup rolled to a stop, gravel crunching beneath its tires like the ticking of a clock counting down to an inevitable confrontation. The house before them stood unassuming among the lush greenery of Troublesome Creek, but it was the figures on the porch that held their attention.

As they approached, Simon couldn't help but notice the sea of indigo-tinted faces that greeted them. It was clear that Loran's family had come out in full force to welcome them. Each face held a unique blend of curiosity and warmth, making Simon feel instantly at ease. He couldn't help but be drawn in by the vibrant colors and diverse features of Loran's clan.

"Must be a Smith thing," Lori whispered, the hint of a smile fleeting across her lips despite the gravity of their visit.

They unfolded themselves from the truck with the ease of long familiarity, Simon's boots hitting the dirt first, followed by Lori's quieter step. Jack and Mark joined them, falling into step as they approached the porch where Greg Smith stood—a mountain of a man whose presence seemed to command the very air around him.

"Pa," Loran said, her voice carrying that slow southern drawl that spoke of deep roots and unwavering strength. "This is Simon, Lori, and you've met Jack. And Mark."

"Welcome." Greg's handshake was firm, enveloping their hands in his like a bear would a salmon, but his eyes were kind, a soft contrast to the steel in his grip.

"Thank you for havin' us," Simon replied, tipping his head in respect.

"Let's not stand on ceremony," Greg suggested, gesturing towards the living room. "Come on in, and we'll talk."

Inside, the conversation flowed as naturally as the creek outside. Simon outlined their situation, the words heavy with the weight of lives at stake. Lori's hands twisted together, her knuckles white, as she listened, the fear for her daughter a silent scream between each sentence.

"Greg, we're not here to drag your boys into danger," Simon assured him. "But we're up against something bigger than us, and we need all the help we can get."

Greg nodded, his expression unreadable for a moment before he spoke. "I understand your concern, and I share it. This cartel... if they take root here, none of us are safe. Our home, our way of life—it's all on the line."

He paused, glancing back at the indigo-faced youth who had gathered quietly in the doorway, watching with solemn eyes. "The boys can show you what they can do with those drones. And if it comes to it... We're willing to stand with you."

"Thank you, Greg," Simon said, relief threading through his voice. "That means more than I can say."

"Family looks out for each other," Greg replied simply.

As the meeting drew to a close, there was a sense of unity that hadn't been there before—a bond forged not just by necessity, but by the understanding that some fights were too important to face alone. They were no longer strangers; they were allies, linked by a common cause and a shared determination to protect what was theirs.

"Let's see what those drones can do," Simon said, a spark of resolve lighting his eyes.

"Follow me," one of the boys said, a grin spreading across his face as he led them outside.

And with the sun dipping low in the sky, casting long shadows that stretched toward the encroaching night, they stepped back into the fresh air, ready to witness the skill that could turn the tide in a war they never asked for—but one they were determined to win.

The evening air buzzed with an unexpected levity as the Smith boys, armed with remote controls that looked far too sophisticated for simple play, coaxed three sleek drones into the sky. The hum of the propellers melded with the laughter and chatter of the onlookers, creating a symphony of modern country life that seemed out of place given the grave circumstances that had brought everyone together.

"Watch this, y'all," the youngest Smith boy called out. With deft flicks of his thumbs, he sent his drone spiraling upwards before it dove down, narrowly missing the branches of an old oak and eliciting gasps from the crowd.

Simon stood at the edge of the gathering, his broad shoulders relaxed in a way that Loran hadn't seen since they'd started this grim undertaking. His gaze followed the drones' aerial dance, a hint of admiration flashing in his normally stoic blue eyes. It was clear these weren't just kids playing with toys; they were pilots commanding their crafts with precision and skill.

"Them boys could give any military drone operator a run for their money," Lori said.

"Looks like it," Simon agreed, the corner of his mouth tilting up ever so slightly.

One by one, the drones weaved through the forest's natural obstacle course, zipping between trees and underbrush with the agility that belied their operators' casual demeanor. At one point, a drone dipped low, its camera locking onto a couple of unsuspecting raccoons that scurried across the forest floor.

The critters froze, eyes wide as saucers, before darting into a thicket, the drone hot on their trail until they disappeared from sight.

"Almost makes you forget what we're up against," Loran remarked, standing on tiptoes to get a better view. Her blue eyes reflected the last rays of sunlight piercing through the canopy.

"Almost," Simon echoed, his voice barely above a whisper.

"Wouldn't mind having one of them drones myself," Jack muttered, rubbing his chin thoughtfully. "Imagine the advantage in scouting."

"Advantage and then some," Mark added, nodding. "Especially if those boys are behind the controls."

As the demonstration continued, the atmosphere grew lighter, the tension that had been coiled tight around everyone's shoulders unwinding strand by strand. Laughter floated on the breeze, mixing with the chirps of crickets that signaled the approach of night.

"Feels like a carnival," Lori mused aloud, the corners of her eyes crinkling with a smile that had been absent for far too long.

"Best kind," Loran replied, her indigo-tinted skin glowing in the dusky light. For a brief moment, the world narrowed to this pocket of joy amidst the chaos—a reminder of what they were fighting to protect.

As the drones finally descended, coming to rest gently on the grass, applause broke out among the group. The boys took a bow, their cheeks flushed with pride. And even though dark clouds loomed on the horizon, threatening the peace of their small Kentucky enclave, tonight they allowed themselves the luxury of hope, bolstered by the spectacle of flying machines and the bond of newfound allies.

"Reckon you'll be needing their help sooner than later," Greg said, clapping Simon on the back.

"Let's hope it's later," Simon responded, his mind already shifting gears back to the mission at hand. But for now, he let the sounds of celebration fill the space where worry usually resided, if only for a moment.

Chapter 6

Simon crouched behind the weathered trunk of a massive oak, its gnarled roots snaking across the forest floor just off the front of the barn between them and the abandoned adult bookstore—a perfect natural barrier for what they were about to witness. Beside him, Jack was almost imperceptible in his camouflaged gear, eyes fixed through the binoculars pressed against his face. The Kentucky woods around them were thick with underbrush, giving cover and a certain primeval comfort that only seasoned operatives like them could appreciate.

"Anything?" Simon whispered, his voice barely rustling the leaves that blanketed the ground.

"Four tangos outside, armed. Looks like an AK-variant for each. Two by the door, two roaming. They're not here for the scenery."

Simon's blue eyes narrowed as he processed the information. He didn't need to see for himself; Jack's observational skills were as sharp as the knife Simon kept sheathed at his ankle. They both knew this was no small-time operation—the cartel had sunk their claws deep into Hart County soil.

A commotion stirred beyond their line of sight, and the muffled sound of raised voices filtered through the trees. Instinctively, Simon reached for the compact monocular clipped to his belt and peered through it, angling for a better look at the unfolding drama.

"Damn," he muttered under his breath. A group of locals, faces etched with fear and anger, confronted two cartel members in the parking lot of the strip mall near the CB shop that served as the facade for this rural drug nexus. A scrawny teen, no older than seventeen, stepped forward, his chest puffed out in a brave attempt to stand his ground.

"Big mistake, kid," Jack said, almost to himself.

One of the cartel enforcers sneered, something wicked glinting in his hand—a blade, catching the slanting sunlight that managed to pierce the canopy. The other thug grabbed the boy by the collar, shoving him back against a car so hard that the fender dented slightly.

"Let's hope he doesn't do something he'll regret," Simon said, though they both knew regret wasn't something men like these trafficked in.

The scene escalated quickly. The cartel member with the knife gestured wildly, the threat clear even without hearing the words. The locals shuffled uneasily, casting glances at each other that screamed of desperation and a creeping sense of doom.

"Time?" Simon asked, his gaze never leaving the binoculars.

"Three past two. They're right on schedule if the intel is solid."

"Ready when you are."

Jack nodded curtly, and they both knew what came next—wait, watch, and learn. Every detail mattered: the faces, the movements, the subtle cues that spelled out the hierarchy within the cartel's ranks.

"Let's just hope we can get what we need without diving into that mess," Jack added, though the unspoken sentiment hung heavy between them: if it came to it, they wouldn't hesitate to jump into the fray. For now, they were shadows among the trees, silent witnesses to the cruelty that had infested the tranquil hills of Kentucky.

Simon felt the tension coil in his gut, a familiar sensation that always preceded action. He watched through the green foliage as one of the cartel thugs grabbed a young woman by the arm, yanking her closer with unnecessary force. Her eyes, wide with fear, flicked around, searching for a savior in a sea of hostile faces.

"Jack," Simon murmured, his voice barely a whisper, yet carrying the weight of impending conflict.

"Got it," Jack replied, already shifting from his spot, his body language calm but his eyes sharp and assessing.

They had planned to remain unseen observers today, but some lines weren't meant to be crossed—not on their watch. The woman's silent plea was enough to spark the decision, and within seconds, they moved.

Simon slipped from the cover of the trees, his footsteps muffled by the underbrush. Jack took a wider arc, intending to cut off any escape or interference from the other cartel members. They were a blur of motion, synchronized and silent as ghosts.

In a swift movement, Simon closed the distance from the trees, across the open patch of grass, and into the parking lot. His hand shot out, grabbing the assailant's wrist and twisting sharply. A pained gasp escaped the thug's lips as he released the woman, who stumbled back, her breath hitching in her throat.

Jack was there in an instant, incapacitating another cartel member with a precise strike to the sternum followed by a swift chop to the neck. The man crumpled to the ground like a felled tree.

"Run," Simon urged the woman, but she froze, her gaze flickering between him and the unconscious bodies of her aggressors.

"Who are you?" she asked, her voice shaky but laced with a hint of awe.

"Friends. We're here to help."

Her eyes brimmed with tears of relief. "I... I can tell you things. About them," she gestured towards the fallen men, "about Poteet Valley."

"Let's get you somewhere safe first," Simon interjected, scanning the area for more trouble. They needed to move—now.

"Thank you," she whispered as they ushered her away from the scene, her gratitude palpable.

Once secure in the relative safety of the abandoned barn they had been watching from, the young woman's composure began to return, and with it, a flood of information. She spoke of the holdup house nestled on the edge of Mammoth Cave National Park, where others like her were being kept. She detailed the guards' shifts, the hidden paths leading to the grand house, and even the times when the cartel bosses would visit.

As the sun dipped low, casting long shadows over the Kentucky hills, Simon and Jack listened intently. Each piece of intel was a weapon in its own right, and they knew the value of what they were given. This young woman, once a victim, had become their informant—and perhaps the key to dismantling a part of the Ortiz Cartel's vile enterprise.

"Thank you," Simon told her. "You've been incredibly brave."

"Will you stop them?" she asked, a hopeful tremor in her voice.

"We will," Jack assured her, his tone as steady as his resolve.

And as they made plans under the cover of twilight, the promise hung in the air, a vow made not just to the woman, but to all those suffering at the hands of the cartel. The fight was far from over, but tonight, they had scored a quiet victory.

Huddled behind the thick veil of Kentucky underbrush, Simon and Jack studied the holdup house with clinical detachment. The setting sun gave way to a creeping twilight that painted the two-story structure in deepening shades of gray. With each passing moment, the environment became an ally, cloaking their movements as they prepared for their assault.

"Four guards on rotation," murmured Simon, his eyes never leaving the lookout perched by the second-floor window. "Two by the main entrance. One roving."

"Roving's your wildcard," Jack whispered back, the faint lines around his eyes tightening as he scanned for patterns in the guard's patrol. "We'll need to time it just right."

"Agreed. We go when he rounds the corner—gives us a twenty-second window." Simon's voice was calm, every word measured and deliberate.

"Back door?"

"Unmanned. Our informant said it's their blind spot."

"Let's not make it our own." Jack's cautionary tone was a reminder that overconfidence was as deadly as any bullet.

"Never," Simon replied, the corner of his mouth twitching with a grim sort of humor. They both knew the stakes.

The two men shared a nod, a silent accord formed from trust and shared experience. Then, they slipped from the shadows, blending into the night like specters.

Silent as the breeze whispering through the leaves, they moved towards the house. Jack's hand signals were crisp, and clear even in the dim light, guiding Simon to the left as they split to flank the building.

Simon approached the back door, his steps so light he might have been another shadow among many. He reached into his pocket, pulling out a small lock pick set, and within seconds, the lock gave way with a hushed click. He eased the door open, pausing to listen. Nothing but the distant sound of a night bird calling to the moon.

Inside, the air was stale, heavy with the scent of fear and unwashed bodies. Simon's throat tightened, but he pushed the emotion down. Now wasn't the time. Head on a swivel, he crept forward, his hands ready to silence any threat.

Jack, meanwhile, had found his way beneath the lookout's window. With the precision of a man who had scaled more dangerous facades, he ascended, finding purchase on the smallest of ledges. His fingers wrapped around the edge of the windowsill, and with a controlled exhale, he hoisted himself up and through the opening before the lookout could so much as shift in his seat.

The guard's surprise was quickly silenced as Jack's muscular arm snaked around his neck, pulling him back into a vice-like grip against a chest as solid as a brick wall. With a swift motion, Jack expertly cut off the man's oxygen, rendering him unconscious in an instant. The guard hung limply in Jack's grasp, supported only by his unyielding strength. A knife sticking out of his chest had punctured his heart as intended. A quiet "shh" escaped Jack's lips as he whispered into the man's ear, his voice surprisingly gentle for such a deadly act. It was over before it began, with the guard left slumped at Jack's feet.

One by one, Simon and Jack neutralized the threats within the holdup house. A shadowy dance of sorts, where they anticipated moves, countered, and subdued with the efficiency of men who had long ago learned that hesitation meant death. There were no grand flourishes here, no wasted movement— just the quiet thuds of bodies hitting the floor, too fast to raise the alarm.

Together, they cleared room after room, their presence still unknown to the rest of the cartel members scattered throughout the house. They communicated with glances and subtle gestures, a language forged in the fires of countless missions.

It wasn't until they reached the last guard, the one whose path had seemed so random, that their rhythm faltered. The guard turned suddenly, an instinctive reaction to some imperceptible change in the air. But Simon was already there, his arm locking around the man's throat. There was a brief struggle, a grunt of exertion from Simon as he applied pressure.

Then, nothing but the quiet patter of a body gently lowered to the ground.

"Clear," Simon whispered into the comms unit nestled snugly in his ear.

"Clear," came Jack's response, echoing from the other side of the house.

They met in the hallway, their gazes locking in silent acknowledgment of what they'd accomplished—and what was yet to come. With the guards taken care of, they had a moment to catch their breath, to prepare for the next phase of their plan. But there was no mistaking the hard set of Simon's jaw or the fire burning in Jack's eyes.

This was just the beginning.

Simon's muscles tensed as they rounded the corner into the dimly lit basement, their boots silent on the cold concrete floor. The faint hum of a generator reverberated through the walls, and the pungent scent of mold mingled with the metallic tang of fear. It was here, in the bowels of the hideout, that they encountered the die-hard defenders of the cartel's sinister operation.

Two brute-like figures emerged from the shadows, their eyes narrowing at the sight of the intruders. There was no time for subtlety now; this was going to be a brawl. Simon felt the familiar surge of adrenaline course through his veins as he locked eyes with the nearest assailant—a mountain of a man with knuckles scarred from countless fights.

"Jack," Simon muttered, the name barely leaving his lips before the hulking figure charged.

Jack nodded, understanding the plan without words. They'd been in scraps like this before, each one a deadly dance they knew by heart. As the first thug lunged at Simon with meaty fists, Jack swung around, aiming a precise kick at the second attacker's knee, the crack echoing in the confined space.

Simon ducked under a wild swing, feeling the whoosh of air as a fist sailed over his head. He pivoted, delivering a sharp jab to the man's midsection. The thug grunted, more surprised than hurt, and Simon seized the moment, driving a punishing elbow into the man's jaw. The crack was sickening, but Simon didn't flinch; he couldn't afford to.

On the other side of the room, Jack grappled with his own opponent, the two of them locked in a fierce struggle. Jack's discipline and training shone through as he absorbed a hit only to retaliate with a swift uppercut, his attacker's head snapping back. But these were no ordinary street thugs—they were hardened criminals, driven by desperation and loyalty to the cartel.

The fight was chaos, a whirlwind of strikes and counters. Simon could hear his own breathing, heavy and controlled, as he dodged another punch and responded with a quick combination of his own. His fists were a blur, each hit calculated to incapacitate, not kill. They needed answers, after all.

A sudden shout signaled Jack's success as his foe crumpled to the ground, but there was no time for celebration. Simon's adversary was relentless, shaking off blows that would've felled lesser men. But Simon was a force unto himself, every move honed by years of covert operations. He sidestepped a haymaker and swept the man's legs, sending him crashing down.

"Stay down," Simon growled, his voice low and dangerous. But the thug struggled to rise, spitting blood and defiance.

"Enough," Jack said, stepping beside Simon and offering a hand—not to help the man up, but to signal the end of the fight. The message was clear: they were not to be trifled with. The cartel outlaw would not give up, he had declared his loyalty to Juan Ortiz, and he would die before failing his job.

Together, Simon and Jack stood over their fallen adversaries, chests heaving. It was over, for now. They had won, but this victory was just a small triumph in a larger war— a war they were determined to win, whatever the cost.

Simon's knuckles ached with the satisfying throb of victory as he surveyed the dimly lit room—finally silent except for the ragged breaths of the defeated man sprawled across the floor. Jack gave him a terse nod, his eyes still scanning for threats out of old habit. They both knew they had to move quickly; time was a luxury they couldn't afford.

"Let's tear this place apart," Simon said, his voice resonant with the kind of grim determination that came from years of chasing shadows. He felt in his bones that they were close to something big, something that could tip the scales in their long struggle against the Ortiz Cartel.

"Right behind you," Jack replied, already moving towards a desk piled high with papers and clutter—a chaotic mess that concealed more than it revealed.

They rifled through drawers, flipped over mattresses, and shook out books. This wasn't just about finding evidence; it was personal. Simon could almost see Jennifer's face, her vibrant spirit dulled by the fear these monsters peddled. He shuddered at the thought of her being moved, used as a pawn in the cartel's sick game.

"Got something," Jack called out, holding up a ledger with scribbled notes and names. "Looks like a schedule—transport times, locations... and look here, rooms for holding."

"Those bastards," Simon muttered, taking the ledger and flipping through the pages. His eyes caught on a detail, a note scrawled in the margin: 'JH moved pre-raid'. Jennifer Hawkins.

Anger flared in his chest, but he tamped it down. They needed to stay focused.

"Means we're striking fear into them at least. They're changing tactics," Jack noted, his tone more analytical than emotional. He was right; it was a sign of their impact, but cold comfort when lives hung in the balance.

"Let's keep looking. There's got to be more." Simon's gaze swept the room, settling on a seemingly innocuous section of wall. Something didn't add up. It was too clean, untouched by the grime that layered everything else.

"Jack, help me with this," he said, pushing against the wall. Together they searched, pressing and tapping until a hollow sound echoed back. With a collective effort, they pushed harder until a section of the wall gave way, revealing a hidden chamber bathed in the harsh glow of fluorescent lights. As they stood and studied the chamber before going in, Simon felt rather than heard a disturbance behind him. He turned and saw the cartel outlaw he had fought with a knife held above his head in both hands posed to strike Simon in the back of the neck. Before he could react, Jack had swiftly slid his knife to the hilt into the outlaw's temple. His eyes bulged, he coughed and then Jack removed his knife and pushed the dead outlaw backwards.

Simon looked from the outlaw to Jack and said "Damn, now I owe you." Both men smiled that warrior smile which said they had each other's back no matter what.

"Jesus," Jack whispered as they stepped inside the chamber. Rows of shelving held bricks of narcotics, stacks of cash bundled neatly, and an arsenal that would make a small army envious. The air was thick with the scent of gun oil and greed.

"Look at all this..." Simon trailed off, unable to fully process the extent of the operation. This wasn't just a local problem; it was a veritable hub of criminal enterprise stretching far beyond Hart County.

"Enough firepower here to start a war," Jack said, picking up an assault rifle and checking its magazine with practiced ease. "And drugs... enough to poison half the state."

"Or fund their next move," Simon added grimly. He pulled out his phone, snapping pictures of the room.

Evidence—they needed all they could get to bring the cartel to its knees.

"Let's document everything. We'll need it for the briefing," Jack suggested, already cataloging the weapons with quick, efficient movements.

"Agreed." Simon's mind was racing, overlaying plans and contingencies. They'd struck a blow today, but the fight was far from over. As they worked to record the cache before them, Simon knew one thing for certain: the cartel had underestimated them—and that was a mistake he intended to make them regret.

Simon's finger lingered over the last of the drugs he had photographed with his phone when a distant shuffle of boots on gravel reached his ears. He exchanged a look with Jack, who had also frozen, his senses heightened. The two men shared an unspoken understanding; they weren't alone anymore.

"Time to ghost," Simon murmured, pocketing his phone. Their eyes locked onto the door leading to the back of the house where they had come in—a narrow escape route they had noted earlier for just such a contingency.

"Got your six," Jack replied, slipping the assault rifle's strap over his shoulder. They moved as shadows, blending with the dim interior, their footsteps muffled against the cold floor. Each man was acutely aware of how the walls of the holdup house could turn into their tomb if they didn't act fast.

"Left hallway—clear," Jack whispered, peeking around the corner with military precision.

"Go." Simon's command was barely audible, but it carried the weight of urgency. They advanced, each covering the other's blind spots, the rhythm of their movement a dance they had mastered over countless missions.

As they neared the exit, the murmur of voices grew louder, the clatter of approaching boots more distinct. Simon's pulse thrashed in his temples; he could almost feel the adrenaline coursing through Jack's veins as well. They were close— dangerously close.

"Back down the stairs," Jack mouthed, pointing to the decrepit staircase to their right that led to the basement. It was a risky move—the wooden steps could groan under their weight and betray their presence—but it offered a momentary shield from sight.

"Lead the way," Simon said, trusting Jack's instincts. They descended with the stealth of hunters, each step deliberate, avoiding the spots where the wood looked weakest.

As they descended the ladder, hasty footsteps and shouts echoed from above. The air was filled with a cacophony of panic and alarm as the doors were kicked open, shaking the very foundations of the holdup house. The previously still and silent corpses of outlaws had been discovered by their comrades, only moments away from being caught.

"Quickly, the tunnels," Simon breathed out, recalling the blueprint of the old bootlegger paths that snaked beneath the property. Jack nodded, already moving toward the concealed entrance they had stumbled upon earlier. Their research had paid off; the cartel hadn't bothered to find all the secrets this old place hid.

They slipped through the opening, the narrow passageway enveloping them in darkness. Behind them, the search continued, the cartel members none the wiser to the escape route hidden beneath their feet.

"Keep it silent," Simon instructed, though it was hardly necessary. Jack was a ghost behind him, his presence only confirmed by the faint brush of fabric or the controlled exhale of breath. They navigated the labyrinthine tunnels, relying on memory and the faint glow of Simon's watch face to guide them.

Minutes stretched like hours, the tension winding tight until at last, a sliver of moonlight beckoned from above—an exit, just as they had mapped it out. With a boost from Simon, Jack ascended the ladder rungs, then pulled his comrade up into the cool night air of Poteet Valley.

They emerged amidst thickets of wild brush, nature's cloak of invisibility. Pausing only to ensure they left no trace, they vanished into the Kentucky wilderness, the sounds of pursuit fading into the night.

In the sanctuary of shadows, Simon allowed himself a moment to catch his breath, his blue eyes scanning the treeline. They had made it out, not just with their lives but with evidence that could cripple an empire of corruption. And for now, that was enough.

The Kentucky night air was thick with tension as Simon and Jack sprinted through the dense underbrush, their breaths coming in short, sharp bursts. The rhythmic pounding of their boots against the soft earth was a desperate drumbeat urging them forward, away from the danger snapping at their heels.

"Left, up ahead!" Simon called out, his voice low but urgent, directing them toward a narrow deer trail he'd memorized days before. Jack nodded, trusting Simon's knowledge of the terrain implicitly. They banked sharply, branches whipping at their faces, leaving thin red marks that were quickly forgotten in the adrenaline rush.

They could hear the cartel members crashing through the foliage behind them, voices raised in frustration as they lost ground to the two men who moved like specters through the night. Occasionally, a shot would ring out from someone in the cartel as they thought they saw movement. None of the rounds found their mark. Simon and Jack were an efficient team, each movement calculated and every decision based on practiced coordination.

As they neared a clearing, Simon signaled for a sudden stop, pressing close to a large oak tree. Jack mirrored the action, both men going still, their breathing controlled. The sound of their pursuers faded, muffled by the natural barriers of the forest. It was risky, stopping like this, but it was necessary—like the eye of a hurricane, a momentary reprieve before the onslaught continued.

Minutes ticked by, and when no sounds betrayed the presence of the cartel, Simon gave a curt nod. "We're clear for now," he said, his tone conveying relief mixed with caution. They moved again, this time at a steadier pace, conserving energy for the long trek back to safety.

After what seemed an eternity, they arrived at their rendezvous point, a secluded cabin nestled between towering pines. The warm glow from within promised rest and a respite from the chaos they'd left behind.

Inside, Loran and Lori awaited, anxiety etched into their features. Simon gave them a brief, weary smile as he and Jack crossed the threshold. He dropped a heavy duffel bag with a thud onto the wooden floor, its contents vital to their cause.

"Got something you might want to see," Simon said, his voice rough from exertion as he unzipped the bag and revealed stacks of documents, several encrypted drives, and a collection of photographs.

Lori stepped forward, her blue eyes reflecting the gravity of the situation. She reached out, her hand trembling slightly as she picked up one of the photos. It depicted a group of young women, fear evident in their eyes—a stark reminder of what was at stake.

Loran, silent until now, leaned over the table. "This is it, ain't it?" she asked with her characteristic slow southern drawl, the weight of the evidence not lost on her.

"Yep, that's the heart of the beast," Jack confirmed, his broad shoulders sagging slightly as the adrenaline left his system.

For a moment, they simply stood there, absorbing the reality of their success. They had infiltrated the heart of darkness and emerged with more than just their lives—they held the key to dismantling the cartel operations in Hart County.

"We did good tonight," Simon finally said, allowing himself a small nod of approval. His gaze met Lori's, and a silent promise passed between them. They would stop at nothing to bring her daughter home.

"Let's get to work," Jack said, rolling his sleeves up. "We've got a cartel to take down."

Dawn painted the horizon with bruised purples and fiery oranges as Simon sat on the hood of their dusty pickup, parked in the shadow of an old barn. Jack leaned against the vehicle, a half-eaten energy bar in one hand, his eyes scanning the treeline. They'd spent the night poring over the intel, connecting dots that formed a grim picture of the Ortiz Cartel's reach.

"Looks like Juan's been busy," Jack mumbled, his voice rough with fatigue.

"More like a plague," Simon replied, staring at the map spread across the hood, marked with notes and lines. "But now we know the veins feeding the disease."

"Cut off the supply, starve the fever," Jack said, finishing Simon's thought.

"Exactly." Simon folded the map with precise creases. "We need to go bigger on this one. It's time to bring in the heavy hitters."

"Briggs and his crew?" Jack arched an eyebrow, his tone skeptical.

"Briggs, Larry, and... the CIA Director herself." Simon reached into his pocket, pulling out a phone that had seen better days but held secure lines to the most powerful people in espionage.

"Going straight to the top, huh?" Jack tossed the remnants of his snack aside, wiping his hands on his jeans. "You sure she'll take the meeting?"

Simon dialed the number he'd memorized long ago, the phone pressed against his ear, the ringing tone echoing slightly in the crisp morning air.

"Briggs," came the gruff answer after three rings, a voice accustomed to urgency and command.

"Briggs, it's Wilson. We need to meet. The full monty," Simon stated, his voice low but steady.

There was a pause on the line, a momentary silence that spoke of calculations being made, risks weighed.

"You have something solid?"

"Solid and actionable. We've charted the network, identified weak spots, and got enough dirt to plant a garden of justice," Simon said, allowing a hint of dry humor to color his words despite the gravity of their situation.

"Give me two hours. I'll get Harlow and the Director. Where?"

"Let's meet at the farm."

"Got it. Two hours."

"Two hours," Simon echoed, ending the call.

He locked eyes with Jack, his blue gaze hardening with resolve. "Let's gear up. This is where the real fight begins."

"About damn time," Jack responded, pushing off from the car with a renewed sense of purpose.

The two men set about preparing their equipment, checking weaponry for future needs, and securing the precious data they had bled for. They were no strangers to violence, each scar and callus a testament to battles fought—both physical and mental. But this... this was the turning point they had been working towards, the moment when the tide would begin to turn in their favor.

By the time the sun fully cleared the horizon, casting long shadows across the Kentucky landscape, Simon and Jack were ready. Ready to confront the darkness with unyielding light, to strike at the heart of corruption with unwavering determination.

The glass-and-steel monolith of the CIA headquarters towered above them, reflecting the clear skies in its polished facade. Simon led his motley crew through the revolving doors with a sense of purpose that belied his casual attire. The reception area was bustling, yet their entry seemed to carve a moment of stillness as onlookers took in Loran's indigo hue and Lori's nervous poise.

"Wilson, party of four," Simon announced to the receptionist, whose eyes lingered curiously over Loran. A nod from behind the desk directed them to a set of leather couches in the lobby. "We'll be escorted shortly," Simon added, noting Jack scanning the room with military precision.

"Feels like we're inside the belly of the beast," Jack murmured, his voice low enough only for their ears.

"More like the brain," Simon replied, leaning back and crossing his arms, watching the ebb and flow of operatives and analysts.

Loran sat quietly, her eyes tracing the intricate patterns on the marble floor, while Lori fidgeted beside her, her gaze darting around the imposing space. Time stretched until a well-dressed man approached with an efficiency that spoke of countless such errands.

"Mr. Wilson? Please follow me."

The conference room was stark, yet functional, with a long table dominating the center. Amanda Sawyer stood at the head, her presence commanding attention without a word. Briggs and Larry were already seated, their expressions unreadable.

"Director Sawyer, allow me to introduce my team," Simon began, gesturing to each member in turn. "Jack Thompson, former Air Force Security Forces. Loran Smith, from Troublesome Creek—her insights have been invaluable." He paused as some of the CIA members exchanged glances at Loran's distinct appearance. "And this is Lori Hawkins, she's had a firsthand experience with the cartel's impact."

"Welcome," Amanda said, her voice measured. "Let's get down to business."

Simon nodded, and they all took their seats, the tension hanging in the air like static before a storm. As they settled, the room filled with the silent acknowledgment that the game was about to change. With Simon's team at the vanguard, the Ortiz Cartel wouldn't know what hit them.

Simon leaned forward, the light from the overhead fixtures glinting off the surface of the portable hard drive as he passed it to Amanda Sawyer. "What you're about to see," he said, his voice carrying a weight that quieted the murmurs around the table, "is everything we've uncovered."

Amanda examined the device briefly, her eyes meeting Simon's for a moment before she called for the IT specialist. Within minutes, a young man in glasses entered, taking the hard drive with practiced care. He connected it to a laptop, ran a quick scan, and then nodded to the director. The room darkened slightly as the screen on the front wall flickered to life, displaying folders neatly organized by date and location.

"Ms. Smith will walk us through it," Simon said, gesturing towards Loran who, until now, had been a silent observer, seemingly lost in the room's grandeur.

Loran stood up, her slight stature becoming somehow magnified as all eyes fixed on her. Her fingers danced across the keyboard, bringing up images, maps, and documents, each click revealing another layer of their painstaking investigation. With her slow southern drawl cutting through the sterile ambiance of the conference room, she narrated the findings.

"Here's the layout of the Holdup house in Poteet Valley, and here are the surveillance photos of the cartel's comings and goings."

The details unfolded on the screen—a digital tapestry of clandestine operations and covert recon, evidence of the cartel's sprawling network meticulously documented for the CIA to dissect. When the briefing concluded, a silence settled over the room, punctuated only by the soft hum of the projector.

"Where did this intel come from?" Amanda finally asked, her gaze sharp as she assessed Simon.

"Groundwork. My team covered Hart County. We got close—closer than comfortable." He avoided specifics, leaving out the more dangerous encounters, the narrow escapes. "And I spent some time in Mexico, gathering what I could."

"Your team has done impressive work," Amanda said, though her eyes still held questions. Simon knew that dance— the push and pull of information, the measured give-and-take.

"Thank you," Simon said, acknowledging the compliment but ready to move past pleasantries. "We have a window of opportunity now. The Ortiz Cartel is vulnerable."

"Indeed," Amanda mused, tapping the hard drive thoughtfully. "Let's make sure we use what you've brought us effectively."

As the lights came back on, the room stirred into action, analysts and operatives huddling around monitors, dissecting Loran's presentation frame by frame. Simon watched them, knowing that the real fight was just beginning, and the path ahead would demand every ounce of their collective cunning and resolve.

"Accuracy," Amanda insisted, her voice cutting through the murmurs of discussion. "I need to be certain. Is this intel as precise as what we've got?"

Simon leaned forward, his gaze steady despite the fatigue that edged his eyes. "Every data point was cross-checked with local sources. We covered a lot of ground to confirm."

Amanda's eyes flicked toward Loran, who had remained quiet, almost blending into the background of the conference room. "Ms. Smith, can you corroborate?"

Loran nodded, her slight figure unassuming yet resolute. "Yes, ma'am. We made sure to verify information with folks from Hart County. They know the land, the people."

"And the holdup house?" Amanda pressed, her eyebrows knitting together.

"Seen it with our own eyes," Simon interjected. "The intel on the location and operations—it's solid."

"Show me," Amanda said.

With a nod, Simon stood and crossed to the projector. The click of the keyboard was punctuated by his narration, detailing the safehouse surveillance, and the patterns they'd identified. On-screen, satellite imagery zoomed in on Poteet Valley, overlaid with heat maps and movement trails—the clandestine world laid bare in bytes and pixels.

"Explain how you obtained these images," Amanda demanded, scrutinizing the screen.

"Observation posts, drones, the civilian kind, high-powered lenses, a bit of old-fashioned sneaking around," Simon replied, his explanation casual but not without pride. Loran added a soft "Mmhmm" in agreement.

"Without detection?"

"Without detection," Simon affirmed, thinking back on the close calls they'd omitted from their report.

"Very well," Amanda conceded, though her eyes still searched Simon's face for any telltale signs of evasion. She seemed to weigh her next words carefully. "This is commendable work. But remember, you're playing in a bigger arena now. We can't afford mistakes."

"Understood." Simon exchanged a glance with Loran, their shared experiences unspoken but understood. They had walked the razor's edge together and would do so again.

"Good." Amanda leaned back, a small nod indicating her satisfaction—for now. "We'll take it from here. Make sure your team is ready for what comes next."

As the meeting disbanded, the low buzz of conversation picked up once more. Loran quietly collected the hard drive, slipping it back into her bag. Simon watched her, his mind already racing ahead to their next move.

"Thanks," he murmured as they left the room, the hum of CIA activity fading behind them.

"Anytime," Loran replied, her slight indigo tint barely noticeable in the corridor's fluorescent lighting. They walked side by side, partners in a mission far from over, each step taking them deeper into the shadows where the real battles lay.

Chapter 7

The dense canopy of the Kentucky woods muffled their voices, a natural cone of silence around the clearing where Simon Wilson stood waiting. He was a solitary figure against the backdrop of tangled underbrush, his brown hair almost blending into the twilight shadows.

Sheriff Mark Thompson's truck rumbled up the dirt path, gravel crunching beneath heavy tires. The vehicle halted, and Mark stepped out, his tall frame filling the space between them as he approached. His piercing blue eyes carried the weight of a man who'd seen too much yet still clung to hope that things could change.

"Simon," Mark greeted with a cautious drawl.

"Mark," Simon nodded. "We don't have much time. The cartel is digging its claws deep into these parts. You know it, I know it, and if we don't act, this place will turn into a battleground."

Simon watched the sheriff's sturdy build tense, conflict playing out in the furrows of his brow. Mark's hand subconsciously drifted to his sidearm—a gesture of vulnerability rather than threat.

"Simon, you're talking about a war with men who've made fear their business. They don't take kindly to resistance, and they come after families. Mine. Yours. Anyone's."

"Which is why we can't let them take root here," Simon insisted, his tone steady but fervent. He stepped closer, bridging the gap between hesitation and action. "I've been down this road before, Mark. We hit them hard and fast, using their own shadows against them. They think they're untouchable, but I've touched them—brought them down. We can do it again."

"Stories are one thing, Simon. But this is real life, not some action flick where the good guys always win."

"Real life is where people like us make a stand," Simon replied, locking eyes with the sheriff. "You've sworn to protect this community, and I'm here offering you a chance to keep that promise. It won't be easy, and it sure as hell won't be safe. But since when has doing the right thing been about safety?"

There was a pause, the kind that stretched out like the land itself, full of potential and waiting for a decision to be planted. Mark looked away, scanning the tree line, maybe searching for an answer or perhaps an escape.

"Look, I'm not asking you to trust me blindly," Simon continued. "Just trust in what you've already done for this county. Trust in your damn badge, Mark. If not for yourself, then for those girls at the holdup house, for every family that calls Hart County home. I know you have helped from the edge of things. Now is the time to step up and be part of the team, as we had discussed earlier. Get front and center!"

A muscle twitched in Mark's jaw, a small spasm that signaled the internal struggle reaching its peak. Simon had seen that look before—the moment before resolve sets in, before courage overrides fear. He waited, giving Mark the space to fight his demons.

"Alright, Simon," Mark finally said, the words coming out like a dam breaking. "I'm in. God help us, I'm in."

"Good man," Simon said, a surge of relief flooding him, though his face remained impassive. "We'll need every good man we can get."

Mark nodded, a fragile smile cracking the surface of his worry. "Let's just hope our good is good enough."

"Trust me, it will be," Simon assured him, clapping a firm hand on the sheriff's shoulder. Now they were united, a strong alliance forged in the twilight, ready to face the darkness together.

Under the cloak of a moonless night, Simon led Sheriff Mark Thompson down a path that seemed to swallow their steps, a deep silence punctuating each footfall. The shadows played tricks on their eyes, but Simon walked with certainty until they reached an old, neglected shack that looked like it hadn't seen life in decades.

"Inside," Simon murmured, pushing open the creaky door. Mark hesitated for just a heartbeat before following him into the darkness.

The shack was barely more than four walls and a roof, but a man sat at a solitary table, a dim lantern casting eerie shadows across his face. This was their informant, a former cartel member with a price on his head and secrets in his heart.

"Mark, meet Luis," Simon said, gesturing to the man. "Luis, Sheriff Thompson."

"Hello," Luis greeted, his accent heavy. His hands were clasped tightly together, knuckles white as if holding onto his composure by sheer force of will.

"Simon tells me you've turned against the cartel," Mark said, skepticism woven through his drawl.

"Si, Sheriff. My sister... they took her," Luis's voice cracked like dry earth. "To make me pay for my mistakes."

Simon watched as empathy softened Mark's features. "We're going to shut them down, Luis. And we'll start with what you can tell us."

Over the next hour, Luis painted a picture of the cartel's operations so vividly that even the stoic Simon felt a flicker of horror. Names, places, schedules—all spilled forth from Luis's lips, each word a piece of the puzzle they desperately needed to solve.

"Thank you, Luis," Simon said as they prepared to leave. "Stay hidden, stay safe. We'll handle the rest."

"Gracias, amigo," Luis replied, nodding solemnly. "I trust you."

As they emerged back into the night, Simon knew the real work was about to begin. He glanced at Mark, whose jaw was set in determination, the earlier uncertainty now replaced by resolve.

"Let's get your boys up here, Jack," Simon said into his radio, and moments later, three silhouettes materialized from the trees—Greg's sons, each carrying a drone controller.

"Alright, listen up," Simon instructed, his gaze sweeping over the young men. "We need footage of the holdup house and any other cartel locations you've scouted. You know this terrain better than anyone. Use it to your advantage."

"Got it," one of the brothers, the tallest, replied with a nod, his voice betraying no hint of fear.

"Keep communications open, but only if absolutely necessary. Stealth is key," Jack added, his military background evident in his clipped words.

"Remember, boys," Mark chimed in, his blue eyes piercing in the dark, "those girls are counting on us."

With a final nod, the brothers split up, each heading in a different direction. Simon and Jack followed the middle brother, their bodies moving with practiced stealth through the underbrush. They had to cover several miles of rugged forest, the terrain uneven and treacherous underfoot.

Each step was measured, each breath controlled as they closed in on the holdup house—a fortress of despair nestled in the valley. The drone whirred softly overhead, a silent sentinel capturing the atrocities below.

"Jack, left flank," Simon whispered, his eyes catching movement in the distance. A guard patrolled the perimeter, oblivious to the eyes watching him.

They moved like ghosts, undetected, until the sharp snap of a twig under Jack's boot sliced through the stillness. The guard spun around, his hand reaching for his weapon.

Without hesitation, Simon launched forward, his body a weapon honed by years of training. He collided with the guard, a swift strike to the throat silencing any cry for help. Jack was there a second later, securing the area as Simon caught his breath.

"Good save," Jack muttered, clapping Jack on the shoulder.

"Let's not make a habit of it," Simon replied, his eyes scanning the horizon.

The drone continued its flight, the camera capturing every detail—faces of the captives, license plates, armed sentries. Each frame was evidence, of possible salvation.

"Footage is clean," the youngest brother's voice crackled through the radio. "Heading back."

"Copy that," Simon responded, relief threading through the tension. "See you at the rendezvous point."

They retreated as silently as they had come, leaving no trace but the vital intelligence now stored within the drones. The mission was a success, but it was only the beginning. There was still much to do, and time was a luxury they didn't have.

"Nice work tonight," Simon said to the boys once they had regrouped. "Your father would be proud."

"Let's just hope it's enough," the tallest brother replied, his expression grim.

"It will be," Simon assured him, though he knew the hardest part was yet to come—the assault on the cartel stronghold. But with the intel they'd gathered tonight, they were one step closer to bringing the cartel to its knees and saving the innocents trapped within its grasp.

Simon's phone buzzed in his pocket, a silent vibration that immediately set his nerves on edge. He glanced at the caller ID—Amanda Sawyer—and stepped away from the group, his boots crunching softly on the gravel as he moved into the shadow of an old oak tree.

"Wilson," he answered, the phone pressed against his ear.

"Simon, we need to talk—one-on-one," Amanda's voice was firm, laced with the gravity of their situation.

"Understood," Simon replied, his gaze instinctively scanning the treeline for any sign of eavesdroppers.

"First things first," Amanda began. "Your badge, consider it reinstated. You're active again, effective immediately."

Simon felt a weight settle in his chest—a mix of responsibility and determination. The badge wasn't just a piece of metal; it was a symbol of the trust placed in him, a trust he intended to honor.

"Appreciate it, ma'am," he said, his voice low. "But I have to say, Briggs is the one who got us this far."

"Briggs did his part, but don't sell yourself short," Amanda countered. "Your work on the ground has been invaluable. We wouldn't have eyes on the holdup house without you."

"Speaking of eyes on the ground," Simon interjected, seizing the opportunity. "We've got a new addition to our motley crew—Sheriff Mark Thompson."

"Thompson?" There was a note of surprise in Amanda's voice. "Isn't he...?"

"Jack's brother, yeah," Simon confirmed. "And the sheriff here in Hart County. He's in, all the way."

"Good," Amanda said after a brief pause. "We need people like him—locals who know the terrain and can rally the community."

"Exactly my thoughts," Simon agreed, hearing the faint sound of leaves rustling behind him. He turned sharply, hand drifting toward his concealed sidearm, only to find a raccoon scuttling across a branch overhead. The little bandit seemed indifferent to the life-and-death conversation unfolding below.

"Stay sharp, Wilson," Amanda warned, as if sensing his momentary distraction. "We're playing a dangerous game here."

"Always am," Simon assured her. He ended the call and slipped the phone back into his pocket, taking a deep breath of the crisp night air.

The moonlight filtered through the trees, casting dappled shadows on the ground. Somewhere in the distance, an owl hooted—a solitary sentinel in the quiet night. Simon turned back to his team, ready to face what was to come.

Simon leaned against the hood of his matte black SUV, a portable floodlight casting long shadows across the gravel clearing that served as a makeshift base. In his hand was a worn leather-bound notebook, brimming with hastily scribbled notes and dog-eared pages. He flipped it open to a page marked with a folded corner, its contents a meticulously itemized list of supplies.

"Here's what we're looking at," Simon said, his voice steady despite the gravity of the situation. The phone pressed to his ear, he could almost picture Amanda Sawyer on the other side, her keen eyes scanning over similar lists in her well-lit office, far removed from the dangers of Hart County.

"Go ahead," came Amanda's crisp reply.

"First off, we need weapons. Nothing flashy—subdued, silenced, suited for close quarters and woodland skirmishes." He paused, waiting for any hint of hesitation but found none. "Surveillance equipment is next. Drones with thermal imaging, long-range cameras, and some decent comms gear. We're blind out here without it."

"Understood," Amanda responded. Her tone was businesslike, yet Simon detected an undercurrent of concern. It was the weight of responsibility—the lives that rested on the resources she would provide.

"Lastly, intel analysis," Simon concluded. "We've got a mountain of data coming in, but without sharp minds to piece it together, it's just noise."

"Done. I'll have everything on your list en route by sunrise. We recognize the importance of what you're doing, Simon. You'll have what you need to succeed."

"Appreciate it, Amanda," Simon replied, a tightness easing in his chest. The CIA's support was critical, and it felt like a lifeline had been thrown to them in the murky waters they were navigating.

"Before I let you go, I'm giving you my personal cell number." There was a brief pause, and Simon heard the soft click of keys. A message with the number appeared on his phone's screen. "Use it if you need to bypass the red tape. This goes beyond our official channels—you have my full trust, Simon."

"Thanks," Simon said, the significance of the gesture not lost on him. It was a lifeline of another kind—a direct connection to someone with the power to move mountains or, in this case, sanction a covert operation against a ruthless cartel.

"Keep me posted, Wilson," Amanda instructed before ending the call.

Simon stood alone for a moment, absorbing the stillness of the night around him. The stakes couldn't be higher, and every decision carried the weight of consequence. But there was solace in knowing they weren't entirely in the dark; they had the might of the CIA behind them, albeit from the shadows.

He pocketed the phone and gazed up at the stars, their distant light offering a silent promise of guidance through the battles ahead. With a deep breath, he pushed away from the vehicle and moved towards the treeline where shadows danced, ready to prepare his team for the dawn that would soon break.

Simon squinted against the glare of his laptop screen, the blue hues from the encrypted chat with Amanda Sawyer reflecting off his face. Amanda's words appeared on the screen: "What's with the girl? The one who was with you, at the initial briefing—her skin."

"Ah, Loran," Simon typed back, glancing over his shoulder to ensure he was still alone in the dimly lit motel room. "She's from Troublesome Creek. The Blue Fugates, they call her kind. A rare genetic trait, methemoglobinemia. It gives her that tint."

"Interesting," came the swift response, followed by a pause. Simon knew Amanda was scouring the internet for information on this peculiar lineage.

"Her brothers are helping us with drone surveillance," Simon continued. "All with that same blue hue."

"Resourcefulness runs in the family, then," Amanda replied after a minute. "Keep them close. We need people like that."

Simon paused as he heard a soft knock at the door. Pushing the laptop aside, he moved silently towards the sound, every muscle primed for trouble. But when he opened the door, it was Jack Thompson, his face grim with resolve.

"Ready for the next step?" Jack asked.

Simon nodded. They had work to do.

The drive to the Amish community was shrouded in darkness, the moon a silver sliver in the sky. When they arrived, the smell of fresh earth and the sound of nocturnal creatures filled the air. Simon stepped out of the truck, his boots crunching on gravel, and approached the gathering of Amish men and women who waited for them, their expressions solemn.

"Thank you for coming," Simon said, his voice steady despite the churn of adrenaline in his veins. "We don't take your help lightly."

"Nor we yours," replied an elder with a thick beard and hands roughened by labor. "Our way is peace, but we know evil must be faced."

"Your skills—your knowledge of the land—it's invaluable," Simon said, locking eyes with each person in turn. "Whatever happens, we keep your involvement quiet. You have my word."

Nods met his gaze, and a sense of unity settled among them. These were people unaccustomed to the violence that now lurked at their doorstep, yet ready to defend their homes.

"Let's get started," Simon said, and the group dispersed to discuss logistics and strategy. In the hush of the night, they planned a takedown that would strike at the heart of the cartel, using every resource at their disposal—including the quiet strength of the Amish and the unique abilities of the Blue Fugates.

The moon hung low and full, casting a silver glow over the fields of Zechariah's farm as Simon Wilson followed the Amish leader and his companion Jack Thompson through rows of corn that whispered secrets in the night breeze. Simon's eyes, sharp as a hawk's, scanned the shadows, picking out the silhouettes of barns and sheds against the dark horizon.

"Over here." Zechariah led them toward the back end of his property, where an old barn loomed like a ghost from the past, its weathered wood telling tales of seasons come and gone.

Simon could almost taste the danger in the air, metallic and sharp. They halted a safe distance from the structure, hidden by the cloak of night and the tall crops that swayed gently around them.

"See there?" Zechariah pointed to a set of tracks leading into the barn—tire treads imprinted deep into the soft earth, betraying recent activity. "They come and go at odd hours, always the same path."

"Cartel's not big on subtlety, are they?" Jack's gaze followed the trail. Simon noticed the way his friend's posture tensed, ready for action, every muscle coiled like a spring.

"Those tracks might as well be breadcrumbs," Simon added, his eyes narrowing as he spotted movement within the treeline that bordered Zechariah's land. He counted three... no, four figures standing guard, their stances relaxed yet vigilant.

"Armed men," Zechariah continued. "They've been watching the barn day and night. Any who wander too close... well, I needn't say more."

"Understood." Simon felt a surge of protectiveness for the man beside him. The Amish were peaceful folk, unaccustomed to the violent undercurrents that now pulsed beneath the surface of their quiet lives.

"Have you seen what they're hiding in there?" Jack squinted towards the barn as if trying to pierce its walls with his stare alone.

Zechariah shook his head. "No. Since they arrived, that barn's been off-limits to us all. It may as well be on the moon."

"Whatever it is, it's important to them," Simon mused, rolling his shoulders to shake off the tension that clung to them. "And it's going to be important to us."

Jack nodded in agreement, the scar along his jaw catching the moonlight as he turned his face. "Time to find out what they're so keen to protect."

"Be careful," Zechariah implored, his eyes reflecting the pale light as they fell upon Simon and Jack. "We wish no harm to come to any soul, but we understand—some battles must be fought."

"Nobody's getting hurt on our watch, Zechariah," Simon promised, feeling the weight of responsibility settle on him like a mantle. The mission was clear: uncover the secrets held within the barn and dismantle the threat looming over Hart County.

"Let's move," Simon instructed, his voice firm yet low, slipping into the role he knew all too well—the protector, the loner, the agent who'd walked through fire and emerged tempered and ready for whatever darkness lay ahead.

The moon was a silent witness to their grim procession as Simon led the way, his gait silent, predatory. Beside him, Jack moved with the precision of a man who'd spent his life readying for moments like this. Behind them, Lori's slight figure hunched beside an oak tree, her fingers wrapped around the rifle with a grip that betrayed both her fear and determination.

"Stay low," Simon whispered back to Lori, his eyes never leaving the shadowy outline of the barn. "Your job is to cover us. Nothing more."

She nodded, her blue eyes almost luminous in the dark. "I got you," she whispered, her Kentucky accent thick with tension.

Simon and Jack advanced, threading through the trees like shadows merging with the night. The guards were just visible, silhouettes against the dark wood of the barn, rifles cradled casually but ready. Simon counted three—no, four—in quick succession, his mind already mapping out their takedown.

"Spread out," Simon breathed. They split apart, moving like specters on a path of retribution.

The first guard went down silently, Jack's hand clamped over his mouth as he twisted, a precise, violent dance that left the man limp on the ground. Simon watched from his peripheral vision, noting the efficiency—the scar along Jack's jaw flexing with controlled force. The next two guards went without sound.

A twig snapped under Simon's boot, thunderous in the stillness. He froze, heart hammering, as the fourth and only guard left turned. Time slowed. The guard's eyes widened in recognition, his rifle coming up.

"Jack!"

The warning was all Simon could offer before gunfire shattered the night. Jack grunted as he dove for cover, rolling behind a tree. Simon closed the distance to the guard, his movements a blur.

His hand found the guard's throat, steel slipping through flesh with sickening ease. The man's eyes bulged, his rifle firing into the sky as he fell. Simon felt nothing—there was no room for emotion, not now.

"Jack! You hit?"

"I'm good!" Jack's voice came, strained but solid.

Another guard burst from the barn, weapon raised, finger tightening on the trigger aimed at Simon. A shot rang out, but not from the guard's rifle. The man's head snapped back, and he crumpled to the ground—a clean shot from Lori's position.

"Good shot," Simon breathed, but as he turned to Lori, he saw her face. It was ghostly pale, the rifle shaking in her hands. Simon strode over to her.

"I... I killed him." Her voice was a broken whisper, her eyes fixed on the fallen guard.

Simon approached slowly, placing a gentle hand on her shoulder. "You did what you had to do. You saved my life."

Lori looked up at him, searching his face for condemnation or horror, but finding none. Shakily, she said, "The only other life I have taken was trying to save my Jennifer, and it was spontaneous. This time…this time I knew exactly what I planned to do. I couldn't let him kill you. I've lost enough."

"Look at me, Lori," Simon urged softly. "This isn't about us—it's about protecting what we love. Your daughter, our town. Sometimes, we have to make impossible choices."

Her gaze held his, the internal struggle waging behind her eyes. Slowly, the tremor in her hands stilled, fortified by the truth in his words.

"Okay," she finally said, the word carrying the weight of acceptance.

"Let's finish this," Jack called out.

With one last reassuring squeeze to Lori's shoulder, Simon nodded. "Let's go."

The barn loomed ahead, a silent behemoth casting long shadows across the dewy grass. Simon moved forward cautiously, his boots crunching softly on the gravel as he neared the large double doors.

"Clear," Jack whispered, his breath visible in the cold Kentucky night.

Simon pushed one of the doors open, the metal hinges protesting with a groan that seemed too loud in the quiet. Inside, the darkness was thick, but his flashlight beam cut through it like a knife, revealing rows of high-tech drones and several off-road vehicles, their matte black surfaces gleaming dully under the light.

"Jackpot," Simon muttered, sweeping the light across the barn. No drugs or paperwork in sight, just the tech and a stack of cash that would make a bank manager blush.

"Let's get Mark on the line, then Loran." He pulled out his phone and dialed the sheriff's number.

"Mark, it's Simon. We hit the motherlode—drones, vehicles... and funds. Lots of funds." He paused. "No, no dope or paper trail. But we need to move this, now."

After giving Mark a quick rundown, Simon dialed Loran. The line clicked.

"Simon?"

"Loran, I need you to rustle up some locals with trucks and trailers. Six should do it—we've got vehicles to transport."

"Ah'll see what Ah can do."

"Thanks, Loran. Be quick, please."

"Will do, Simon."

Simon pocketed the phone and turned to Jack. "Help's on the way. Let's start moving these beauties outside."

They worked in sync, muscles straining as they pushed the first of the off-roaders toward the door. The engine roared to life at Jack's touch.

"Like stealing candy from a baby, huh?" Jack smirked as he maneuvered the vehicle outside.

"Let's not count our chickens just yet," Simon replied, glancing back at the barn.

One by one, they rolled the vehicles out, positioning them for an easy getaway. The pile of cash followed, stuffed hastily into duffel bags that bulged at the seams.

As the last vehicle cleared the threshold, headlights pierced the darkness. A convoy of trucks and trailers rumbled down the dirt road, led by Loran herself.

"Didn't expect you to drive one," Simon noted as she climbed down from the truck.

"Someone's gotta show you boys how it's done. I got a ride to Pa's place in an Amish buggy and got the family truck."

Under the cover of darkness, they loaded the contents of the barn, the community working together seamlessly. The off-roaders were chained down, the drones carefully packed away, and the money stowed securely.

"Jack's place next," Simon confirmed once everything was loaded. "We'll sort through it all there."

"Lead the way," Loran said, climbing back into the truck.

Leaving the now-empty barn behind, they set off in a caravan of purloined goods. The drive was tense, but the roads remained clear, their passage unchallenged.

When they finally pulled into Jack's property, the first hints of dawn were touching the horizon. They unloaded in silence, the barn swallowing the evidence of their night's work.

"Let's keep this between us," Simon addressed the small crowd. "Not a word to anyone."

Nods of agreement met his gaze.

"Good. Now let's get some rest. We've got a big day ahead of us."

As the group dispersed, Simon leaned against the side of the barn, the adrenaline slowly ebbing from his veins. They had taken a significant step tonight, but the path ahead was fraught with danger. For now, though, they had won a small victory, and that was enough to close his eyes to.

In the quiet predawn light, the barn stood watch over its new treasures, a steadfast guardian ready for the battles yet to come.

Simon paced the length of Jack's cluttered living room, his boots thudding softly on the wooden floor. The morning light filtered through the windows, casting a hopeful glow on what would be a crucial meeting. Mark Thompson sat at one end of a worn-out sofa, his fingers drumming an anxious rhythm on his knee.

"Alright," Simon began, his voice steady as he faced the team assembled before him. "We've got intel from our informant that's gold. Plus, we managed to snag some drone footage that gives us eyes on the cartel's holdup house."

The group leaned in, their expressions a blend of determination and the weight of what was to come. On the makeshift coffee table lay a spread of maps and photographs, each depicting different angles of a large, innocuous-looking farmhouse nestled deep within Poteet Valley.

"Here," Simon pointed to a section of the image, "is their stronghold. The layout's a damn maze. We need to be smart about this."

Mark cleared his throat. "They'll have guards posted, surveillance, maybe even dogs. It won't be easy getting in—or out like you and Jack did. They will be more careful now."

"Which is why we train," Jack interjected, standing up. "We start today. And we don't stop until we're ready."

The training ground was a stretch of land behind Jack's barn, now emptied of its illicit contents. Simon strapped into the off-road vehicle, his hands gripping the wheel as Jack explained the controls. The engine roared to life, the sound echoing across the open field.

"Remember, it's about control, not just speed," Jack shouted over the din.

Simon nodded, easing the vehicle into motion. The land was uneven, pocked with dips and rises, but he maneuvered with growing confidence, learning the quirks of the machine beneath him.

Meanwhile, drones buzzed overhead like oversized insects, their cameras capturing every move. Simon took turns piloting them, his brow furrowed in concentration as he coaxed the devices into sweeping arcs across the sky.

"Keep it steady," Jack advised, watching the screens that displayed the drone's perspective. "Think of it as an extension of your own eyes."

The days blurred into a relentless cycle of drills and briefings. They practiced takedowns and hand-to-hand combat, the air thick with grunts and the smack of flesh on flesh. Camouflage techniques were refined, turning bodies into ghosts against the backdrop of the Kentucky woods.

"Again!" Simon would command after each scrimmage. Sweat dripped from his brow, his blue eyes fierce with the fire of a man who had seen too much to back down now.

As dusk fell, they gathered again in Jack's living room, muscles aching and faces drawn with fatigue. Simon looked over the team, a motley crew bound by a shared purpose.

"Every single one of you is vital to this mission," he said, his tone leaving no room for doubt. "We're going to take them down, but only if we do it together."

Mark met Simon's gaze, his earlier hesitation replaced by a steely resolve. "Let's make sure those bastards never forget Hart County."

"Damn straight," Simon replied, the ghost of a smile touching his lips.

The sky darkened to a deep indigo as Simon and Lori found themselves side by side, checking and re-checking their gear in the dim light of the barn. The air was thick with the scent of oil and earth—a sharp contrast to the tension that crackled between them.

"You sure this Kevlar vest is gonna hold up?" Lori asked, her voice betraying a hint of vulnerability as she adjusted the straps around her slender frame.

"Bulletproof," Simon assured her, meeting her questioning gaze with a steady one of his own. He reached out, his fingers brushing hers as he helped fit the vest snugly against her. Their eyes locked for a moment, charged with an unspoken understanding.

"Thanks, Simon," Lori murmured, a blush spreading across her cheeks. She quickly turned away, busying herself with the other items laid out before them.

Simon watched her for a moment, admiring her strength and the way she'd stepped into this unfamiliar world with unwavering determination. Her resilience stirred something within him—a protective instinct mingled with a warmth that had been absent from his life for too long.

"Hey," Simon said softly. Lori looked back at him. "We're going to get your daughter back. You have my word."

Lori nodded, her blue eyes glistening with unshed tears. "I know. It's just... all this," she gestured to the array of weapons and tactical gear, "it's a lot to take in."

"None of us were born ready for something like this. But you've got grit, Lori. More than you realize."

A moment passed between them, a silent acknowledgment of the bond that had formed amidst the chaos—the shared purpose that drove them forward. It was a fragile thing, this growing connection, but it was real and it gave them both the solace they desperately needed.

"Let's go over the plan one more time," Simon suggested, guiding her towards the makeshift table where maps and drone images were spread out.

Together, they leaned over the detailed layouts, Simon pointing out the entry points they'd identified, the patrol patterns of the cartel guards, and the likely location of the hostages. His hand occasionally brushed against hers, each accidental touch sending a ripple of awareness through them both.

"Once we're in, timing will be everything. We stick to the shadows, take them by surprise."

"Like phantoms," Lori added, a determined glint in her eye.

"Exactly," Simon replied, impressed by her quick grasp of the strategy.

As the hours waned, the rest of the team filtered into the barn, each person carrying their own weight of anticipation and resolve. They gathered around, their faces etched with the gravity of what lay ahead.

"Alright, everyone. This is it," Simon began, his gaze sweeping over the group. "We've trained for this. We know the risks. But remember, we're not only fighting for ourselves— we're fighting for the lives of those who can't fight back."

Nods of agreement met his words, the shared conviction uniting them as they finalized their preparations. Weapons were checked, radios tested, and backpacks hoisted onto shoulders.

"Stay sharp, stay silent, and watch each other's backs," Simon instructed. "We move out at 0400 hours."

The team dispersed, each member retreating into their own thoughts and rituals. Simon caught Lori's eye once more, and in that glance, there was a promise—a silent vow that they would see this through together, come what may.

The team readied at the edge of dawn, poised on the brink of a mission that would test them to their core. The journey ahead promised danger at every turn, but they were resolute, bound by courage and the faint whisper of hope that danced like a firefly in the darkness. The stage was set, and as the first light of morning crept across the Kentucky sky, they stepped out into the unknown, ready to face the cartel head-on.

Chapter 8

The rusty hinges of the tractor-trailer moaned a foreboding welcome as a sliver of daylight pierced the dim interior, casting an oblique light on the huddled forms within. Cramped between rows of other women, Jennifer Hawkins tried to draw a shallow breath, but the air was thick, laced with the pungent mix of sweat, fear, and exhaust fumes. The suffocating heat clung to her skin like a second layer, and she could feel the perspiration trickling down her back.

"Can't hardly breathe," muttered another girl from nearby, her Kentucky accent thickened by distress. Her voice barely carried over the collective murmur of despair. She pulled at the collar of her blouse, trying to let in the non-existent cool air.

"Stay strong," Jennifer whispered, her vibrant green eyes scanning the shadowed faces for some sign of hope that refused to show itself. She reached out, gripping the girl's hand, her own resolve hardening amidst the tremors of fear that threatened to shake her apart.

The truck lurched forward, resuming its journey toward an uncertain fate. At every stop, the back doors would open, and more women, eyes wide with terror, were shoved inside by Miguel Alvarez, known as El Lobo. His tattooed arm flexed as he pushed another captive into the crowded space. "Move in! Make room!"

"Please, no more," someone pleaded, the voice thin and breaking.

"Shut up," El Lobo spat, slamming the doors shut, and plunging them back into darkness. Each new addition to their grim cargo intensified the sense of desperation, the air growing heavier with hopelessness.

Miles passed, marked only by the rhythm of the road and the stifled sobs of the captives. The truck's engine growled relentlessly, indifferent to the lives it carried, as they moved closer to a border that promised nothing but more despair. In the oppressive atmosphere, even time seemed to have surrendered, each moment stretching into an eternity of waiting for a rescue that felt increasingly like a distant dream...

Hidden in the shadow of towering oaks, Loran Smith hunkered down before a makeshift command post—a tangle of monitors connected to her laptop, that was connected to an inverter, stood across a rough-hewn table. Her slight frame belied the steel in her gaze as she surveyed the infrared images flickering on the screens. The indigo tint of her skin seemed to merge with the dusk, rendering her nearly invisible among the dense foliage of Poteet Valley.

"Anything?" she murmured into her headset, her voice a slow southern drawl that crackled over the radio.

"Clear so far," came the reply from one of her brothers, his eyes glued to the drone controls. They were camped out a safe distance from the holdup house, the buzz of the drones barely audible above the chorus of cicadas.

The house itself was a nondescript construction, but what transpired within those walls was anything but ordinary.

Through the thermal imaging, the silhouettes of cartel members moved like specters—each one a potential threat, each room a possible battleground.

"Got movement," another brother said tersely, adjusting the drone's position for a better view. "South corner room."

Loran squinted at the screen, noting how the figures clustered, their heat signatures a stark contrast to the cool blues of the empty rooms. Her jaw tightened. They were not just watching a house; they were watching a ticking time bomb.

"Stay sharp, boys," she cautioned, the tension in her voice mirroring the anticipation that crackled through the humid air. It was a waiting game now, every second ratcheting up the intensity of what was to come.

Nearby, concealed by the cover of trees, Simon Wilson stood with Sheriff Mark Thompson and a small contingent of FBI agents. Their presence was a testament to the importance of this operation—an uneasy alliance forged by necessity.

"Your team's got point on this, Wilson," Mike said, his New England accent tinged with anxiety. He was a man more accustomed to white-collar crimes than the sinister web of cartel operations. His piercing blue eyes flicked toward the house, then back to Simon, searching for reassurance.

"We'll get them out, agent," Simon assured him, his tone calm but commanding. His muscular build tensed, ready for action, yet his expression remained unreadable. This was his element—the brink of chaos where lives hung in balance.

"Time's ticking, people," an FBI agent reminded them curtly, checking her weapon. "We need to move before they change location again."

"Agreed," Simon nodded, turning back to Loran's station. "Loran, keep an eye out for any changes. We're about to shake the hornet's nest."

"Copy that," Loran acknowledged, her focus never wavering from the task at hand.

As nightfall shrouded the valley in darkness, the stage was set. Each player knew their role, and each understood the stakes—rescue any captives and dismantle the operation, or risk losing everything to the ruthless grip of the cartel. And for

Loran, Simon, and the rest, there was no choice but to see it through, whatever the cost.

Simon crouched low, the grip of his pistol familiar in his hand as he scanned the faces of his team. They mirrored his resolve, their bodies tensed like coiled springs, ready to unleash hell on his command. He pointed to each member, his gestures sharp and deliberate.

"Jackson, you take point. Quiet entry through the back. No surprises," Simon instructed. Jackson nodded once, his jaw set in grim determination.

"Kara, with me. We'll flank from the side. Eyes sharp for any movement." Kara's response was a curt nod, her dark eyes locked onto Simon's, full of trust and unwavering focus.

"Rest of you, backup positions. I want angles covered, no blind spots. We do this clean, we do this fast." The nods came in unison, a silent symphony of readiness.

With a final glance at Loran, who was stationed behind a bank of monitors, Simon led the way. The world seemed to shrink to the space between them and the holdup house, every step a measured beat in the symphony of the night's operation.

They approached the house with the caution of hunters stalking their prey. The air was thick with tension, each breath a muted gasp in the stillness of the valley. The house loomed ahead, an ordinary structure now transformed into a battleground for souls.

The darkness was their ally, cloaking their movements as they split up and moved into position. Simon could feel his heart thrumming in his chest, a drumbeat that pulsed through his veins. Adrenaline surged, sharpening his senses to a razor's edge.

He signaled to Kara; they were in sync, two shadows gliding toward the house's vulnerable flank. Their pistols, equipped with silencers, were extensions of their will—silent sentinels that promised swift retribution.

The faintest click of a lock yielding under Jackson's skilled hands was a clarion call to advance. Simon and his team filtered through the dim corridors like wraiths, their footsteps hushed whispers against the floor. They were inside now, deep in the belly of the beast, where every shadow could conceal a threat, and every creaking board might betray their presence.

Eyes darting to every corner, they pressed on, guided by the infrared imagery relayed to them by Loran's vigilant gaze. Each room they cleared ratcheted the tension higher. Empty... then another empty. But they knew, as certain as the blood coursing through their veins, that danger lurked close—coiled and waiting.

Simon's hand signals cut through the gloom, commanding and precise. With each directive, his team responded, a deadly dance choreographed by years of training and trust.

"Stay sharp," Simon whispered. "We're close."

The silence was a tangible thing, wrapping around them, seeping into their bones. It was the quiet before the storm, the held breath of the world. And somewhere, hidden within the walls of this innocuous house, the captives waited, their fates intertwined with the actions of Simon and his team.

It was time to strike, to reclaim lives from the clutches of darkness. For Simon, failure was not an option. This was more than a mission; it was redemption, a chance to right the wrongs of a world too often indifferent to suffering.

As they moved deeper into the house, each second stretched into eternity, a slow march towards an inevitable confrontation. The anticipation was a live wire, crackling through the charged air. Every sense was on alert, every muscle tensed for the fight to come.

The hallway stretched before them, a gauntlet that seemed to pulse with unseen threats. Simon led the way, his every step a statement of lethal intent. The muffled thuds of their boots on the carpet were the only sounds in the oppressive silence.

"Contact!"

A door flung open and time contracted as adrenaline surged. Figures emerged from the shadows, their intentions spelled out by the glint of moonlight on cold steel. Simon's finger tightened on the trigger; the silencer muffled the pistol's report to a soft cough, and the first assailant crumpled without a sound.

His team flowed behind him like water—no hesitation, no second-guessing. They moved through the rooms with the precision of a well-oiled machine, their silenced weapons whispering death. Each takedown was clean and clinical. A ballet of violence choreographed on the fly.

They swept through the rooms, clearing them with ruthless efficiency. Then, amidst the methodical chaos, it happened.

"Mark's hit!"

The shout shattered the surgical calm. In an instant, the stakes skyrocketed. Mark staggered back against the wall, his hand clamped over his shoulder where a bloom of red was spreading fast.

"Cover me!" Simon moved to shield his wounded teammate. His gaze never left the danger zones, his weapon tracking any hint of movement.

The team adapted seamlessly, closing ranks. The fight intensified, each shot a potential life-saver, each miss a possible tragedy. The cartel members fought with the desperation of cornered animals, but Simon's team was relentless.

"Stay with me, buddy," Simon muttered to Mark, who was gritting his teeth against the pain. Rounds cracked past, close enough to feel their passing heat. Simon returned fire, his aim unerring. Cartel members fell, one by one, their threats extinguished before they could fully ignite.

It was a fight measured in heartbeats and split-second decisions. Every action, every choice, carried weight. And as the last threat dropped to the floor, the team exhaled a collective breath they hadn't realized they'd been holding.

Simon's fingers tightened around the grip of his pistol, the slide slick with a sheen of perspiration. The house, once a silent abode in Poteet Valley, now echoed with the sharp report of silenced gunfire and the heavy breaths of exertion. Amidst the chaos, Simon moved like an avenging shadow, each step calculated, each shot a harbinger of finality for the cartel members who dared to oppose them.

"Clear left! No hostages." one of Simon's teammates called out, sweeping through the sparse interior of what used to be a bedroom, now emptied of comfort and filled instead with fear.

"Right side and basement clear. No hostages," another voice confirmed, the tension in the air dissipating as the last pockets of resistance were snuffed out by precise, disciplined fire.

Only three cartel members remained, huddled together, their weapons clattering to the floor as they realized the futility of further struggle—their faces twisted in a cocktail of anger, fear, and defeat.

"Secure them," Simon ordered. His team moved with well-rehearsed efficiency, zip-tying the cartel members' wrists with swift, practiced movements. The threat inside the house was neutralized, but the real work was just beginning.

"Medic!" Simon's call cut through the aftermath, his tone shifting from command to concern. The team might have won this skirmish, but with Mark wounded, the victory was far from complete.

"Mark, how bad is it?" Simon knelt beside his wounded teammate, the man's blood seeping through the fabric of his tactical gear.

"Feels like I've been punched by a damn gorilla," Mark grunted, attempting a strained smile that didn't quite reach his eyes.

"Let's patch you up," Simon said, signaling for the medic. They worked with quiet competence, cutting away the sleeve to reveal the angry wound beneath. The medic applied pressure, staunching the flow as he prepared a field dressing. Mark's jaw clenched at the touch, but his focus never wavered from the task at hand.

"Still with us, Mark?" Simon asked, maintaining a light tone despite the gravity of the situation.

"Wouldn't miss this party for the world," Mark replied, though his pallor spoke volumes about the pain he concealed behind humor.

"Good. We'll need your sharp eyes on the next go-around." Simon clapped him gently on the uninjured shoulder.

Professionalism and composure were their armor, shielding them from the horrors they faced, and keeping them grounded when the world tilted into madness.

As the medic secured the bandage, Simon rose, surveying the aftermath. Shell casings littered the ground like macabre confetti, a testament to the fierce battle waged within these walls. But the mission wasn't over—not until every captive was safe, every enemy vanquished.

"Team, let's secure the perimeter," Simon instructed. "Make sure no surprises are waiting for us."

"Roger that, boss," came the unified response.

They moved through the house, a silent dance of vigilance, checking every corner, every shadow. This was their world—where every second counted, where every decision could mean life or death. And as they stood united in the aftermath of conflict, they were reminded that in the face of danger, it was not just their skills, but their bond that kept them alive.

Simon watched as the three surviving cartel members were cuffed and led out of the house, their faces betraying little of the defeat they had suffered. Jorge Lopez's dark eyes flickered with a defiance that seemed almost misplaced given his circumstances. Miguel Alvarado, or El Toro as he was known, struggled against the tight grip of the officer, his tattooed forearm flexing in protest. Ricardo Lopez walked with his head held high, yet fear shimmered in his green eyes.

"Get anything you can out of them," Simon told Mike. "We need to know how deep this goes."

Mike nodded solemnly. "We'll get them talking, Simon. We'll do whatever it takes."

The FBI agents escorted the captives to a fleet of black SUVs. The vehicles peeled away from the gravel driveway, dust swirling in their wake as they headed towards the local office where interrogation rooms awaited. This wasn't just about putting these three behind bars; it was about chipping away at the cartel's foundations.

Back inside the house, Simon's team worked methodically to secure evidence. Rows of firearms were lined up on the kitchen counter, each tagged for processing. Stacks of drugs were cataloged, bagged, and sealed, ready for the DEA's scrutiny. Computers and paperwork were next—potential gold mines of intelligence.

"Look at this," one of his team members called out, holding papers aloft.

"Anything useful?" Simon asked.

"Shipping routes, contacts... It's a start."

"Good. Box it all up. Every scrap could lead us to the next link in the chain."

As the last of the contraband was being loaded into evidence boxes, Simon felt the weight of their responsibility. This was more than just a raid—it was a blow against an empire of fear and violence. And they were the hammer.

"Let's wrap it up here," Simon announced. "We've got what we came for."

His team exchanged silent nods, their movements now familiar, almost ritualistic in their precision. They knew the drill: leave no trace, take everything of importance. The house would soon be just another empty shell, but the echoes of tonight's victory would resonate through the cartel's ranks like an unspoken threat.

In the dim light filtering through the curtains, Simon took a moment to let the stillness wash over him. Tomorrow would bring new challenges, but for now, they had won. And every win, no matter how small, kept the darkness at bay.

Simon stood outside his cabin, his muscles aching from the night's exertions. He pulled out Amanda's cell number—memorized from necessity—and dialed it on his phone, preferring the personal line over the traceable office one. The ringtone cut through the silence of the early morning air before her familiar voice answered.

"Wilson," Amanda said.

"Operation's done. Three in custody, the rest neutralized. We're collecting intel now," Simon reported, keeping his voice low and even.

"Any complications?" Amanda asked.

"Mark took a hit, but he'll live. Our medic patched him up," Simon replied, glancing back at the cabin where Mark was resting, a grimace etched onto his face even in sleep.

"Good work, Wilson. Keep me posted on the intelligence you gather. It's crucial we use this momentum to our advantage."

"Understood." Simon ended the call. He slipped the phone back into his pocket and turned to survey the scene once more before heading towards the motorhomes parked discreetly at the edge of his land.

The largest of the three motorhomes had been transformed into a makeshift command center, while the other two were for sleeping and eating for the analysts assigned to Simon. Inside, analysts from the CIA huddled around laptops, their fingers dancing over keyboards as they sifted through digital files and scanned documents. The hum of generators and the clink of coffee mugs filled the space with a sense of urgency.

"Anything jumping out at you?" Simon asked one of the analysts, peering over a shoulder at the scrolling lines of data on the screen.

"Still sorting through the noise, but we've found references to shell companies. Could be how they're funneling funds."

"Keep digging. We need a clearer picture of their network," Simon instructed, his gaze traveling across the room where maps and photographs were pinned to the walls, forming a web of connections that they hoped would lead to the heart of the cartel.

As the hours stretched on, fatigue set in. The adrenaline that had fueled them through the night began to wane, giving way to the toll of their labor. Simon could feel it in his bones, the weariness creeping up like a shadow. But there was solace in the methodical nature of their task; each piece of evidence brought them closer to dismantling the beast they hunted.

Finally, with the first hints of dawn painting the sky a soft blue, Simon gave the order to rest. They had earned a brief respite, a moment to breathe before they would dive back into the fray. The team dispersed, finding corners in the remaining two motorhomes to catch some sleep.

In the quiet that followed, Simon sat alone at the small table in his quarters, the glow of his laptop casting a pale light on the stoic planes of his face. He scrolled through the freshly acquired intel, each click a step on the path to their next move. As sleep beckoned, he resisted its call, determined to wring every last drop of usefulness from the night's haul.

The world outside might still be dark, but within the confines of the motorhome, the mission continued to burn bright, a beacon guiding Simon and his team through the uncharted waters of the night.

Dawn crept over the county like a cautious intruder, its pale light brushing against the clustered trees and quiet homes. But there was no peace in its arrival for Simon Wilson and his teams as they prepared to strike at the heart of the cartel's local operations. Today, no quarter would be given.

Simon's team approached their target house—a nondescript single-story dwelling that belied the venomous activities within—moving with an economy of motion. At precisely 6:00 AM, they breached the front door with a practiced kick. The interior was dim, the air thick with the stench of unwashed bodies and sour fear.

"Clear left!" one of the operatives called out.

"Clear right," responded another.

They moved through the house like specters, pistols drawn, silencers affixed—the soft phut-phut of rounds fired punctuated the stifled gasps of startled cartel members. Simon led from the front, his blue eyes cold and focused, each movement deliberate and lethal. He dropped two gunmen before they could fully rouse from sleep, their weapons clattering uselessly to the floor.

Across the county, Mark's team executed their assault with similar precision. The second house, a two-story structure with peeling paint, became an instant battleground. Mark's team moved through the rooms systematically. Cartel thugs scrambled to mount a defense, but it was dismantled swiftly. Bullets found their marks in silent bursts, leaving only echoes of struggle behind while a wounded Mark stayed in the background as backup.

Meanwhile, Jack Thompson's unit descended upon their target, a ramshackle farmhouse that had seen better days. Jack's military discipline shone through as he directed his squad with terse commands. His broad shoulders turned into the breach, pistol leading the way. They swept room to room, engagement after engagement—each time Jack's steady hand and unerring aim contributed to the swift conclusion of the fight. Not even the scars of past battles slowed him down; if anything, they spurred him on, every scar a testament to his survival and resolve.

No new intelligence was gleaned from these simultaneous strikes—only the cold certainty that the cartel's grip had been weakened. Bodies lay in silence where they had fallen, the clear message sent: the reach of justice was long and unyielding.

As Simon and his team withdrew to regroup from the morning raids, they knew that the battle against the cartel was far from over. It was a war fought in the shadows, with victories measured not just in lives saved but also in the relentless pursuit of a scourge that refused to simply fade away.

While at the same time, at the holdup house, as the sun climbed higher in the sky, the FBI made their move. Special agents, dressed down to fit in as locals, arrived at the previously secured holdup house, their presence a clear sign of the operation's gravity. They set up surveillance equipment with practiced ease, casting a watchful eye over the scene.

"Keep sharp. We're not done here by a long shot."

"Vigilance is the name of the game," came the reply, as the horizon was scanned.

With the FBI settling in, their surveillance gear casting an electronic net over the property, special agents whispered commands, their eyes never leaving the monitors as they prepared for whatever the night might bring.

"Anything moves, we'll know," one agent assured his partner.

"Let's hope it's a quiet night," the other replied, though they both knew better than to expect it.

The ongoing nature of their mission was manifest in the careful placement of cameras, the murmured conversations between agents, and the occasional crackle of radio comms.

In the quiet that followed, Loran watched as her oldest brother manned a drone, his indigo-tinged fingers moving with a dancer's grace over the controls. She watched through the infrared lenses as the FBI agents crept into the periphery, their presence a necessary reinforcement for what would be a long night of vigilance.

And so, another day of conflict closed, and the anticipation of what was yet to come loomed large. The operation continued the commitment to ending the cartel's reign of terror unwavering. The next moves were already forming in Simon's mind, each potential scenario playing out like a chess match where the stakes were life and death. The game was far from over, and they were all too aware that the next move was crucial.

The sun dipped below the tree line, casting long shadows over the house Simon surveyed the aftermath of this raid. The air was thick with gunpowder and tension, tinged with an unspoken resolve that hung heavy among the team members.

Simon's blue eyes scanned the horizon, his gaze as steady as his hand had been when he took down the last cartel member in a silent, precise shot. Simon and his team loaded up and headed back to his cabin.

"Clear!" Mark's voice echoed from the southern end of Simon's property upon his return, his silhouette outlined against the fading light. Jack responded with a similar call from the north, signaling the end of their coordinated assault. Three houses, three swift takedowns—each executed with lethal efficiency. Simon nodded, acknowledging the unyielding focus of his team, even as Mark, standing on the porch, clutched his shoulder where a bullet had struck him earlier, a stark reminder of the risks they faced.

Simon turned to address his team after they had reassembled, his voice low but clear. "We've dealt a blow today, but this is far from over. We regroup at 0600. Check your gear, and rest up. Tomorrow we push harder."

Nods of agreement met his words, each member feeling the gravity of his command. They were a unit, bound by purpose and the silent oaths they'd taken to see this mission through. As night enveloped the cabin, Simon's thoughts drifted briefly to Lori Hawkins, the worry etched on her face a constant image in his mind. Her daughter, Jennifer, was out there somewhere, and he made a silent vow to bring her home.

Simon stood on his porch, his gaze fixed on the horizon where darkness met the river. There was a palpable sense of something brewing just beyond their line of sight, a storm waiting to break. As the last light faded, he felt the familiar itch of anticipation under his skin. The next chapter loomed, fraught with uncertainty and the promise of challenges yet to come—a chessboard set against the backdrop of Kentucky's rolling hills, where every move could mean the difference between life and death.

"Tomorrow," Simon whispered to himself, the word a promise and a warning, as he turned to join his team in the shadows.

Chapter 9

The dim glow of a laptop screen cast a pale light over the worn map stretched out on Simon Wilson's kitchen table. It was nearing midnight, and the silence of the Kentucky countryside enveloped the old cabin, save for the occasional hoot of an owl or the rustle of leaves in the gentle night breeze. Simon, with his muscular frame folded into a chair that creaked under his weight, traced a route with his finger from their current location to North Mexico.

"We'll have to cross at McAllen," he muttered, more to himself than to Lori Hawkins, who sat across from him, her blond hair pulled back into a ponytail that revealed the worry lines etched on her forehead.

"Can we trust the contact there?" Her blue eyes scanned the map as if it held the fate of her daughter within its tangle of roads and symbols.

"Raul's solid. Larry vouched for him when I met him in Kingsville earlier. He also helped me when I was coming out of Reynosa."

"Reynosa..." Lori whispered, her accent drawing out the vowels. "That's where they took Jen, isn't it?"

"We're getting her back, Lori. We've got the element of surprise on our side." His voice was steady, the confidence of a man who had danced with danger too many times to count.

"Simon, I know you're trained for this, but I'm just... I'm scared. Scared for Jennifer, scared for us. This cartel—"

"Hey," Simon interjected softly, reaching across the table to lay his hand over hers, an unexpected gesture that made her flinch, then relax. "It's okay to be scared. But we can't let fear call the shots. We stay focused, stick to the plan, and we bring your girl home."

In the quiet that followed, Lori found herself studying Simon—the way his brown hair fell just so over his furrowed brow, the intensity in his blue eyes that now held a flicker of something gentler. She drew a shaky breath, bolstered by the strength she saw in him. "You ever get scared, Simon? Really scared?"

"Every damn time. But fear doesn't get to win. Not when it matters most."

Lori nodded, feeling a kinship with this man who was once a stranger, now her closest ally in the darkest of times. They were two souls, united by a common cause—a mission that was personal for one and a duty for the other.

"Thank you," she said, her accent softening the words. "For everything."

"Nothing to thank me for," Simon replied, though his eyes betrayed the sincerity he felt. "Now, let's go over the plan one more time. We need to have every detail nailed down before we cross that border."

They leaned in closer, their heads nearly touching as they poured over the map, plotting and planning until the first light of dawn began to creep through the farmhouse windows. Simon and Lori knew the road ahead would be fraught with peril, but in this moment of solitude, away from the chaos that awaited, they found solace in each other's presence—a quiet strength in their shared resolve to face whatever lay ahead.

Simon's hands wrapped securely around the worn leather of the punching bag as Lori landed another rapid sequence of jabs. Her knuckles were red, but her determination was unyielding, each strike echoing through the otherwise silent holdout house. The muscles in her arms flexed with every jab, a testament to the hours they had dedicated to training.

"Keep your guard up, Lori. Imagine it's the one thing standing between you and Jennifer."

Lori's eyes blazed with renewed intensity at the mention of her daughter. She shifted her weight and threw a powerful cross that made the bag sway, her Kentucky accent swallowed by the sound of impact. "Like this?"

"Exactly like that," Simon replied, giving her an approving nod. The corners of his mouth lifted in a faint smile, which did not escape Lori's notice. It was these small gestures of kindness amidst the grueling training that reminded her they were in this together.

They moved on to sparring, circling each other warily under the shade of the large oak tree. With each calculated step, Simon admired Lori's quick progress. She was no longer the scared single mother he had met weeks ago; she was becoming a force to be reckoned with.

"Come on, don't go easy on me," Lori taunted playfully, bouncing lightly on her toes.

"Wouldn't dream of it," Simon responded, his blue eyes locking onto hers.

The air between them crackled with an electric tension as they exchanged blows, each block and counter showcasing their growing synergy. Simon could feel the trust building, the unspoken assurance that they had each other's backs. When Lori stumbled slightly, he reached out instinctively to steady her. His touch was gentle, yet firm—enough to remind her that he was there, without undermining her strength.

"Thanks," Lori said, her breath coming in short gasps. She looked up into Simon's eyes, finding that same reassuring smile that had become her anchor in these stormy seas.

"Anytime," he replied softly, releasing her arm but not the invisible thread of connection that had formed between them.

As they resumed their training, pushing each other to the brink of exhaustion, neither mentioned the gesture again. But it lingered in the air, a silent promise that, despite the chaos and uncertainty of their mission, they would find hope in the bond they had forged—a bond that was quickly turning into something more profound than either of them had anticipated.

Simon's knuckles were white against the wrap of the punching bag, each blow a testament to his determination. The rhythmic thud echoed through the makeshift gym they'd set up in the abandoned barn on Lori's land after it got to hot outside.

He was a machine, every muscle coiled and released with precision—a predator honing his skills.

"Hey," Lori's voice broke through the cadence of his training, softer than the crack of leather on canvas but carrying a weight that immediately drew Simon's attention. She stood in the doorway, her silhouette painted by the fading Kentucky sun, eyes searching for something unspoken in his gaze.

"Everything alright?" Simon lowered his fists, wiping a bead of sweat from his brow as he stepped towards her.

Lori hesitated, biting her lip in a way that told Simon this wasn't just a casual check-in. "I... Can we talk? Away from all this?" She gestured vaguely at the surrounding equipment—their war room turned gymnasium.

"Of course." Simon led her outside, where the evening air held the day's warmth like a lingering embrace. They found solace under an old oak tree, its leaves whispering secrets to the setting sun.

"Simon..." Lori's voice trembled as she started, her hands fidgeting with a loose thread on her worn jeans. "I'm scared.

Terrified, actually. For Jennifer. I can't shake this feeling that... what if we're too late?"

Her blue eyes, mirrors of a storm-tossed sea, met his own. In them, Simon saw the reflection of every nightmare he had been trained to confront. But this—this fear was personal, and it cut deeper than any blade.

"Hey, look at me," Simon said gently, cupping her cheek in his hand. His thumb brushed away a tear that had escaped her defenses. "We're going to get her back. Do you know why? Because I've seen what you're made of, Lori. You're stronger than you give yourself credit for."

Lori leaned into his touch, allowing herself a moment of vulnerability. "But what if our best isn't enough?"

"It has to be," Simon said with quiet intensity. "We'll make it enough. We have to believe that, or we've already lost."

Emboldened by his unwavering determination, Lori flung herself into Simon's arms. She desperately sought solace in his embrace, allowing her tears to flow freely as she crumbled under the weight of a mother's unyielding love and overwhelming fear. Simon held her close, enveloping her in warmth and security as he silently conveyed his unwavering support and understanding. His heart ached at the sight of her pain, but he knew that this was a necessary release for her. He held her tightly, letting her cry out all the pent-up emotions until she was spent, feeling grateful that they could find comfort in each other during this trying time.

As her cries subsided, Simon felt Lori's breath steady against his chest. He lifted her chin, meeting her gaze once more. "We won't fail her, Lori. I promise you."

At that moment, something shifted between them, an invisible line crossed. Without another word, Simon's lips found Lori's in a kiss that spoke volumes. It was a kiss born of shared burdens and whispered promises, a testament to the raw emotions they'd kept at bay.

Their hearts beat in tandem, each pulse chasing away the shadows of doubt. The world outside their embrace fell away; there were no cartels, no rescue missions—just two souls clinging to each other amidst the chaos.

It was a kiss that neither would forget, sealing an unspoken pact between them. Whatever lay ahead, they would face it together.

The sun dipped below the horizon, casting the Kentucky landscape in hues of burnt orange and deepening purple. Inside Lori's house, the atmosphere was a stark contrast to the serene twilight outside. Simon moved through the sparsely furnished living room, his muscular frame a silhouette against the fading light. The air was thick with the scent of antiseptic and sweat—a reminder of the day's grueling training.

"Hey," Lori called out from the kitchen. "Dinner's ready."

Simon turned, his blue eyes seeking her out. He found her by the stove, stirring something that filled the space with a homely aroma. She wore an apron over her clothes, a small defiance against the chaos that had taken over their lives.

"Thought we could use some comfort food tonight," she said with a hint of a smile, her Kentucky accent wrapping around the words like a warm blanket.

"Smells good," Simon replied, walking over to join her. On the table lay a spread that spoke of simpler times—fried chicken, mashed potatoes with gravy, and a side of green beans along with two glasses of sweet iced tea. It was a meal rooted in tradition and memories, a culinary embrace amidst their current turmoil.

They sat across from each other at the table, plates generously heaped with food. For a few moments, they ate in silence, allowing the act of sharing a meal to ground them in normalcy.

"Simon," Lori began, breaking the quiet. She paused, gathering her thoughts. "Have you ever thought about what life might be like after all this is over?"

He looked up from his plate, meeting her earnest gaze. "I'd be lying if I said no."

"Tell me," she prompted gently.

Simon set down his fork, leaning back in his chair. "Honestly? It's hard to imagine. My life has always been...complicated. Then the lightning struck, hell I am an old man. I am ninety but in the body of a thirty-year-old, but somehow God put me here. But lately, I've been thinking about a future where it doesn't have to be."

"Like what?" Lori prodded, her curiosity piqued.

"Like a place where waking up isn't immediately followed by checking for threats. Maybe somewhere far away from all this madness." He gestured vaguely, encompassing more than just the room they were in.

"Could you really leave it all behind?" Lori asked. Her eyes searched his face, looking for a truth that even he wasn't sure existed.

"Before, I couldn't," Simon admitted. "But now—" He hesitated, unsure how much to reveal.

"Go on," she urged softly.

"Now, there's something—or someone—worth leaving it for." His hand reached across the table, fingers brushing against hers.

Lori's breath caught at the touch, a blush creeping onto her cheeks. "And do you see that someone in your future?"

"I do," he said with a certainty that surprised even him. "If she'll have me."

Their hands intertwined, a tangible connection that bridged the gap between their worlds. For a moment, they allowed themselves to dream of a life untethered from fear and duty—a life together.

"Let's promise each other something," Lori whispered, her thumb tracing circles on his skin.

"Anything," Simon responded, his voice low but resolute.

"Whatever happens, we won't let this mission define us. We'll find a way to start anew, to build something that's ours. Just Simon and Lori, not the spy and the desperate mother."

"Deal," Simon agreed, feeling the weight of her words anchor him to a hope he hadn't dared entertain before.

Their dinner forgotten, they stayed locked in conversation, exchanging dreams as easily as they shared the meal. Each word wove a tapestry of a possible future, a world where love was their guiding star, far from the reach of danger and despair.

As the night deepened, so did their bond, fortified by promises made over comfort food and the silent vows reflected in their gazes. Together, they would carve out a path toward the life they yearned for—one where peace was the norm, and chaos was nothing but a distant memory.

The next night was Simon's turn to cook and the sizzle and pop of the grill broke the silence as Simon deftly flipped the steaks, their juices hissing against the hot metal. Lori watched from the porch steps of his cabin, the amber glow from the setting sun casting a warm light on her face. She seemed more relaxed than usual, her shoulders untensed, and even managed a smile as she observed him.

"Almost ready," Simon called out over his shoulder, his voice carrying a faint hint of excitement. He glanced back at her, their eyes meeting for a moment before he turned his attention back to the food. The savory aroma of grilled meat filled the air, mingling with the earthy scent of the surrounding woods.

"Smells amazing, Simon," Lori said, her Kentucky accent wrapping around each word like a comforting blanket.

"Wait until you taste it," he replied, giving her a wink that made her heart flutter unexpectedly.

Dinner was simple yet satisfying; perfectly grilled steaks, fluffy baked potatoes topped with melting butter, and a side of crisp green beans. They ate mostly in silence, stealing glances at each other between mouthfuls. Afterward, Simon cleared the table and brought out a homemade apple pie, its crust golden-brown and flaky, with coffee to wash it down.

"Simon, you didn't have to go to all this trouble," Lori said, her blue eyes shining with appreciation.

"It's no trouble at all," he assured her, pouring the rich, dark coffee into two mugs. "And I have something for you."

He reached into his pocket and pulled out a small object, carefully wrapped in a piece of cloth. Unfolding it, he revealed a delicate silver chain with a tiny pendant—a compass rose etched into its surface.

Lori's breath hitched as she took the necklace, her fingers trembling slightly. "Simon, it's beautiful."

"It's to remind us that no matter how lost we get, we'll find our way back to each other," Simon said, his voice thick with emotion. "To our future."

Tears welled up in Lori's eyes as she let Simon clasp the necklace around her neck. The cool metal rested against her skin, a tangible symbol of their shared resolve.

"Thank you," she whispered, turning to him. Their faces were inches apart, and the air between them crackled with intensity.

"Thank me by coming back safe," Simon murmured before closing the gap between them.

Their lips met in a passionate kiss, conveying all the fear, hope, and love they held within. It was a fervent promise made without words, a pledge of devotion amidst the uncertainty of their mission. Lori wrapped her arms around Simon, pulling him closer as if she could merge their souls into one indomitable force.

They broke away briefly, their foreheads resting against each other as they caught their breath. Whispers of love and vows of return echoed softly in the space between them, each syllable a lifeline to cling to in the days ahead.

"Nothing will keep me from coming back with you," Lori breathed, her voice laced with determination.

"And nothing will stop me from protecting you," Simon vowed, sealing their pledge with another deep, longing kiss that spoke of a future they were willing to fight for, whatever the cost.

The moon hung high over the cabin as Simon and Lori lay entwined in the soft cocoon of an old quilt, their breaths mingling in the cool night air that slipped through the cracks of the rustic cabin. The silence was heavy with anticipation, punctuated only by the occasional hoot of a distant owl.

"Tomorrow's it," Simon whispered against Lori's hair, his hands tracing the curve of her spine. The weight of the mission pressed down on them, but here in this intimate cocoon, everything else fell away.

Lori lifted her gaze to meet his, her blue eyes reflecting the determination that matched his own. "Together," she affirmed, her voice steady despite the tempest brewing inside her.

"Always," he replied, sealing their pact with a kiss that slowly deepened, savoring the taste of her, memorizing the feel of her lips moving perfectly against his—this was their armor against the chaos to come.

Their bodies moved in a silent dance, each touch a testament to their unspoken vows. It was more than just a physical union; it was a fierce melding of souls, a declaration of trust and unwavering loyalty. The room filled with the sound of whispered names and soft gasps, the creak of the wooden bed frame keeping time with their heartbeats.

Later, spent and still wrapped in each other's arms, they lay quiet, the warmth of their bodies warding off the chill that seeped in from outside. Lori's fingers traced the lines of

Simon's muscular arm, feeling the strength that lay beneath the skin—the strength she'd come to rely on.

"Simon?" Her voice broke the silence, tentative yet needing to voice the fears that clawed at her heart.

"Shhh, I know," he said before she could continue, his hold tightening around her. "I'm scared too. But we've got each other, and that's more than most have."

She nodded against his chest, taking solace in the rhythmic beat of his heart. "It's Jennifer I'm thinking about. What if—" The words caught in her throat, unable to bear the weight of her dread.

"We'll get her back, Lori. We'll bring her home." His tone left no room for doubt, his conviction a beacon in the darkness that threatened to engulf her.

They lapsed into silence once more, each lost in thought. In the embrace of the Kentucky night, they allowed themselves a moment of vulnerability, acknowledging the gravity of what awaited them across the border. Their shared fears and hopes wove together, creating a bond stronger than the steel of Simon's weapons or the resolve etched into Lori's face.

As dawn threatened to break, casting a soft glow on the horizon, they shared one last look—a silent promise of protection, a vow of return. They would step into the unknown, but they would do it as one, their love a shield against whatever perils lay ahead.

The dim light of dawn barely infiltrated the room as Simon checked his gear for the final time. The weight of his pistol was a familiar comfort against his side. Beside him, Lori methodically packed her bag, her movements precise and deliberate. Her blue eyes, usually warm and inviting, were steel today, tempered by the fires of determination.

"Hey." Simon's voice was soft but firm as he caught Lori's hand, pausing her actions. She turned to face him, and in that moment, the world outside their bubble ceased to exist. Their gazes locked, each filled with unspoken understanding, fears, and fierce resolve. Without words, they leaned into each other, their lips meeting in a final, passionate kiss. It was a kiss of promise, a seal on the vows they'd made to each other and Jennifer. A kiss that infused them with hope, a silent reassurance that they would face whatever came their way together.

As they parted, there was a lingering warmth, an ember that would remain kindled within them through the trials ahead.

"For luck," Simon murmured, his breath ghosting across her cheek.

"We make our own luck," Lori replied, a wry smile curving her lips despite the gravity of the situation.

They shouldered their bags and walked out of the cabin together, emerging into the crisp morning air. The rest of the team was already gathered around the vehicles—a mix of rugged faces set in grim lines of focus mixed with the soft faces of youth. The group comprised of misfits, it seemed, all thrown together, each one aware of the stakes at hand.

Simon and Lori joined them, standing shoulder to shoulder. There was a palpable sense of unity among the team, a shared commitment that was almost tangible. They exchanged brief nods with their comrades, acknowledging the road ahead without the need for speeches or dramatic goodbyes.

"Alright, let's move out," Simon commanded, the authority in his voice a clear signal to begin. They piled into the vehicles, engines rumbling to life as they kicked up gravel in their wake. The team moved out, trailing dust clouds along the winding roads that would lead them to their destination.

The journey was tense, every mile bringing them closer to the danger that awaited in Mexico. Yet, as the miles ticked by, Simon felt the steady presence of Lori beside him. Her quiet strength was a constant source of inspiration, and the love blossoming between them was a flame that fear could not extinguish.

Their thoughts were on Jennifer, the vibrant young woman who had been thrust into a nightmare. But they were also on each other, on the bond that had formed in the crucible of their shared mission. Each knew that no matter what lay ahead, they would face it as one, their resolve as unbreakable as the love that held them together.

Loran sat in the back seat with her youngest brother Alva, her nose constantly in the laptop she had plugged into a USB adapter to the car. Her phone was also plugged in so she could use the hotspot for internet connectivity. The laptop and phone, supplied by the CIA, were far better than her own. Mark, who was nearly mended, rode with Jack and Loran's two other brothers, Frank and John, in the car behind.

The sun dipped below the horizon, painting the sky in hues of blood and fire as the convoy snaked its way to the border. Simon's hands gripped the wheel, his eyes scanning the road ahead while his mind played through every possible scenario they might encounter. Beside him, Lori sat in silence, her gaze lost in the rapidly approaching twilight.

The two vehicles pulled up to the Love's Truck Stop after getting into Memphis and turning South on 240 from the interstate. Loran's intel had been that there was a cartel stronghold using a warehouse on Amido Ave and Stiler Ave. This was a complex of warehouses and the cartel was supposed to be in the two on the West end.

While the team looked over the maps and photos once more, the three boys prepared their drones fitted with infrared cameras. They would do an aerial recon before the others went in. Simon called Amanda on her cell.

"Where are you, Simon?"

"We are at the Love's on 240 on the South side of Memphis. Go ahead and call the FBI and tell them where we are. We will wait for them and get the best places to go in after the boys show us what the drones pick up."

"On it, Simon," Amanda replied and the phone went dead.

Ten minutes later, three cars with four agents each pulled up to the team's cars.

"Which one of you is Simon?" asked a female agent. She looked to be about twenty-three and was looking at the three men of the team.

"That would be me."

"Angie Winn, Agent in Charge of this detail." Simon shook her hand. "Glad to meet you. Let me brief you on our latest details and then with your knowledge of the area we'll set up our command center, get some live drone feed, and take it from there."

Simon and the team briefed the agents on what they knew. They found the best location for the command center that would be out of harm's way and then hit the road in a convoy. Once everything was set up, the boys launched the drone. The agents leaned over Loran's shoulder and watched the footage come up.

The footage showed activity in only one warehouse. The East end looked like a sleeping area for a large number of people. Towards the middle were more people in prone positions with only a few walking around or sitting.

"This will be the captives," Simon said, pointing to the screen. "Boys, whoever is flying near the loading docks on the far end, drop as low as you can and get us some images of the doors down there."

The drone moved into position.

"Hold it right there," Simon ordered. "This is where we need to go in. That will put us between the captives and the cartel. Four of your agents will breach this door on the West end, and two more will stand guard. If any get by, it will be their job to neutralize them, Angie."

She nodded and pulled her team back to give assignments.

"Lori, I want you to stand guard at our door with one of the agents. Be ready to come in as soon as I call. If these are girls like I think they will be, you will need to help comfort them until medical arrives."

Lori nodded.

With the teams in position at the designated doors and the drones keeping watch as Loran and her brothers stood by at the command center, Simon gave the order: "Go, go, go."

Battering rams slammed into the doors and the teams made their entry. They were met with immediate gunfire. They responded in kind but had the advantage of Loran telling them where the cartel members on patrol were right before they entered.

Screams could be heard from behind the wall at their backs. In less than three minutes, the gun battle was over. All the cartel members were dead and one agent was KIA. His team attempted first aid but it was no use. Angie got on her phone and ordered medics and a clean-up crew from the agency. Suddenly, shots came from the room where they believed the captives were held.

"Jack, Mark, hit it," Simon shouted as he ran towards the interior door that separated the room. He threw open the door and rolled inside. One shot was all it took to take out the guard. Unfortunately, three captives were dead before Simon and the others reached the room.

"Get Lori and Angie in here. No men allowed from this point on," Simon ordered.

"I'll get 'em," Jack replied as he looked away from the captives and their condition. He wanted to be sick from what he saw.

"Lori, you and Angie need to get in there," Jack told them as they were looking around at the carnage.

The two women took a step forward and Jack grabbed Lori's arm. "Be strong, it is bad in there."

Lori's eyes stared into Jack's, then she nodded and continued. Tears came to her eyes as she took in the surroundings inside the room.

Chapter 10

The stale air hung heavy in the cavernous room, thick with despair. Fifty pairs of eyes, once bright with dreams and aspirations, now dulled by trauma, glanced warily at their rescuers. The captives, huddled together for warmth and solace, bore the marks of unspeakable horrors on their naked bodies. Bruises flowered like dark petals across their skin, ranging in shades from sickly green to deep purple. Some wounds were scabbed over, while others still oozed fresh blood. The faint tang of metal filled the air, a reminder of the violence inflicted upon them. It was a tableau of violation and neglect, the aftermath of assault still clinging to them in the form of bruises, scratches, and scars. Their once pristine bodies were now marred by the filth and brutality forced upon them. And yet, despite it all, they stood strong, refusing to be defined by their abusers' actions.

Lori, along with Angie, moved among them like ministering angels, their faces set in masks of professional calm, but their eyes betrayed a deep well of sorrow. They whispered words of comfort, handing out blankets they had found to cover shivering forms and offering gentle touches that spoke volumes—a promise that the nightmare was over, that they were no longer alone. Except for the three that were alone in death.

"Get backup on the way," Angie said into her comms. "We need medical and psych teams at the loading docks, stat."

"Copy that," came the crisp reply. Within minutes, a convoy of unmarked vehicles and ambulances rolled up, a symphony of slamming doors and urgent footsteps as agents swarmed the scene. Paramedics, with their kits and compassion, began triaging the captives, soothing their fears while assessing their wounds.

Simon Wilson stood slightly apart from the flurry of activity, his muscular frame a silent sentinel amidst the bustle. His piercing blue eyes scanned the room, taking in every detail—the way Angie directed the rescue efforts with practiced ease, the way Lori's presence seemed to offer a balm to the traumatized women.

"Angie," Simon called out, his voice barely rising above the din, yet somehow cutting through it. He waited until she met his gaze before continuing. "I'm turning the op over to you. We're heading to Waco as soon as we can."

Angie gave a curt nod, her focus never wavering from the task at hand. "Understood. We've got this covered here. Go get the rest of them."

With a final survey of the room, Simon motioned to his team. They understood the unspoken command—they were moving out. As they exited the warehouse, the weight of what had transpired pressed down on Simon's broad shoulders, but he shrugged it off with practiced ease. This was just another chapter in a long career of service—a career that often asked more of him than he thought he could give.

The drive to the Holiday Inn was a silent one, the team too exhausted for conversation. They checked in with minimal fuss, each member disappearing into their respective rooms with the mechanical movements of those too tired to feel.

Simon entered his room, the door clicking shut behind him. In the solitude, the adrenaline that had sustained him began to ebb away, replaced by an all-consuming fatigue. He peeled off his clothes, stepping into the shower with a sigh. The hot water sluiced over his muscular frame, washing away the grime and blood, though he knew the stains lurking beneath his skin would take longer to fade.

He slept that night—though sleep was a generous term for the restless hours spent tossing and turning, images of the raid flashing behind closed eyelids. When dawn broke, Simon was already awake, staring at the ceiling, his mind churning with plans for the next rescue.

"Time to move," he muttered to himself, the loner in him ready to face whatever dangers lay ahead in Waco. But first, a few hours of respite—a brief reprieve in a world where peace was as elusive as the morning mist.

"Let's get moving," Simon said as he knocked on the doors to the hotel rooms his team occupied. His voice was calm, but those who knew him could hear the steel edge beneath the measured tones.

The drive to Waco was a blur; the highway stretched out before them, a monotonous tapestry of tarmac and painted lines. Lori sat beside Simon, her hand finding his whenever the weight of silence grew too heavy. Each touch was a balm, steadying her as thoughts of her daughter intertwined with the faces of the women they had just left behind.

As they entered the warehouse district of Waco, the atmosphere shifted palpably. The buildings stood like dormant beasts, their hollowed windows gazing blankly at the intruders in their midst. Simon pulled out his phone, his thumb hovering over the screen for a moment before he dialed.

"Amanda, it's Simon. We need FBI support in Waco. There's another cell holding captives here."

"Consider it done," Amanda replied. "I'm sending a team now."

With that, Simon coordinated with Loran, who was already at the makeshift command post with her three brothers. They were a formidable sight: blue-tinted skin, slight in build but with eyes that spoke of mountains and untold resilience. Their drones hummed overhead, providing a bird's-eye view of the cartel's stronghold.

"Positions, everyone," Simon ordered after the FBI team had arrived and been briefed, his gaze sweeping over his team. They moved like a well-oiled machine, each person a cog necessary to the grim task at hand.

The breach was explosive—a symphony of chaos and precision. Gunfire erupted, the sound ricocheting off the metal walls. Simon led the charge, every muscle coiled and ready. The cartel members fought with the ferocity of cornered animals, but one by one, they fell. It was over in minutes, the air thick with gunpowder and the stench of death.

"Clear!" someone called out, their voice ringing in the sudden stillness.

Simon took a moment, his breathing steadying as he surveyed the aftermath. He had walked through the valley of death more times than he cared to count, but it never got easier. The sounds of the captives emerged from the shadows in the room they were kept in.

"Let them know it's over," Simon instructed, his eyes meeting Lori's once more. She nodded, stepping forward to embrace the role of comforter once more. However, now as she walked, her Glock 23 was at her side in case there were more guards lurking, as in Memphis.

"Come on out," Lori beckoned softly. "You're safe now." And though her voice wavered, the promise didn't feel hollow this time. With Simon by her side, and the determination that coursed through her veins, she believed it. They would make it right, somehow.

After the raid, the Waco warehouse was illuminated by harsh fluorescent lights. Angie, who had requested to be assigned to the operation until its conclusion and had been granted her wish, arrived just minutes before the raid as the FBI agent in charge. She flicked on the overhead lights, flooding the once dim space with brightness. The sudden illumination revealed a harrowing scene: rows upon rows of young women, their faces etched with the trauma of captivity.

They huddled together, shivering and exposed, their naked bodies bearing the brutal marks of beatings and worse— terrible evidence of the vile acts they'd been subjected to.

"Get some blankets in here, now!" Angie's voice cut through the thick silence, commanding and clear. Within moments, agents scurried in, arms laden with fabric that would provide at least a modicum of dignity. "Call in some medics and get these girls some medical attention now."

Lori, her heart lodged firmly in her throat, moved among the captives like a guardian angel, draping blankets over quivering shoulders. Her eyes never strayed far from Simon drawing strength from his unwavering presence as he stood watch by the entrance, his blue gaze vigilant and cold.

One girl, barely out of her teens, caught Lori's attention— a fragile bird with haunted eyes.

"Can you tell me what happened?" Lori asked, her Kentucky accent soft but firm.

The girl told her story, but what made Lori pause, was when she said; "A man... he came sometimes. They called him Larry... or Harlow," the captive whispered hoarsely.

"Did you see his face?" Lori pressed gently, though her pulse raced with the implication.

"Only once. He was careful not to show it much," the girl murmured, and others around her nodded in silent affirmation.

"Thank you," Lori said, squeezing the girl's hand before rising. She crossed the room to where Simon stood, her blanket-clad charges watching her go. "Simon, they mentioned a visitor—Larry or Harlow. It could be important."

Simon and Lori walked back over to the girl who had informed Lori about Larry Harlow.

"Please tell him about this Larry Harlow," Lori said, pointing to Simon.

The girl described his old friend to him. Some parts might have been skewed, but he knew from what she said, that it was in fact Larry Harlow she told him about.

Simon's jaw clenched an imperceptible shift that Lori wouldn't have noticed if she hadn't been looking for it. He turned away from her, facing the grim tableau of the warehouse. His mind raced, grappling with the possibility that betrayal had wormed its way into their operation.

"Harlow..." The name was like a splinter in his thoughts. Larry Harlow—a colleague, a fellow CIA operative, a friend. Could he really be involved? The notion sent a tremor of anger through Simon, undercut by the bitter sting of betrayal. His fists clenched at his sides; trust was currency in their line of work, and he felt robbed.

"Simon?" Lori's voice was tinged with concern, pulling him back from the precipice of his inner turmoil.

"Keep interviewing them," he instructed his tone even despite the storm raging inside him. "We need all the information we can get."

As Lori nodded and returned to the captives, Simon withdrew to a quiet corner of the warehouse. This was a challenge he hadn't anticipated, and it weighed heavily on him. The mission was always paramount—rescuing the captives, dismantling the cartel—but the thought of an insider playing them gnawed at him with sharp teeth.

"Damn it, Harlow," Simon muttered under his breath. If the betrayal proved true, it meant reevaluating every move they made, every plan they laid. But there was no time for hesitation; lives hung in the balance. With a deep breath, Simon steeled himself. Whatever it took, whoever was involved, he would see this through to the bitter end.

Simon pulled the team together in an empty corner of the warehouse, now including Angie. "We have been informed of a mole. Not that it makes any difference who it is, but it is an old CIA agent who has firsthand knowledge that I, we, are after Ortiz."

"Simon, we can't just leave things like this," Lori implored, her voice strained with emotion as she glanced up at him, her blue eyes a mirror of the turmoil he felt within.

"Nobody's suggesting we do," Simon replied, his gaze lingering on the faces of the captives, each one a silent plea for justice.

"Then we push forward," said Jack, breaking the heavy silence. "We can't let Ortiz get away with it."

"Push forward?" Mark countered skeptically, crossing his arms over his chest. "With a rat in our ranks? That's suicide."

The room became a battleground of conflicting opinions, voices rising and falling in heated debate. Some advocated for pressing on, driven by righteous anger and a refusal to be cowed by fear. Others argued for caution, the recent betrayal casting a long shadow over their trust in the operation.

"Think about what you're saying," Mark snapped, his frustration palpable. "Continuing blindly could cost us everything."

"And what? We just abandon these girls to their fate?" Loran shot back, her hands clenched tightly at her sides. "That's not why we signed up for this."

Simon listened, the muscle in his jaw twitching as the tension mounted. The air was electric with the crackle of raised voices, the team's unity fraying at the edges as desperation clawed at their resolve.

"Enough!" Simon's command cut through the cacophony, silencing the group. He met each pair of eyes in turn, his blue gaze steely. "We knew this mission wouldn't be a walk in the park. But we also knew the stakes. Lives are hanging in the balance—lives we vowed to protect."

The room held its breath, the team exchanging uncertain glances as they grappled with the weight of their choices.

"Betrayal or not, we have a job to finish," Simon continued, his voice steady despite the storm of emotions brewing beneath the surface. "We adapt, we watch our backs, and we see this through. Are we clear?"

"Clear," came the reluctant murmur, the team's commitment flickering like a flame in the wind, challenged but not extinguished.

"Good." Simon nodded, the matter settled for now. But as he looked around at the faces of his team, he knew the road ahead would test them all, perhaps more than any mission had before.

Simon stood amidst the chaos, his gaze lingering on the heart-wrenching sight before him. The room was filled with the aftermath of brutality, a stark reminder of the cruelty that had prompted their mission. Women huddled together, their eyes reflecting unspeakable traumas. Some were motionless, lost in their own worlds of anguish, while others sobbed softly, their bodies marked by violence and neglect.

"Damn it," Simon muttered under his breath, his fists clenching at the sight of such torment. These were daughters, sisters, friends—people who had been living their lives until they were snatched away into this nightmare. His heart ached for Jennifer, for the vibrant young woman whose spirit must not be broken by monsters like these.

The team watched him, their own emotions a turbulent storm behind their professional masks. They knew what Simon was about to say before he even spoke, yet they waited for his command, the linchpin that would decide their next move.

"We're not leaving anyone else behind," Simon declared, his voice resonating with a strength that seemed to anchor the room. "Not now, not ever. We came here to end this, and that's exactly what we're going to do."

His declaration was met with silence at first, the team processing the weight of his words. They each knew the risks, the potential cost of pushing forward when every instinct screamed to take cover, to protect themselves from the fallout of betrayal.

But then, one by one, they nodded. They had seen the horrors firsthand, and the images were etched into their minds, fueling their determination. Their trust in Simon had been forged in fire by now, tempered by missions and shared dangers. It held firm, even now.

As they prepared to face what lay ahead, Simon felt the weight of leadership heavy on his shoulders. But alongside it, there was something else—a fierce sense of purpose that blazed brighter than any fear or doubt. He would lead them through whatever battles awaited, and together, they would bring each and every captive back into the light.

Simon's hotel room felt like a crucible, the air thick with tension and the aftermath of adrenaline. The ragged breathing of his team filled the space as they crowded in, each person carrying the weight of the day's harrowing rescue. It wasn't the sterile environment of their usual bases; it was a Holiday Inn room, replete with mundane details that clashed with the gravity of their mission—a floral bedspread, an innocuous landscape painting on the wall, the faint hum of the air conditioning. Each had a drink in their hand, alcohol for the adults, and sodas for the kids.

"Everybody ready?" Simon asked, his voice betraying none of the turmoil churning inside him. His blue eyes scanned the faces of his comrades, finding grim determination mirrored back at him.

He dialed Amanda Sawyer, the CIA Director, and set the phone in the center of the group. The ringtone coming through the speaker cut short, and her voice came through, crisp and authoritative.

"Wilson, report."

Simon didn't mince words. "Amanda, we've got a situation. We just found out Larry Harlow is dirty. He's been spotted with the cartel at the Waco warehouse."

There was a sharp intake of breath from the other side of the line, followed by a moment of heavy silence. When

Amanda spoke again, her tone was laced with an edge of betrayal. "Understood. I'm pulling him in now."

Angie's normally stoic demeanor cracked for a moment as she recounted the state of the young women in her mind, all in their prime yet subjected to unspeakable torment. The visceral impact of her words left a palpable anger hanging in the room.

"Those bastards are going to pay for what they've done," Jack muttered, clenching his fists until the knuckles turned white.

"Focus that anger," Simon instructed, his voice steady but his mind racing with the same fury. "Use it to stay sharp out there. We have one more push, and every single one of those girls is counting on us." With that, the team separated into their own rooms.

In the adjoining hotel room, Loran Smith watched Lori unpack a small case, her normally shy demeanor giving way to sisterly concern. The faint indigo tint of her skin seemed more pronounced in the dim light, a spectral reminder of her Blue Fugate heritage.

"Go on, honey. Be with Simon tonight," Loran encouraged, her slow southern drawl carrying a hint of mirth. "He needs you, and Lord knows you need him too."

Lori paused, her worried look betraying the inner turmoil that simmered beneath her caring exterior. She thought of her daughter, of the horrors unfolding around them, and the man who stood as both protector and anchor in the storm.

"Are you sure?" Lori asked, her voice barely above a whisper.

"Sure as the creek runs clear in Troublesome Creek," Loran replied with a soft giggle, nudging Lori toward the door. "Now go, before I have to push you out myself."

With a small smile, Lori repacked and zipped up her case and headed towards the door, the weight of the night ahead settling in her heart, yet somehow made lighter by the prospect of finding solace in Simon's steadfast presence.

With trepidation, Lori found herself outside Simon's door, her fingertips hesitating before they rapped softly against the wood. It was a timid knock, one that spoke volumes about the vulnerability she felt in this moment of seeking comfort.

The door swung open, revealing Simon in just a pair of shorts, his blue eyes reflecting a storm of his own. He stood there, the embodiment of strength wrought by a life spent in service of others, yet it was the flicker of tenderness in his gaze that drew Lori in. Without a word, Simon stepped aside, allowing her passage into his temporary sanctuary.

"Thanks for letting me come over," Lori said, her Kentucky accent threading her words with a warmth that seemed out of place in the sterile hotel room.

"Of course," Simon answered, his voice low. He took her bag from her, setting it down with a gentleness that contrasted his muscular frame. His presence was a balm, and as she looked up into his eyes, Lori felt the first threads of tension unravel within her.

"Loran almost pushed me out of our room telling me to come here. Evidently, she has seen something in us, or she just knows, you know, that hillbilly intellect thing you hear about," Lori said.

Simon closed the distance between them and drew her in for a lingering kiss. "Guess we were fooling ourselves that no one would know," he replied after releasing her lips from his.

Their lovemaking was slow—a dance of two souls seeking and giving solace in equal measure. Simon worshipped her with his touch, reverent and unhurried as if understanding the depth of healing they both needed. Every brush of skin, every shared breath, was a silent vow of support and connection.

They found their rhythm, a languid exploration that allowed them to lose themselves in each other. Lori clung to Simon, her fingers tracing the contours of his back, memorizing the feel of him. In these quiet hours, they were not defined by the turmoil around them but by the peace they found in each other's arms, not the chaos of their lives but by the intimacy that bloomed between them.

Exhaustion eventually claimed them, and they fell asleep entwined, Lori's head resting on Simon's shoulder. In slumber, their defenses lowered, and they found peace in the steady beat of each other's hearts—a lullaby that promised if only for a night, respite from the world outside their door.

The next morning Simon was sitting on the edge of the bed after having just showered when the sound of his ringing phone interrupted the silence.

Amanda Sawyer's voice crackled through the phone. "We've got Harlow singing like a canary. He's confessed to feeding intel to Ortiz's gang about our moves. Says he's been compromised for months. I'm going to play you a portion of the recording we made, hang on."

The sounds of computer keys being tapped could be heard over the connection. While Amanda was queuing up the recording, Simon shook Lori awake and placed the call on speaker. "Amanda, I have you on speaker and Lori is listening as well." Hearing Amanda's name, Lori sat up quickly, letting the sheet slip off her, exposing the breast Simon had feasted on the night before.

"Okay, here it is," Amanda said. Then the next thing Simon and Lori heard was the frail voice of Larry Harlow.

"Please, I just... I was trying to protect myself," Larry's frail voice broke, quivering with fear or perhaps regret. "Juan

Ortiz—he knew things, he made threats. I fed him bits and pieces, nothing major, just enough to keep him off my back."

"Information about our operations?" Amanda's voice was like steel.

The confirmation came as a sob. "Yes. I'm so sorry."

Amanda stopped the recording and pinched the bridge of her nose, her voice tight with frustration. "So we've had a mole in the operation. You still want to proceed with the Reynosa raid?"

"More than ever," Simon replied, his tone resolute. "We can't let this betrayal stop us. Those girls need us, Amanda."

She sighed into the receiver, the lines of command and care blending in her response. "It's a fool's mission, Simon. But I trust your judgment. You'll have our support."

"Thank you," he said simply. "Keep him there. We'll handle it from here." Disconnecting the call, Simon looked at Lori, seeing her expression shift from shock to resolve. While the revelation stung, it only served to harden her resolve. They were the last line of defense against monsters like Juan Ortiz, and they would not falter now.

"Alright. We know what we're up against," Simon declared. "Let's finish this."

They dressed and Simon made his walk through the hall waking his team. "Time to get up. We'll meet for breakfast downstairs and then get going." He knew they would be ready to go without much delay. He went back to his room, grabbed their bags and he and Lori went downstairs to find a hot breakfast waiting in the small dining area next to the lobby.

Chapter 11

The sun had just dipped below the horizon when Simon Wilson guided the cars following his into the parched parking lot of a Super 8 in Harlingen, Texas. The last rays of daylight gave the hotel a golden glow against the encroaching twilight. He killed the engine and let out a long breath, feeling the weight of the long drive from Waco settle into his muscles.

"Everyone out," he ordered, more out of habit than necessity.

The team occupants met behind Simon's car as the others were parked on each side of it. Jack Thompson was stretching his arms above his head, the bones in his spine popping audibly. His vigilant eyes scanned the area, always the protector, even in the mundanity of a motel parking lot.

"Place looks quiet enough," Jack commented, his voice carrying that ever-present undertone of authority fine-tuned by years in the Air Force Security Forces.

"Let's hope it stays that way," Mark replied, joining Jack as they both surveyed the surroundings.

Simon reached for his cell phone, scrolling through his contacts until he found Emilia Salgado's number. With a press, the call connected, and her voice, crisp with an edge of anticipation, filled the line.

"Simon, ¿estás cerca?" Emilia's tone was a mix of business and concern.

"Yep, we're at Harlingen, just checking in. How are things on your end?" Simon kept his voice low.

"Everything is set. Be careful, I have a feeling the cartel has been more alert lately," she warned, her voice dropping to a whisper that sent a shiver of foreboding down Simon's spine. We need to change the entry to La Reforma.

"Understood. We'll keep our heads down. Thanks, Emilia."

Ending the call, Simon pocketed his phone and turned to see Lori Hawkins leaning against the car. Her blue eyes were wide with unspoken fears, her hands fidgeting with the hem of her shirt. She drew a shaky breath, trying to muster a smile for Simon's sake.

"Are you okay to share a room with me tonight?" Simon asked, his voice gentle, laced with the concern he felt for her.

Lori nodded, her lips pressing into a thin line. "Yes, I'd prefer it, actually," she whispered, barely audible.

"Alright then, let's get settled in," Simon said, offering her a small, reassuring smile as he grabbed their bags.

Loran Smith trailed behind them as they made their way to their rooms after leaving the lobby, her slight build and the faint indigo tint of her skin almost making her blend into the dusky shadows. She moved with a reticence that belied her tough mountain upbringing. When they reached Angie's door, Loran paused, turning back to face Lori with a mischievous glint in her eyes. She raised her eyebrows in a playful wiggle, eliciting a nervous chuckle from Lori before vanishing into the room she'd be sharing with Angie.

Simon watched the exchange, a wry smile tugging at the corner of his mouth. In this grim business, any moment of levity was a precious commodity. He led Lori to their room, the key card sliding into the slot with a soft beep.

"Home sweet home, at least for tonight," Simon quipped as he pushed open the door, stepping into the simple but clean space that would serve as their sanctuary before the storm that was sure to come.

The Super 8's neon sign flickered in the rearview mirror as Simon steered the car onto the road, the engine's low growl cutting through the silence of the early morning. Emilia's latest message had been brief but clear: La Reforma was correct in being picked as the crossing point instead of the McAllen area. No reason was given for the change, and none was asked. In their line of work, adaptability wasn't just an asset—it was survival.

"La Reforma," Lori muttered from the passenger seat, her gaze fixed on the darkened horizon. She seemed lost in thought, the uncertainty of what lay ahead etching lines of worry across her brow.

"Trust in Emilia," Simon reassured, his voice steady. "She knows the lay of the land better than anyone."

"Doesn't make it any less nerve-wracking," Lori replied but nodded with reluctant acceptance.

La Reforma materialized out of the shadows like a ghost town, its streets deserted and bathed in the pallid glow of sparse streetlights. Simon guided the convoy of vehicles—two sedans and an SUV—into an unassuming lot tucked behind an abandoned gas station. The location was strategic enough cover to hide their presence, with sightlines that would give them the advantage if things went sideways.

"Everybody good?" Simon called out as the engines died down. His team—Jack, Mark, Loran, her brothers, Lori, and

Angie—emerged from the vehicles, quiet nods and focused expressions their only replies.

"Gear up," Simon instructed, popping the trunk to reveal an arsenal carefully laid out in foam padding. They moved with practiced efficiency, each person grabbing their preassigned weapon—a mix of assault rifles, handguns, and knives—and checking them over with meticulous care.

"Remember, we're not looking to start a war," Simon reminded everyone as he slung his rifle across his back. "But we damn well better be ready for one."

"Always am," Jack grunted, the former Air Force Tech Sergeant cracking his knuckles with a grin that didn't quite reach his eyes.

The sheriff of Hart County, Mark, cautioned the team as they prepared for their mission. He checked and double-checked the equipment in his backpack, making sure it was secure. "Stay alert," he reminded them. "Keep your eyes on the skies and ears open for any signs of trouble."

Loran was silent, her fingers deftly securing the straps on her bulletproof vest. Her brothers mirrored her actions, the familial bond between them unspoken but unmistakable in their synchronized movements.

Angie double-checked her medical bag, making sure every bandage and syringe was accounted for. "Hope I don't have to use this," she murmured.

"Here's hoping," Lori echoed softly.

Simon surveyed his team one last time, their faces illuminated by the dim light spilling from the SUV. They were a motley crew, each drawn into this fight for reasons as varied as their backgrounds. But in this moment, they were united by a single purpose.

"Alright," Simon said, his words slicing through the tension. "We move in thirty minutes. If you have to pee or anything else, now is the time to do it."

He watched them disperse, finding spots around the vehicles to catch a few minutes to reflect on what was about to happen in their own way. Simon sat on the trunk of one of the sedans, the weight of the upcoming mission settling heavily on his shoulders.

In the quiet of the night, under the watchful stars, the team waited for Simon's signal.

At four-thirty, Simon said, "It's time." Simon and his team were already on the move. The rising sun was still about two hours away as they traversed through the sparse terrain, the scrub and mesquite offering scant cover. Their boots crunched softly on the gravel and dry earth, each step measured to avoid drawing unwanted attention.

Simon led the way, his blue eyes scanning the horizon. His hand rested casually near the pistol holstered at his side, a gesture that belied the adrenaline coursing through his veins. With every step, the border drew closer, and so did the danger.

"Stay off the ridgelines," he instructed quietly over his shoulder. "We'll use the arroyos for cover."

Jack, ever the dependable second-in-command, nodded and relayed the message with hand signals to those behind him. The team adjusted their path, descending into the shallow depressions in the land that would shield them from prying eyes.

The stillness of the morning was deceptive, giving no hint of the peril lurking just beyond their line of sight. But Simon's instincts—which had kept him alive in darker places than this—were sounding silent alarms. He could almost feel the cartel's gaze upon them, a predator sizing up its prey.

"Drone overhead," Frank whispered urgently, the youngest of the trio pointing skyward.

Simon didn't need to look, he trusted the warning implicitly. "Cover!" he hissed, motioning toward a cluster of dense brush nearby.

The team scattered silently, each member finding refuge among the thorny undergrowth and dusty earth. Simon pressed his back against a large rock, his breathing controlled as he peered through a gap in the foliage. A small, dark shape buzzed across the sky, sweeping the area in a methodical pattern.

"Cartel scouts," Mark murmured beside him, barely audible. "They're searching for something—or someone."

"Us," Simon confirmed grimly. The drone hovered for a moment longer before continuing on its path, disappearing into the distance.

"Wait for it," Simon commanded, holding his team in place with a steady gaze.

Minutes stretched into an hour, the sky changing as the darkness began to give way to the pending sunrise. But Simon knew better than to move too soon, the cartel was cunning, often doubling back to catch the unwary.

Finally, when he was sure the coast was clear, Simon gave the signal to move out. They emerged from their hiding spots like wraiths, leaving no trace of their presence behind. The crossing loomed ahead, the promise of danger—and the chance to save lives—drawing them inexorably onward.

Simon led his team in a zigzagging advance through the scrubland, his eyes scanning for signs of surveillance. He considered sending a drone up to check the area but knew they might need every minute of battery life later. He had relied on his own skills long enough to decide it would be a waste of resources. Jack and Mark also had skills that, combined with his, he hoped would keep them alive and out of harm's way. Loran's brothers also showed skills as hunters back home, and he knew he did not have to worry about them until the prey became human and the fight was up close.

"Keep it loose," he murmured over his shoulder, "but keep it tight." The paradox wasn't lost on him, but it was the only way to describe their formation—spread out enough to avoid one sweep taking them all, close enough to support each other at a moment's notice.

Dust devils danced across the landscape as they approached Reynosa, a city that seemed to rise mirage-like from the heat haze. Ringed with the steel teeth of border fences and the watchful gaze of guard towers, it was a place that thrived on the edge of lawlessness.

As they reached the outskirts, the team huddled behind an abandoned building, its windows shattered and walls scarred by graffiti. Simon's blue eyes flicked across the street, where a stray dog rummaged through garbage, oblivious to the human drama unfolding around it.

"Simon." The voice pulled his focus, and he turned to see Rudy emerging from the shadows of an alleyway, Emilia a silent specter at his side. Her green eyes met Simon's with an intensity that belied her calm demeanor.

"Rudy, Emilia," Simon greeted, giving a nod as the rest of his team acknowledged the pair with curt nods and hand signals.

"Let's walk," she said, leading them away from the exposed area into the relative privacy of a crumbling adobe wall draped with bougainvillea vines.

Simon took a deep breath, the humid air of Reynosa filling his lungs as he sat across from Emilia at a nondescript cantina. The aroma of strong coffee mingled with the sweetness of pan dulce on their table, an odd counterpoint to the gravity of their discussion. Emilia's gaze was unwavering, her green eyes fixed on Simon as she leaned in closer.

"Twenty-four guards in total," Emilia said, the words deliberate and precise. "Six stationary at all times, two at each entrance, and the rest are either resting or patrolling."

"Armed?" Simon asked, sipping his coffee to mask his tension.

"Always. Semi-automatics, sidearms. And the K9 units— three German Shepherds trained to kill. They're let loose at night, primarily."

"Fantastic," Simon muttered under his breath, his sarcasm lost in the clatter of dishes from the kitchen. He turned the sketch around, studying it again. The compound was a fortress, and Juan Ortiz had left nothing to chance.

"Surveillance?" Jack interjected from beside him, his attention momentarily diverted from the drone controller Loran's brother seemed to be calibrating.

"Cameras cover every angle," she confirmed. "No blind spots outside, but there might be one or two inside you can use to your advantage."

"Roving patrols are your biggest concern," Emilia continued. "They change their patterns, but I've been able to time them somewhat. You'll have a seven-minute window during the shift change at 0300 hours. It's the best opening you'll get."

"Seven minutes to breach, neutralize, and enter without tripping any alarms," Simon mused aloud. The odds were far from ideal, but he'd faced worse.

"Exactly. And once inside..." Emilia paused, her expression darkening. "You need to be quick. Juan won't hesitate to use the hostages as leverage."

"Then we won't give him the chance," Simon stated firmly, his blue eyes reflecting a steeliness that matched Emilia's intensity.

"Let's iron out our entry," Loran piped up, her brothers nodding in agreement as they meticulously checked over their drones, ensuring every battery was charged, and every lens clear.

"Mark, you'll take point on the ground. Jack and I will cover the flanks. Loran, Lori, keep those drones quiet but ready. We need eyes inside before we make our move," Simon directed, each member of the team absorbing their roles, the unspoken communication between them as vital as the spoken orders.

"That's bullshit, Simon. Not gonna happen!" Lori exclaimed. "That is my daughter in there and I am going in with you when you go. No arguments. You have seen already I am able and willing to do what it takes."

"Lori..." Simon stopped himself after looking at the resolve on her face. "Okay, if you feel you can do it. I won't argue."

Emilia watched them, a mixture of admiration and concern etched on her face. "You have my intel, Simon," she said, standing up, her chair scraping softly against the floor. "Now it's up to you and your team. Remember, those girls are counting on you. Jennifer is counting on you."

Simon nodded, his resolve hardening like forged steel. "We won't let them down," he promised, the weight of the responsibility settling on his shoulders like a mantle.

The team spent the next hour poring over maps and recon photos, discussing contingencies, escape routes, and rendezvous points. Every scenario was dissected, every potential pitfall examined until their plan was as close to foolproof as it could get. This was more than a mission, it was personal—each of them keenly aware of the lives hanging in the balance.

"Alright, let's load up. Quiet and quick, just how we like it," Simon said, rising from the table. Emilia gave him a curt nod, her faith in him unspoken but evident.

As they filed out of the cantina and headed to the Salgado home where they could prepare without watchful eyes on them, the sun dipped below the horizon, casting long shadows across the dusty streets of Reynosa. In the fading light, Simon couldn't help but feel the gravity of the night ahead. They were about to walk into the lion's den, and only the most meticulous planning, unwavering courage, and a little bit of luck would see them through.

Simon stepped out into the cool night air, drawing in a deep breath to clear his head after the intensity of the planning session. The rough-hewn stones of the Salgado home felt solid beneath his boots as he walked around the corner of the house, seeking a brief moment of solitude before the storm they were about to enter.

There, in the dim glow of the crescent moon, he found Lori, her silhouette hunched against the wall, shoulders shaking silently. Her sobs were soft but carried a weight that seemed to fill the space between them. Simon approached cautiously, not wanting to startle her.

"Lori?" His voice was gentle, an offering of comfort in the vast desert silence.

She looked up, her eyes glistening with tears, reflecting the sparse light like twin stars lost in the darkness. "Simon," she choked out, her Kentucky accent thick with emotion. "I can't shake this feeling... this dread. It's like... it's like I'm staring down a barrel, and there's no dodging the bullet."

"Hey, hey now," Simon said, crouching beside her, his blue eyes locking onto hers with a steadiness that belied the turmoil within him. "We've got this. We've planned for every twist and turn. Your girl—Jennifer—she's tough, just like her mom. And we're gonna bring her back."

Lori nodded, attempting a smile through her tears. "I know you will. It's just hard, you know? Waiting. Wondering." She wiped her face with the back of her hand, her slim figure trembling slightly.

Simon reached out, resting his hand on her shoulder. "It's okay to be afraid. Fear keeps us sharp. But don't let it paralyze you. We need you with us, all the way."

"Thank you, Simon," she whispered, taking a shuddering breath. "For everything."

"Come on," Simon urged gently, helping her to her feet. "Let's join the others. Time to gear up."

Together, they walked toward the side of the house where the rest of the team was gathered, each member absorbed in their final preparations. Jack and Mark were checking their weapons with practiced ease, while Loran and her brothers meticulously calibrated the drones, ensuring every battery was fully charged.

"Alright, listen up," Simon called out, his voice cutting through the quiet bustle. The team turned to him, a collective sense of purpose in their stance. "This is it. We go over everything one last time. No stone unturned, no question unanswered. We do this right, and we all come back alive."

The team crowded around, poring over the maps and photographs spread out on the hood of a dusty pickup. Simon pointed to the compound's layout. "Remember, two guards here, cameras on these corners. K9 units likely patrolling this quadrant. We take out the power here," he continued, his finger tapping a critical junction on the map.

"Silent and smooth," Jack said, his eyes scanning the aerial view. "We get in, find the girls, and get out before they even know what hit 'em."

"Keep your comms open and clear," Mark added, adjusting the frequency on his radio. "No chatter unless it's mission-critical."

"Drone support will give us eyes in the sky," Loran said, holding up one of the sleek, black quadcopters. "We'll see them before they see us."

"Everyone clear on their roles?" Simon asked, sweeping his gaze from face to determined face. Nods and murmurs of assent met his question. "Good. We move out in ten. Let's bring our people home."

As the team dispersed to don their tactical vests and holsters, Simon felt the familiar adrenaline surge that came with impending action. They were ready, each of them finely tuned instruments of resolve and skill. The fate of Jennifer and the other victims rested in their hands, and Simon Wilson, CIA operative and loner by nature, knew that tonight, more than ever, it was the strength of their unity that would see them through.

The night air in Reynosa was thick with tension, a barely perceptible hum that seemed to emanate from the very ground they tread upon. Simon stood before Emilia, his team flanking him like silent sentinels. The gratitude he felt for this woman along with her husband, who had become their guide through the treacherous labyrinth of cartel territory, was palpable.

"Emilia," Simon started, his voice steady despite the swirling chaos of the mission ahead. "We owe you more than words can express. Without your intel, we'd be flying blind."

Emilia's green eyes, sharp and discerning under the moonlight, met his with a silent understanding. She nodded once, a crisp, professional gesture belying the dangerous liaisons she navigated daily.

"Bring them back, Simon," she said, her tone carrying an edge of command that matched her determined gaze. "All of them."

"We will," he assured her, the promise hanging between them like a sacred vow.

With one last nod to Emilia, his team turned away, their gear rustling softly as they moved in unison toward the outskirts of town where Rudy waited, a shadow among shadows.

"Ready?" Rudy asked, his voice low.

"Let's move," Simon replied, the weight of leadership sitting squarely on his shoulders.

They set off into the cover of the night, leaving behind the relative safety of the Salgado homestead. As they traversed the uneven terrain, Simon kept pace beside Rudy, the poor farmer turned unlikely ally whose knowledge of the land was invaluable.

"Rudy," Simon began, his tone casual but the topic anything but, "there's something you should know about Larry Harlow."

"Qué pasa con él?" Rudy asked, his brows knitting together in concern.

"He's been working with the cartel," Simon revealed, watching closely for Rudy's reaction.

"¡Maldito sea!" Rudy spat, the disgust clear in his face and the venom in his voice. "Traitor to his own people."

"Exactly," Simon agreed, his jaw tightening at the thought of Larry's betrayal. "But right now, our focus is on getting those girls out safely."

"Si," Rudy conceded, his expression hardening into a mask of resolve. "We do what we must."

Their footsteps were nearly silent, a testament to the rigorous training and intense focus each member of Simon's team possessed. They wove through the darkness, every sense heightened, every muscle coiled and ready for action.

"Compound's just beyond that rise," Rudy whispered, pointing ahead to a slight elevation in the darkened landscape.

Simon gave a curt nod, signaling to his team. The figures of Jack, Mark, Loran, and the others were barely distinguishable from the night itself as they readied themselves.

"Stay sharp," Simon cautioned, his voice barely audible. "This is where it gets real."

Every step took them deeper into enemy territory, every breath could be their last before engagement. In this world of shadows and whispers, Simon's team were phantoms moving towards an uncertain dawn, driven by a singular purpose—to rescue those who could not save themselves.

Rudy halted, his hand raised in a silent command that froze the team in their tracks. In the dim light of the waning moon, his eyes met Simon's, the gravity of the moment hanging between them like a weight.

"From here on, you're in the devil's playground," Rudy muttered, his voice threadbare with tension.

Simon nodded, his gaze following Rudy's outstretched arm to where the cartel compound loomed in the distance—a hulking mass of shadows and danger. "We've got it from here, Rudy. Go home and take care of Emilia. Thanks for guiding us this far."

"Be careful, amigos," Rudy said, before turning back into the night, the soft sounds of the brush swallowing his departure.

The team scattered like specters among the trees, every move calculated, every breath measured. Jack and Mark took point, their figures blending seamlessly with the foliage as they approached the designated area to set up a makeshift command center.

Loran's brothers, with their slight builds and indigo-tinted skin that made them almost part of the night itself, were already unpacking the drones—sleek machines of surveillance and strategy. The soft beep and whirr of the drones coming to life punctuated the silence, an overture to the chaos that would soon unfold.

"Keep the noise down," Loran whispered, her deep mountain drawl barely audible as she checked the connections on the drone controllers. "Don't want to spook the game before we even have a shot."

"Quiet as church mice, ma'am," Frank responded his fingers deftly setting the coordinates.

"Check your six!" Jack suddenly hissed, the words slicing through the stillness.

A pair of cartel members, patrolling the perimeter, had stumbled upon their location. They were talking in hushed tones, unaware of the deadly audience observing them.

"Take 'em," Simon breathed, his eyes never leaving the approaching figures.

In a fluid dance of shadow and steel, Jack and Mark materialized from their cover. There was no hesitation, only the silent efficiency of predators. The glint of the blades was the last thing the cartel members saw before they were silenced forever.

With practiced ease, Jack and Mark dragged the limp bodies away, disappearing into the underbrush to hide evidence of their grim work. The choreography of death had been performed flawlessly—no alarm raised, no trail left behind.

"Let's keep moving," Simon ordered, his voice steady, betraying none of the adrenaline coursing through him. He glanced at the tree line where the command center was now fully operational.

"Ready the drones," Simon instructed, his eyes scanning the horizon. "We need eyes in the sky before we make a move."

"Roger that," Loran acknowledged, her voice betraying no emotion despite the stakes. Her fingers flew over the keyboard. "Send them up," she spoke to her brothers, who sent the hummingbirds of technology into the night sky.

As the drones soared, their cameras piercing the darkness with their infrared lenses, the team prepared for the final act—the rescue of Jennifer and the others. Weapons checked, plans reviewed, they were an orchestra poised for the crescendo, the notes of their impending battle etched in the tension that crackled in the air around them.

"Time to bring our people home," Simon murmured to himself, the promise of a silent oath to the shadows.

Chapter 12

The dimly lit room was void of any comfort. The damp, musty air hung heavily in the space, assaulting the senses and adding to the oppressive atmosphere. The room, once designed to be a sanctuary, now served as a prison for the one hundred twenty-odd girls who huddled together on the cold, concrete floor. Their bodies were weak, their spirits even weaker, but Jennifer Hawkins, a senior in high school with a promising soccer career ahead of her, refused to give in to the despair that threatened to consume her.

As the door creaked open, the room plunged into chaos. The captives screamed and scrambled, desperately clinging to one another as five burly men barged in, their intentions clear. One by one, they grabbed three girls by the hair, yanking them to their feet with savage grace. The chosen ones kicked and thrashed, their muffled screams muffled by the soiled rags shoved in their mouths, but it was to no avail.

Jennifer's heart pounded in her chest as she watched the scene unfold, her breathing ragged and uneven. She knew it was only a matter of time before it would be her turn, and the thought of the unimaginable horrors that awaited these girls, and eventually herself, sent a shiver down her spine. She closed her eyes, trying to block out the pandemonium around her, and instead, focused on her soccer games, the cheering crowds, the rush of adrenaline as she scored a goal.

The two guards stood with weapons waving over the captives, making sure there was no interference with the rape going on behind them. Jennifer couldn't help but notice how their weapons, ready to shoot into the sobbing girls. The guards were all hardened criminals, their eyes cold and emotionless. Her heart pounded in her chest as she watched, knowing her time would come soon. She recognized one of them as Pedro Rodriguez, a well-known cartel underling. His eyes met hers for a moment before he turned away, uncaring about any fear or pleading she might have shown.

As the selected girls were being taken away to a bare wall, Jennifer could hear their muffled screams and slaps echoing across the room. The smell of sweat and desperation filled her nostrils, making it hard to breathe. She held onto hope that maybe today wouldn't be her day, maybe she'd survive this ordeal. The remaining girls curled up tighter together, trying to find some semblance of comfort in their misery. Jennifer's heart raced as she listened to the rhythmic groans and grunts of the girls being taken, their pain and humiliation palpable even from where she sat. She tried to block out the sickening noises, focusing instead on her soccer team and the thoughts of escape. But all around her were reminders that freedom was a thing of the past for her and the others. Minutes passed like hours as the rape continued.

The two guards who were standing over them with their weapons were looking around the room selecting their victims. The ones they would defile for their pleasure. One locked his eyes on what Jennifer thought was her. Then they turned and half watched the rape going on laughing with each slap and scream.

When the three cartel members were done, they drugged the used and abused girls back to the edge of the captives and dropped them like they were nothing. Maybe to the cartel, they were nothing, but to Jennifer, they were all humans who deserved more, then moved back to guard.

The remaining two cartel members made their way through the bodies sitting on the floor. One grabbed a redheaded girl and started dragging her to the bare wall. The other headed straight for Jennifer. He stopped and grabbed her naked breasts and kneaded them. He then pinched her nipple and twisted until she cried out in anguish. Laughing he then grabbed the girl next to her and took her to the "rape wall" as Jennifer thought of it. There the rape continued.

El Fantasma enters the room of captives. He waits with a smirk on his face as the two men finish with the captives and threw them back into the crowd. El Fantasma tells the captives, in a heavy Mexican accent they will be sold into slavery. Some will have good lives being concubines for a sultan or a king somewhere, some will be a mistress for others, and those the cartel doesn't feel are worth much money, will wind up as whores in cheap bars throughout Mexico and other South American countries or maybe be traded to pirates at sea for exchange of trouble-free routes in their drug trade.

Carlos Ramirez also known as El Fantasma after his speech walks slowly through the room. Finds Jennifer and drags her behind the wall of five guards and rapes her. He forces himself in her mouth and when she starts to bite down he slaps her, knocking her backwards. "For that Puta, you will get my special treatment." El Fantasma spoke then to the guards "Ven a sostener a esta perra." He has three of the guards hold her, one on her arms and the other two on her legs, and starts to violate her. Before his climax, he pulls his shaft from her and has her turned over with her knees under her. Carlos then spits on her anus and before she could protest he slammed into her ass.

Jennifer cried out in pain as the cartel members, including Carlos, laughed at her. "su culo es tan jodidamente apretado" El Fantasma roared as he fired his semen deep into her bowels. Her cries filled the room causing all captives to huddle and cry more.

The guards and Carlos left the room laughing and praising their performance and how much fun it was to take the putas anytime they decided it was good to do so. Several of the girls move to Jennifer who has passed out to see about her. She is breathing fine, just passed out from the brutal rape.

"Jennifer." one of the girls spoke softly near Jennifer's ear between sobs. "Can you hear me? Please be okay," the girl, known to Jennifer as Amy, sobbed. "You are the strongest one here. We won't know what to do if you die."

Jennifer moaned.

Amy pulled Jennifer's head into her lap and began to stroke her forehead and hair. Over the next hour, all the guards in the compound come in four or five at a time to rape captives. They would look at Amy and Jennifer, who was still mostly out of it, and then decide there was more prime picking among all the girls.

As the sun began to set, casting long shadows across the compound, Carlos Ramirez, 'El Fantasma,' leaned back in his chair and steepled his fingers together. Today had been a productive day, he'd overseen the distribution of drugs leaving Mexico for the United States, overseeing the packaging process for transport across the Rio Grande. His cold gaze flickered to Miguel Alvarez, 'El Lobo,' and Pedro Rodriguez, 'El Sombra,' as they stood on either side of him, taking orders without hesitation. The men were valuable assets to the Ortiz cartel, and he knew they wouldn't let him down.

From his elevated position on the second-floor balcony overlooking the main room below, he listened intently to their chatter about missing guards but remained unperturbed. This wasn't unusual, sometimes people got careless, went to sleep, or even had some drugs or tequila stashed and stopped to partake. If that was the case, it would be their last mission and they would be a lesson to those still alive. Orders were given swiftly - one team would search for each guard with trained dogs sniffing out any potential threats while another would go without a dog, but they were more experienced. It was an old-fashioned technique but effective nonetheless.

"Simon, you see that? Looks like El Fantasma himself is here."

The drone hovered low, level with a window, capturing a clear image of Carlos leaning back in his chair, observing his subordinates search for missing guards below him.

"Good work, Loran. Keep an eye on him, send the other two drones to follow those search teams while the one on El Fantasma stays back to watch the compound."

The two search teams, one on each side of the gate, moved swiftly and silently through the dense foliage. The one to the right of the gate had a Rottweiler with them, its nose to the ground, sniffing out any scent that might lead them to their target. The guard walking by the dog seemed preoccupied with something else. He grumbled under his breath in Spanish about how the two men on the lost patrol were lazy, always causing problems for him. The other guard on that team nodded along, not really listening but sharing the same frustration. They didn't notice the drone hovering above them, keeping watch from above like an eagle eye.

Meanwhile, on the left side of the gate, no dogs were used this time around. Miguel Alvarez 'El Lobo,' walked at the head of his team, his eyes scanning every tree trunk and bush they passed by. His cold gaze scanned for any signs of movement or an ambush as they moved deeper into the woods where even drones with normal lenses couldn't reach anymore. If he had known there was a drone above keeping an eye on him with an infrared lens. Pedro Rodriguez 'El Sombra,' followed close behind him, hand resting on his holstered handgun as they both knew that anything could happen.

Simon called in Angie, Jack and Mark to the command center where Lori, Loran, and her brothers were. "Looks like we are going to have some company," pointing at the screen. The others looked at the screen as Loran pointed quickly to the two teams on the move. "The team on the right appears to be a K9 unit." All the team agreed.

Lori had already been there watching.

"Jack, I want you and Mark to take the team on the left. Angie and I will take the K9 team. Loran will keep us informed on where we need to go, and when we are in proximity of the Tangos. Boys, how are your batteries holding up?"

"I am good for now, but will have to come in and swap in about 15 minutes," Frank, the one on the compound, said.

"I have about 25 minutes left," John answered next.

"I am like Frank and only have about 15 minutes on mine," Alva said.

"Okay, the patrols are moving slowly enough. Frank, bring yours in and get swapped out. John, cover the compound for now, and when Frank gets back in the air, you and Alva come in and swap out. We will wait until everyone has fresh batteries and all the Tangos have been relocated before we move out," ordered Simon.

"What about me?" asked Lori with a little heat in her voice.

"You stay right here and guard Loran and the boys. We know where these patrols are. What we don't know is if any others are coming up from behind us," Simon responded calmly. He knew Lori wanted to be part of this, but the truth was the command center needed protecting too. He knew Lori had become close to Loran and would protect her and the boys with her life.

The battery swap was done, and the coverage exchange was done with precision and ease. It only took John and Alva about three minutes to find their assigned teams once back in the air. Jack and Simon had watched it all, looked at each other, grinned, and shook their heads at the blue-tinged drone operators.

"Load up with silenced pistols and knives. It should be as silent as possible, remember, sound travels farther at night. We don't want the compound to know we are here yet."

The team got their equipment, including the wireless comms, so Loran could tell them where they were in relation to the Tangos.

"Okay, I have made a decision," Loran started. "If we are going to be an operational unit, we need call signs, so I have assigned them. It's your job to remember them. Now, Simon, you are going to be G-Man. Angie, you are Rouge. Jack, you are Flyboy and Mark, you will be Badge. You will call me Command, and Lori, when you are out there, you will be Mama. Questions? No, good!"

Everyone looked at Loran with stern looks, then broke down laughing. It felt good for everyone to laugh, even if it would only last a few minutes. Simon pulled her into a hug and kissed her on the forehead. "We love you, but there may be a time you need to be out and about, so we don't agree with your call sign." Simon pretended to be thinking and winked so the rest of the team could see him. "Nope, your call sign is Smurfette."

The whole team except Loran was laughing, even her brothers. The shocked look on her face was priceless, and she was stunned, frozen in place for an instant. She then punched Simon on the arm and started laughing as well.

"Okay, I can do that." She then turned to her brothers and said, "Remember, you are smurfs too. I can see Grouchy, Clumsy, and hmmm, maybe Handy coming into play as well." That stopped the boys from laughing.

"Let's head out," Simon ordered. Before he and Angie took off, though, he went over to Lori, looked deep into her eyes as if seeing her soul, and kissed her. "See you in a bit," he said, then turned away and moved beside Angie as they headed through the brush.

"You two serious?" Angie asked.

"Don't know yet. Ask me again when this shit is over," Simon replied in a tone that said he was not talking about it anymore.

"G-Man to Flyboy," Simon spoke into the mic on the side of his face, still not believing communications equipment like this existed.

"Flyboy, go," was the return in the earpiece.

"For this op, and to make it easier on Smurfette, your two Tangos will be one and two. Ours will be three and four, with the K9 being Lassie."

"Copy that," Jack replied.

"Smurfette copies as well," Loran interjected. Angie giggled at the call sign being used.

"G-Man, you and Rouge need to angle right. Flyboy, you and Badge are headed right where you need to be."

"Copy that," was repeated into the comm sets. Simon and Angie turned slightly right and continued forward.

With a few slight corrections on both teams, the drones would follow the cartel members and then move to briefly watch the intercepting teams, then back to the cartel.

"Flyboy, you and Badge are right where you need to be. Find a place and get ready."

"Copy."

Five minutes later, Loran reported the same to Simon and Angie. Simon and Angie started looking for a place to conceal themselves when Angie asked, "What about up in those two trees?" pointing at two trees that draped over the trail, providing a good sightline for about one hundred yards.

"Perfect. It and the wind blowing into our faces might keep the dog from alerting on us too soon," came the reply from Simon as he started to move to the tree he would be in. Angie moved to the other. Both found good, fat branches to lay on and wait.

"G-Man and Rouge are in position, waiting."

"Copy."

"Badge and Flyboy in position as well."

"Copy that. Both teams, the Tangos are still making progress but do not seem to be moving fast. Standby and I will let you know when they are close."

"Esa, check in with the patrols. I want to know something," Carlos told his communications guy.

"I will, one moment," the operator said before turning to the radio equipment and checking in with the cartel patrols.

Both teams reported their location, about a quarter of the way around the trail, and they had still seen nothing of the lost patrol.

"They need to move faster, but keep looking hard," Carlos told the operator, who passed along the message.

Jack and Mark found some bushes to blend in with, one on each side of the trail. They had discussed guns if needed, but knives would be better. Miguel and Pedro were walking along and just talking as if they were on a casual walk. They expected to find their counterparts drunk somewhere along the path. Mark and Jack could both hear them well from a distance.

"Flyboy to Smurfette, we can hear the Tangos approaching."

"Copy."

Lori moved closer to Loran and watched the screen as the figures kept moving. Slowly they could make out Jack and Mark as they lay in wait.

"We have visual," Simon whispered into his mic. Looking at Angie, she was still as a mouse hiding from a cat in plain sight and had her pistol aimed towards the Tango in the rear holding the dog on a leash.

The K9 patrol moved within 15 yards of Simon and Angie. Feeling much pain for his actions, Simon took aim and shot the dog. Angie, at the same time, shot the K9 handler. Both dropped in silence where they were shot. The other person, speaking to what he thought was his friend behind him, had moved just under the tree when he realized his companion was not answering him. He turned and saw both the K9 and the handler dead. Simon jumped from the tree and knocked the guard out as he did.

Angie dropped next to Simon and moved to check on the others. The dog, though down, growled as she approached. Not slowing in her steps, Angie took aim and fired at the dog once, and it became quiet as blood seeped from a new hole just below its ear.

Confirming both were dead, Angie stripped the weapons and radio equipment from the man and then started pulling them both into the brush. She followed that up by mixing the dirt in the trail to conceal part of the blood, hoping if someone else came along, they would miss what was still visible.

Meanwhile, Simon had stripped the weapon and comm gear from the one he had knocked out. He zip-tied his hands behind his back and made a hobble out of the zip ties so he could not run fast or far. Stuffing a piece of the man's shirt in his mouth and then tying another strip around his head, the man was securely gagged.

With Angie's help, Simon threw the man over his shoulder and nodded to Angie, who had the weapons and radios. She took the lead on the way back to camp. "Call it in," Simon told her.

"Smurfette, this is Rouge. We have one Tango down, one K9 down, and are bringing one Tango in."

"Copy that."

"You know, G-Man, I kinda like these call signs. Smurfette did good," Angie said with a giggle.

Simon just shook his head.

Miguel and Pedro, the other cartel patrol, not aware of what had taken place on the other side of the path from them, walked past Jack and Mark without seeing them. Just as the patrol got past, Jack nodded at Mark, and they eased up from the brush they were in, behind the patrol. Jack, taking Miguel with his hand on the Mexican's forehead, sliced his throat before he realized he was even in trouble.

In a matter of milliseconds, Mark's hand shot out to grab Pedro's shoulder, attempting to mimic the swift move that Jack had just made. However, Pedro's keen peripheral vision caught the action, and he swiftly turned his body to face Mark. In a quick and fluid motion, Pedro swung his arm in a roundhouse punch, connecting with Mark's jaw before he could fully complete his intended action. The impact sent Mark stumbling backward, his head spinning from the unexpected blow.

Mark, dazed by the punch, was not ready when Pedro charged him. They both went to the ground and struggled. During the struggle, Mark was able to stab Pedro. As Mark rose to his knees, he stabbed Pedro again, this time in the heart, and with the knife buried to the hilt, he gave a twist.

"Brother, you seem to have all the luck," Jack chuckled. "First getting shot, now getting into a fight."

"Jack, do the words 'Fuck you' mean anything to you?" Both men chuckled and began cleaning up the area. Weapons and radios in hand, bodies moved, and the trail scraped. They headed back towards camp.

"Smurfette, this is Badge. Coming in. Two Tangos down."

"Copy."

Once everyone was back at the base camp, debriefings took place. Simon and Angie went first, then Jack and Mark.

Jack made light of Mark getting into a wrestling match, to which Mark's only reply was to flip Jack the bird.

Just as the group calmed down and was getting ready to eat some MREs they had packed, the cartel radio went off.

"Damn, wish we spoke Spanish. They are going to come with reinforcements if it is not answered."

"Señor Simon. It is me, Rudy. Maybe we can help."

"Rudy, what the hell are you doing here?" Simon asked.

"Señor Simon, we could not leave you here alone to fight your battle. Some trusted friends are with me too, like my Esa José here. They are watching you from behind. Let us answer the radios."

Simon handed the radio to Rudy, who checked in for the dead cartel team, then handed it to José, who did the same when the other team was called. The cartel operator did not seem to notice the voices being different and signed off for another half hour.

"Rudy, you should not be here, but we are damn glad you are," said Lori after the radio traffic was made.

"This is our fight too. We are not trained as you, but as you just saw, we can be of service."

"Thank you so much for your help. You might work well here at the command center, but if it gets too heated, y'all go home to your families," Simon told him.

Mark offered Rudy and José an MRE, which they turned down, but they did pull out two thermoses of coffee that were appreciated by Simon and the team.

Following the meal, Simon distributed the sleep guard duties. Two children and two adults would take turns keeping watch for the next four hours, switching halfway through.

"I'll take Loran's spot," said Lori. "Her mind needs time to really shut down before it hits the fan. She and that computer are busy all the time."

"I can stand my watch," Loran replied to the comment.

"I know you can, but I said I am taking your place, so don't argue with me. I want and we need you fresh when we go in later."

Chapter 13

Juan Ortiz

Juan Ortiz's ascent was a crimson spoor etched across the underbelly of Mexico's criminal world. His rise to power bore the hallmarks of both a master tactician and a savage beast, leaving a legacy written in blood and whispered in fear. In the beginning, he was just another foot soldier, but with each act of shocking violence, and each ruthless decision, he clawed his way up through the ranks of the cartel.

Ortiz's hands never trembled when they gripped the hilt of his machete, a blade he wielded with a painter's finesse, only his canvas was human flesh. With every enemy he dispatched, his infamy grew—his name spoken like an invocation of death. He was an artist of intimidation, manipulating men of lesser resolve as easily as he sliced through their defenses. The scar that marred his face, running jagged from left eye to chin, was not just a mark of survival, it was a testament to his indomitable will.

No one saw it coming when he finally seized power, but in hindsight, the signs were all there—the bodies left hanging from bridges, the clandestine meetings with corrupt officials, and the strategic eliminations of rivals. Ortiz became the head of the Ortiz Cartel not because he sought it, but because he was simply the last man standing, the apex predator in a jungle where only the most brutal survive.

Simon Wilson

As Ortiz's memories faded into the ether, another series of recollections surged forward with the force of a riptide, pulling Simon Wilson back to a past stained by covert operations and clandestine warfare. It was the 1960s, and the world was a chessboard of shadowy figures and geopolitical gambits. Simon had been a different man then, a ghost moving through the fog of the Cold War, his blue eyes cold mirrors reflecting the necessary evils of his trade.

One mission eclipsed all others, a high-stakes operation that would forever haunt him—a plot to assassinate President Kennedy. It wasn't just the magnitude of the operation that burdened his soul, it was the web of lies, the deceit that cloaked every move. Simon was chosen for his exceptional skills, his ability to blend into the backdrop of any scene, and his knack for making the difficult choices that others shied away from.

But even a man carved from stone feels the weight of history's judgment. As whispers of the plan circulated among the shadows, Simon grappled with the enormity of what they were about to do. Being ready to turn in a report of the plan. Notes everywhere and the eight by eleven and a half sheet of paper in the typewriter, the third sheet in the report he had gotten to. Then he just had to take that break. The lightning, the waking in the cave, and then Simon's world fractured. History had shifted on its axis, and he was left with the shards, the what-ifs, the ghosts.

The aftermath was a silent cacophony that only he could hear, a symphony of screams and sirens that played on a loop in the deepest recesses of his mind he had seen on the TV documentaries. It was this torment, this unresolved chapter of his life, even if vengeance had been served cold, that fueled his relentless pursuit of justice, driving him to dismantle the very empires of corruption he once helped to uphold. And now, facing the vile empire of Juan Ortiz, Simon felt the old rage stir within him, a tempest that would not be quelled until he had torn down everything Ortiz had built.

His muscular frame, hardened by years of covert operations, was ready to bear the burden of this crusade. Simon stood resolute, his past sins and failures converging into a singular purpose: to topple the Ortiz Cartel, to right the wrongs that haunted him, to silence the demons once and for all.

<u>Angie Winn</u>

The gymnasium was stale with the scent of sweat and ambition when Angie first stepped onto its polished wooden floors, her FBI badge still a distant dream glimmering in her determined eyes. The other recruits towered over her, their broad shoulders and confident stances a stark contrast to her slight frame. But what Angie lacked in stature, she compensated for with a tenacity that clawed itself from the very core of her being.

"Remember, it's not about how hard you hit, but how hard you can get hit and keep moving forward." His words were a mantra that Angie clung to as she navigated the trials of Quantico. Each grueling fitness test, each sleepless night poring over criminal psychology texts, each simulated hostage negotiation where the margin between success and failure was razor-thin, they were all blows she absorbed, fueling her resolve.

Her fellow trainees whispered doubts, questioning her endurance, but with every derogatory remark, Angie's spirit sharpened like a blade on a stone. When they saw a diminutive woman, she showed them an unyielding agent in the making. She sacrificed friendships, love, and the comfort of a routine life—all laid upon the altar of her aspirations.

And when the day came that Agent Angie Winn stood before her superiors, badge gleaming under the fluorescent lights of the bureau, she knew every sacrifice had been worth it. Her journey had seared into her a resilience that would later become her hallmark, her weapon against the darkness she vowed to combat.

Lori Hawkins

Meanwhile, in the rugged heart of Kentucky, Lori Hawkins bore the weight of a different trial. The news of her husband's death in a timbering accident struck like a winter storm, leaving her world blanketed in cold silence. Single motherhood thrust upon her without warning, Lori grappled with grief and the relentless demands of raising a child alone.

The weather-worn house that had once echoed with laughter now resounded with the cries of her infant daughter, Jennifer. Every night, after lulling the baby to sleep, Lori would sit on the porch steps, staring up at the vast Kentucky sky, searching for answers that never came.

"Yer strong, Lori. Stronger'n any man I ever did know," her father's voice would echo in her memory, his words a lifeline in the solitude. With hands calloused from tending to the land, Lori embraced her new reality with a fierceness that belied her soft-spoken nature. She became the mountain—

unyielding, enduring, rising above the valleys of despair that sought to claim her spirit.

She toiled in the fields, fixed the creaking boards of the farmhouse, and soothed Jennifer's teething pains, all with a quiet strength that spoke volumes of the tough woman she had become. Through the hardships, Lori's blue eyes retained their warmth, her blonde hair its luster, and her body a testament to the physical demands of her new life.

In both women, the crucible of their pasts had forged an indomitable will. Angie, with her shrewd acumen and undying commitment to justice. Lori, with her maternal love and survival borne of necessity. Their paths, though divergent, were etched with the same unspoken creed: to face the tempest head-on and emerge not just unscathed, but victorious.

Loran Smith

Loran Smith's childhood was a tapestry of isolation and scrutiny woven by the whispers and stares that followed her wherever she went. The indigo hue of her skin, a genetic inheritance from the Blue Fugate clan of Troublesome Creek, set her and her brothers apart in a world reluctant to embrace difference.

"Here comes the blue bunch," the other children would snicker as Loran and her siblings walked the dust-ridden path to school.

"Blue devils," they'd jeer, throwing stones that stung less than the names.

Her mother would wrap her arms around them, whispering tales of the Fugates who carried the blue through generations like a secret pact with the past. But in the town, their legacy was not one of wonder, it was an oddity that made cashiers double-glove their hands and mothers pull their curious children away.

"Keep yer chin up, Loran," her eldest brother would say, his voice holding a tremor that betrayed his brave front. "Ain't nothin' wrong with us."

But the ridicule didn't end with childish taunts. It seeped into every facet of their lives, branding them as outsiders, unworthy of the same kindness and opportunities afforded to others. When they entered shops, the air would grow heavy with unspoken revulsion, the shopkeepers eyeing them with a mix of intrigue and disgust.

"Y'all best be quick with yer buyin'," the grocer would grumble, never meeting their gaze.

"Thank you kindly, sir," Loran would reply, her voice soft but resolute, that slight indigo tint glowing a bit brighter with the flush of embarrassment and anger that never quite dulled.

The echoes of the past lingered as Loran stood among Simon's crew at the command center camp, the weight of history a silent companion in their grim resolve. They had been resting, but rest brought little comfort when the task ahead clawed at their minds, breeding doubt where confidence once thrived.

Simon Wilson surveyed his team, noting the shadows beneath their eyes, the lines of tension etched into their faces. He could see Loran's fingers twitch, the muscle memory of defiance playing out in the restless dance of her hands.

"We've got one shot at this," Simon said, his voice a low rumble of command that resonated within the sparse room. "Those girls are counting on us."

He caught Loran's eye, seeing in her the reflection of battles fought long before any of them were born. Her resilience, born of a lifetime of being underestimated and shunned, now served as an unspoken vow that they would not fail.

"Let's go over the plan one more time," Simon continued, igniting a spark of focus in his team as he laid out their tactics with precision.

They listened, each nodding as the details cemented in their minds. The despair that had threatened to consume them was now fuel for the fire that burned in their hearts—a fire that would either forge their success or reduce their efforts to ashes.

"Remember, stay sharp, and watch each other's backs," Simon concluded, his gaze lingering on Loran. "We're not just fighting for those girls, we're fighting for each other."

Loran felt the familiar surge of determination rising within her, the scorn of the past transforming into strength for the present. She knew what it was to be looked down upon, to be seen as less than. But today, she and her companions would prove their worth—not just to the world, but to themselves.

"Let's do this," she said, her drawl thickening with emotion, the blue hue of her lineage gleaming like a warrior's paint in the dim light. They rose as one, stepping towards destiny with a shared conviction that transcended their individual fears. Today, they would be the saviors in the darkness, the hope amidst despair.

Simon's mind drifted, unbidden, to the one memory he had fought so hard to suppress—the assassination of President Kennedy. "Focus, Wilson," he murmured to himself, but the images surged forth with the relentlessness of a flood. He was back in '63. "Could've saved him," he whispered, the weight of history pressing down on his shoulders like a physical force. The guilt never faded, it was a ghost that haunted his every step, a specter of failure that clung to him more tightly than any shadow.

"Dammit, Simon, pull yourself together." Shaking his head, he forced the phantom pains of the past back into the recesses of his mind. He couldn't change what happened in Dallas, but here, now, he had a chance to make things right. To save lives that were still within his grasp.

"Alright, team," Simon called out, his voice steady despite the turmoil within. "We're going in, and we're not coming out without those girls."

The team gathered around, faces set in grim determination. Simon's eyes met each of theirs in turn, reading the silent questions that lingered there. Could they do this? Was their plan foolhardy or genius?

"Here's how it's gonna go down," Simon said. "Loran, you know your job. I'll take point with Lori and Mark with me. Jack, Angie—you're our cover at least twenty yards off the side and back. You will be able to keep eyes on us and the surroundings as needed. Anything moves that isn't supposed to, you take it down. Quietly."

"Got it," Jack nodded, his expression taut.

"Silent as the grave," Angie added, a fierce glint in her eyes.

"Good. We hit them fast, hit them hard, and get out before they know what's happening."

"Boys, you know your jobs, so I don't need to tell you. Eyes on us, eyes on the camp, and eyes in between."

"Got it, boss," all three of the boys replied as one, going back to their prep work.

"And if things go south?" Loran asked, her voice steady but her eyes betraying the flicker of concern shared by all.

"Then we adapt. We always do," Simon replied, a wry smile touching his lips. "Remember, folks, this is what we do. We're not just fighting for Jennifer and those girls—we're fighting for a chance to look ourselves in the mirror tomorrow morning."

The team exchanged glances, their resolve hardening. They checked their weapons one last time, the sound of magazines clicking into place and rounds being charged into the barrels a grim symphony in the quiet night.

"Let's move out," Simon ordered, and they slipped into the darkness, moving toward the compound with the stealth of predators on the hunt. The scent of danger was thick in the air, but so too was the scent of hope—a dangerous cocktail that drove them forward into the unknown.

Under the cloak of night, Simon's team moved like shadows across the desolate landscape that hugged the perimeter of the compound. Their footsteps were muffled by the underbrush, each member acutely aware that silence was their greatest ally in the moments leading up to the assault.

"Drone's up," Alva told Loran, her eyes on the tablet screen that showed a bird's eye view of the compound, one on the team moving towards the compound and a third sweeping back and forth in between in random patterns to get the whole area covered. The infrared signatures of the guards appeared as glowing specters against the colder backdrop of the building and surrounding forest. "Power station's on the northeast corner. The guard on rotation every five."

"Time it right, and we can kill the lights without them noticing for a solid minute. That's our window," Simon stated, his voice low but clear. He had memorized the layout of the compound, every entrance, every blind spot—an architect of destruction fine-tuning the final details.

"Angie, you're with me on the power. Jack, you take point on entry. Loran, make sure we have drone coverage for our six." His instructions cut through the tension, a steel thread binding them all to the mission.

"Copy," came the crisp replies from each member and Loran from the comm unit—the soft clinking of weapons and equipment a tangible measure of their readiness.

With a nod from Simon, Angie slipped away with him toward the power station, her movements fluid and precise, a testament to years of training. Meanwhile, Jack counted the seconds, synchronizing his advance with the guard's predictable path. They each had a role, a part to play in this deadly performance.

The moment arrived, the drone overhead gave the signal. A suppressed shot whispered through the night, and the guard at the power station crumpled silently. Angie, swift and efficient, cut the wires with precision, plunging the compound into darkness.

"Go, go, go!" Simon's command was a catalyst, and the team surged forward.

The entry was swift—Jack took out the first two guards with silent precision before a bullet grazed his arm. A sharp hiss of pain escaped him, but he pressed on, determination etched into every line of his face. Around them, chaos erupted as the cartel's forces scrambled in the sudden blackout.

"Contact!" Angie's voice rang out as she returned fire, her silhouette illuminated by the muzzle flashes. A bullet seared through her leg, and she stumbled, but her aim never wavered. She gritted her teeth, using the pain to fuel her resolve as she provided cover for Simon, who was already moving deeper into the compound.

The fight intensified, a cacophony of gunshots and shouted commands. Simon's team maneuvered with lethal grace, their training taking over in the dance of combat. Each move was calculated, each shot precise, as they pushed forward with a singular focus: to rescue the captives and dismantle the cartel's stronghold. Each corner turned, and each room cleared bringing them closer to the hostages—and El Fantasma.

Amidst the fray, Jack, suppressing the throbbing in his arm, took down another assailant with a well-placed shot. Angie, limping, refused to yield, her shots finding their marks even as her blood painted a crimson trail behind her.

"Keep pushing!" Simon urged, his focus razor-sharp as he led the charge. Bullets whizzed past, embedding into walls and shattering windows. But the team was relentless, driven by a purpose greater than any fear or pain they endured.

As they breached the heart of the compound, the stakes were palpable, the air thick with the weight of lives hanging in the balance. This was their only chance to succeed, and they poured every ounce of their being into the fight—to rescue the hostages, to topple a tyrant, to emerge from the darkness triumphant.

As the last of the cartel's soldiers fell, Simon's breaths came hard and fast, his body slick with sweat and grime. He scanned the dimly lit corridor of the compound, the blood pounding in his ears a grim counterpoint to the silence that had descended. The flickering emergency lights cast long shadows, turning the once-imposing stronghold into a macabre tableau of death and defiance.

"Clear!" The call echoed down the hallway, each member of his team confirming the absence of further threats. But there was one more demon to face.

He moved toward the reinforced door at the end of the hall, where intelligence suggested they would find El Fantasma. As Simon approached, the door swung open slowly, revealing Carlos Ramirez, silhouetted against the stark light of a room beyond.

"El Fantasma," Simon said, his voice steady despite the adrenaline coursing through his veins.

"Simon Wilson. I was wondering when we would meet."

The standoff was palpable. Two predators, circling, each aware that the next few moments would seal their fates. Behind Carlos, Simon could see the frightened faces of the hostages, including Jennifer Hawkins, whose green eyes were wide with terror.

"Let them go, Carlos. This ends now," Simon demanded, his gun trained on the man before him.

"Ah, but you see, it is not so simple. You've cost El Jefe much today, señor."

In a blur of motion, Carlos reached for his own gun. But Simon was faster. His finger tightened on the trigger, two shots ringing out in quick succession. Carlos staggered back, a look of surprise etched on his otherwise impassive face as he crumpled to the ground.

"Move in!" Simon yelled, breaking the spell. His team surged forward, securing the room and attending to the hostages. Simon's gaze found Jennifer, her relief tangible as she ran into the arms of Mark.

"Is she...?" Lori's voice quivered over the comm link, desperate for confirmation.

"Jennifer's safe," Simon assured her, his relief a heavy weight lifting from his chest.

The emotional aftermath was overwhelming. Hostages sobbed, embracing one another, their ordeal finally at an end. The team, battered and bloodied, shared weary smiles and nods of respect. They had done what many had thought impossible.

"Simon, we need to get these people out of here," Angie said, limping over to him, her injured leg a testament to her tenacity.

"Agreed. Let's get them home," Simon replied, his thoughts already shifting to the cleanup ahead. The cartel would be reeling after the loss of El Fantasma, but others would rise to fill the void. The fight was far from over.

As they cautiously guided the hostages through the exit, the cool night air enveloped them like a comforting embrace. Lori's heart raced as she scanned the crowd until her eyes finally landed on Jennifer. The sight of her daughter ignited a surge of emotions within her - joy at seeing her alive and safe, but also sorrow for all that had been endured. Their reunion was an explosive mixture of relief and grief, their tears mingling in a bittersweet embrace. With trembling hands, Lori cupped Jennifer's face, taking in every detail to reassure herself that she was truly here, in the flesh. The crisp breeze carried away the lingering fear and replaced it with hope for a new life ahead.

"Thank you," Lori whispered to Simon, her gratitude raw and powerful.

"Ma'am, it was my honor," Simon replied, tipping an imaginary hat, a small smile playing on his lips.

"How do we get them out of here? We can't stay. If they had a chance to call Ortiz, he is on his way. If they didn't, it's only a matter of time," Mark asked.

"I don't know, but you're right, we can't stay here, nor they, and for that matter, I am not in a condition to walk far," Angie added.

"Simon, call Amanda and see if she has access to any Chinook helicopters. That would be the fastest and also get more people out all at once," Jack suggested.

Simon pulled out his phone and dialed the number.

"Damn, Wilson, I was beginning to think the operation had gone tits up on us. What have you got for me?" Amanda answered.

"Good to hear your voice as well, Amanda. I have about one hundred and twenty or so beaten, battered, raped, malnourished, and naked hostages. Two friendlies wounded and no way out of this shit. Jack asked if you have access to any Chinook helicopters, whatever they are. He said it would be the best way out."

"Let me put you on hold a minute, Simon, so I can make another call," Amanda said, and the phone went quiet.

Two minutes later, Amanda was back on the phone. "I have someone working on it. Can you, Jack, and Loran find you a relatively safe place to hide until we get there and then call me back with some coordinates or something?"

"I don't see we have much choice in the matter. I will call back as soon as we are somewhere safe." Simon ended the call, then found the number he was looking for and dialed it.

"Emilia, I don't know how to contact Rudy, but we need to get out of here. Travel will be difficult, but we have to find somewhere safe until we can be flown out of here. Any ideas?"

"I will be there in about ten minutes and will have Rudy and some others with me. If at all possible, can you start moving east?"

"I don't think these girls can do it, plus Angie and Jack were both hurt, and I don't know how far they can go."

"How many people are with you, Señor Simon?"

"Besides my team, I am estimating about one hundred and twenty hostages."

Emilia crossed herself in the sign of the trinity. "We will be there soon, Señor Simon."

Simon looked at a stand of trees to the east of the compound that was about one hundred yards away. "Lori, we have to get away from here right now. Emilia is on her way and has a better place to be, but for now, we need to get everyone under cover. We need to get to that stand of trees if we can. Can you start the girls that way?"

"I don't know if they can make it, but we will start them that way. If they know it means freedom, I am sure they will give it their best effort."

"Okay, I am going to carry Angie over there and then come right back and help with any that can't make it."

"Okay. I'll get them moving."

Simon walked over to Angie and picked her up.

"What the hell, Simon?"

"We are headed to a stand of trees. I am going to carry you because you can't walk, and then I am coming back to carry any of the girls who can't make it. You will need to be there for support when they get there."

"Okay, but warn a girl next time," Angie said with a smile.

Simon had dropped off Angie, and he and Mark had carried three girls each to the tree line. The ones who could find the strength to do it had walked about a quarter of the way there. Simon's phone rang.

"Yes," he answered.

"Señor Simon, it is Emilia. We are almost to the compound. I just wanted to let you know it was us and not Ortiz. I didn't want to scare anyone."

"Thanks, Emilia. I will pass the word." Simon ended the call and shouted, "There are friends coming in vehicles. They should be here any moment. Do not be frightened when you hear them coming."

Everyone nodded and kept walking. Simon was moving in to carry another hostage because he knew he couldn't stop, the mission had to go on.

Soon Emilia and friends with six pickups showed up. The pickups were loaded to capacity with the girls and Angie and moved to a barn. It took three trips to get everyone, but they all made it to safety. Simon called Amanda back after Jack had found their location on the map app.

"Amanda, I am handing the phone over to Jack, and he is doing something I don't understand but said you would. Hang on.

"Amanda, I am going to drop a pin of our location. It should be close enough that when they see a barn, they know it will be us."

"Got it. That will work perfectly. Jack, get me a good count on the number of people needing transport. What do you need other than a ride?"

"It will take too long to get clothes. Lots of blankets, food, water, and medics would be great."

"I can make that happen. The birds will be in the air within fifteen minutes and they are coming from San Antonio so they should be there about one hour after takeoff."

"Got it. Thanks."

The group settled in to wait for the arrival of the airlift. Emilia and a group of women she had called upon seeing the shape of the girls were trying to comfort and tend to them as quickly as they could. Mark and Jack sat at the barn doors on either end as lookouts.

Simon walked over to Lori and Jennifer. He removed his shirt and handed it to Jennifer, who took it and put it on.

Lori took his hand in hers and Jennifer looked at the two of them. "Looks like there is a story here."

"Jennifer, this is Simon. The man who has come into our lives to save you. In the process he saved me."

"Simon, I am so glad you and the others came. I don't know how much longer we would have been alive or been here. But it looks like I need to thank you for taking care of my mom too."

"I am glad I was able to do it. But I was not alone. That is something we will talk about when we all get back to Hart County though. I need to see if I can help elsewhere right now."

Simon started to rise but Lori pulled him back down and put her hands on his cheeks. "I know it is not the time or place. But I want to thank you again." She leaned in and kissed him passionately. "That is to hold you until you are better paid by me." Her eyes moved to Jennifer who sat open-mouthed and Lori blushed.

Simon stood and started making his way through the group of girls. Not taking into account the nudity, but the pain they were all in. Stopping to talk to a few as he moved.

As the team waited and worked on what injuries they could, Amanda was on the phone with the president informing him of the operation and the results so far. She was just boarding a private plane headed to San Antonio. The battle was won, but the war against the shadows of the cartel's influence lingered on. Simon knew that their success would send ripples through the Ortiz cartel, and maybe others. Retribution would come, but for now, they savored the victory. They had saved lives, and in this moment, that was all that mattered.

Chapter 14

Simon Wilson's breath hung in the chilled air of the Mexican barn as he checked his gear one last time. The musty scent of hay mixed with the tang of anticipation among his team, a motley crew bound more by purpose than camaraderie. They moved with a practiced ease that belied the tension gripping each of them—holsters snapped, radios crackled, and eyes flicked to the entrances, where Mark and Jack sat waiting.

"Five minutes out," came Amanda Sawyer's clipped tone through the receiver on Simon's phone, her voice slicing through the hush that had settled over the team. No one needed to see her to know she was all business, her authority was as unmistakable as the crack of a whip.

"Copy that," Simon responded, as he ended the call.

"Chinooks incoming," Jack shouted over the noise in the barn. One hundred and twenty hostages, plus the team, then add Emilia and her crew tending to the girls. The distant whirring grew louder, a mechanical heartbeat growing ever more insistent.

"We wait for them to come to us. Let's arrange the order the girls will be taken by worst injured to least," Simon told Loran. "You and Emilia can identify who is who. I want all guns to be ready just in case. I've got a feeling this won't be as easy as we wish."

"We will take care of it, Simon. I just hope you are wrong about that," Loran replied. She took his hand and gave it a squeeze to let him know she had his back, just like he had hers.

Loran had always been a loner due to her skin tone, except around her family. She had been what others would call a nerd. If she was not reading, she was using the computer and learning. By Simon including her in his team, but not treating her differently because of her skin, she felt whole. She was useful and had proved herself over and over. Sure he called her Smurfette, but she knew that name came with the love an uncle, a brother or even a dad would give her if they had thought of it. From him and the team, her new extended family, she did not mind it. It was not delivered with the hate her schoolmates had shown.

Simon could feel the thrum of the Chinook blades now, a promise of support and the threat of war rolled into one. His heart pumped not with fear but with the adrenaline of a predator closing in on its prey. This was where he belonged, on the razor's edge between life and death, making the kind of decisions that left scars on the soul.

He watched as Loran and Emilia with the help of Emilia's friends began moving girls closer to the door who were the most badly hurt, at the same time having those with injuries not as bad move away from the door they would use to egress. Lori had relieved Jack from his post by the door and she was keeping watch with an AR across her legs while Jack lay against the wall next to her to rest from his injury.

Amanda Sawyer's gaze swept across the horizon from the window of the private jet, the golden hues of dawn spreading like a warm blanket over the landscape below. She was a woman carved from the same stone as those she served—a pillar of strength and resolve, her face set in determination, her mind always two steps ahead.

"Approaching San Antonio," the pilot's voice crackled through the cabin, pulling Amanda back from her thoughts. She straightened her tailored suit, a uniform of power that spoke volumes before she uttered a single word.

"Thank you," she responded crisply, her tone betraying none of the urgency coursing through her veins.

As the jet descended, she ran through the operation details one final time. She was about to brief the highest echelons of law enforcement and the Vice President of the United States— a meeting where every detail mattered. The stakes were sky-high, and there was no room for error.

The plane touched down with a gentle jolt, and Amanda disembarked with purposeful strides. She was escorted to a secure conference room where the FBI Director and the Vice

President awaited. Their expressions were grave, the weight of the impending operation etched into their features.

"Madam Director," the Vice President greeted, his voice resonating with authority.

"Mr. Vice President, Director," Amanda nodded, acknowledging each with a respect that was mutual. She took her place at the head of the table, her eyes locking onto theirs.

"Let's get right to it," she began, her tone all business. "Operation Freedom's Dawn is in its critical phase. In less than five minutes, our rescue team led by Simon Wilson will be airlifted out of Mexico with one hundred and twenty hostages. Most are badly beaten and have been repeatedly sexually assaulted."

The FBI Director leaned forward, his fingers laced together. "That many? How was this done under our noses?"

"Yes," Amanda replied. "Wilson's team is the best we have—they are a well-trained band of misfits, and if I had not seen the fruits of their efforts I never would have believed it, let alone gone along with the operation. They are well-equipped, and by rescuing the hostages without a single fatality to the team, they have proved themselves again. They knew what was at stake."

"Good." The Vice President's eyes hardened. "We can't afford any slip-ups getting them out. The public outcry would be..."

"Understood, sir," Amanda cut in. "The Chinooks should be on the ground as we speak."

As the briefing continued, outlining contingencies and extraction protocols, the distant throb of Chinook helicopters began to resonate in the air. Far away, the sound grew louder, vibrating through the bones of the barn where Simon and his team lay in wait.

"We got incoming! Shit, there is a bunch of 'em," Mark yelled out.

Simon moved to see what he was talking about. There were probably fifteen pickups and jeeps coming for them at a very fast pace. "Lori, put Jack back in that chair and you get to that window," he pointed to where he wanted her.

"Loran, get in our packs and get us a shit ton of ammo. We're gonna need it," Simon ordered.

Moving to his window to fire from if needed, Simon hollered at Frank, "You three get next to one of our shooters. You will be reloading magazines and keeping us supplied."

"Yes sir," Frank replied and sent John and Alva to a window. Alva went to Simon, John to Lori, and Frank went to stand by Jack.

"Señor Simon, I am a good shooter. I can help," Rudy said, running up to him.

"Grab a rifle from that pile and find someone to load for you, then go over there. Do you have someone who can help Mark with his ammo?"

"Si. It will be done." Rudy took off to get him a weapon the team had taken from the night they ambushed the patrols. Yelling in Spanish got a couple of men moving to be assistants.

Hidden within the weathered structure, the team members exchanged tense glances, their bodies taut with anticipation.

The Chinooks were close now, their twin rotors slicing through the air, churning up dust and leaves in their powerful wake.

"Shit!" Simon cursed under his breath, blue eyes narrowing as he peered out from the barn's dusty window. The cartel's vehicles skidded to a halt, encircling the barn like vultures ready to feast. The light glinted off the metallic surfaces of the vehicles, an ominous vision of entrapment.

And then, it was upon them—the deafening roar of the helicopters as they flew overhead to where they were going to land, drowning out all other sounds and sending clouds of dust everywhere. The very earth seemed to tremble beneath the might of the approaching machines, their downdraft sending ripples through the tall grasses surrounding the barn.

The Chinook helicopters, those gargantuan beasts of burden that danced through the skies with a mechanical grace, touched down with a heavy thud. Their massive frames, armed with a cargo bay large enough to carry two dozen soldiers and their gear, cast long shadows over the barn.

"Take off! Take off!" he yelled into his radio, knowing the pilots of the Chinooks could hear the telltale pop-pop-pop of gunfire even over the roar of their engines. With a gut-wrenching lurch, the helicopters lifted, disappearing into the sky, leaving Simon and his team grounded and vulnerable.

Almost immediately, the barn erupted into chaos. Bullets zipped through the air, puncturing the old wood with ease and sending splinters flying. The staccato rhythm of gunfire became the soundtrack to hell itself. Simon flinched as a bullet whizzed past, narrowly missing his head and embedding itself in the wall behind him.

"Stay down!" he barked at the hostages, who were huddled together, their wide-eyed stares fixed on the pandemonium around them. Screams pierced the cacophony as explosions shook the very foundations of the barn. Simon could taste the fear and gunpowder as if they were tangible things, thick in the air and choking.

The rescue team, though outnumbered, was not outgunned. They returned fire with precision, each shot calculated and deliberate. The barn became a warzone, with Simon orchestrating the defense, moving from one position to another, after one of the other men from Rudy's group took his place, firing with lethal accuracy.

"Keep them back!" he shouted over the din, locking eyes with Lori across the room. They nodded, a silent understanding passing between them—they would hold this line or die trying.

A grenade detonated close by on the outside of the barn, its blast wave slamming into Simon's body, nearly knocking him off his feet. He stumbled but regained his balance quickly, his training kicking in. Another explosion followed, closer this time, and the freed hostages screamed again, their cries mingling with the relentless sound of warfare.

Simon's world narrowed to the barrel of his gun, the faces of his enemies, and the lives he was here to save. Each pull of the trigger was a promise, a vow that he would not let these innocents be dragged back into the darkness they'd just escaped.

"Fight, damn it, fight!" he roared, the intensity of battle etching itself into every line of his muscular frame. This was more than a mission, it was a testament to his resolve, to the ferocity of the human spirit when cornered by evil.

And fight they did, with everything they had, until the barn itself seemed to scream in protest, its walls shuddering with the impact of bullets and bodies alike.

Simon ducked behind an overturned table, his breaths measured despite the chaos. The musty scent of old hay mingled with the acrid bite of gunpowder as bullets chipped away at his makeshift cover. He glanced over to Loran, who was crouched beneath a window sill, her eyes fierce and focused. She had a rifle in her hand, ready once again to get into the battle if needed. Mark and Lori were just shadows in the dusty air, firing from behind the solid beams of the barn's structure.

"Keep 'em busy!" Simon called out, his voice rough with urgency.

Loran gave a sharp nod, rolling out from her position and taking aim. Her shots were methodical, each one meant to disable or deter, honing in on the shadowy figures that darted between the vehicles outside.

The cartel came at them hard, emboldened by numbers, their shouts rising above the gunfire. Simon felt the heat of a bullet as it whizzed past his ear, embedding itself into the wood behind him. His weapon kicked back against his shoulder with every squeeze of the trigger, a steady rhythm he'd grown accustomed to.

"Keep your heads down!" he barked at the hostages huddled in the corner. They were a sea of wide, terrified eyes and trembling limbs, but they obeyed, pressing themselves closer to the ground.

The air grew thick, almost tangible, with smoke and debris. Explosions intermittently lit up the interior of the barn, casting grotesque shadows that danced along the walls. Grenades lobbed by the cartel burst with deafening cracks, sending splinters and dirt flying. Simon's world shrank to the space between breaths, the heartbeat moments of reloading, the split-second decisions that could mean life or death.

"Simon!" Lori's voice cut through the haze, tense with adrenaline. "They're pushing forward!"

He peeked around his cover, spotting a surge of cartel members charging, their guns blazing with reckless intent. It was now or never. With a grunt, he propelled himself to another position, firing in controlled bursts. Each round spat from his gun found a mark, stalling the advance.

Then, over the cacophony, came a sound sliced through the air—rotor blades chopping rhythmically against the sky. Simon's heart thumped harder as he recognized the welcome noise, it was the guttural growl of Chinook helicopters. Reinforcements! One from the North and one from the South.

The door-gunners filled the air with hot lead from their .50 cal machine guns. Lighting into the cartel from their perch above the ground.

The battle morphed into a relentless tide, with both sides locked in a deadly dance. Shouts turned to screams, screams to groans, as the fight claimed its toll. But amidst the violence, Simon's mind was eerily calm, analyzing, calculating. His body moved on muscle memory, honed by years of training that had taught him how to survive—to turn the tide.

Simon reloaded swiftly, his fingers working deftly to slot in a fresh magazine. He spared a glance towards the hostages, ensuring they remained unharmed, then refocused on the fray. His team moved like parts of a well-oiled machine, each covering the other's blind spots, each shot purposeful and precise.

"Push them back!" he shouted, rallying his team as they gained momentum.

Their counter-attack was relentless, and for a moment—a brief, resounding moment—the barn held its breath as the gunfire tapered off.

The smell of gunpowder hung heavy in the air, a testament to the ferocity of their defense. And as Simon took cover once more, panting from exertion, he knew this was just the beginning. There would be no retreat, no surrender. Not until every last one of them was safe, not until the threat was extinguished.

"Stay sharp," he muttered under his breath, reloading again. "We're not done yet."

As the massive twin-engine birds hovered as best they could, their silhouette cast an imposing shadow over the battlefield. Rounds flying into the enemy from above Simon's team began to see the light at the end of the battle. Now was the time. Take the battle to him.

"We are going to take it to them now. Hit the doors shooting when I say." Simon yelled. After a few brief more minutes it was time.

"Move! Move! Move!" Simon commanded, seizing the opportunity to press their advantage.

Amidst the renewed chaos, a figure emerged from the swirling dust and gunsmoke, almost theatrical in his audacity. Juan Ortiz. The man was unmistakable, his dark features twisted into a snarl, the infamous scar on his face like a grotesque badge of honor. He barked orders in Spanish, his thick accent slicing through the din as he rallied his men to mount a counterattack.

Simon's blue eyes locked onto Ortiz, his body tensing like a coiled spring. This was the man responsible for so much pain, and so much fear. He felt a visceral urge to end it now—to put a bullet between those brown eyes and watch the cartel crumble without its ruthless leader.

"Ortiz!" Simon growled, his voice almost lost in the roar of gunfire. "You're done!"

The Chinooks loomed overhead, their gunners unleashing hell upon the cartel's exposed positions. A relentless downpour of lead chewed through anything in its path.

Simon used the cover fire to his advantage, maneuvering closer to Ortiz, every sense heightened. The smell of sweat and blood mixed with the earthiness of the surrounding landscape, and the distant wails of sirens promised more backup was on its way.

"Today, Ortiz," Simon whispered to himself. "Today it ends."

Simon darted from the splintering wooden cover of the barn, his eyes never leaving the figure of Juan Ortiz. Clad in a tactical vest that bore the scars of near misses, Ortiz moved with a deadly grace, commanding his men even as chaos reigned around them.

His finger tightened around the trigger, his aim steadying despite the pandemonium that raged around him. This was the moment of truth—the climax of their desperate battle. And Simon Wilson, loner, killer, CIA spy, would not falter.

Ortiz was shouting orders now, his voice a guttural roar that cut through the gunfire. Simon's eyes narrowed as he watched the cartel leader duck behind an armored SUV, issuing commands with a venomous urgency.

"Damn it," Simon muttered, adjusting his grip on his weapon. He needed to get closer—close enough to ensure that this time Ortiz wouldn't walk away.

Another explosion rocked the ground, sending plumes of dirt skyward. The Chinooks continued their relentless assault from above, providing enough distraction for Simon to inch forward, using the battered vehicles as cover.

The firefight intensified, blossoming into a maelstrom of violence where every second counted and hesitation meant death. Bullets whizzed by, some finding flesh, others burrowing into wood and metal. The air was thick with the acrid stench of gunpowder, and sweat dripped into Simon's eyes, stinging and blurring his vision.

"Focus," he growled to himself, wiping his brow with the back of his hand. There was no room for error—not when the lives of his team and the hostages hung in the balance.

"Simon, Ortiz is on the move!" Lori's voice crackled in his ear. Her warning was punctuated by the sharp report of her rifle firing in controlled bursts.

"Tracking," Simon replied, eyes locked onto the shifting figure of Ortiz. He could see the desperation in the cartel leader's movements, the realization that his empire was crumbling around him. This fueled Simon's resolve, turning it into an unquenchable fire.

He advanced, each step measured, his finger resting lightly on the trigger. The world seemed to slow, the sounds dimming to a distant echo as he found his moment.

"Ortiz!" Simon's shout sliced through the noise, his gaze locked onto the man responsible for countless atrocities. There was a flicker of fear in Ortiz's eyes—an animal caught in the headlights of inevitability.

Squeezing the trigger, the bullet flew true, cutting through the air with lethal intent. Ortiz stumbled, his weapon clattering to the ground as he gripped his arm, blood seeping between his fingers. It wasn't a fatal shot, but it was enough. Enough to stop him. Enough to send a message to those who remained.

A cartel member close to Juan grabbed him and threw him into the bed of a pickup, then got behind the wheel. Soon the pickup was leaving at a high rate of speed. The rest of the cartel members who were still alive and could, retreated as well. Some in vehicles, some on foot.

The deafening silence was almost as startling as the chaotic gun battle that had just taken place. The smoke, thick and acrid, still lingered in the air, mixing with the scent of burnt gunpowder. In the distance, birds chirped cautiously, unsure if it was safe to resume their songs. The ground beneath their feet was littered with spent casings and bullet holes, a grim reminder of the violence that had erupted just moments ago. It was a stark contrast to the peacefulness that surrounded them now.

"Lori, go check on the people in the barn. Loran, go help. Make sure you check on Jack and Angie as well."

The two ladies took off at a run to follow the orders given to them.

Simon knew this was far from over. The battle was won, yet the war raged on—a war against darkness that sometimes felt endless. Looking at the bodies that littered the farm, and the damage to the barn, he shook his head in wonder of it all.

In the barn, Lori and Loran found a few of the hostages had been hit by stray bullets. The wounds were bad but not any more life-threatening than many of the women already were. Lori looked up and saw Simon standing in the door, so she went to report the injuries and casualties to him.

"A few of the hostages were hit, but nothing too serious on that end. Emilia was also hit, but she will live."

Rudy's crew didn't make it. Angie and Jack are no worse for wear.

As she was telling Simon the condition of those inside, his eyes darted around the room. "Thanks."

He walked to Emilia and took in her wound. Lori was right, she would live but would need a hip replaced it appeared. "I am so sorry this happened, Emilia."

"Señor Simon," Emilia's voice was strained but determined, "there is a price to pay for freedom. I paid mine today, but it will be worth it. Did you get that son-of-a-bitch?"

Simon's face was etched with concern as he replied, "He is wounded, but he managed to escape. Don't worry, I will get these girls home safely, tend to my injuries, and then I will be back. And when I return, he will not escape my wrath. I promise you that."

Despite the searing pain in her hip, Emilia mustered a small smile and took Simon's hand in hers, giving it a grateful squeeze before nodding in understanding. The adrenaline from their harrowing escape was wearing off, leaving her body trembling and weak. But she had never been more thankful for her team and their unbreakable determination to bring justice to those who sought to enslave them.

Simon then moved to Rudy who was praying over the bodies of the friends he had lost. Not knowing what to say, Simon placed his hand on Rudy's shoulder and just stood. Rudy raised his face to see Simon there. He then closed his eyes and began praying again.

Medics from the helicopters came into the barn and began assessing the situation. "Who is Simon?" one asked.

"That will be me," Simon waved.

"The area is secure and we are ready to load up and get the hell gone from here," stated the medic before calling for all hands on deck in the barn over his radio.

"Let's get these people out of here," Loran called out from where she had stood listening to the conversation, her voice echoing Simon's thoughts. There was no time to waste, the hostages were their priority now.

The team moved quickly, ushering the frightened hostages out of the barn. The women, young and terrified, clung to one another, their eyes wide with the shock of sudden deliverance. Some were moved on stretchers and some were able to walk.

"Staff Sergeant," Simon called out and the medic he had spoken to earlier came over.

"Yes sir?"

"I need you to take a minute and do what you can for our friend. My team and the others will load the hostages. She is a local who was shot in the hip. I know you don't have the equipment to do much. Like I said, what you can please."

"Sure thing, where is she?"

Simon pointed out Emilia and the medic immediately went to do what he could.

"Stay close! We're getting you out!" Mark reassured them, guiding them toward the waiting helicopters.

Simon helped load the hostages, his heart pounding with the urgency of the moment. As the last of them climbed aboard, he took one last look at the barn, its walls pocked with bullet holes and smeared with soot. They were leaving behind a battlefield, a testament to the violence they had endured and overcome.

"Let's go home," Simon muttered as the helicopter lifted off, the desert landscape receding below them. Beneath the roar of the engines, he could hear the soft sobs and murmurs of relief from the hostages. They were safe now. And for a brief moment, as the barn became a speck in the distance, Simon allowed himself to feel the weight of their victory.

But the fight wasn't over—not while Juan Ortiz drew breath. As the Chinook banked toward the horizon, Simon's mind was already plotting the next move, the next battle in this relentless war against darkness.

The Chinook's descent onto the tarmac at Lackland AFB was a controlled plummet, its massive blades churning the air with a rhythmic thump that reverberated through Simon's chest. He watched from the open ramp as the ground crew dashed forward, their movements practiced and precise under the bright lights of the airstrip. The freed hostages shuffled past him, some stumbling in their haste, their faces etched with exhaustion and the ghostly pallor of trauma.

"Keep moving, folks. You're safe now," Simon called out, his voice lost in the din of the helicopter's engines.

As they disembarked, blue buses and ambulances lined up like vigilant sentinels, ready to ferry the group to Wilford Hall. Simon caught glimpses of Lori shepherding a few of the young women, her soothing Kentucky accent cutting through the chaos like a lifeline. Loran stood nearby, her eyes scanning the horizon with fierce protectiveness.

"Come on, we've got doctors waiting," Mark urged, guiding the dazed hostages toward the buses with gentle firmness.

The doors of the blue buses swung open, and the hostages who were able were ushered inside, the others placed in ambulances. Simon watched as they departed, knowing that within the walls of Wilford Hall, a swarm of hospital staff would be hustling to treat wounds both visible and invisible.

"Let's head over," Lori said, her voice barely above a whisper but carrying an undercurrent of steel. She pointed at the people standing in front of the Base Ops building. "They'll need us."

Simon nodded, leading the way toward the building where high-ranking officials awaited them. The walk gave him time to replay the operation in his mind—the gunfire, the adrenaline, the desperate fight for survival. It had been a close call, too close.

They entered a nondescript conference room, where Amanda, the FBI director, and the Vice President stood in a huddle of quiet conversation. At their entrance, heads turned, and the murmur of discussion ceased.

"Simon, team, good work out there," Amanda began, her tone stern but her eyes betraying a hint of relief. "We need to debrief—every detail matters."

"Understood," Simon replied, taking a seat opposite the trio of authority. They launched into the retelling, each voice adding a layer to the narrative of the rescue: the planning, the execution, and the unexpected ambush by the cartel. Simon's account was measured, each word weighed with the gravity of their mission.

"And Jack? Angie?" Amanda asked.

"Wilford Hall," Lori responded succinctly. "They're being treated. Angie took a hit, but she'll pull through. Tough as nails, that one."

"Good," Amanda murmured, her gaze dropping to her hands folded tightly in her lap.

The debrief continued, the Vice President interjecting occasionally with questions that pierced to the heart of the operation. Simon answered without hesitation, the details etched into his memory like the scars he bore from countless missions before.

"Your team performed admirably," the FBI director concluded, his voice gruff but not unkind. "It was a hell of a thing you did today."

"Thank you, sir," Simon replied, though the weight of unfinished business pressed heavily on his shoulders. There would be more to do, more battles to fight. Juan Ortiz was still out there, and Simon couldn't—and wouldn't—rest until that threat was eliminated.

"I do have one more question for you," the Vice President stated, looking at Loran. "Young lady, are you and those fellows back there behind you okay?"

"How do you mean, sir?" Loran started, being young she didn't know really to leave it with that. "Yes, I am uninjured. Mentally, myself and my brothers are still trying to figure that out. It may take a while. Why do you ask, sir?"

"Well, I have never seen anyone with the pigment to their skin that y'all have. I am not seeing any paint lines for it to be a kind of camouflage or something like that. I was wondering if you were exposed to something down in Mexico."

"No, sir, we are what people call Kentucky blue people. We were a freak of nature due to our ancestors. But now, we know we are not freaks. We matter! Simon, Lori, Jack, Mark, and Angie have all proven that to us." Loran replied with some anger in her tone.

"I am sorry, Ms. I just have never seen anyone like you four. I meant no harm in my question. It was just concern for your health. Please forgive me," said the Vice President.

Loran nodded and cut her eyes to see if Simon was going to be mad at her. She should not have worried, he had a slight pull to his lip like he was trying to hide a smile.

Simon rose from his chair, ready to make the calls that would reunite families with their loved ones. He felt a surge of resolve. The war wasn't over, but tonight, they had saved lives. And that was something worth fighting for.

The Vice President stood as well, his presence commanding the room as he extended his hand toward Simon with a firmness that spoke of gratitude. "You and your team have the nation's thanks," he said, his voice resonating with sincerity. "Heroes, one and all."

"Thank you, Mr. Vice President," Simon replied, shaking the offered hand, though his eyes betrayed a storm brewing beneath the surface.

"Tell me," the Vice President continued, leaning against the solid oak conference table, "what are your plans now? This operation is behind you. What comes next?"

Simon's jaw tightened, the muscles working as if chewing over the question. He remained silent for a moment, his gaze distant before snapping back to the present. When he spoke, his voice was edged with a steely resolve that filled the room.

"Sir, with all due respect, this isn't over," Simon said, his words clipped. "Juan Ortiz is still out there. If we leave him be, he'll just regroup, and take more innocents. We've cut the head off the snake, but it can still bite."

The Vice President's expression shifted, a mix of understanding and concern etching his features. "I see," he said, nodding thoughtfully. "I suppose I shouldn't be surprised. Men like you, you never stop fighting the good fight."

"Where can we find some privacy to make calls?" Simon asked, glancing at Lori, Loran, and Mark, who stood resolute by his side. "Families are waiting to hear their daughters are safe."

"Of course," Amanda interjected, pointing towards a corridor. "There's a conference room down the hall. Four lines, all secure."

"Thanks," was all Simon managed before leading the way, his companions close behind. They found the room easily enough, phones lined up on a long table like sentinels awaiting orders.

Taking a collective deep breath, they each picked up a receiver, the weight of what lay ahead settling in their chests. Dialing the numbers that Lori and Loran had gathered and written on pads supplied by the helicopter crews, they prepared to deliver news that would change lives forever, voices steady despite the emotional maelstrom churning within.

"Hello, this is Simon Wilson," he began, his tone carefully measured. "I have someone who's been dying to talk to you. However, she is in the hospital getting checked out at Lackland Air Force Base. When can you be here?" As the first sobs and cries of relief echoed over the line, Simon knew that no matter how hard the road ahead, moments like these made every battle worth it.

Chapter 15

The couple of days since the harrowing events at the Mexican compound had been a blur. Angie Winn and Jack Thompson had been whisked away to Wilford Hall hospital at Lackland AFB, where they were treated for their injuries sustained during the rescue mission. Jack's shoulder was aching, but he knew it could have been much worse. Angie's leg was in a cast, but she insisted it was nothing compared to the lives they'd helped save.

Simon, Lori, Loran, Mark, Frank, John, and Alva had been moved to on-base temporary housing, where they were taking some much-needed rest and enjoying the sights of San

Antonio. The news of the successful operation had made headlines, and the authorities were busy unraveling the web of corruption that had been spun around them.

During this time, the families of the one hundred and nineteen hostages began to pour in, their faces etched with worry and relief as they were ushered into the hospital. Slowly, the sound of sobs and cries of joy filled the halls, as each girl was reunited with their loved ones.

Angie and Jack watched from afar, their own reunion temporarily on hold as they recovered. Angie observed a young girl, no more than sixteen, who looked like she'd seen a ghost, rush into the arms of an older woman, presumably her mother. The woman's eyes were red and swollen as she held onto her daughter for dear life, as if afraid she'd vanish into thin air.

"It's never easy, is it?" Jack asked, his voice gruff with emotion.

"No," Angie agreed, her own eyes moistening. "But at least we got them back."

As the last of the families left with their daughters, Angie and Jack were finally discharged. They returned to the temporary housing, where the other rescued greeted them with hugs, backslaps, and expressions of gratitude.

Simon and Lori shared a private moment, their relief and happiness palpable as they held each other close. Loran, Mark, Frank, John, and Alva traded stories of their time in Mexico, their voices filled with awe and disbelief at the successful mission. Jennifer sat off to the side, legs drawn up in the chair with her arms wrapped around them, bruises still visible on her arms and legs.

"You two should rest up," Lori said, looking in the direction of Jack and Angie.

Jack nodded in agreement. He went to his and Mark's room while Angie went to her and Loran's room. It had been decided Lori would be sharing a room with Jennifer.

The group dispersed, each finding solace in their own ways. Some slept, and others simply sat in silence, trying to process the events that had transpired.

During the night, several times Jennifer would cry out. The first time scared Lori so bad she thought she was back in Mexico. When she noticed Jennifer was having a bad dream, Lori made her way to Jennifer's bed, shook her awake making her jump.

"Baby, you were having a nightmare. How about I crawl in here with you and hold on to you? Hopefully, it will make you feel better. I know it will make me feel better," Lori told her.

Jennifer just nodded and made room. Lori climbed into the bed and held Jennifer until she slept.

The team returned to Hart County, each of them trying to find solace in their own ways. Simon and Lori's romance blossomed, fueled by their shared experiences and the understanding they found in each other. They spent long nights talking, first as friends, then as something more. As this phase of the mission was completed and they began the healing they all needed, their relationship developed in the safety of their secluded cabins, far from prying eyes.

As the days passed, Jennifer's guarded walls began to crumble under Simon's gentle presence. Her trust in him grew stronger with each passing moment, and she found herself opening up more than she ever had before. The three of them would spend precious evenings together, sharing in each other's company and creating new memories. Laughter, which had been scarce in their lives, slowly started to return as they bonded over movies and stories. Their once dull and somber existence was now filled with warmth and joy, thanks to the newfound friendship between them.

As for Jack and Loran, their connection grew slowly but surely. They found themselves drawn to each other, bonded by their shared trauma and the healing that only they could provide one another. They would take walks in the quiet woods, fish in the serene lakes, and share meals together. Each moment together was a step closer to closure, a step towards reclaiming their lives.

Jack had talked to Greg, Loran's father. "Yes sir, I am aware of her age. I tell you on my honor, sir, I have nothing but the purest of feelings for Loran. When you spend time in battle together, you develop a bond. I will never hurt her, or let you down, Mr. Smith."

"Jack, it's not just the age difference, but you are worldly, and Loran has been in these timbers all her life, well until y'all went down there. I do appreciate you and the rest looking after her and my boys for sure. Just if things are going to get to be different, come talk to me please."

"Yes sir, I sure will," Jack answered.

"Good, now let's grab a bite to eat," said Greg.

The days passed in a blur of healing and recovery. The FBI and CIA task force that had been formed had taken over the case, leaving the team to focus on picking up the pieces of their shattered lives, only calling on the team when they needed something clarified. But each team member knew, deep down, that their work wasn't done. They had made a difference, but the fight against injustice was far from over.

One night, as the sun set over the horizon, the team gathered. They exchanged knowing glances, each understanding the thoughts running through their minds. It was time to go back to their normal lives, back to the world that needed them.

The crackling fire cast a warm glow over the group of friends gathered around it. Simon and Lori sat comfortably in each other's arms, watching the flames dance.

"This is the life," Simon said with a contented sigh.

Lori smiled and leaned into him. "It sure is."

Jennifer lounged on a nearby chair, soaking up the last rays of sunlight before it disappeared behind the trees. "I used to hate it here growing up in this podunk place, but after this last adventure which I did not want, this is heaven to me now."

Loran nodded in agreement, her normally stoic expression softened by memories of the cabin and its inhabitants.

Jack chuckled, handing out cold drinks to everyone. "Well, we sure have made memories together in a short time. I have come to think of you all as family, not just that ass over there I call a brother," pointing to Mark.

"Next time we go somewhere and you get in a jam, I'll just leave your ugly ass," Mark replied and they all laughed.

As they chatted and laughed, the calm atmosphere was soothing their minds and souls. They were all too aware that soon they would have to say goodbye to this peaceful haven, to finish the mission, but for now, they were happy with the downtime.

And as the night grew darker and the stars twinkled above them, they knew that this was a moment they would always cherish - a rare lull in their chaotic lives where they could simply relax and be together, forever bonded by their shared experiences at the cabin.

As the sun set over the northeast side of Mammoth Cave National Park; in Reynosa, Mexico Juan Ortiz's house bustled with activity. A six-bedroom house, it was the epicenter of the cartel's human trafficking operations. The air was heavy with tension and barely restrained fury as Juan Ortiz, the head of the cartel, paced the main room. His 5'10" frame was dwarfed by his large, scarred hands, and his dark complexion flushed with anger.

"¿Qué coños ha pasado?" he roared, a vein bulging in his neck.

His subordinates, both those in slings or on crutches and those unhurt, cowered before his wrath. They knew better than to cross him, especially after such a humiliating defeat. The loss of the girls, the destruction of their operation, and the mounting bodies left in their utilized compound and barn weighed heavily on his mind.

"Señor, no tengo las palabras..." one man began, his voice shaking.

Juan whirled on him, his fist connecting with the man's jaw and sending him reeling. "¡No me mientas! ¡Yo no quiero excusas, quiero respuestas!" he bellowed, spittle flying from his lips.

The men cowered, avoiding his gaze. They knew their boss well enough to know he wanted results, not excuses. The room was tense as they scrambled to come up with some sort of explanation for their failure.

"Señor, fue un grupo bien entrenado. No teníamos ni idea..." another man stammered.

Juan stabbed a finger in his direction. "¿Un grupo? ¿Quiénes eran esos hijos de puta? ¿Fueron los federales?"

The men shook their heads, unsure. "No, señor, no creo que fueran la ley. Tenían..." he trailed off, unsure how to explain the level of violence they had witnessed.

Juan's eyes narrowed. "¿Y bien?"

"Tenían... contacts," the man finished lamely. He knew it sounded ridiculous, but what else could he say? They had been outmatched and outgunned by a seemingly unstoppable force.

"Y que alguien descubra quién es este Simon Wilson," Juan shouted.

Juan paced the room, his knuckles white at his sides. The last thing he needed was to be shown up in front of his rivals. He couldn't afford to look weak. He stopped abruptly, turning to his men.

"Mis cabrones," he growled, his voice low and deadly, "I want those responsible found. I don't care what it takes or who you have to go through. ¿Entienden?"

A chorus of "Sí, señor" filled the room as the men straightened, newfound determination in their eyes. They would not fail their jefe again.

In a secluded location deep in the timbers of Kentucky, Simon's cabin was abuzz with activity. The Vice President had flown the families and the rescued hostages in and now, they were enjoying a well-deserved cookout. Laughter and the tantalizing smell of barbecue filled the air as everyone tried to forget the hell they had been through.

Simon circulated among his guests, a beer in hand, watching as they laughed and shared stories of their loved ones. He couldn't help but feel proud of his team. They had pulled off a miracle, rescuing these women and reuniting them with their families.

Amanda, looking radiant in a sundress, approached him, her eyes shining with unshed tears. "Simon, I... I can't thank you enough," she began, her voice trembling.

"You don't have to thank me, boss," he replied, suppressing a grin. "We're just doing our jobs."

"No, I mean it, Simon. You and your team, you've given these families their lives back. I... I wish..." Her voice trailed off, but Simon knew her meaning.

"Hey," he said, placing a comforting hand on her shoulder. "We're all in this together. And who knows? Maybe one day we'll find a way to bring your sister home too."

Amanda managed a watery smile. "I appreciate that, Simon. I really do."

As the sun began to set over the westerly horizon, the group gathered around the fire pit. S'mores were roasted, stories were shared, and for one night at least, they were able to forget the darker side of their world.

As the sun dipped below the horizon, casting a warm, golden glow over the picturesque Green River as it flowed past Simon's property, Amanda pulled Simon aside for a private conversation.

"Simon, I have some news. Juan Ortiz...he's started rebuilding his cartel. And your team... you're at the top of his hit list."

Simon ground his teeth. "You and I, we're CIA operatives and Angie is with the FBI, Amanda. We're used to being targets. But those people over there, my team, they are civilians. Battle-tested for sure, but still civilians. Don't you have someone who can take him out and protect them?"

"Simon, if it were that easy it would have been done. I have lost three operatives since your mission trying to get close. They are just so cautious now," Amanda answered, then added, "He's got nothing to lose now. He's been quietly amassing an army, and he's more ruthless than ever. We need to be prepared for the fallout."

Simon looked over at his teammates, laughing and enjoying themselves. "Understood. I'll let them know and we'll be ready."

Amanda patted him on the shoulder. "That's why you are right for this mission, Simon. I know you and your team can handle it. Just... be careful, alright?"

Simon gave her a small smile. "You know it."

As they rejoined the party, Simon's mind started to hone in on the beauty of the Kentucky wilderness. The scent of pine and hardwoods lingered in the air, mingling with the enticing aroma of barbecue and spices. The sun slid further down the horizon, casting golden hues across the rolling hills. The weight of their accomplishments settled upon them, but the looming threat of Juan Ortiz's retaliation lurked just below the surface.

Simon took a moment to observe his teammates, their faces etched with relief and happiness. They deserved this respite, but he knew it wouldn't last long. He made a silent vow to do everything in his power to protect them from the storm he knew was brewing.

As the evening wore on, the party turned more introspective. The survivors shared stories of their harrowing ordeal, and how Simon and his team's arrival had been nothing short of a miracle. Wives, husbands, and children embraced their loved ones, tears of relief and gratitude shining in their eyes.

Simon, however, found himself watching Amanda. She moved gracefully through the crowd, ensuring everyone was cared for and comfortable. Her beauty, intelligence, and strength were captivating, and he thought she must have been a damn fine field agent in her time. She could mingle with the females and flirt with the males. It had to have served her well.

As the last of the guests began to trickle out, Amanda approached him, a slight smile playing on her lips. "Well, Simon, I must admit, you and your team have surpassed my expectations."

Simon squared his shoulders as he stepped closer to her. "I'm just glad we could help."

"Can we talk tomorrow, you, me, and the rest of the team?" Amanda asked.

"Amanda, I will have everyone here by ten in the morning. Show up then and we will have a fresh pot going. I guess you want to tell them what you told me?"

"I do, Simon, and want to read you all in on our latest intel."

"Okay, I'll pour your cup at ten, so don't let it get cold."

Simon went and gathered the team, telling them to be at his place in the morning before ten so they could meet with Amanda.

He nodded to them, fighting the disappointment welling up inside him. With one last lingering look, they parted ways, each consumed by their own thoughts and the knowledge that their mission was far from over.

The next morning, the team had gathered at Simon's cabin. Jennifer had come with Lori and was now entrenched into the team. They were sitting and eating biscuits Lori had made when she and Jennifer were the first to arrive. Honey and some homemade apricot preserves along with some butter were on the table to dress the biscuits.

At exactly ten, Simon stood and poured another cup of coffee and set it at an empty spot on the table. Then he went to get another chair and placed it in front of the coffee cup, causing the others to scoot closer together. That done, he walked over and opened the front door just as Amanda was pulling up.

Amanda took her place, grabbed a biscuit, and broke it in half, loading one side with honey and the other with preserves. She took a bite of the side with honey and moaned at its wonderful taste. Sipping the coffee, she asked, "Simon, did you tell them?"

"Nope. Figured that was your story to tell."

She looked each member in the eye for a split second before moving to the next, then said, "We have new intel. Juan Ortiz is preparing for war. Unfortunately, you are his enemy in this."

"Do you have a timeline?" Jack asked.

"No, I was hoping to get someone within the house who could feed us information, but I have lost all three of those men we sent in," Amanda told the group. "I have a bit of intel in the back seat of my car if someone wouldn't mind grabbing it while I finish this biscuit and then we can talk more about what is in it."

"I'll grab it," Mark said.

They meticulously combed through the intelligence, analyzing every detail and piece of information. Most of it centered around the new arrivals who had joined forces with or were possibly even a part of, the notorious Ortiz cartel. The names and faces on the dossier blurred together, but the danger they posed was crystal clear. The weight of their findings sat heavily on their shoulders as they strategized their next move in this high-stakes game of cat and mouse.

"What are you thinking?" Loran asked Simon as she had been watching him while he looked out the window after stretching from being bent over the table for so long.

"My thought is to get a group of operatives and paramilitary together and go down there and kill that fucker. I don't want him back here on our soil where innocent people will get killed," Simon replied.

"Well, that is all fine and good, when do we go?" Loran spoke.

"Not we, me," Simon replied, looking at her.

All at once the house was in an uproar with the team all trying to talk at once. Lori held up her hand and everyone got quiet. "Now you listen to me and you listen well, Mr. Wilson. You are my man, know it or not, like it or not, you are! Now that's out of the way, let me just tell you where you go I go, and from listening to the team here they all feel the same way. So, there is no 'Not we, me' in this conversation anymore. Got it? Good."

Amanda stood and smiled. She knew Simon was beaten before he could even get on the field to play the game.

"Yes ma'am. But I want to say this first. Know we have already been down to Reynosa, we have fought like hell and managed to come back, some a little worse for wear than the others. We might not make it back this time."

Jack spoke, "We all know the risk, Simon. We are now a team and we go where our leader goes."

"Okay, but I want to hear it from the rest of you each. Mark?"

"I'm there, buddy. I've been thinking about retiring this badge anyway."

Simon looked at Angie and before he could ask she spoke, "I am still assigned to the operation so I am in."

Loran didn't even wait for his gaze to leave Angie when she said, "Don't even think of leaving me out of this. Also I will talk to Pa and ask about the boys and if they are in, I'll let you know."

Simon looked at them all once again, shook his head, and threw up his arms. "I guess we are going in Amanda. Do we have your support?"

"All of it," was her reply.

"Wait," said Jennifer.

"What is it, Jen?" Simon asked.

"You didn't ask me."

"Jen, with all you went through, there's no way I would ask you to go."

"Well, as my mother just told you, Mr. Wilson, you are her man, and I am her child, so when you get one of us, you get us both because we come as a package deal. That is here at home as a family unit and on the battlefield as one badass fighting team, so you really don't need to ask. But since you are about to, I'll save you some wind. Yes, I am in!"

Simon looked at Lori who had tears in her eyes. He did not know whether it was from the thought of Jennifer going with them or the fact she said they were a family unit. Simon's mind was not that fast when it came to women.

The following days passed in a blur of strategy sessions and vigorous training. The team honed their fighting skills and sharpened their instincts, preparing for the inevitable showdown with Juan Ortiz's men. Simon, Lori, Loran, and Jennifer threw themselves into their training even when Jack and Mark could not be there, fueled by their shared goal of dismantling the cartel and exacting justice.

Loran Smith and Lori Hawkins sat by the campfire, roasting marshmallows and sipping steaming cups of coffee. The night air was chilly, but the warmth from the fire kept them company, along with the shared knowledge that they were no longer alone in this fight. The recent events, the revelations about the cartel, and of Ortiz weighed heavily on their minds, but they found solace in each other's presence.

Loran tapped her indigo-tinted fingernails on her mug, the sound muted by the crackling fire. "I never thought I'd be here, fightin' against a cartel, tryin' to save our home."

Lori nodded, her blond hair falling over her shoulders. "Me neither, Loran. I never thought I'd be part of this...this war." She shuddered, but there was a spark in her blue eyes that hadn't been there before. A fire that had been ignited by the flames of injustice.

"But look at us now," Loran said, her voice soft but sure. "We've come so far. We've survived more than most people could even imagine. That's somethin' to be proud of, Lori."

Lori's eyes filled with unshed tears, but she blinked them away. "You're right, Loran. We've come a long way. And we've got each other."

Jennifer draped an arm around her mother's shoulder. "We're a team now, Mom. We're gonna get through this, together."

Loran smiled at the mother-daughter duo, her heart swelling with pride. "And we ain't alone. We got the whole town behind us, and we got Randolph and his boys too."

Randolph, aka Wildman, sat across the fire from them, his eyes reflecting the flames. He'd been quiet since the news about Ortiz had reached them, but his silence spoke volumes. He was mourning the loss of a friend, but he was also fueled by a burning rage, a need for justice that wouldn't be extinguished anytime soon.

In Reynosa, Mexico, the same kind of discussion was happening. Emilia, who sat next to her husband Rudy, squeezed his hand. "Si, mi amor, we will get through this," she whispered in her lilting accent, her green eyes shining with determination. "We are stronger together, and we will bring these bastards down. The people who will help us here are not as strong or as many as Juan Ortiz, but God will send us what we need."

Rudy, his face a stone mask, squeezed her hand in return. "We will, mi corazón. We will avenge our lost and protect those we love."

In Hart County, the night wore on, the conversation ebbing and flowing like the flames of the fire. Laughter mingled with tears, as they shared stories of better times, of the future they would build together once this was over. And as they sat there, the survivors of this small town, they found strength in one another. A strength that couldn't be broken, no matter how hard the cartel tried.

Because they were no longer just a group of individuals. They were a family, forged by the fires of tragedy and hardship, and together, they would endure. Together, they would win.

The days passed by in a blur of activity. The people in Poteet valley along with Loran, Jack, and Simon, worked tirelessly to rebuild their homes and their lives after the destruction that took place in the area the night they destroyed that group of cartel members. Unfortunately, the damage was not isolated to the house the cartel had taken over. Jennifer and Lori, their bond stronger than ever, helped out where they could, their laughter and love a balm to the weary souls around them.

As the town of Hart County slowly mended, so too did the scars left behind by the cartel. The physical wounds were easy enough to heal, but the emotional ones would take time. Time, and the love and support of those around them.

Loran found herself thinking about Simon more often than she cared to admit, his haunted eyes and quiet strength drawing her in like a moth to a flame. He was a man with demons of his own, she could tell, but there was also a goodness in him, a light that refused to be extinguished.

One afternoon, as they took a break from repairing one of the houses, she found the courage to speak to him. "You know," she drawled, wiping the sweat from her brow, "you've been pretty quiet these days. Something on your mind?"

Simon, who had been lost in thought, started. "Oh, sorry. Just... thinking."

"About?"

He hesitated as if weighing his words. "About the future, I guess. About what's next for us."

Loran understood all too well. The cartel may have been dealt a blow, but they weren't finished yet. The Ortiz Cartel was ruthless and relentless, and they wouldn't stop until they had what they wanted. And what they wanted was right here in Hart County.

"Ain't no use borrowin' trouble 'fore it's due," she said, quoting her father. "We'll face that bridge when we come to it."

Simon nodded, a half-smile playing on his lips. "You're right, of course. Guess I just... I don't know. I've gotten used to having something to fight for, I guess."

Loran surprised herself by laying a hand on his arm. "You'll always have something to fight for as long as we're here, Simon Wilson. And don't you ever forget it!"

Simon's eyes met hers, and for a moment, Loran thought she saw something that felt like family between them. But it was gone as soon as it appeared, replaced by his customary cool demeanor. "Thanks, Loran. I... appreciate it."

As the weeks passed, life in Hart County began to return to some semblance of normalcy. The streets were repaired, the houses rebuilt, and the people of the town worked to put their lives back together since many of the hostages came from right there in the county. They knew that the cartel was out there, lurking in the shadows, biding their time. They knew that one day, they would have to face them again.

But for now, they found solace in one another's company, in the knowledge that they had survived together. They could do this, they told themselves. They could face whatever the future threw at them, so long as they did it as a team.

One sunny afternoon, Loran found herself sitting on her porch, sipping a glass of lemonade and watching the world go by. A shadow fell across her and she looked up, squinting against the sun. Simon stood there, his Stetson in his hands. "Mind if I join you?" he asked his voice gruff but with an undercurrent of tenderness.

"Wouldn't have it any other way," she said, patting the space beside her on the swing. He sat down, and for a moment, neither of them said anything. They didn't need to. The air between them was that of a family – an uncle and niece, a big brother and little sister – someone who belonged in each other's life forever. For Simon, he thought if he had a daughter he would feel for her just like he did Loran.

Loran set her glass down and turned to face him. "So, partner," she said, a mischievous glint in her eye, "tell me, just how does a man in his nineties get a young chick like Lori to fall so hard for him?"

Simon's cheeks flushed slightly, but he grinned. "Well, little lady, as it so happens..."

Their laughter rang out over the quiet valley, mingling with the sounds of reconstruction and the promise of new beginnings. And as the sun dipped below the horizon, the two of them remained there, side by side, facing whatever the world had in store for them together. After a bit, Loran's mother brought out a pitcher of lemonade and two extra glasses. She bent and kissed Simon on the cheek, which made him blush again.

"Simon, you are a good man, and what you, Loran, the boys, and your team have done makes you heroes. I know the world weighs heavy on you now, as it does with Loran there. But it makes me so happy to hear you both laugh and to see her more confident. You, sir, have been a blessing to her." It was Loran's turn to blush.

Chapter 16

Simon Wilson's gaze was unyielding, locked onto the target as beads of sweat traced the edges of his taut brow. His fingers danced across the weapon with a lover's finesse, checking every component with practiced ease. The dull clack and metallic slide of magazines being loaded formed a rhythmic cacophony in the background.

"Steady... breathe..." Simon murmured to himself, each word punctuating the still air of the makeshift training ground. Around him, his team mirrored his focus, their movements precise and deliberate, a ballet of controlled aggression and silent communication.

The crack of gunfire shattered the quiet, sending echoes bouncing off the walls of the makeshift urban warfare house on Simon's land. It wasn't just any session, it was a symphony of preparation, each round fired a note in the crescendo building toward the inevitable confrontation. Today they used sandbag targets Simon had placed in the different rooms in preparation for the war they knew would come in Reynosa, Mexico. They were ready—or at least as ready as they could be for the unknown chaos that awaited them.

Meanwhile, Angie Winn's phone vibrated against the oak desk, its urgent pulse demanding attention. Her brow furrowed as she snatched it up, her blue eyes scanning the message that lit up the screen. Her posture stiffened, this was it—the intel she wished was not coming.

Frustration boiled up inside her, spilling out as she muttered "Damn it" under her breath. In one swift movement, she pushed back from her desk with such force that her chair skidded across the floor and collided with the wall behind her with a loud thud. Snatching up her jacket, she shrugged it on while striding purposefully out of her cramped office space. The sound of her angry footsteps echoed down the hallway, mingling with the faint sounds of chatter and laughter from coworkers. She had reached her breaking point, and there was no stopping her now.

She got in her FBI-assigned sedan and headed out.

The sharp sound of gunfire echoed through the urban warfare practice house as Angie made her way towards Simon's team. Her voice rang out above the chaos, causing all to stop their practice. In her hand, she held up her phone and displayed a message that sent a chill down their spines. "Folks, we've got some serious trouble. Multiple gangs are converging on Kentucky. It looks like Hart County is their target...again." The gravity of the situation weighed heavily on their minds as they thought back to what had recently happened here in their own backyard.

Simon lowered his weapon, his muscles tensing further, if that was even possible. The news hit like a gut punch, but there was no room for hesitation. He nodded curtly to Angie, acknowledging the gravity of the situation. "Shit, here we go again. I thought they would have still been rebuilding. Angie, do we know anything about these gangs?"

"It seems they are from all over. As you know, we have people assigned to gang task forces all over. They all started reporting their assigned gangs on the move. They are coming from California, Texas, and Georgia, and they all seem to be coming here."

"Mark, get the local LEOs read in. I will call Amanda."

"Go Simon," Amanda answered after two rings.

"Amanda, I have Angie here with me. She just got a message about gangs all headed to what looks like our way. This may be Ortiz retaliating already."

"What?"

"Angie said they look to be coming from the West and Southeast coasts and even some from Texas. Who knows what they will pick up along the way? All seem to be headed to Kentucky and to me that only means one thing."

"I'll call the FBI and get that message. I'll see what we can do, but above all else Simon. Be careful, that means the whole lot of you."

"We will."

"Time to gear up," he said, his tone leaving no room for debate. "We're moving out. Jack, you take the North from Munfordville, West of sixty-five. Mark, you take East of sixty-five. Angie, if you are able I would like you to take from Munfordville South from sixty-five east. Lori and I will take West." Simon paused and let out a breath.

"Loran, can you get your brothers? If so, get two to ride with Mark or Jack, then you and the other can ride with the other. Jennifer, you ride with Angie."

"Calling Pa now to get the boys here," Loran spoke.

"Angie, I need you to get as much information as you can on these gangs from those Task Force folks. We need numbers and when we can expect them."

"Copy that," Angie replied, her determination palpable. She knew what was at stake—innocent lives hanging in the balance, a community under siege. And she knew Simon and their team were the best shot at preventing an onslaught that would leave nothing but devastation in its wake.

Their training had been relentless, but now it was time to see if it would pay off when faced with the raw violence and brutality of a battle they could only partly anticipate. The team exchanged glances, a silent agreement passing between them. They would stand together, come hell or high water.

As they prepared to confront the threat head-on, the sense of urgency was a living thing among them, propelling them forward with a grim resolve that only those who walk in the shadows of danger truly understand.

"The boys will be here within the hour," Loran said. Simon nodded.

With all this coming at them, he thought about adding on to his cabin. It seemed every time they prepped, his cabin was the meeting place, and when people got tired they just crashed out where they could. It got awfully small inside his place when these sessions happened.

Darkness enveloped Cave City, a small town just south of Hart County, as reports of vandalism and theft spiked overnight. The once quaint storefronts now lay shattered and the streets were no longer safe for residents to roam. The chaos soon spread to neighboring towns like Rowletts, Uno, and Hardyville, each succumbing to a calculated wave of destruction. It was as if someone had carefully orchestrated this chaos to draw attention from those in power - specifically, Simon Wilson and his team. The night was filled with an eerie silence, broken only by the sound of shattered glass, the roar of motorcycles, and decked out lowriders the gang members drove, and the distant cries for help. Fear hung heavy in the air as the townspeople huddled together, wondering who or what could be behind these violent attacks.

The news reached Simon as he sat in a dimly lit room, poring over maps and satellite imagery. Angie burst in, breathless.

"Simon, they've hit Horse Cave. They're tearing the place apart."

Simon's blue eyes hardened, the muscles in his jaw clenching visibly. He stood up, towering in the cramped space, his six-foot frame all coiled energy and imminent action. They had expected to fight, but not one so close to home, not one so brazen. It was a message—a challenge thrown at their feet.

"Come on, everyone ready," Simon commanded. "We roll out in ten."

"Don't look like we will need to start those patrols now. They are here. Angie, did you ever get your intel to warn us?" Jack asked.

"I didn't," Angie replied, already moving towards the gear boxes.

As the team gathered their gear, there was no banter, no bravado—only the sound of clasps snapping shut and magazines being loaded with methodical precision. Each member donned their tactical vests, checked their weapons, and prepared mentally for the confrontation ahead.

Simon surveyed his unit, seeing the reflection of his resolute determination mirrored back at him. These men and women were more than operatives, they were guardians against the shadows poised to engulf innocent lives.

"Stay sharp, stay alive, protect the innocents," Simon reminded them, his gaze meeting each pair of eyes in turn. "Let's end this."

With nods of acknowledgment, they filed out to the convoy of black SUVs they had gotten for their trip to Mexico, waiting outside. Engines roared to life, cutting through the still night air as they set off toward Horse Cave, the town's name now synonymous with danger.

As the vehicles tore down the road, sirens blaring in the distance joined the chorus of urgency. Mark had called the sheriff's office as soon as he had the time. Simon's mind raced with tactical possibilities, his focus narrowing to the threat that lay ahead. There would be time later for introspection, for the weight of what they were about to face. But now, as the darkness enveloped them, only one thing mattered—the mission and the lives hanging in the balance.

As the convoy skidded to a halt on the outskirts of Horse Cave, dust billowing around the tires, Simon Wilson's gaze snapped to the figures emerging from the treeline. Greg Smith led the way, his massive frame unmistakable even in the dim light, followed closely by Frank, John, and Alva—their faces set in grim determination.

"Figured you could use some mountain muscle," Greg rumbled, his deep voice barely rising above the chaos unfolding in the distance where sporadic gunfire cracked the night.

"Welcome to hell," Simon replied, clapping Greg on the shoulder with a nod of gratitude. "Let's get to work."

Simon spoke into his comm gear: "Smurfette and all others, your Pa and brothers just showed up to help."

"Smurfette copies, and thank God, it looks like we are gonna need 'em," Loran replied.

They moved swiftly, a silent unit blending into the shadows as they approached the besieged town. The air was thick with tension, each breath laced with the acrid sting of smoke and the undercurrent of danger that awaited them.

Suddenly, the stillness shattered. A hail of bullets whistled through the air, ricocheting off the abandoned cars that littered the street. Simon's team hit the ground, rolling behind cover as the gangs unleashed their fury. The initial clash was electric, a maelstrom of violence that erupted without warning.

"Move, move, move!" Simon barked orders, his voice cutting through the cacophony as he led the charge. They returned fire with practiced precision, each shot calculated to protect and neutralize.

Greg loomed like a behemoth beside him, his weapon an extension of his imposing presence, while Frank slipped through the shadows, his indigo-tinted skin a blur against the night. Bullets zinged past, too close for comfort, but they pressed on, relentless in their advance.

The gangs were numerous, a rabid swarm descending upon the town. Their laughter was manic, their movements erratic, and their intentions deadly clear as they ransacked what remained of Horse Cave.

"Left flank, Frank!" Simon called out. Frank nodded, his response immediate as he pivoted, taking down two assailants with swift, sure shots that belied his slight frame.

Alva, not one to be outdone, danced through the chaos, his movements almost balletic as he dispatched gang members with ruthless efficiency. John's steady hand provided cover, his focus unyielding amidst the bedlam.

Simon caught a glimpse of Loran, her indigo hue now smeared with grime and blood, as she fought alongside her kin. Her drawl had turned into a snarl, her every shot echoing her ferocity.

In the heart of the fray, it was a symphony of adrenaline and instinct. Each member of the team wove through the battle, their individual strengths coalescing into a force to be reckoned with. They were outnumbered but undeterred, their resolve as unbreakable as the mountains that had forged their newest allies.

The gangs, sensing the tide turning, grew more desperate, their attacks more frenzied. But Simon's team, bolstered by the raw power of the Blue Fugate clan, met them head-on, their unity unwavering in the face of sheer bedlam.

It was a brutal dance of survival, each movement, each decision, a step towards reclaiming the town from the clutches of lawlessness. And in this moment, under the cloak of night, Simon Wilson and his team fought not just for victory, but for the very soul of Horse Cave.

"Come on!" Simon bellowed over the din of gunfire and shouted orders, his voice a rallying cry in the murky twilight that had settled over Horse Cave. The town was alive with the sounds of battle, with every new explosion and cry underlining the urgency of their struggle.

As Simon's team pressed forward, flanked by Greg, Frank, John, and Alva, an unexpected sight unfolded before them. Emerging from the shadows of the surrounding buildings, a group of Amish men advanced, their somber attire stark against the backdrop of chaos. With grim determination set upon their usually peaceful faces, they moved with a purpose that spoke of deep-seated conviction.

"Simon!" shouted a voice that cut through the tumult. It was Ezekiel, the Amish community's elder, his beard flecked with sweat and dirt. "We cannot stand by while our neighbors fall. We bring our strength to join your cause."

"Your help is welcome, Ezekiel," Simon replied, a surge of respect welling within him for these unlikely warriors.

The Amish men, though devoid of modern weaponry, carried tools repurposed as weapons—pitchforks, scythes, and hammers gripped with the same proficiency as their plows and saws. Their presence reminded Simon that sometimes, the heart of a fighter beat strongest in those who lived by peace.

"Form up! Use what you know," Simon instructed, and without hesitation, the Amish men fell into ranks beside his team. Together, they executed a series of maneuvers that Simon had drilled into his squad: movements that were now amplified by the Amish's unexpected agility and knowledge of the land.

"Cover the left flank!" Ezekiel commanded his brethren, his voice steady. They moved as one, their formation tight and disciplined, shielding the left side of Simon's team as they pushed forward into enemy territory.

"Push them back, inch by bloody inch!" Simon roared, his own body moving with the practiced ease of a seasoned operative. He could feel the tide of the battle shifting beneath their feet, the gangs' lines buckling under the combined force of his team and the Amish community.

Amidst the fray, the unique skills of the Amish became evident. One man, Jacob, turned a fallen tree limb into a formidable weapon, swinging it with a precision that belied its crudeness, knocking gang members off their feet. Another Levi, used his knowledge of horse-drawn carriages to maneuver a commandeered vehicle, turning it into a makeshift barricade that provided cover and disrupted the gangs' advance.

"Keep pressing! They're faltering!" shouted Simon, his gaze locking onto the next strategic point, a cluster of buildings that would give them higher ground.

"Follow Simon's lead!" Ezekiel echoed, his people seamlessly adapting to the rhythm of combat, their actions born of necessity and a fierce desire to protect their homes.

Together, Simon's team and the Amish moved like a wave across the battlefield, their coordinated efforts slowly but surely reclaiming the beleaguered town from the clutches of the marauding gangs. The raw courage and unity displayed by this band of defenders grew stronger with every fallen foe and every inch of ground regained.

It was a testament to the power of community and the unwavering spirit of those who fought not just for themselves, but for the future of Horse Cave. As they continued their advance, there was no doubt left in Simon's mind: together, they would triumph.

Simon ducked behind a battered pickup truck, its engine still ticking from the heat of gunfire. Bullets ricocheted off the rusted hood with angry zings as he reloaded his weapon, his movements practiced and smooth despite the chaos erupting around him. The relentless barrage from the gangs had been met with equal ferocity by his motley crew and their unexpected allies—the Amish.

"Out of ammo!" Alva shouted from across the street, his back pressed against the wall of what used to be a quaint bakery.

"Cover me," Simon grunted to Greg, who nodded, lifting his rifle to provide suppressing fire.

With a deep breath, Simon sprinted into the open, the sound of his boots pounding against the asphalt blending with the cacophony of battle. He skidded next to Alva, dropping spare magazines into his waiting hands. He gave him a quick nod of thanks before returning to the fight, his aim steady and unforgiving.

The gangs were using hit-and-run tactics, but Simon's team adapted quickly, communicating with hand signals and curt shouts to those without the comm units. They were like a living organism, each cell responding to the needs of the whole. When a gang member lobbed a makeshift Molotov cocktail, it was Frank who leaped forward, batting it away with a shovel taken from an abandoned hardware store.

"Nice save," John yelled over the din, his eyes flashing with adrenaline-fueled excitement.

"Let's not get too cocky! They're pushing on the left flank!" Simon called out, directing attention to a new threat.

In response, the Amish men, led by Ezekiel, formed a human chain, their broad shoulders interlocking to create an impromptu barrier. Women and children, seeking refuge under an old house, peered through from under the porch, their prayers whispered fervently for the brave souls above.

"Keep 'em out of the cave!" Simon instructed, hoping the sheriff deputies would cause a barrier as the gangs started to retreat.

Like a well-oiled machine, Simon's team and the Amish worked in concert. John and several Amish youths flanked the gangs, funneling them away from the cave entrance. The gang members stumbled, caught off guard by the sudden shift in strategy, their ranks breaking as they scrambled to avoid being trapped.

"Look at them run!" Alva crowed, a triumphant grin spreading across his face as he took down another assailant attempting to flee.

"Stay focused. This isn't over yet," Simon reminded him, though he couldn't help but feel a surge of pride at the sight of their enemies in disarray.

The tide had indeed turned, the once brazen gangs now fought defensively, their numbers dwindling under the relentless assault of a community united. The setting sun cast long shadows across the battlefield, a visual metaphor for the dark fate that awaited those who dared threaten Horse Cave.

"Keep at it!" Simon barked, his voice hoarse but resolute. "We've got them on the ropes!"

Sweat mingled with gunpowder and blood, the air thick with the scent of determination. Each member of Simon's team found a reserve of strength they didn't know they possessed, fueled by the knowledge that surrender was not an option—not when so much was at stake.

And as the last rays of daylight faded, giving way to the cool embrace of twilight, Simon knew without a shadow of a doubt—they would emerge victorious.

Simon's breath came in measured gasps as he surveyed the scene, his team seamlessly blending with the Amish to form a formidable force. The gangs, once a looming threat, now appeared scattered and desperate, a stark contrast to their earlier bravado. He could see John and Frank, communicating wordlessly, moving together like a well-oiled machine, picking off gang members who strayed too close.

"Push forward!" Simon commanded, his fingers tightening around his weapon as he led the charge, the Amish flanking him, their somber expressions etched with determination.

A blur of movement caught Simon's eye—Greg Smith, an imposing figure even amid the chaos, was barreling through enemy lines, paving a path for others to follow. The gangs' resolve crumbled under the combined assault, their gunfire sporadic and misdirected as panic took hold seeing not only a hulking figure of a man in Greg but his indigo-tint, something they had never seen or heard of. Thoughts of a demon ran through more than one mind before it was blown away in the gang members.

"Let's end this," Simon growled, feeling the adrenaline surging through his veins. With a final, concerted effort, they cornered the last of the gang members against the stone walls of the bakery, or what was left of it. There was no escape, and one by one, they dropped their weapons, hands raised, defeat etched on their faces.

As nightfall draped the valley in darkness, the sounds of battle subsided, replaced by a heavy silence. Simon allowed himself a moment to take it all in—the pounding in his chest, the relief washing over him, the triumphant gleam in Alva's eyes as he joined him, his fatigue masked by the exhilaration of victory.

"Damn good work, everyone," Simon said, his gaze sweeping over his ragtag team and the stoic Amish, standing shoulder to shoulder. Together, they'd done the impossible.

The deputies, whose part in the actual fight was small, as they had to uphold the law and could not shoot indiscriminately as the defenders of the town had, were gathering the gang members, zip-tying their hands, and getting them ready for transport.

The aftermath was sobering. Horse Cave lay in ruins, the small town's charm shattered by bullet holes and broken glass. Residents emerged from hiding, their faces haggard but eyes filled with fierce resolve. They gathered in huddles, assessing damage, sharing water and provisions, their conversations a mix of grief and gratitude.

"Looks like we've got our work cut out for us," Simon remarked quietly to Angie, who nodded solemnly beside him while Lori came up on his other side and slid her arm around his waist. The town might be battered, but the spirit of its people remained unbroken, their hands ready to rebuild, their hearts undeterred.

"Starting tomorrow, we begin again," she replied, her voice steady despite the tremors of the day's events. "Together."

Jennifer and the rest of the team, along with Greg and the Amish, all gathered loosely around Simon, Lori, and Angie, taking in the sight.

Under the blanket of stars, amidst the wreckage of their homes and livelihoods, the people of Horse Cave found solace in unity as would the other towns hit by these gangs. They would rise from the ashes, stronger and more connected than ever before. And Simon, once a loner, realized that he too was part of something larger—a community that fought fiercely, not just for survival, but for each other.

The sun rose over the remnants of Horse Cave, casting a golden hue on the faces of those who had emerged to reclaim their town. Simon Wilson stood back for a moment, hands on hips, the muscles in his arms flexing as he surveyed the scene. Men and women, young and old, worked together in a seamless choreography of resilience, clearing debris with a quiet determination that hummed through the air like electricity.

"Never seen anything quite like it," Simon mumbled under his breath, his eyes tracking the Amish men as they hoisted splintered beams off the road, their broad shoulders set against the weight.

"Community's stronger than any damn gang," Angie replied, standing beside him, her voice tinged with pride. She was right; the people of Horse Cave, united by adversity, were a force unto themselves.

Later that day, inside the relative calm of his cabin, Simon leaned back in a worn leather chair, phone pressed to his ear. "Amanda, it's time. Ortiz won't stop until he's put in the ground. I need your word you're with us."

"Simon, you know I've got your back," Amanda Sawyer, CIA Director, reassured him from the other end of the line. Her voice was steady, the sound of support and unspoken promises. "Whatever you need in Mexico, consider it done."

"Appreciate it, Amanda," Simon said before hanging up. He didn't allow himself the luxury of doubt, action was the only path forward.

There was a knock at the door, and Simon's contemplative solitude was interrupted as Jack Thompson strode in, his frame filling the doorway. Behind him trailed twelve people, each bearing the hardened look of those who knew the stakes of the game they were about to play.

"Hope I'm not interrupting," Jack began, a wry smile playing on his lips as he introduced the people. "Came across some folks eager to join the cause. Actually, that is not true. I served with each one of these folks, and when one heard what we were up against, they called and asked if they could help."

Simon eyed the newcomers, noting their cautious glances toward Loran Smith, Greg, and her brothers, who stood nearby, their indigo-tinted skin a stark contrast to their surroundings. It was a rare sight for most, but in the presence of shared purpose, awe gave way to respect.

"Welcome to the team. We'll need every ablebody we can get."

"Never seen anyone like 'em," one of the recruits whispered, unable to hide his fascination.

"Get used to it. They're part of what makes this team special."

As the group settled into an uneasy silence, Loran stepped forward, her slight build belying the toughness beneath. "Hello, my name is Loran. My callsign is Smurfette, and I am sure you can figure out why. We'll teach ya what we know," she offered in her slow southern drawl, a deep mountain folk accent that seemed to resonate with the very earth beneath their feet. She pointed at Simon, "That's Simon or G-man, he's the one in charge."

With introductions out of the way, they gathered around an old oak table, maps and plans spread before them. The next move was clear, and Simon wasted no time in laying out the preliminary plan for the Ortiz house. It was going to be a long night, but Simon could feel the tide turning in their favor. They would take the fight to Ortiz, and they would win.

Simon ran a hand through his brown hair, the muscles in his forearms standing out as he reached for another map from the pile. It was late, the only light in the cabin coming from the dim glow of a single bulb overhead. The walls seemed to close in on them, heavy with the weight of the mission ahead. His blue eyes scanned the faces of the new team members, gauging their reactions as he pointed to the high-resolution satellite images laid out like a patchwork quilt on the table.

"Alright, listen up. This is the Ortiz house." He tapped the photo where the stone walls and guard stations of the cartel's stronghold were visible amidst the lush greenery of Reynosa. "It's fortified, crawling with armed men and attack dogs. We're not going on a field trip, we're walking into the lion's den."

He moved his finger over the layout, indicating entry points, vantage positions, and escape routes. Each member leaned in, their expressions a mix of determination and apprehension. Simon noticed Jack's eyes narrow, the man's mind already turning over the information, calculating risks.

The recruits exchanged glances, the air thick with unspoken promises and resolve. They understood. This wasn't just about taking down a cartel, it was about saving lives, and restoring peace to those who had been terrorized by Juan Ortiz's reign of fear.

"Get some rest. We start moving out tomorrow."

The group dispersed, leaving Simon alone with the maps and plans while Lori went to make a fresh pot of coffee. He let out a long breath, the silence of the room settling around him like a cloak. With practiced movements, he folded the maps and tucked them into his pack.

He stepped outside, the cool night air brushing against his skin. Retrieving his secure satellite phone from his pocket, he dialed a familiar number and waited for the connection.

"Rudy, es Simon. We are starting our trip South tomorrow. Each team will be two vehicles and we will all meet in Santa Anna Refuge. When we are all in place, I will call you to arrange to meet. Meet us on the outskirts of Reynosa, two clicks west of the old farm road."

There was a pause, and then Rudy's voice came through, rough but steady. "Entendido, amigo. Estaré ahí."

"How is Emilia recovering my friend?"

"Ella está mucho mejor. Ella está levantada y sigue siendo tan mandona como siempre," Rudy replied with a chuckle.

"Good. Keep your head down until we call."

"Siempre," Rudy said, a hint of steel in his voice belying his usual disheveled appearance. "Nos vemos pronto."

"See you soon," Simon echoed and ended the call. He stared at the sky, the stars indifferent to the chaos below. With any luck, they'd bring an end to the nightmare that Ortiz had created.

Steeling himself for what was to come, Simon turned back inside. He grabbed the coffee cup Lori was holding out for them and they moved to the porch as one. Holding hands, they were one.

Chapter 17

The warm glow of the setting sun cast long shadows across the porch of Lori and Jennifer's house, where a congregation of purpose had gathered. Simon Wilson, a man whose life was etched with secrets and scars, stood before his team, a mosaic of resolve and raw muscle. The group had swelled in size, now bolstered by the addition of Jack Thompson's twelve Air Force colleagues—men and women who knew the taste of danger—and Ezekiel Yoder, an Amish man with a quiet strength, alongside Greg Smith, Loran's towering father.

"Listen up," Simon began, his voice steady as the oak that sheltered them. "What we're stepping into is a surgical strike at the heart of the Ortiz Cartel. Juan Ortiz's house, our target, is fortified like a fortress. Stone walls, guarded stations, patrols with attack dogs." His finger traced the perimeter outlined in red on the map spread across a large folding table. "We're not walking into some backwoods skirmish, this is Reynosa, Mexico—a hornet's nest."

Greg nodded solemnly. Beside him, Loran leaned in. "How we gonna get past them walls, Simon?" Her mountain drawl thick with concern.

"Precision and teamwork," Simon asserted, locking gazes with each person present. "Every one of you has your own skills and we are going to use them. We'll approach under cover of darkness. Two teams, two entry points. One distraction, one breach. Silence is our ally until it isn't."

"Distraction's my game," Jack chimed in. "My crew knows how to raise hell without firing a shot."

"Good," Simon replied. "Mark, your knowledge of silent entry will be invaluable. And Greg, we'll need that brute strength if things go south."

"Count on it," Greg's deep voice rumbled.

"Once inside," Simon continued, "we neutralize opposition, and exfil when the last of those fuckers is dead."

"Prisoners?" Jackie Haston asked.

"None. This is a seek-and-destroy mission, nothing less," Simon said.

A murmur of agreement swept through the group, a blend of determination and the weight of what lay ahead. They knew the stakes, they were fighting for past lives stolen, for futures derailed by the insidious reach of the Ortiz Cartel.

"Loran, dole out the assignments for me, please. I need another cup of coffee," Simon told her.

"Sure Simon," Loran replied as she moved next to the map. All eyes were on her.

Greg looked upon his daughter with pride, seeing how much trust and responsibility Simon gave her.

"Jack, you and your team are on recon," Loran started. "You know what to look for. No engagement unless absolutely necessary."

Jack nodded. "Copy that Smurfette," he replied with a grin and a wink.

Greg rose at that, and Loran motioned him back down. "Pa, it's okay, I even like it coming from these knuckleheads. I know when they call me Smurfette, it's because they care about me and not being mean. It's my callsign! And if you're mean to me, you might be Poppa Smurf." The room filled with laughter. "Speaking of which, I'll be assigning callsigns to each of you when we get to Texas."

Greg shook his head and laughed with the rest of them.

"Mark, Angie, you're with Simon on the front line. You'll breach, you'll clear," Loran directed.

"Pa, you'll be handling support with Jackie and Wayne. Keep the escape routes open and secure. We may need a quick exit."

"Understood," Greg affirmed, sharing a look with Jackie and Wayne.

"Frank, John, Alva, you should know where you'll be and what you'll be doing," Loran continued. "For those who don't know, they fly our drones. Each is equipped with an infrared lens if needed and they are so silent, you can barely hear them from ten feet away. They are fed into my computer and I'll change your direction as needed due to that. By the way, I am at the command center directing everything."

"Jacob, Ezekiel, y'all will be the eyes on the perimeter. Radio silence unless you've got a situation. I hope our comm units won't go against your beliefs."

"We will do what it takes. These scoundrels have invaded our land and taken some of our women too," Ezekiel said.

"Remember," Simon concluded, his blue eyes sweeping over the assembled group, "precision, teamwork. We're a single unit with one objective: dismantle Ortiz's operation and watch each other's backs. If you were not given an assignment by Loran, you may be later, or you will be placed on a team with someone who was mentioned."

"One last thing and I'm only gonna say it once. If any of you think you can't do this, or it causes some conflict, we will all understand and there will be no hard feelings for anyone who says they can't go. It is up to you to decide. 'Nuff said on that topic."

A collective murmur of assent rose from the team, each member mentally running through their assigned tasks. They were ready, their resolve hardened knowing what was in store for them.

Simon leaned back against the wall of Lori and Jennifer's porch, watching his team huddle over maps and photos scattered across the table. The atmosphere was thick with anticipation, each breath a silent testament to the gravity of what lay ahead.

"Okay, so we're clear on entry points," Mark said, tapping a finger on a marked-up satellite image. "But what about contingencies? If things go sideways, how are we pulling out?"

"Good question," Simon replied, his tone even. "We'll have two SUVs stationed here and here." He pointed to two spots just outside the perimeter of the Ortiz House. "Smith boys, you're our eyes in the sky. If you catch wind of trouble, Loran will signal Greg's team for extraction."

A flicker of concern crossed Lori's face as she pushed a stray blonde lock behind her ear. "And if the SUVs are compromised?" Her voice barely rose above a whisper, yet it carried the weight of her fears.

"Then we fall back to rendezvous point Bravo," Simon said, addressing her directly. "We've got additional resources waiting. We won't be pinned down."

"Are these comms secure?" Wayne asked, holding up a sleek, black communication device. "Last thing we need is Ortiz listening in."

"Encrypted, military-grade," Simon assured him. "I triple-checked them myself. No one's listening unless we want them to."

The porch fell into a brief silence as the reality of their mission set in. Each member seemed lost in their thoughts, mentally preparing for the confrontation ahead.

"Hey, Simon," Greg piped up, breaking the quiet. "What's the protocol if we encounter locals? Reynosa's not exactly gonna be empty."

"Evade and avoid," Simon responded sharply. "Our beef isn't with the locals. Stay focused on the goal."

Jennifer, who had been standing away from the group, finally spoke up. "What if I see... him?" Her voice was steady, but the fear in her green eyes betrayed her.

"Juan Ortiz?" Simon's gaze softened momentarily. "Leave him to me."

"Alright," Jennifer said, nodding slowly. "I'll try, but..."

Tension hung between them like a physical barrier, each knowing that despite the planning, the variables were many, and the risks, were high. They had trained, and prepared, and now they stood on the precipice of action, the unknown stretching ominously before them.

"Listen up," Simon began, his voice low and commanding. "This is more than just a mission. It's personal for all of us. But remember, we're not just fighting for ourselves. We're fighting for anyone Juan Ortiz has ever harmed or those he will harm if we fail. Keep your heads cool, watch your corners, and trust each other."

He looked around at his ragtag team—Air Force veterans, two Amish men with an unexpected knack for strategy, and a father driven by the need to protect his family—and felt a surge of pride.

"Let's take down Ortiz and end this nightmare," he finished resolutely.

"Here, here," they echoed, a chorus of determination rising on the porch.

The early morning haze still clung to the landscape as the first SUV's engine hummed to life. Simon checked the rearview mirror, noting the placid faces of his companions. Lori sat beside him, her fingers tapping an anxious rhythm on the armrest. Behind them, Jennifer was checking her gear once more—the restless energy in her movements betraying her nerves. Loran, gazed out the window, her expression unreadable. Young Alva and Ezekiel Yoder completed the ensemble, their presence a silent vow of solidarity.

"Get some rest. It's gonna be a long drive," Simon murmured as they pulled away from Lori and Jennifer's house, the second SUV falling into formation behind them. The road ahead was a ribbon of uncertainty, each mile bringing them closer to their quarry.

As they crossed the Kentucky state line, the team's focus was palpable. They spoke only when necessary, their words hushed whispers against the rumble of the SUVs. Outside, the verdant hills rolled past, a serene backdrop to the tension that filled the cabin of the SUV.

"Checkpoints ahead," Loran said quietly, her mountain drawl slicing through the silence. Her eyes had caught the telltale signs of a highway patrol up ahead. Simon nodded his acknowledgment.

"Diverting to Route 45," he said, his voice even. He trusted Loran's instructions—her connection to the land was almost supernatural.

The convoy slipped onto the back roads, bypassing the potential snare. Tennessee came and went, the sun climbing higher as they traversed the state, its rays glinting off the chrome finishes of the SUVs. They avoided the main thoroughfares, opting instead for the less-traveled paths where the chances of being spotted were slimmer.

As the two-team convoy rumbled down the highway, their engines roaring in unison, they made regular stops for gas, food, and restroom breaks. The drivers would swap places, allowing the current driver to get a much-needed rest or possibly even a proper nap. Exhausted from the long hours on the road, they eagerly welcomed these brief respites before continuing on their journey through endless stretches of asphalt and waning daylight. Each break was a chance to recharge and keep them going until they reached their destination.

Arkansas provided its own challenges, the terrain shifting, the heat oppressive. Simon could see the strain on Lori's face, her concern for Jennifer a constant ache.

"We're doing everything we can," he reminded her softly, offering a brief touch on her shoulder.

"I know," she replied, her Southern lilt heavy with worry. "Just feels like we're driving straight into the lion's den."

"Except this time, the lions don't know we're coming," Jennifer chimed in, her green eyes fierce with determination.

The sun beat down on the convoy as it snaked its way through the desiccated Texas landscape. Inside the lead SUV, the murmur of conversation competed with the hum of the engine and the occasional crackle of static from the radio.

"Ever think we'd end up on a mission like this?" Alva asked, his gaze fixed on the road ahead.

"Feels like a high-stakes poker game," Jennifer mused, eyes scanning their surroundings. "Except we can't bluff our way out of this one."

"Who needs to bluff when you've got an ace like Simon?" Lori cut in, offering a supportive glance towards Simon who was staring pensively out the window.

"Thanks, but remember, it's not about any single ace," Simon said, meeting her eyes briefly before returning his gaze to the horizon. "It's the hand we play together that'll win this."

"Speaking of playing hands," Alva chimed in, breaking the tension, "Anyone up for a round of cards tonight? I feel like I could take you all down with my Amish Rummy skills."

"Keep dreaming, kid," Ezekiel teased, eliciting a round of chuckles. The laughter was a brief respite, a momentary release from the weight of their shared purpose.

"Let's just make sure Juan Ortiz folds first," Simon concluded, his voice steady as the miles continued to roll by beneath them.

At the Ortiz house in Reynosa, fury radiated from Juan like the unforgiving Mexican sun. He paced the opulent living room, his scarred face contorted in rage.

"Useless! Every single one of them!" he spat out in Spanish, hurling a glass across the room where it shattered against the stone wall. The remnants of his temper glinted dangerously amid the shards.

"Patron," one of his lieutenants ventured cautiously, "we underestimated Simon Wilson and his team. But we will find another way—"

"Another way?" Juan interrupted the edge in his voice sharp enough to slice through the tense air. "I have no use for excuses. They should have been dead long ago!"

"Simon Wilson is not an ordinary adversary," the lieutenant tried to explain. "He has resources, connections—"

"Then we will sever those connections," Juan interjected coldly. "I want every rat in this city who can shoot or slice with a knife. We know his town, we know he has putas on his team and we can use them as leverage against the rest. And when we find them..." His hand mimicked a gun firing, the gesture final.

"Simon Wilson will regret ever setting foot in my kingdom."

Juan Ortiz's fingers drummed a staccato rhythm on the mahogany desk, the sound echoing through the quiet of his office. His gaze was fixed on a grainy photo pinned to the wall – Simon Wilson's determined face staring back at him.

"Chepe Diego," he murmured into the phone, his voice low and dangerous. "I need fighters. Merciless. Hungry. The kind that doesn't blink at blood."

"Consider it done, Juan," the voice on the other line promised, oily and obsequious. "They'll be ghosts in the night, knives ready. This will set the score to even."

"Good." Juan hung up with a click, a slow smile spreading across his face. He would bolster the ranks of the Ortiz Cartel with the most desperate, those with nothing to lose. They would be his instruments of vengeance, and Simon Wilson's downfall.

In the southwest corner of the Santa Ana National Wildlife Refuge, the sun dipped low, casting long shadows among the mesquite trees and thorny underbrush. The team gathered silently, their faces set with determination as they set up their camp, checked and rechecked their gear.

"Remember, stay sharp out here. We are close enough to the border to spit and hit Mexico," Simon said, his eyes scanning the group. "We're not just fighting a man, we're fighting an idea—fear, oppression. We end it here."

The team members nodded, their own resolve reflected in the set of their jaws. The air was thick with anticipation, each breath heavy with the weight of what was to come.

"Comms check," Lori said, her voice crisp as she adjusted her earpiece. Jennifer stood beside her, her expression unreadable, but her hands steady as she loaded her weapon.

"Check," each member responded in turn, their voices a chorus of readiness before storing their comm equipment. Loran and Lori would be in the command center and using their comms when people were out on patrol while her brothers would rotate shifts flying drones, batteries to be recharged from a USB port in one of the vehicles.

"Friday," Simon stated plainly, looking at the sunset as if trying to read the future in its fiery colors. "That's when we call Rudy. For now, we will wait and watch what we can from here."

"Let's hope he's got good news," Loran muttered, his eyes dark pools in the fading light.

"This Rudy's solid?" Ezekiel Yoder interjected his Amish upbringing a stark contrast to the weapons he now carried with ease. "He'll come through?"

"He hasn't failed us yet," Lori responded.

As darkness enveloped the refuge, the group settled into their camp, each lost in their own thoughts but united by a common thread—their unyielding spirit to fight against the darkness that Juan Ortiz had spread across their world. Patrol times were set and those not on patrol crawled into their tents for a night's rest.

Under the veil of a cloudless night, Simon crouched beside the crackling fire, his blue eyes reflecting its flickering flames. His team, an assembly of weary warriors, sat huddled in the shadows of the Santa Ana National Wildlife Refuge, their profiles etched against the darkness. The air was laden with the scent of mesquite and anticipation.

As the day wore on, drones were sent out to observe the activities of people just across the river. The sleek machines hovered silently in the air, their cameras capturing every movement and action below. At times, groups of men could be seen patrolling the area, their rifles held firmly in their hands as they scanned for any potential threats. The tension in the air was palpable, a constant reminder of the unrest and danger that lurked just beyond the river's edge.

Patrols and drone footage each day and night showed the same as Monday afternoon and night, and as each new arriving team arrived they were paired with someone who had already been there for patrolling until all the SUVs had arrived. The team had driven in this way to keep suspicion down.

"Rudy's on the line," Jennifer murmured, handing Simon a rugged satellite phone, its buttons worn from use.

Simon took the phone, pressing it to his ear, his voice low and steady. "Rudy, you in position?"

"Si, Simon. I'm just outside Reynosa like we planned."

"Good. Any changes on your end?"

"I think maybe Ortiz is planning something big, Simon. It seems there are more banditos in town and around the area. Rumor has it he has brought in men from an El Salvadorian cartel. That's what Emilia's contact has informed her of. Juan's getting paranoid," Rudy replied, the sound of cicadas chirping in the background.

"More reason for us to stay invisible until the last second. Remember, we blend in, hit hard, and vanish," Simon instructed his thoughts meticulously piecing together each segment of the plan.

"Understood. I'll be ready with the extra gear," Rudy assured before the call ended with a click.

Simon turned to face his team, his expression a mask of determination. "Okay, listen up. Rudy's confirmed our entry point. We stick to the backstreets and keep interactions minimal. Disguises on before we cross over."

Lori, her hair pulled back tight, nodded as she held out a collection of weathered hats and shawls. "Local garb. Enough to make us look like part of the scenery."

"Make sure your comms are synced. We can't afford any slip-ups once we're in there," Simon continued, his hands methodically checking his own device, an earpiece so small it was almost invisible.

"Frequency's secure," Alva interjected, his youthful face belying the cold precision with which he handled his tech.

"Emergency rendezvous?" Jennifer asked, her hand instinctively resting on her sidearm.

"Two exits, north and west of Ortiz's compound. If things go south, we split and regroup at the secondary rendezvous. No heroics—we leave together or not at all." Simon's tone left no room for argument, the unspoken memories of past missions hanging heavily between them.

"Let's get some rest. We move just before dawn," Simon concluded, his gaze lingering on each member of his team. They were an odd mix of military and civilians, bound by a shared purpose, each carrying the scars of battles past.

As they settled down, the refuge around them seemed to hold its breath, the calm before the storm that was about to break upon Reynosa. And in the heart of that impending tempest stood Simon Wilson, the loner who had become a leader, ready to bring the fight to Juan Ortiz's doorstep.

The set of cartel patrols had just passed the entry point designated for the team. John, who was flying a drone, had watched them until they had entered the city of Reynosa. If things held as they had been, the next patrol shouldn't be there for at least an hour, and by then they would be in country away from the Rio Grande.

The river was a dark ribbon under the predawn sky, sluggish and deceptively serene. Simon crouched at the water's edge, the cold lapping at his boots. Beside him, five rubber rafts lay deflated, their clandestine crossing complete. It was the sort of thing they'd done a dozen times in training along the Green River, but this wasn't an exercise—this was the real deal.

"Everyone check-in," he murmured into the comm, voice low, heart hammering against his ribs. From the shadows, hushed confirmations trickled back, each one a testament to their readiness, to their unity as a team despite the motley paths that had brought them here.

"Let's stash these and move out," Lori whispered, her fingers deftly rolling up the nearest raft. The others followed suit, stowing the evidence of their border breach beneath a scrub of mesquite, the thorny branches a natural deterrent to any prying eyes.

With the remnants of their crossing concealed, they ghosted through the sparse vegetation, each step calculated, silent. The tension was a living thing among them, a coiled spring ready to snap. They were close now, so damn close to the culmination of all their planning and sacrifice.

As they neared the rendezvous point, Simon's gaze constantly swept the area, alert for any sign of trouble. It wasn't long before Rudy's silhouette materialized from the gloom, his form bolstered by the unexpected numbers clustered behind him. Eighty men, grim-faced and resolute, stood ready to support the takedown of Juan Ortiz.

"Didn't think I'd come empty-handed, did you?" Rudy quipped, a wry smile playing on his lips as he approached Simon. His clothes hung off his frame, the mark of a hard life etched into every line of his face, but his eyes sparkled with a steely determination that belied his ragged appearance.

"Never doubted you for a second," Simon replied, clapping him on the shoulder. He surveyed the new additions to their force, an unspoken respect passing between them. These were not soldiers polished by formal training, but they carried the weight of personal stakes, each man driven by reasons deep and varied just like his initial team.

"Any last questions on the plan," Simon announced, his voice carrying the authority that had seen them through countless dangers. "We do this right, we end Ortiz's reign of terror for good. Rudy, I would like you and your people to be our overwatch, all around the compound. Also if you could have some men with the fast exit vehicles we talked about that would free up a few more of our team."

"Not a big deal, we can handle that." Rudy then moved to his team and explained their assignment in rapid Spanish.

The group huddled closer, eighty-one pairs of eyes fixed on Simon, the promise of dawn casting the first light upon their resolve. They were ready for the fight, ready for the risks. And if death stared them down, they would meet it head-on, together.

The ensemble of warriors, the Rio Grande at their backs and the heart of darkness ahead, slowly and stealthily made their way towards a battle that would be etched into the skin of Reynosa with blood and defiance.

Chapter 18

Rudy Salgado led the team, his tattered clothes blending with the dust and rubble that littered the streets of Reynosa. Behind him, Loran Smith and her brothers followed expressions set in grim determination as they closed in on the fortress-like stone walls of Juan Ortiz's opulent stronghold.

"Almost there," Rudy murmured over his shoulder, his voice barely audible above the distant echoes of barking dogs patrolling the compound's perimeter.

Loran adjusted the straps of her pack, her slow southern drawl cut through the tension as she spoke to her brothers. "Keep sharp, y'all. This ain't no Troublesome Creek."

They had just begun to set up their makeshift command center when the night erupted into chaos. A thunderous explosion shook the ground, a bright flare illuminating the sky above Ortiz's house. Gunfire crackled like a deadly downpour, punctuated by the screams of men and the relentless reports of automatic weapons.

"Down!" someone shouted, and the team hit the dirt, eyes wide as they took in the carnage unfolding before them. A rival cartel had launched a surprise attack, and the Ortiz compound was a maelstrom of violence and destruction. Bullets whizzed overhead, finding flesh and stone with equal ferocity, while explosions sent shards of the once-impenetrable walls flying like deadly shrapnel.

"Damn," one of Loran's brothers cursed, his voice a whisper lost amidst the sounds of battle.

"Stay low," Loran hissed her tough mountain woman instincts on full display. "We ain't part of this... not yet."

The team crawled to a better vantage point, finding cover behind a crumbling wall. They watched as the assault on Ortiz's house intensified, the glow of fires casting dancing shadows across the frenzied scene. The attacking cartel members were relentless, moving like shadows among the flames, their guns spitting death with ruthless efficiency.

"Can y'all believe this?" Rudy's voice was a mix of awe and fear. "Los Zetas... they're tearing the place apart."

"Could be our chance," Simon murmured, his eyes never leaving the battlefield. "Once they're done, we move in. Clean up what's left."

"Ortiz's men will be scattered," Jack added, his voice steady despite the pounding of his heart. "Weak. Vulnerable."

"Exactly," Rudy agreed, nodding sharply. "We just need to stay out of sight until then."

The team settled into their hidden position, muscles tense as they waited for the right moment to strike. Every new explosion, every scream, every burst of gunfire brought with it the promise of opportunity—and the weight of danger.

"Keep your heads down," Simon's voice came over the radio, calm and collected even now. "Let them soften each other up. We'll have our turn soon enough."

As the battle raged on, Loran and her team remained unseen, specters in the night waiting for the dawn of their deadly encounter.

Simon crouched behind the crumbled remains of what had once been an ornate fountain, shards of marble, and sprays of water his erratic companions as chaos unfolded before him. The air reeked of gunpowder and scorched earth, punctuated by the roar of assault rifles and the staccato percussion of grenades.

"Talk to me," Simon's voice was a low growl into the comm unit, his blue eyes scanning the fray for any advantage. "Options?"

"Could take years waiting for another chance like this," Loran replied, her tone urgent yet calculated. She was poised in the shadows, her sharp gaze dissecting their grim tableau.

"Damn straight," one of the brothers chimed in, echoing her sentiment. "But do we really want to dance with the devil?"

"Sometimes you have to sway with the worst to bring down the bad," Simon countered, his jaw setting firm. The idea tasted foul, but desperation made strange bedfellows. "We consider aligning with Los Zetas—just until Ortiz is out."

"Align? With those psychos?" Rudy's incredulity crackled through the line. There was a collective pause, the team considering the gravity of such a pact.

"Temporary," Simon pressed on, feeling the weight of every word. "It's about survival. And let's face it, they're doing a damn good job tearing Ortiz a new one."

"Too good," another brother muttered, the implication hanging heavy in the air that the enemy of their enemy was hardly a friend.

"Okay, say we go through with this crazy idea," Loran said, her voice steady despite the obvious risks. "What's stopping them from turning on us the minute Ortiz falls?"

"Nothing," Simon admitted, his gaze never wavering from the battlefield. "Which is why we stay one step ahead, use them to take the heat off us until we strike."

"High risk, high reward," Rudy finally conceded, the grudging acceptance palpable even over the radio. "But if we pull this off..."

"Big if," someone pointed out, but the seed of audacity had been planted.

"Let's say we go in, guns blazing with Los Zetas at our backs," Loran mused aloud, weighing the deadly gamble they were entertaining. "We'd need a solid exit strategy. Can't trust snakes not to bite."

"Agreed," Simon responded, his mind already racing with tactical maneuvers and fallback plans. "We would need absolute control over the how and when. We play this smart, or we don't play at all."

"Smart doesn't usually involve siding with cartel hitmen," Rudy's voice now held a hint of resignation, the kind born from the knowledge that sometimes the worst decisions led to necessary outcomes.

"Better the devil you know," Simon quipped darkly, his lips a thin line. "We watch. We wait. And when the time is right, we move in hard and fast. No mercy."

"Never is with us," Loran affirmed, her conviction strengthening the resolve of the team. They were united in purpose if nothing else.

"Alright," Simon said with finality, determination laced with a dangerous edge. "We play the long game. Watch the show, and learn their moves. But keep your trigger fingers ready. This dance could turn into a brawl real quick."

The agreement was silent but unanimous. From the relative safety of their covert location, Simon and his team watched the rival cartels tear each other apart, knowing full well the inferno they might be stepping into. It was a twisted sort of patience, the kind only honed by those intimate with death and driven by vengeance.

"Stay sharp," Simon murmured, more to himself than anyone else. "This is far from over."

The staccato rhythm of gunfire echoed through the air like a macabre symphony, punctuated by the deep-throated roars of explosions that shook the ground beneath their feet. Simon's team hunkered down among the scrub and debris, eyes fixed on the opulent stone fortress that was Juan Ortiz's house, now transformed into a war zone where death held court.

"Teaming up with them is off the table," Simon concluded grimly, scanning the chaos with a tactical eye. The rival cartel's assault was relentless, a tsunami of violence crashing against the once unassailable walls of the Ortiz stronghold.

"Good call," Loran muttered. "We don't need to be in bed with another set of devils."

"Speaking of which," Rudy interjected, his voice low but carrying a weight that defied his disheveled farmer's appearance, "you should know exactly who we're dealing with here. Los Zetas don't play by any rules but their own."

"Tell us something we don't know," John replied dryly, though his gaze never left the sight of his sniper scope, tracking targets with lethal precision.

"Los Zetas... they're not just ruthless, they're a whole other breed of monster," Rudy continued. "And those monsters are tearing each other apart out there." He paused, looking at each member of the team, ensuring his words hit home. "If they win, it's not just Ortiz we'll have to worry about—it's what comes after."

Simon nodded, his expression unreadable. They all knew the stakes. It wasn't about taking sides, it was about survival and hitting when the enemy was weakest.

Outside the relative safety of their hideout, the battle raged on. The air was thick with gunpowder and fear, the night sky ablaze with the fires that consumed parts of the compound. Shouts and screams painted a visceral soundscape, a grim reminder of the human cost of this turf war.

"Focus on the endgame," Simon instructed tersely. "We clean up whatever's left after they've had their fill of each other."

"Got it, boss," Alva responded, his fingers dancing over the drone controls, sending their electronic eyes into the fray to capture every bloody detail.

The fight between the cartels was a brutal ballet of bullets and bloodshed. Bodies littered the ground, some still clutching their weapons even in death, while others writhed in agony, their cries lost amidst the cacophony of combat. Explosions sporadically tore through the air, sending shrapnel and debris flying, adding to the carnage.

"Stay sharp," Simon repeated, his voice barely above a whisper as he watched another explosion rock the compound, the flames reflecting in his cold, determined eyes. "This isn't our fight yet, but hell if we won't finish it."

In the lull between the detonations, in that eerie silence that followed the shockwaves, the team's resolve hardened. They were no strangers to violence, to the necessity of wading through blood and sorrow to achieve their aims. But tonight, they were witnesses to an annihilation that would change the balance of power in Reynosa forever.

As the firefight began to wane, the night air heavy with the stench of smoke and spilled life, Simon signaled his team. They moved like ghosts, positioning themselves for whatever came next, ready to end the reign of Juan Ortiz. As they lay in wait, the distant sound of approaching sirens melded with the fading echoes of battle, a haunting prelude to the storm that was yet to come.

The night air was split by the disconnected rhythm of gunfire, a symphony of chaos that Juan Ortiz had orchestrated many times before. But this time, the melody was off—a jarring dissonance that set his teeth on edge. The Los Zetas cartel had come to call, and their reputation for visceral savagery sent shivers even down the spine of a man like Ortiz.

"¡Formación! ¡Defiendan la casa!" Ortiz barked orders in rapid-fire Spanish, his voice cutting through the panic like a machete through the underbrush. His men, once disciplined soldiers of the drug trade, now scrambled like frightened children as the reality of facing the Los Zetas cartel sank in.

Ortiz's brown eyes, hard as flint, darted across the compound, assessing the damage, and tallying up the cost of survival. The acrid stench of gunpowder mingled with fear, thickening the air until it was almost too dense to breathe. He'd survived prison, police raids, and rival gangs, but the Los Zetas were a different beast altogether—one that wouldn't be cowed by reputation or firepower.

"¡No dejen que avancen!" he yelled, pushing his men forward, only to watch one of them falter. The man's eyes were wide, reflecting the inferno that raged around them. He turned, making a break for an exit, thoughts of desertion clear as day.

Without hesitation, Ortiz drew his pistol. The report of the gunshot was almost lost amid the cacophony, but its message was unmistakable. The deserter's body jerked and crumpled to the ground, a stark reminder that betrayal was a sin paid for in blood.

"¡Nadie abandona la lucha!" Ortiz roared over the tumult. His visage, marked by that jagged scar from eye to chin, became the embodiment of relentless cruelty. "¡Luchen como los diablos que son!"

His remaining men rallied, their resolve steeled by the display of ruthless leadership. As bullets whizzed by, they returned fire with a renewed fury, driven by fear of their enemies and their own merciless leader alike.

Ortiz paced behind the frontlines, his scruffy face set in grim determination. Death had come to his doorstep wearing the mask of Los Zetas, but he would not go gently into that good night. He would fight, claw, and kill to protect what was his—until the bitter end or a triumphant dawn.

Simon crouched low behind the husk of an overturned vehicle, his blue eyes fixed intently on the chaos that unfolded beyond the stone walls of Juan Ortiz's opulent fortress. The night air was thick with tension and the bitter tang of gunpowder. Explosions punctuated the darkness, casting brief, lurid light across his team's grim faces.

"Alright," Simon murmured, voice steady despite the adrenaline coursing through his veins, "we hold position. Let these bastards thin their own ranks." Simon then headed to the makeshift command center.

Loran nodded, she watched the computer screens as she readied to have the drones launched and images come to life on her computer. Beside her, Frank, John, and Alva were ready with their three drones, each one humming softly as it lifted into the tumultuous sky.

"Let's see what we're dealing with," Loran said, her drawl slow but her intent clear. Each brother pushed forward on the controller, causing each drone to move forward. One would go to each side of the house, while the other would move directly overhead. Again Loran was happy about the CIA drones being quiet, though with the firefight in progress, it hardly mattered.

The small, buzzing machines rose above the walls, sending back a stream of video to Loran's rugged, portable computer. The screen flickered with images of terror and violence. Simon leaned in, watching as the camera feeds painted a vivid picture of bedlam within the cartel compound.

"Feed looks good," Loran remarked quietly, her Appalachian accent softened by focus.

"Keep 'em high," Simon instructed. "I don't want those drones spotted."

"Copy that." Alva's affirmation was almost lost in the concussive roar of another explosion.

Through the lens of the hovering drones, they saw Ortiz's men scrambling like cornered animals, their bravado dissolving under the relentless assault of Los Zetas. The rival cartel's reputation for brutality seemed well-deserved as the feed showed glimpses of savage retribution against any who dared resist.

"Damn, this is one hell of a mess," Wayne muttered, squinting at the screen.

"Exactly why we wait," Simon replied. His tone was casual, conversational even, belying the gravity of their situation.

"Patience isn't exactly my strong suit," Jennifer confessed, her eyes never leaving the monitor.

"Mine neither," Simon agreed, "but rushing in there now would be suicide. We'll get our shot when the dust settles."

"Assuming there's anything left to shoot at," Mark added darkly.

The drones continued their silent dance above the battlefield, recording every instance of carnage—each burst of gunfire, every shattering explosion. Beneath the violence, though, Simon sensed the tide turning. Los Zetas was gaining ground, and Ortiz's stronghold was crumbling beneath their onslaught.

"Once Los Zetas pulls out, we make our move," Simon decided, his gaze locked on the drone feeds. "Ortiz and any lieutenants left standing won't know what hit them."

"Reckon they'll leave much for us?" Angie asked, his tone skeptical.

"Doesn't matter," Simon said. "We're not here to pick over scraps. We're here to end this."

They settled in to watch and wait, the distant echoes of battle a jarring counterpoint to the stillness around them. In this lull, Simon felt the weight of every decision he'd made, every life he'd taken. But there was no room for doubt or hesitation—not when the mission was all that mattered.

As the sounds of conflict began to wane, signaling the nearing end of the brutal skirmish, Simon straightened up. He directed his team with a series of hand signals, each member moving with practiced ease to their assigned positions.

"Time to finish this," Simon whispered, his voice barely audible over the dying roars of war. With a final glance at the drone feeds, he signaled the advance, his team moving like shadows toward the uncertain fate that awaited them within the bloodied walls of the Ortiz compound.

Static crackled over the radio, a harsh whisper against the backdrop of fading gunfire. Simon crouched behind a crumbling wall, his eyes fixed on the Ortiz compound as he keyed his mic.

"Jack, you and your team are up. Stay frosty," Simon's voice was low but clear, the command etched with the calm assurance of a man who had orchestrated chaos into victory more times than he cared to count.

"Copy that," came Jack's terse reply. The former Air Force man moved with the stealth of a panther, his team flanking him in disciplined silence. They were shadows among the ruins, their movements almost spectral.

"Loran, status?" Simon asked as he walked back up close to Loran's laptop screen, carrying a cup of coffee for himself and the blue girl, which glowed eerily in the dim light.

"Got somethin' here," Loran's voice, tinged with the mountain drawl of Troublesome Creek, held a note of urgency. "Northeast quadrant, near the old guardhouse. Looks like a handful of 'em waitin' for an invite."

"Coordinates, Alva," Loran interjected, her fingers dancing across the keys, plotting the position on the digital map. Despite her normally shy demeanor, in this moment, she was all precision and focused.

"Sending now," Alva responded, and Loran relayed the info to Jack through her headset, her southern drawl stretching out each syllable. "Smurfette to Flyboy, you're gonna wanna take ten paces to your left, then straight ahead. They're tucked away behind that pile o' rubble. Can't miss it."

"Roger that, Smurfette," Jack murmured, adjusting his path slightly. His team followed suit without question, their trust in her directions absolute.

"Keep it quiet," Jack whispered into his comms. "Silenced pistols only. Knives if you need 'em."

The pocket of cartel members came into view, unsuspecting sentinels in a battle already lost. With the efficiency born of grim necessity, Jack and his team closed in. Silenced shots punctuated the air—a soft phut-phut-phut—in rapid succession. Bodies thudded to the ground, their final gasps swallowed by the night.

"Clear," Jack breathed into the radio moments later, his voice barely concealing the adrenaline rush of the swift engagement.

"Good work," Simon praised, allowing himself a brief moment of relief. "Maintain positions and hold for further orders. And keep your heads down, this ain't over yet."

"Understood," came the collective response, a symphony of gritty determination.

As the night wore on, the radio remained a lifeline, a constant hum of status reports and murmured conversations that wove together the fabric of their precarious operation. Each member of Simon's team, bound by a common goal, waited with bated breath for the final act to unfold.

"Stay sharp," Simon reminded them, his anticipation a tangible thing. "We're close now. Very close."

As the distant echo of gunfire petered out, Simon crouched behind a stone barricade, his eyes scanning the horizon painted with the orange hue of fires raging within the Ortiz compound. His heart thumped in his chest—not from fear, but from the adrenaline-fueled clarity that came with knowing every decision carried weight. Lives hung in the balance, their fates entwined with his actions.

"G-Man," Loran's voice cut through the static of the radio, steady despite the chaos, "I got movement to the east wing. Looks like they're regrouping."

"Copy that, Smurfette," Simon replied, his gaze shifting to the movement she reported. He observed the huddled shapes of Ortiz's men rallying, desperate to mount a defense against the Los Zetas onslaught.

"Watch 'em, but don't engage," he instructed. "We can't afford to get caught in the crossfire."

"Understood. Badge, do not, repeat do not engage," she responded, her tone betraying none of the concern that Simon knew she harbored for her teammates—somewhere out there in the dark, risking their lives just as she was.

The team's motivations were clear: take down Ortiz and cripple the cartel's infrastructure. Yet, beneath that unified goal lurked a web of personal stakes. For Loran, it was about protecting her kin and avenging the wrongs done to her community. For Lori Hawkins, it was the revenge for her daughter Jennifer's kidnapping, her bright future darkened by abduction.

Simon felt the gravity of responsibility, knowing his decisions impacted not only the mission but also the lives attached to each of his team members. He couldn't let them down. Not now. His motivation was not revenge, but the security of those who would come next if they failed.

"Rudy, status?" Simon's voice was calm but carried an edge.

"East side's quiet... too quiet," Rudy's reply crackled through the comms, tinged with suspicion. "Feels like a trap."

"Stay vigilant," Simon warned, sharing Rudy's unease. "And everyone, remember why we're here. We end this tonight."

A deafening explosion shattered the peaceful stillness, ripping through the ground and sending a billowing cloud of smoke into the sky from the heart of the compound. The earth trembled beneath their feet as screams erupted, piercing through the air like daggers to the soul. Panic and chaos reigned as people scrambled for safety, their cries echoing off the walls of nearby buildings. The once serene atmosphere was now consumed by fear and destruction, leaving nothing but devastation in its wake.

"Damn it," Simon cursed under his breath. He could imagine the terror etched on Juan Ortiz's face as he realized the Los Zetas cartel had brought hell to his doorstep.

The night air was thick with tension, the silence between gunfire growing longer as if both cartels were catching their breath for the final push. And then...

"Team," Loran's voice was a whisper, yet it pierced through the lull with urgency, "I see something. On the west side. A breach—a chance."

Simon's muscles tensed, ready to spring into action. This was it—their window of opportunity. He signaled to his team, each member already primed for his command.

"Positions, now! We go in silent, we go in swift. Our moment's coming."

The night was eerily quiet as they made their way through the aftermath of the day's brutal battle. The destruction and debris around them served as a somber reminder of the toll this war had taken.

"Wait for my signal," Simon's voice was barely audible, even to himself.

Chapter 19

Under the veil of a moonless sky, Simon Wilson led his team through the dense underbrush toward the Ortiz House compound. Their movements were ghost-like, deliberate, and quiet, each step calculated to maintain silence. The oppressive darkness was both ally and enemy—shielding their advance but threatening to betray them with every unseen twig underfoot.

Simon's breath was a ghost in the night, condensing briefly in the cool air as his team moved with practiced silence toward the breach in the stone wall. The treeline provided a cloak of darkness just yards from their target, and every step they took was calculated, and measured to avoid detection. The moon hung like a silent sentinel above, its light filtered through the branches, casting shifting patterns on the ground.

"Stay sharp," Simon whispered, his voice barely audible even to those closest to him. His blue eyes were fixed ahead, alert for any sign of movement. Beside him, Lori's face was set in determination, though her hands betrayed a slight tremble. Jennifer, vibrant under any other circumstance, now exuded a steely resolve that belied her youth. Ezekiel Yoder, the wise elder whose white beard seemed to blend with the night, traveled with them, an unexpected warrior in a conflict far removed from his peaceful existence. And Jacob Miller, the gentle giant, kept pace with a quiet ferocity that promised violence to anyone who would threaten his kin or community.

As they approached the hole, Simon signaled a halt with a raised hand. He crouched, motioning for the others to do the same, and peered through the gap in the enclosure. What met his gaze was a tableau of horror: bodies strewn across the compound's dirt floor, some motionless, others writhing in the agony of their final moments. Blood painted the scene in stark, brutal strokes, and the air was thick with the metallic scent of death.

"God Almighty..." Ezekiel murmured, his voice a low rumble of dismay. His compassionate eyes took in the sight, finding no solace in the shadows that danced around the fallen.

"Looks like a damn massacre," Jacob added, his tone edged with disgust and anger. The reality of the cartel's ruthlessness was laid bare before them, fueling a fire within that would not be easily quenched.

Lori's lips parted, a silent gasp escaping as she clutched at the cross hanging around her neck—a tether to hope in a sea of despair. Her mind raced with thoughts of her daughter, praying a silent thanks she had been spared this fate.

"Keep it together," Simon said quietly, though his own heart hammered against his ribs like a relentless drum. "We knew it wouldn't be pretty."

Jennifer's jaw clenched, her green eyes hardening with each passing second. "Let's make these bastards wish they had never come to Hart County, or any other for that matter," she said, the edge in her voice slicing through the tension.

Simon nodded, his muscular frame poised to spring into action. "Smurfette, get Rooster on his way. I want a party of ten to rendezvous with me as quickly as possible," he instructed, his gaze locked onto the chaos within. They were ready—to fight, to avenge.

"Roger that, G-Man. Rooster, grab a team and rendezvous with G-Man ASAP," Loran spoke into the comm set following Simon's instructions.

"Stay sharp," Jack murmured, his voice a low rumble in the stillness, the scar on his jawline tightening with anticipation. His eyes scanned the terrain, every sense alert for the telltale signs of the enemy's approach.

It didn't take long.

Like phantoms, several Los Zetas cartel members materialized from the underbrush, moving stealthily toward Simon's team positioned at the hole. They were intent on drawing blood, their deadly mission clear in their hushed whispers and the glint of moonlight on steel.

Jack's hand tightened around the grip of his rifle, every muscle coiling like a spring. He nodded at his team, and without a word, they understood—it was time to strike.

"G-Man, hold position. We are about to light up some Tangos approaching you."

"Copy, Flyboy. Let 'er rip," Simon said as he signaled to the group to lay flat on the ground.

"Take them down," Jack commanded, his voice no louder than a whisper but carrying the weight of iron.

The first shot broke the night's calm, a precise burst of violence that dropped a cartel member before he knew what hit him. Jack's team worked with practiced efficiency, firing with disciplined control, their shots weaving a lethal tapestry of protection around Simon's advancing group.

One by one, the would-be ambushers fell, their plans unraveled by the swift retribution of Jack's team. As the last aggressor slumped to the ground, Jack allowed himself the ghost of a smile. "Advantage: ours," he called out on the radio.

Simon clicked the comm unit nestled in his ear, the static crackle breaking the oppressive silence that hung over them like a shroud. "Rooster, status?" he whispered, his voice barely above the hum of the night.

"Two hundred yards, closing fast," came the terse reply. Moments later, the unmistakable sound of footsteps approached, disciplined and light. Wayne's silhouette materialized from the darkness, Jackie right on his heels with the eight other operatives fanning out behind them, their shadows blending with the night.

"What is the plan?" Wayne asked as he stepped into the dim moonlight, his eyes scanning the area like a hawk. Jackie gave Simon a curt nod, her sharp brown eyes missing nothing, her body tense and ready.

Simon's gaze flickered to the hole in the fence where the gruesome tableau lay beyond. The new arrivals followed his gaze. "We're going in hot. I want your team through that fence first. Enter, fan out, and provide cover fire for us."

"Understood," Wayne acknowledged, his hand resting on the butt of his sidearm.

"Jackie, you're on point with me," Wayne instructed, turning to face her squarely. The briefest flash of understanding passed between them, a shared history written in scars and gunpowder.

"Always," she replied, the corner of her mouth twitching upwards in a semblance of a smile.

"Rules of engagement?" one of the operatives asked, the grip on his rifle tightening.

"Kill anything that moves," Simon stated coldly, his blue eyes turning steely with resolve. "They've taken enough lives. It ends tonight."

"Smurfette, this is Rooster. How do we look inside the wall at our location?"

Loran's voice, tinged with the twang of her mountain heritage, crackled through the comm unit, steady despite the tension that gripped her. "Clear for entry, Rooster. No heat signatures in immediate proximity."

"Copy that," Simon replied, his tone low and controlled. With a hand signal sharp as the blade he carried, he directed Wayne's team toward the gaping wound in the compound's defenses.

Wayne led the charge, his silhouette slipping through the breach like a ghost haunting the battlefield. Jackie was right behind him, her lithe form bristling with quiet menace. The eight others fanned out with military precision, each one picking their way to cover, their boots whispering against the parched earth, their movements so fluid it was like watching a deadly dance choreographed to the music of war.

They were shadows amidst the chaos, taking up positions amid the rubble and scant foliage. As cartel members stumbled into the yard, disoriented by the violence that had torn through their sanctuary, they met an unflinching fate. Wayne's team functioned as one—a lethal entity that showed no mercy. The crack of gunfire punctuated the night, brief and final.

"Clear for entry," Wayne said over his comm unit when his team had found positions of cover.

Simon didn't need to be told twice. He darted forward, his body a coil of potential energy unleashed. Lori, Jennifer, Ezekiel, and Jacob surged behind him, each driven by their own private hellfire. They trusted Wayne's team, knowing their backs were covered, that every wounded enemy reaching for a gun would be neutralized before they could draw a bead on them.

Ezekiel, the pacifist turned reluctant warrior, moved with surprising grace, his eyes betraying none of the inner turmoil he must have felt. Beside him, Jennifer's green eyes blazed with fierce determination, her rifle an extension of her will to protect her team, which had turned into an extended family at all costs. And Lori, though fear clung to her like a second skin, kept pace with the rest, her desperation lending her speed.

The yard became a deadly ballet where each participant knew their role. Shots rang out—short, controlled bursts— from Wayne's team, dropping cartel members who appeared like specters from the darkened corners of the compound. Each takedown was clinical, devoid of emotion—a job to be done, nothing more.

"Tangos left!" Jackie's voice sliced through the din as she targeted a pair of cartel gunmen attempting to flank Simon's team. Her bullets found their marks, and the threat crumbled to the ground in a heap.

"Good shooting," grunted Wayne, his focus never wavering from the task at hand as he laid down a stream of covering fire, allowing Simon's group precious seconds to cross into the relative safety near the main house.

As they progressed, it was clear that the Los Zetas cartel had caused major damage to the Ortiz cartel. But as they moved forward, Simon's face remained a mask of steely resolve, the weight of leadership and the urgency of their mission etched in every line of his expression.

"Keep pushing," Simon ordered, the sound of his voice barely rising above a whisper, yet carrying the force of a command that would not be disobeyed. His team responded, moving with him as they closed in on the heart of darkness—the opulent stronghold that housed their nemesis.

Inside, they knew, was the ultimate target, Juan Ortiz.

Simon, Lori, Jennifer, Ezekiel, and Jacob fanned out as they advanced towards the main house. It wasn't long before the cartel members began to respond. Gunfire erupted from a nearby guard tower, but the bullets thudded harmlessly into the thick stone walls around them.

"Get those towers!" Simon barked into his comms. Wayne's team popped out from behind cover long enough to take down the shooters with two clean headshots. The bodies fell lifelessly to the ground below.

In the distance, they could hear the sound of alarms blaring to life, signaling that their presence had been discovered. The team picked up their pace, weaving through the compound's maze-like pathways.

Jace and Maria broke from Wayne's team on his command, both equipped with breaching charges, took point, clearing doors and hallways of any traps or tripwires they might encounter.

As they neared the main house, the fighting intensified. It was as if the cartel members knew exactly what was at stake and were willing to die to protect their leader's secrets. The team was outnumbered, but they were fresh and knew the enemy, already being in one battle, would be licking their wounds.

Simon took cover behind a crumbling stone wall as he reloaded his sidearm. Bullets whizzed past his head, kicking up gravel and stone around him. He took a deep breath, willing his racing heart to slow down. He peeked over the wall, scanning for targets.

The night air was heavy with the scent of gunpowder and blood. Bullets whizzed by, serenading them with their lethal intent, but Simon's voice remained steady and clear over the comm unit. "Ezekiel, on my six. Jacob, take left flank—watch those shadows." He hoped Wayne and Jackie would keep them safe from these stray bullets sporadically coming at them.

"Roger that," Ezekiel grunted, his Amish upbringing a stark contrast to the violence he now navigated with a calm efficiency.

"Got it," Jacob replied, his eyes scanning the darkened corners of the compound for movement.

Simon knew the importance of communication in this chaos, it was the thin line between life and death. He could feel the weight of his responsibility, not just as a leader, but as the shield against the storm of bullets meant for his team. They were his to protect, and he would do so with every last breath.

"Move up!" Simon ordered as they edged forward towards the main house. It loomed before them, a fortress of cruelty that had housed unspeakable horrors. But tonight, it would witness the wrath of the righteous.

Lori's sharpshooter skills came into play as she picked off a cartel member attempting to flank them from a second-story window. The crack of her rifle was a symphony of precision, her focus unwavering even as the man fell with a thud onto the cold ground below.

"Good shot," Simon acknowledged, feeling a surge of pride amidst the terror. Jennifer, right beside him, nodded in agreement, her weapon raised and ready.

They moved like ghosts among the gravestones, darting from cover to cover. The once-opulent garden provided them with makeshift shields—a marble bench, and an ornate fountain now defiled by the splatter of blood. Simon could almost taste the metallic tang in the air, the bitter residue of the cartel's reign.

"Entrance ahead," Jennifer called out, pointing to a set of large double doors. They were nearly there, the heart of the beast within striking distance.

"Breaching in three... two..." Simon counted down, and then the world erupted around them once again. The door gave way under the explosive charge Jace and Maria had set, splintering into fragments that danced in the air like deadly confetti.

"Go, go, go!" Simon bellowed, his voice barely audible over the ringing in his ears. They poured into the house, guns raised, each corner presenting a new threat to neutralize.

"Room clear!" Ezekiel called out, his voice a mix of relief and tension.

"Staircase secured," Jacob added, his breathing heavy with exertion and adrenaline.

They were a machine, each part working in tandem with the other, and Simon was the conductor of this orchestra of destruction. His team's movements were fluid, a testament to the countless hours of training and the unspoken bond between them.

"Upstairs," Simon directed, his gaze meeting Lori's. There was no need for words—their brief shared history spoke volumes in that glance. She nodded, her face set in grim determination, and together they ascended the stairs.

Each step was a step closer to justice, to the end of a nightmare that had claimed too many innocent lives. Simon felt the burn in his muscles, the tightness in his chest—not from the physical exertion, but from the knowledge of what awaited them at the top.

"Ready," he whispered, not to his team, but to himself. This was it—the moment of truth. As they reached the landing, Simon knew whatever happened next, they would face it together. And that was all that mattered.

Jennifer, her face smeared with grime and resolve, swung her rifle with practiced ease, picking off a cartel enforcer attempting to jump out a window. "Not on my watch, asshole," she muttered under her breath, a feral grin slicing through the dirt on her face.

"Where did he come from?" Lori asked.

"I don't know, but I don't like it," Simon said. "We need someone here to watch our six. Jace, Maria, that will be you."

"Got it," they both replied.

Mark's breaths came out in controlled bursts as he led his team through the brush outside the compound on the north side. The night air was thick with no nocturnal animal sounds one would expect. The fierce battle between the two cartels and now their team entering the house had silenced the night.

"Watch your six!" he barked, his voice a gravelly whisper over the din of battle. His team moved with precision, covering each other's blind spots as they advanced.

Suddenly, a group of Los Zetas cartel members burst from a side passage, their retreat cut off by Mark's squad. The distance between them closed rapidly, too fast for comfort. There was no time for hesitation, instinct took over. Mark raised his weapon, sighting on the nearest target, but the cartel fighters were on them in an instant.

The fight became a maelstrom of violence. Mark grappled with a burly enforcer, his sweat-slicked skin slipping beneath his grasp. Mark drove his knee into his groin, eliciting a howl of pain before his elbow found the cartel member's throat. Beside him, his teammates engaged in their own desperate struggles, the sounds of hand-to-hand combat merging into a singular cacophony of fury.

It was in this chaos that fate turned its fickle hand. A glint of steel caught Mark's eye a moment too late. A blade arched through the darkness, finding a home in his abdomen, and then drove upwards. His body tensed, shock momentarily overriding the searing pain. He staggered back, his strength waning, even as his training urged her to keep fighting. With a final, defiant glare at his assailant, Mark Thompson fell, his blood staining the ground of a foreign land as he exhaled his last breath.

Mark's team outnumbered the Los Zetas group but did not have the experience to take them down quickly. After several minutes that seemed like hours to them, they overcame the experienced fighters. It was then they noticed Mark.

After checking his vitals, they moved his body to a tree and laid him beside it. Not knowing what else to do, they took up positions around him and waited. Johannsen took his comm unit and listened to the radio traffic. Knowing there was nothing they could do for Mark now, he decided not to interrupt the mission.

Inside the opulent main house, Simon and his team encountered the heart of the cartel's defense on the second floor. Bullets whizzed through the grand hallways, chipping away at the ornate decor—each ricochet a reminder of the peril they faced.

"Stay sharp!" Simon called out, ducking behind a marble column as gunfire erupted from ahead. His gaze flickered to Lori, who was crouched behind an antique credenza, her blue eyes wide but determined. They communicated silently, a nod enough to synchronize their next move.

They surged forward, room by room, clearing each space with methodical efficiency. But the cartel was relentless, their heavily armed members firing with a ferocity born of desperation.

"Simon! Room to your right!" Lori's Kentucky twang sliced through the chaos just as a spray of bullets tore past Simon's position.

"Got it!" he replied, pivoting to confront the threat. But another hail of gunfire followed, and amid the ear-splitting reports, a strangled cry cut through—a cry distinctly Lori's.

Turning back, Simon saw her clutching her side, a blossom of red spreading across her tactical gear. Adrenaline spiked through him as he laid down suppressive fire, giving him the precious seconds needed to reach her.

"Medic!" he roared into his comm unit, hoisting Lori into his arms. Her breaths were shallow, her face etched in pain, but she managed to grip his arm tightly. "Mama is down."

"Keep... keep going," she gasped, urging him not to stop.

"Like hell," Simon gritted out, carrying her with a protective ferocity. He could feel the wet warmth of her blood seeping through his gloves, a visceral reminder of the stakes they played for.

"Medic one, we need you at the main house, now!" Loran's voice crackled over the comm, urgency threading her tone. "Hold on Lori. Help is coming."

Loran's heart raced as she clutched her chest. Hearing Simon's gravelly voice, she exhaled a shaky sigh of relief. Her relief was short-lived, however, as she processed his words. "Roger that, Simon. Medic One Team, you're inbound to the house. The rest of you, hold your positions until we've secured the compound."

Loran's fingers trembled as she keyed the mic once more. "Rouge, do you copy?"

"Copy that, Loran," Rouge responded, her voice filled with adrenaline. "We're all clear here. No sign of Badge or Flyboy, though."

"Roger that, Rouge. Flyboy?"

"Copy, Loran," Flyboy's chipper voice came through the static. "We're good here. It's quiet... too quiet."

"Copy that. Badge, you there?"

The line crackled with static, but no response came. Loran's stomach dropped. "Badge, do you copy?"

Nothing.

"Loran, this is Johansson, Mark's team." The unfamiliar voice on the other end sent a shiver down Loran's spine. "We... we've got a situation."

"Mark?" Loran whispered, her voice trembling.

"I'm sorry, Loran," Johansson replied, his voice heavy with emotion. "Mark didn't make it. He... we were jumped by a group and all of us fighting, at the end we found him."

Tears welled in Loran's eyes, but she forced them back. "Roger that, Johansson. I'll get someone headed that way to bring him and the rest of y'all back. We'll finish this for him, I swear it."

"Roger that, Loran. We owe it to him."

"Copy that. Stay sharp out there, all of you. G-Man, did you copy, and can you confirm Mama's status?"

"I copy Badge is down. Mama was shot in the side and Jennifer and Jacob are with her now, but stable," Simon's voice crackled through the comm. "Needs medical attention ASAP, though. We're pushing ahead to take out Ortiz."

"Roger that, G-Man. Medic One Team, ETA?"

"ETA two minutes, Loran," the medic's voice came through loud and clear.

"Copy that, Medic One. G-Man, be careful in there. We've got your backs."

"Roger that, Smurfette. Flyboy, you good to move up?"

"Copy that, Simon. On my way."

As Simon sheltered Lori with his body, he could hear the distant calls of his teammates, confirming kills and securing rooms. They were close now, so close to ending this nightmare. But as he looked down at Lori's pale face, the cost had never felt so heavy.

"Jennifer, get over here now!" Simon yelled at her.

Jennifer came close and then noticed the wound on her mother's side. Tears came as she collapsed next to Lori. "Oh my God, oh my God," she broke down.

Simon took her by the shoulders and shook her until she focused on his face. "Jenn, you have to stay here and help her until the medic gets here. Do you understand?"

Jennifer nodded. "What do I do? Oh God!"

Simon took a bandana from his pocket and placed it on Lori's side. "Hold this right here and put a little pressure on it," he said as he took Jennifer's hands and pushed them onto Lori's side. Lori groaned.

"Medics are on the way, and Jacob will stay and cover you until they get here. Okay?"

Jennifer nodded again as she looked at her mother's pale face, tears falling from her eyes.

Simon surged forward, the weight of Lori's condition fueling his ferocity as he darted through the opulent corridors of Juan Ortiz's stronghold. The upstairs cleared, and they began looking for a safe room or something they had missed the first time on the first floor. Cartel members were still inside the house, but where were they hiding, and where was Juan Ortiz? The air was thick with gunpowder and desperation, punctuated by the staccato rhythm of gunfire and the thuds of fallen bodies.

"Room clear!" Ezekiel Yoder called out from the east wing.

"Copy that," Simon replied, pivoting on his heel as another pair of cartel thugs burst into the hallway, their eyes wild with fear and resolve. They raised their weapons, but Simon was faster. His Beretta 92F barked twice, and the first man crumpled without a sound. The second managed to squeeze off a round which went wide, before Simon's return fire caught him square in the chest, dropping him like a sack of stones.

"Found a basement, watching it," Ezekiel's voice crackled over the comm, methodical and calm despite the chaos.

"Watch your six, Zeke," Simon warned, reloading his weapon with practiced ease. He knew every second counted, they had to secure the house before Ortiz could slip away or worse, muster a counterattack.

Simon kicked down door after door, each room revealing more lavish excess—the spoils of a criminal empire built on blood and misery. But the rooms were empty now, save for the discarded weapons and the occasional groan of a wounded cartel member.

"Status?" Simon barked into the comm, moving towards the grand staircase at the heart of the mansion.

"Second floor still covered," Jacob responded, followed by a grunt as he presumably dispatched another threat.

"Good. I am going in the basement with Zeke. We stay in contact," Simon ordered, stepping over a shattered vase, its flowers strewn across the marble floor like a mockery of the violence surrounding them.

He descended the staircase, boots barely making a sound on the plush carpeting. At the bottom, Ezekiel was standing against the wall two steps up. He motioned Simon to listen by cupping his hand to his ear. Simon could hear the cartel members talking but could not make out what they were saying.

Simon counted down from five on his fingers, then jumped past Ezekiel to the floor of the basement, pistol at the ready. They were met with a hail of bullets, the remaining cartel members fighting with the frenzied energy of cornered animals.

"Cover!" Simon shouted, sliding behind a heavy oak desk that splintered under the onslaught. He peeked around the edge, squeezed off a few rounds, and ducked back as return fire chipped away at his makeshift shield.

Ezekiel, who had peeled off to the sides, disappearing into the shadows like a wraith, had found a heavy shelf to take cover behind.

Simon leaped out from cover, advancing with deadly precision. Two cartel members fell before they could react, their faces registering surprise even as they hit the ground.

Two shots sounded behind him where Ezekiel had been, and Simon turned with his pistol raised ready to fire when he saw Ezekiel come out. Simon followed his gaze and saw that Ezekiel had put two more cartel members down.

"Great work," Simon praised, though his mind was already racing ahead to the final confrontation. "Now, for Ortiz."

"Ortiz has to be here somewhere," Simon muttered, his blue eyes scanning the grandeur for anything out of place. "He wouldn't abandon his fortress easily."

"Maybe he's got a panic room," Ezekiel suggested, eyeing the walls critically.

"Let's find it," Simon said, determination hardening his jaw. He felt the weight of every life taken, every sacrifice made—it all led to this moment.

"Check everything," he continued, tapping on walls and examining fixtures. "He's here. I can feel it."

The search was meticulous, each member of the team methodically probing the architecture for hidden secrets. It was Ezekiel who found it—a barely discernible seam along the wall paneling.

"Here," Ezekiel called softly, pressing against the wood. With an almost imperceptible click, a section of the wall swung open, revealing a steel door.

"Jace, Maria, any charges left?" Simon asked.

"Yep, we have some," Maria said as she reached into her backpack.

Maria stepped up, planting a small charge on the door's lock. "Stand back," she warned, and moments later, the charge detonated with a muffled boom, the door swinging inward.

"Juan Ortiz," Simon called into the dimly lit room beyond, his voice steady. "Your reign of terror ends tonight."

Their guns raised, they crossed the threshold into the unknown, ready to face whatever lay on the other side. The stakes had never been higher, but Simon Wilson and his team were resolute. This was their fight, and they would see it through to the bitter end. However, the room was empty.

Checking the room, Maria found a rug that seemed a bit out of place. She moved it and it revealed a trap door for a tunnel.

"Fuck!" Simon yelled.

Loran glanced around the command center and then looked at her brothers, her heart pounding out of her chest. This op had gone south, fast. The medics had stopped Lori Hawkins from bleeding and were headed back with her, but now Mark was gone, and Flyboy was heading into the lion's den with Simon's team.

"Smurfette, do you copy? We will bring Mark and his team in," Rouge's voice cut through her thoughts.

"Copy that, Rouge. Flyboy's moving up with Simon's team. ETA two minutes for backup. Stay frosty, all of you."

"Roger that, Loran. We're on it. We'll bring them home, Mark included. Over."

With Mark's sacrifice weighing heavily on her shoulders, Loran keyed the mic one last time. "Roger that, Rouge. Smurfette out."

She pressed her back against the back of her chair, blinking away the stinging in her eyes. She couldn't afford to fall apart now. Mark's memory and the team's safety depended on it.

She wiped her eyes and glanced at the computer screen. "John, make a sweep back from the way you just came."

"Okay, did you see something?"

"I think so."

"Hold there," she replied.

"G-man, can you copy?"

"Go," was his short answer.

"I just got an infrared image that came from nowhere. It just popped up, it's about thirty yards to the north. Who do you want me to send to check it?"

"I'm going. Ortiz slipped out through a tunnel, it might be him. Flyboy, meet me at the north fence, and send the rest of your team into the house."

"Roger that."

"G-Man, the figure is moving slowly, but it looks like he is on the road. He will bypass us if he doesn't go into the brush," Loran spoke.

"We are moving fast. Defend yourself if you need to, but only if you need to, and keep me posted," Simon replied, and you could tell he was running fast.

John kept his drone on who everyone believed was Juan Ortiz. Alva had moved to Angie's team to provide coverage, and Frank was watching Simon and Jack. Once John's drone was able to see both parties, Loran said, "Frank, I can see 'em on both cameras. I want you to pick up the medics with yours." With that, Frank began to maneuver to where the medical team was located.

As the two parties drew closer to the command center, Loran picked up her rifle. At the same time, Rudy called over the comms that he was moving in as well to help Simon. Loran could see him on the camera as well and acknowledged him. Juan would be covered on three sides, and beyond the command center, three hundred yards away, was her Pa if he made it past them.

"Ortiz! It ends now," Simon spoke. They were close enough to the command center that Loran and her brothers could hear.

Ortiz stopped and turned to face Simon and Jack. "It is but two of you, and I am sure I can handle two gringos," Ortiz said in a conceited tone.

Just then, Loran racked her charging handle back on the AR-15. Ortiz heard it and snapped his head that way. On his other side, Rudy did the same, again causing Ortiz to look around.

Chapter 20

Simon's muscles tensed as he squared off against Ortiz, the air heavy with the imminent violence that hung between them like a tangible force. The humidity of Reynosa seemed to press in on all sides, suffocating as if even the weather conspired to add weight to every breath, every movement.

"End of the line, Ortiz," Simon spat, his voice low and venomous with the weight of promises to keep, scores to settle.

Ortiz just smirked, a cold, cruel twist of his lips. "You think you can stop me?" he taunted, circling Simon like a predator stalking its prey. But Simon wasn't prey — he was a hunter too, driven by memories of Mark's lifeless form and Jennifer's haunted eyes.

They clashed like thunder, fists meeting flesh in a symphony of violence. Simon's training manifested in each precise strike, each calculated block. His body moved with the honed instincts of a man who had made survival his art form. He was a CIA operative, not some brute force brawler, but today he channeled raw anger into his techniques, giving and taking hits that would down lesser men.

Ortiz, for all his vile deeds, was no slouch in combat. The cartel boss matched Simon move for move, his rage fueling an impressive display of brutality. They traded blows, their grunts and the sound of impact echoing through the stone-walled compound. Sweat mingled with blood, staining the opulent tiles beneath their feet.

"Mark didn't deserve what was done to him," Simon growled, managing to land a solid punch to Ortiz's jaw that sent the other man staggering back.

"Neither did Jennifer," he continued, throwing a combination of punches that pushed Ortiz back further. Every strike Simon landed was a catharsis, a release of the fury that had been festering inside him since this nightmare began.

The fight wore on, neither willing to relent, both seemingly immune to fatigue. But human limits were slowly encroaching, their movements grew less sharp, their breaths more ragged. Simon felt the burn in his muscles, the ache in his joints from where Ortiz had managed to land punishing hits.

It was a dance of destruction, two forces of nature colliding with the full force of their shared animosity. Simon noticed the slight falter in Ortiz's steps, the momentary lag in his response. It was all the opening he needed.

"Enough!" Simon roared, summoning the last reserves of his strength. With a surge of determination, he launched into a final, devastating assault, determined to put an end to Ortiz's reign of terror once and for all.

Simon's knuckles split open with the force of his blows, blood smearing across Ortiz's contorted face. The two men were locked in a primal struggle, their bodies slick with sweat and the desperation of their fight palpable in the stifled air of the opulent stronghold. With each punishing hit, Simon's rage crescendoed, fueled by every memory of pain Ortiz had inflicted on those he loved.

"Is this all you've got?" Ortiz spat out, his words slurred from the battering. He lunged forward, but his movements were labored, the toll of the battle evident in his slowing reactions.

"Mark... Jennifer..." Simon's voice was a guttural whisper, each name a mantra pushing him beyond human limits. He ducked under a wide swing from Ortiz, feeling the whoosh of air as it missed its mark. Then, with a burst of clarity amid the chaos, Simon saw his moment.

He seized Ortiz's head in a vice-like grip, his fingers digging into the cartel leader's greasy hair. There was a brief look of shock in Ortiz's eyes, a flicker of fear that satisfied the deep, dark part of Simon that hungered for retribution. With a swift twist powered by vengeance and loss, Simon felt the vertebrae give way, a sickening crunch filling the silent space between heartbeats.

Ortiz's body went limp, and as it began to crumple, Simon stumbled backward and was caught by Jack, his chest heaving. "For Mark," he breathed, watching as the life faded from the eyes of the man who had taken so much from them.

The skies above seemed to resonate with the gravity of the moment. Dark clouds had been gathering, unnoticed during the ferocity of their combat. A sudden, jagged bolt of lightning cleaved the air, striking Ortiz's lifeless form just as it hit the ground.

Simon, Loran, Jack, John, Frank, Alva, and Rudy stood rooted to the spot, their eyes wide at the spectacle unfolding before them. The bolt illuminated the scene with an otherworldly glow, and as it retreated, flames licked hungrily at Ortiz's body. The smell of ozone and charred flesh rose up, a macabre incense for the final act of retribution.

"Damn," whispered Jack, the scar on his jaw white against his tanned skin.

"Damn glad when I was struck it didn't do that to me," Simon said with a labored chuckle, then collapsed from Jack's arms to the ground in exhaustion, his eyes never leaving the fire-engulfed body of Juan Ortiz.

As they watched, the fire consumed Ortiz with unnatural fervor, leaving nothing but ash in its wake. The wind picked up, scattering the remains to the four corners of the compound as if even the earth refused to hold the memory of such evil.

"Poetic justice," Loran murmured, her indigo-tinged hands clenched into fists at her sides.

"Let's not stay here any longer than we need to," Frank said quietly, casting a sidelong glance at the others.

"Agreed," Simon managed, his voice hoarse. His eyes remained fixed on the blackened patch of ground where Ortiz had met his end. In that smoldering ruin lay the weight of their pain, the cost of their war, and perhaps, the hope that justice, however brutal, brought closure to the wounds that ran deep.

Simon stood amid the carnage, his breath ragged and his muscles aching from the fight. The scent of rain mixed with the acrid stench of scorched earth and flesh. His blue eyes, once alight with determination, now dimmed as he took in the toll of their victory. He blinked against the rain that began to fall, each drop seeming to wash away the remnants of the fire that had consumed Ortiz.

"Simon," Loran's voice was soft, but it cut through the chaos around them. She stood a few feet away, her slight figure tense and her face shadowed by grief. Her tinted skin looked almost ethereal in the gloomy light.

He turned toward her, acknowledging her presence with a nod. They didn't need words, their shared expression said enough about the cost of their battle.

"Simon, we need to check on Lori," Jack reminded him. "She needs help."

"Right." Simon's voice was hollow, the weight of leadership pressing down on him. He strode over to where Lori lay, cradled in Jennifer's arms. Jennifer's vibrant spirit was dampened by fear, her green eyes wide and troubled as she looked up at Simon for guidance.

Lori was pale, too still, a stark contrast to her usual lively demeanor. Blood seeped through the makeshift bandages, staining Jennifer's pants red. Simon's heart clenched at the sight. "Hang in there, Lori," he murmured, brushing a hand over her forehead.

Taking out his satellite phone, Simon dialed the secure line to Amanda Sawyer, the CIA Director who had become their lifeline throughout this harrowing mission. His fingers were steady, betraying none of the turmoil inside him.

"Director Sawyer, this is Wilson. We need an immediate evac at the Ortiz compound. Casualties and critical injuries. One KIA. Requesting medevac to Wilford Hall," he said, the urgency clear in his tone.

"Understood, Wilson. Coordinates received. Helo enroute. ETA fifteen minutes, I have been holding them close, just for this call. Hold your position," Amanda's voice crackled over the line.

"Copy that. We'll be ready," he replied before hanging up.

Simon returned to Lori's side, crouching down beside her. He met Jennifer's gaze, trying to offer some semblance of reassurance. But what could he say? That everything would be alright? The lie tasted bitter in his mouth.

"Help's on the way," he managed instead, his voice roughened by emotion. "Just hold on a little longer.

"Jennifer nodded, biting back tears. "We're not leaving you, Mom," she whispered fiercely to Lori.

The rain intensified, drenching them all, as if nature itself mourned the loss and pain they had suffered. Simon watched as Jack gently lifted Mark's lifeless body, preparing to carry their fallen comrade home. The sight struck a chord deep within him, the finality of death juxtaposed with the relentless will to survive.

"Let's get everyone under cover," Simon instructed, his gaze sweeping over the exhausted faces of his team. They had won, but the hollow victory echoed with the sounds of their wounded hearts.

The distant thump of helicopter blades stirred hope within him—a promise of rescue and respite. Yet as he waited, holding Lori's hand and sheltering Jennifer with his body, Simon couldn't shake the feeling that things would never be the same again. The road to healing would be long, and the shadows of their ordeal would linger like ghosts in the corners of their minds.

But for now, they were alive. And that had to be enough.

Simon stood sentinel as the distant rumble of the approaching helicopter mingled with the cacophony of raindrops pelting the scorched earth. His eyes, weary with the weight of the day's losses, scanned the horizon until they rested on a figure moving toward them—Emilia Salgado.

Her arrival was like that of an avenging angel, albeit one who bore her own scars from battle. Emilia leaned heavily on her cane, her gait uneven but determined, as she closed the gap between herself, and the battered group huddled beneath the shelter of a tattered awning.

"Simon," she called out, her voice carrying the unmistakable timbre of command softened by a raw edge of gratitude. He met her halfway, noting the way her green eyes blazed with a fire that not even her injuries could dampen.

"Emilia," he acknowledged, his own voice betraying none of the turmoil that churned within him.

One by one, she embraced each member of the team. When Emilia reached Lori, her arms wrapped around the injured woman with a tenderness that belied her fierce exterior. "Thank you," she whispered, pressing a gentle kiss to Lori's cheek.

"Couldn't have done it without everyone here," Lori managed through gritted teeth, her blue eyes reflecting pain and resolve.

Jennifer received a hug that seemed to imbue her with strength, the bond of their shared ordeal palpable in the air. "Your courage is beyond words," Emilia said, pride lacing her tone.

"Learned from the best," Jennifer replied with a wry smile, looking down at her mom, trying to mask her exhaustion.

Loran, slight and shadowed, accepted Emilia's embrace with a quiet nod. "You've given us all something back that we thought was lost," Emilia told her, recognizing the deep-seated resilience in the young woman's gaze.

"Reckon we just did what needed to be done," Loran answered in her slow southern drawl, her tinted skin glistening with rain.

Finally, Jack, standing tall and unyielding despite the chaos and loss of his brother, received a firm handshake followed by a familial peck on the cheek. His scarred jawline tightened as he locked eyes with Emilia. "The fight goes on, but this battle is over," he stated, a silent promise passing between them.

"Is, pero for now, we breathe," Emilia conceded, allowing herself a moment of reprieve.

Before she moved to Mark's body, Emilia's gaze caught Simon's once more, and in that brief exchange, a world of mutual respect was conveyed. She approached the fallen hero, her prayer whispered into the storm, her fingers tracing the sign of the cross with reverence and sorrow.

The chopper's blades cut through the tension of the gathering, signaling it was time to move. With practiced efficiency, Simon, John, Frank, Alva, Rudy, and Greg converged to carry Lori and Mark to the waiting aircraft. Simon felt the familiar ache of muscles pushed to their limits, but the burden was one he shouldered willingly.

"Careful with her," Simon instructed as they lifted Lori onto a stretcher. Her face contorted momentarily with discomfort, but she nodded her thanks.

"Let's get you home," Jennifer said softly, her hand squeezing her mother's before turning to help guide the stretcher.

With Mark's body wrapped in a makeshift shroud, the men maneuvered with grim deference. The silence that enveloped them spoke volumes, honor for a comrade whose laughter would no longer grace their ears.

As the helicopter swallowed them whole, Simon took one last look at the desolate landscape, the remnants of destruction blurred by the relentless downpour. He helped secure the stretchers, then found a seat beside Jennifer, his gaze lingering on her profile.

"Ready?" Jack asked, settling into the seat opposite him with a heavy sigh.

"Let's go home," Simon affirmed, feeling the craft lurch beneath them as they ascended into the turbulent sky. He had placed Wayne and Jackie in charge of cleanup and intel gathering, especially anything that could lead back to the core team. Weapons were to be destroyed using the same techniques that had been used in Desert Storm.

"When you're ready for extraction, call Amanda. She will send you a ride home," Simon told him as he handed Jackie the satellite phone. She took it with a nod of understanding.

The chopper clawed its way through the clouds, leaving behind a world forever altered by violence and valor. As Reynosa dwindled below, Simon allowed himself a moment to close his eyes against the sting of lingering rain—or perhaps something more.

The rhythmic thud of the helicopter blades beat in time with Simon's racing heart as the aircraft cut through the darkening sky. He sat rigid, his hands clenched on his thighs, every muscle tensed against the torrent of emotions threatening to surface. The mission was over, but at what price? The faces of his fallen comrades haunted him, and Mark's still form under the shroud was a silent testament to the cost of their victory.

Simon's blue eyes, usually sharp as a hawk's, now glistened with a sheen of unshed tears. He stared out the window into the abyss of the stormy night, the darkness echoing the turmoil within. With each breath, he tried to push away the creeping despair. They had won, yes, but he couldn't shake the feeling of loss that clung to him like a second skin.

"Simon?" Jennifer's voice, tinged with her Kentucky accent, cut through his reverie. Her green eyes sought his, brimming with a mixture of relief and sorrow.

"Hey," Simon managed, his gruff voice barely above a whisper. "You okay?"

Jennifer nodded slowly, though her gaze lingered on the shrouded figure on the floor. "I should be asking you that," she replied softly.

"Occupational hazard," he said with a wry twist of his lips that didn't reach his eyes. "We did good today, Jen. Your mom... she's gonna be alright."

"I know," Jennifer whispered, leaning against the cool metal wall of the helicopter. "But Mark..."

Silence fell between them, heavy and oppressive. Simon's throat constricted as he thought about the jovial man who would never again share in their victories or console them in defeat.

"Sorry doesn't even begin to cover it," Simon finally murmured, his voice rough with emotion.

"None of this is your fault," Jennifer reassured him, placing a gentle hand on his arm. "You saved us, Simon. You saved me and my mom."

"Didn't save everyone," he countered, his chin dipping as a single tear betrayed him, tracing a path down his stubbled cheek.

"Can't save everyone," Jennifer corrected quietly. "But you try. And that's more than most."

Simon turned his gaze to Lori, lying on the stretcher, pale and fragile-looking, yet her spirit remained unbroken. Her blond hair framed her face like a halo in the dim light, and her blue eyes met his with an understanding that needed no words.

"Hey, Lori," he said softly, moving to sit by her side.

"Simon," Lori responded, her voice weak but filled with warmth. "Thank you. For everything."

"Nothing to thank me for," he replied gruffly. "Just doing my job."

"More than that," she insisted. "You kept your promise. You brought her back to me." She gestured towards Jennifer, a mother's pride evident in her expression.

"Promises are meant to be kept," Simon said, the corner of his mouth twitching in a semblance of a smile.

Loran, seated across from them, her slight indigo features set in a mask of contemplation, broke her silence. "This here fight, it's been a long one," she drawled in her slow southern mountain dialect. "Reckon we all lost a piece of ourselves along the way."

"Too true," Simon agreed, glancing at Loran's resolute face.

"Yet here we still stand," Loran continued, her voice firm. "Ortiz won't be harming no more, thanks to y'all."

"Thanks to us all," Simon corrected gently, knowing full well the part Loran had played.

"Y'all need to heal up now," Loran stated, her tone leaving no room for argument. "Body and soul."

"Body and soul," Simon echoed, a ghost of resolve returning to his voice.

Simon moved across from Jack, who was staring into nothingness. "I am sorry, Jack."

Jack turned back to Simon, his eyes showing all of his emotions at once. "Simon, Mark died doing a good thing. It could have been you, me, or any one of us," he gestured at those seated nearby. "But God himself came and took my brother. He might have used an asshole to do it, but God needed some more Law and Order in heaven, and Mark was the one he needed. Don't be sorry, it is not on you. I don't and will never blame you, so don't go blaming yourself. Ya hear?"

Simon nodded, knowing that was easier said than done, but Jack's words did help him deep down. Jack leaned forward as if to tell Simon something, so Simon did the same. Jack grabbed him and held him in a hug, not a bro hug, but one of love and respect. Simon healed a bit more at that show of kindness.

As the helicopter flew onward, carrying them away from the carnage beneath, Simon's thoughts turned inward once more. He pondered the jagged line between right and wrong, the lives taken, and the ones saved. The weight of leadership bore down on him, and yet, in the midst of the storm, a fragile sense of hope began to take root. Maybe they could find peace after all. Maybe they could learn to live with the scars.

The deep hum of the engines filled the cabin, a lullaby for warriors seeking solace in the skies. Simon's head leaned against the cold window, the silent tears finally flowing free, washing away the remnants of battle, if only for a moment.

The helicopter's blades sliced through the air with an urgent whine, stirring up a tempest of dust and debris as it settled onto the helipad at Wilford Hall. Medics scrambled forward like a well-oiled machine, their movements precise amidst the chaos. Simon Wilson, his muscles still tense from combat, jumped out before the blades had fully stopped, his protective instincts honed in on Lori.

"Let's move, people!" he shouted, more to vent the coiling stress than to hurry the professionals who were already fast at work.

Lori was pale, her features drawn tight with pain, but she managed a weak smile when her gaze met Simon's. "Hey there," she whispered through gritted teeth, her Kentucky accent making the words a soft melody despite the agony behind them.

"Hey yourself," Simon replied, brushing a lock of blond hair from her forehead. He towered over the gurney, his eyes scanning every action the medics took, ensuring nothing was missed. His heart raced, not just from the adrenaline that still pumped through his veins, but from the fear of losing her.

As they wheeled Lori toward surgery, Simon kept pace beside her, his hand finding hers and gripping it tightly. The corridors of Wilford Hall were a blur—a stark contrast to the vibrant and violent memories that played in his mind's eye. Images of the battle, the loss of Mark, and the burning hatred in Ortiz's eyes just before the fatal snap of his neck haunted him.

"Simon," Lori murmured, drawing his focus back. "You did what you had to do."

Her words should've offered comfort, but as she disappeared behind the double doors of the operating room, they left him hollow instead. He stood there for a moment, alone, as the bustle of the hospital moved around him.

What had he become in this quest for justice? A killer, a savior, or something far murkier? With each life he took, he felt a piece of his soul shear away. The morality of his actions—the necessity of violence to prevent further suffering—it was a calculus that never quite balanced. The faces of those he'd saved flickered in his mind, followed closely by the specters of those he couldn't reach in time.

Pain lanced through his body, a mere echo of the emotional agony that ravaged his mind. He had fought to save lives, but at what cost? He thought of Jennifer's relief, Loran's gratitude, and Lori's unwavering trust, and yet he couldn't shake the feeling that he'd crossed lines no man should ever approach.

"Damn it," he muttered under his breath, his voice a low growl that went unnoticed in the sterile hallway. Anger flared hot within him—anger at the world that necessitated such brutality, at the cartel for their unforgivable crimes, and at himself for being the instrument of necessary violence.

"Simon?" A nurse's voice cut through the cacophony of his thoughts. "Are you alright?"

He looked at her, really looked, and saw concern etched into the lines of her face. "Yeah," he lied smoothly, the mask of composure sliding back into place. "Just... thinking about a friend."

"Take care of yourself too. We need to look at those wounds. Your hands look like they've been put through a grinder and your face, well let's just say you won't win any beauty pageants," she advised gently.

Simon nodded absentmindedly, knowing full well that self-care was a luxury he couldn't afford—not yet, not while the job remained unfinished, the wounds unhealed, and the future uncertain. The weight of his choices lay heavy upon him, and as he leaned against the cool wall of the hospital, he understood that healing would be a battle of its own—one he wasn't sure he was ready to face.

"I will get checked as soon as Lori comes out of surgery." The nurse looked at him sideways and he grinned, even that felt good. "I promise."

Simon's gaze lingered on the sterile white doors that had swallowed Lori just moments ago. They seemed to stand as a barrier between the world of the living and the uncertain future that lay beyond them. He felt a hand gently touch his arm, and he turned to find Loran standing beside him, her slight features etched with concern.

"Simon, we're all feelin' this heavy-like. But we gotta hold on together, ya hear?" Loran said, her slow southern drawl carrying a comforting warmth.

Jennifer, standing close by, nodded in agreement, her green eyes brimming with unshed tears. The young woman clasped her hands tightly as if trying to hold herself together. "Mom's strong," she whispered, more to herself than anyone else.

"Your ma's a fighter, Jen," Simon said, managing a strained smile. His blue eyes met Jennifer's, both reflecting the same mix of hope and fear.

Loran stepped closer, her presence somehow grounding despite her small frame. She reached out her other hand to Jennifer, drawing the girl into a gentle embrace. "We're family now. Nothin' gonna change that."

Jennifer leaned into the hug, allowing herself a moment of vulnerability. Simon watched, the tightness in his chest easing ever so slightly at the sight of their shared strength.

Before any of them could say more, the sound of footsteps echoed through the hall. Amanda Sawyer, clad in her usual sharp attire, approached with purpose. Her face softened as she took in the trio, her eyes settling on Simon last.

"Simon, you've done well, despite the high stakes. We're here for you—all of you," Amanda said, her voice authoritative yet tinged with empathy.

"Thanks, Amanda," Simon replied, his voice rough with emotion. "It was hell out there. And it's not quite over yet."

Amanda nodded, understanding the weight of his words. "We'll debrief fully once everyone is safe, but for now, let's focus on getting through this moment. I've arranged for the best care for Lori, and as for the rest of the team... We'll take care of each other. That's what families do."

"Family," Simon repeated, tasting the word like it was something new. It was a foreign concept to the lone wolf inside him, but standing here, surrounded by those who'd been through the fire with him, it felt right.

"Exactly," Amanda affirmed. "Now, let's wait for Lori. Together."

They settled into an uneasy silence, each lost in their thoughts yet bound by the shared experience of the past harrowing days. Simon leaned back against the wall, allowing himself to feel the support of those around him, the comfort of their presence a balm against the storm raging within.

The fight was over, but the healing was just beginning.

Amanda Sawyer's fingers danced over her phone with practiced urgency, the soft click-clacking a stark contrast to the somber atmosphere of the room. Simon Wilson watched from a distance, his blue eyes trailing her every move, a silent storm brewing within their depths. He couldn't shake off the weight that clung to his broad shoulders like a lead cloak.

"Transport is arranged," Amanda announced, breaking the silence that had fallen over them. "Mark's body will be flown to Nashville and then taken by road to Hart County." Her voice was steady, a beacon in the fog of grief that clouded the air.

"Thank you," Simon said, the words scraping out of him like gravel. He stood, muscles tensing as he prepared himself for what was to come.

The journey to Nashville International Airport was a blur, a series of motions and procedures carried out with military precision but devoid of feeling. It wasn't until they arrived and Jack saw the contingent of Sheriff Deputies waiting that the gravity of the situation hit him full force.

Sheriff Jasper Higgins, who took over after Mark retired, stood tall among his men, his posture radiating authority while his eyes told a different story—one of loss and shared pain. Beside him, Angie Winn, her short hair framing her determined face etched with sorrow and resolution, offered a nod of solidarity that spoke volumes.

The flag-draped coffin was carefully transferred to the vehicle, a somber parade that moved with quiet dignity through the airport tarmac. Jack and Angie joined the escort, their presence a silent vow to see Mark home.

As the procession departed, the remaining team members found themselves huddled together outside the hangar, an unspoken need to share and remember drawing them close. They formed a circle, each face a map of the battles fought and the scars earned, both visible and hidden.

Simon and his "family" waited in the waiting room for the surgery to be over. Jennifer had moved to sit next to him and leaned her head on his shoulder.

"You holding up okay, Jenn?" Simon whispered to her.

For a moment she didn't answer, then began to sob. "I'm scared, Simon. She's hurt, and I don't know if she's gonna be okay." Jennifer replied, then turned and threw her arms around his neck and let the tears flow.

The others sat in silence, watching as the two bonded over this dreadful wait. Their thoughts were on what they could do to help ease the pain and fear. Loran took the lead.

Loran chuckled, his eyes gleaming with mischief. "Hey Jennifer, you remember when Mark pulled that epic prank on Jack? He rigged his back door with a bucket of water and when Jack opened it, the bucket of water drenched him!"

Jennifer, pulling herself up from Simon's shoulder and wiping tears, chimed in, joining Loran's laughter. "I remember that and thought Jack was gonna kill us for sure. We were there for a cookout."

The chuckles grew, each team member adding their own tale of Mark's antics, the fabric of his life woven through with threads of humor, bravery, and an undeniable zest for life. Simon remained quiet, listening, absorbing the stories that brought Mark back, if only for a moment.

As the laughter died down, a comfortable silence settled among them. The shared memories seemed to ease the sharp edges of their loss, wrapping them in a collective embrace of camaraderie and understanding. Amid their sorrow, they found strength in each other—the kind of strength that could only be forged in the fires of adversity.

Simon finally spoke, his voice low and rough with emotion. "He lived more in his years than most do in a lifetime." He paused, looking around at the faces of his team, seeing the echo of his own pain reflected back at him. "We should all be so lucky."

Nods of agreement met his statement, a silent pact made to honor their fallen brother not just with mourning, but with living—truly living. Simon felt the first stirrings of peace since the chaos began. It was faint, like the distant promise of dawn after the longest night, but it was there, a sign that perhaps, in time, they would all find their way through the darkness.

Finally, the doors to the operating suite opened and Dr. Emma Jenkins came out. The group as one stood to greet her and get the news of Lori's condition.

"Who is next of kin?" Dr. Jenkins asked.

"I am, but we all need to know," Jennifer responded.

"The bullet was lodged in pretty good, didn't hit anything vital, but she lost a lot of blood. I was able to remove the bullet and repair some of the damage but had to remove her appendix as it was damaged. It was a good thing we started when we did, she might not have made it otherwise. She is doing good now. We gave her blood to make up for what she lost and stitched her up. She is in recovery now and you can go back in about two hours. Go two at a time and don't stay longer than five minutes. Got it? Now what questions do you have?"

Jennifer answered with the one question they all wanted to know to put this behind them: "When can we take her home?"

Dr. Jenkins chuckled. "It will be at least a week."

"Thanks, Doc," Simon said as they all gathered into a group hug as relief washed over them. Again Jennifer was in tears, but these were happy tears.

Amanda made arrangements to get Loran back home when she returned to DC the following morning. Simon and Jennifer stayed at the hospital continuously for the next week, only stepping out briefly to shower. They took turns sleeping, eating, and keeping vigilant watch over Lori day and night.

Simon stood alone on the tarmac as the last glimmers of twilight faded, casting long shadows across the pavement. The air was heavy with the scent of jet fuel and the quiet murmur of distant conversations. He watched as the ground crew busied themselves with their chores, a silent ballet of efficiency and purpose.

He tucked his hands into the pockets of his worn leather jacket, feeling the weight of the day settle upon his shoulders. The mission had taken its toll, not just in flesh and blood but in the very essence of their spirits. They had clawed victory from the jaws of defeat, but it was a victory marred by loss— loss that would linger long after the physical wounds had healed.

"Simon?" Lori's voice, gentle yet laden with the fatigue of recent events, pulled him from his thoughts. She approached, leaning slightly on Jennifer for support, her blue eyes searching his face.

"Hey," he replied, forcing a half-smile that didn't quite reach his eyes.

"Thinking about the road ahead?" Jennifer asked, her green eyes reflecting a maturity beyond her years—a maturity forged in the crucible of terror and resolve.

"Something like that," Simon admitted. His gaze drifted toward the darkening horizon, where stars were beginning to prick the velvet sky. "We've got a lot of healing to do, a lot of rebuilding."

Lori nodded, her blond hair catching the last light. "We'll get there, Simon. Together."

"Right. Together," Simon echoed, allowing the word to resonate within him. The unity they'd found in the face of adversity was more than just a temporary alliance, it was the foundation upon which they could begin anew.

"Mark would want us to keep pushing forward, you know," Jennifer said softly, her voice tinged with the sorrow of loss but also the steel of determination.

"I know," Simon's reply was barely audible, a whisper carried away on the evening breeze.

They fell into silence again, each lost in personal reflection until a faint rumble announced the arrival of the transport that would take them back to Hart County. It was time to leave the battle behind and face the challenges of the ordinary world— a world that now seemed alien and distant.

As they boarded the aircraft, Simon felt a subtle shift within himself. The raw edges of pain were still there, but so too was a burgeoning sense of hope, a stubborn resilience that refused to be extinguished. They had survived the darkest moments of their lives, and in doing so, had discovered an inner strength that would guide them through whatever lay ahead.

"Home," Lori murmured as the engines roared to life, the word hanging in the air like a promise.

"Home," Simon affirmed, his heart echoing the sentiment. With one last look at the retreating landscape, he settled into his seat beside the two women he had learned to love, each in a different way—his family—and turned his face toward the

future, knowing that no matter what it held, they would face it
together.

Chapter 21

As the trio of Simon, Lori, and Jennifer crested the rise that looked out over Hart County, a tableau of renewal unfolded before their eyes. FEMA trailers were dotted around like giant metal caterpillars, volunteers swarming over half-rebuilt structures. The hum of generators and the rhythmic thud of hammers filled the air, stitching together the fabric of a community on the mend.

"Look at this place," Lori whispered, her blue eyes wide as saucers. She stood beside the rugged frame of Simon, her hand finding his in an instinctive search for reassurance. "It's really happening."

"Didn't doubt it for a second," Simon replied gruffly, squeezing her hand back. His gaze swept the scene, the trained eye of a protector scanning for any sign of trouble amidst the bustle of reconstruction.

"We're really home," Jennifer said, her voice tinged with awe. Her athletic frame, poised for action even in this moment of peace, seemed to resonate with the vibrancy of the town's rebirth.

"Home and safe," Lori affirmed, her accent coloring the words with warmth despite the underlying anxiety that still clung to her like a shadow.

"Let's go see everyone." Jennifer tugged at their hands, eager to immerse herself in the community spirit that had always been the heartbeat of Hart County.

They walked together toward the cave entrance on the main street of Horse Cave where the celebration was already in full swing. Banners streamed across the street, proclaiming victory and resilience, while tables groaned under the weight of potluck dishes brought by the townsfolk.

"Simon! Lori!" The crowd parted as Ezekiel Yoder approached, his Amish attire a stark contrast against the casual jeans and T-shirts of the others. His steady gaze and gentle smile embraced them. "Your courage has stitched hope into the very soul of our town."

"Couldn't have done it without everyone's support, especially yours," Simon murmured, uncomfortable with the praise but unable to deny the truth in Ezekiel's words.

"And folks like Jack and Greg," Lori added, glancing over at the two men who were sharing a laugh near the barbecue grill. Both bore the marks of battle—Jack with his authoritative air and gray-flecked hair, Greg with his easy grin against his blue-tinted face, and watchful eyes.

"Let's not forget Jacob, Loran and her brothers," Jennifer chimed in, ever inclusive. "They've been so much part of the rescue and killing of that bastard."

The group looked over the battered but rejuvenating town as the work continued as well as the preparations for the homecoming party.

"Truly, a community effort," Jacob agreed, joining the group. His towering frame and calloused hands spoke volumes about his dedication to rebuilding, his modesty apparent even in this celebratory atmosphere.

As the homecoming festivities progressed, the air filled with stories of bravery and close calls, laughter mingling with tears as they remembered those who were placed in peril along with the fallen friend to each. No one person stood above another; this victory belonged to them all.

"Attention everyone. Please can I have some silence?" Mayor Sandy Kurry spoke in his "official" voice to get everyone's attention. "I would like everyone to welcome Simon Wilson to the mic please."

Simon, surprised to be called upon, and not really a public speaker, was embarrassed by the applause that erupted when his name was called. He attempted to wave off the request, but found himself being pushed towards the podium the mayor was behind.

"Here's to Hart County," Simon finally said, his voice carrying over the crowd. "To its people, its strength, and its future."

Glasses raised, cheers erupted, and for a moment, the weight of the past lifted, carried away on the wings of shared resolve and the promise of tomorrow.

The sun dipped lower in the sky, casting a warm golden hue over the gathering crowd as Simon stepped forward, his broad shoulders squared. Beside him, Loran stood slightly back, her slight indigo tint barely visible in the fading light. She seemed almost ethereal, a stark contrast to Simon's solid presence.

"Friends," Simon began, his voice resonating with quiet authority that demanded attention. "We stand here today, hearts heavy but heads held high. We've lost much, but we've also reclaimed what is ours—our loved ones, our freedom, our safety, and our way of life."

His piercing blue eyes scanned the faces before him, each one marked by the trials they'd endured. "But none of this would have been possible without the courage of those who stood firm against the darkness that sought to suffocate our town. You among us here tonight, those that went with me to fight the battles in Mexico and those towns in between."

A hush fell upon the group as Simon paused, gathering his thoughts. "One man, in particular, embodied the spirit of Hart County in its purest form." He turned slightly, nodding towards Loran, inviting her into his space, and placing a calming hand around her waist.

"Mark Thompson," Loran's voice was soft, a slow southern drawl that carried on the evening air. "He was more than our sheriff. He was a son of this soil, a beacon of hope when shadows crept too close to home."

"Mark gave us something priceless," Simon added, leaning closer to Loran in silent solidarity. "He gave us time—time to fight back, time to save our loved ones. And though fear may have gnawed at him, he never showed it or let it consume his duty."

"His sacrifice will be etched in our memories, a reminder of what one person's resolve can achieve," Loran concluded, her words wrapping around the crowd like a comforting shawl.

"Let us honor him with a moment of silence," Simon said, bowing his head.

As if guided by a single heart, the townspeople closed their eyes, and all the men removed their hats, the only sounds were the gentle rustle of leaves and distant bird calls. Tears traced lines down weathered cheeks and young faces alike, each drop a testament to the collective loss and love for the man they mourned.

When the silence at last gave way to the night's chorus, an undercurrent of excitement began to ripple through the crowd. Simon lifted his gaze, seeing a new fire kindling in the eyes around him.

"Seems we've caught the attention of some mighty high places," Jack Thompson, brother of the late sheriff, announced with a mixture of pride and disbelief. "The Vice President's coming to Horse Cave. I just got the call from up in Munfordville."

Murmurs of astonishment swelled into animated chatter as the news spread like wildfire. Volunteers hustled, clearing spaces and straightening banners, while others set about preparing a welcome fit for a dignitary.

"Never thought I'd see the day," Lori said, her voice tinged with amusement as she sidled up to Simon.

"Me neither," Simon replied, his tone laced with skepticism but softened by the spark in Lori's eyes. "Guess we're full of surprises here in Hart County."

"Best get ready to roll out the red carpet, then," Jennifer quipped, her previous fears momentarily forgotten in the swell of anticipation.

"Indeed," Simon nodded, a wry smile playing on his lips. "Let's show them what this small community can do."

The mayor and his staff were hustling about to make everything just right. Even for a small town where the mayor might have also been a banker or even an undertaker, politics was politics.

The sun hung low in the sky, casting a golden hue over Hart County as its residents gathered on the street, a sense of anticipation buzzing through the air. Amidst the hum of conversation and the clank of folding chairs being set up,

Simon stood with his arms crossed, watching the townspeople with a half-smile.

"Look at all this," Lori said, her eyes gleaming with excitement as she clutched Jennifer's hand. "Can you believe it? The Vice President, here!"

Jennifer bounced on the balls of her feet, her vibrant energy infectious. "Mom, we're like celebrities now!"

Simon chuckled dryly, the skepticism barely concealed behind his blue eyes. "Let's not get ahead of ourselves. It's an election year; they're just looking for photo ops."

"Maybe so," Lori conceded, her Kentucky accent coloring each word, "but it sure feels nice to be recognized."

"Doesn't hurt," Simon admitted, his gaze wandering over the bustling scene before them.

As if on cue, the distant wail of sirens heralded the approach of the Vice President's motorcade. A murmur rippled through the crowd, growing into applause as sleek black vehicles slid into view. Secret Service agents flanked the cars, their eyes scanning the surroundings with practiced vigilance.

"Here we go," Jack murmured from beside Simon, his stance alert.

The Vice President stepped out of the limousine, waving to the cheering crowd. Their entourage maintained a close perimeter as they made their way towards the makeshift stage.

"Simon Wilson, Lori Hawkins, Jennifer Hawkins, Loran Smith, and Jack Thompson," an aide called out. "The Vice President will see you now."

Lori squeezed Jennifer's shoulder, sharing a quick, proud smile before they followed Simon toward the private meeting area.

"Mr. Vice President," Simon greeted, shaking hands with the nation's second-in-command.

"Please, call me Ted," the Vice President replied with a practiced smile, acknowledging each member of the group.

"I've heard a great deal about how your operation ended from Amanda Sawyer. You've done your country a service."

"Thank you, sir," Lori said.

Jennifer nodded, her green eyes wide.

"Y'all did what needed doin' by supporting us with equipment, aircraft, analysts, and especially those drones, and we're mighty grateful," Loran added, her drawl thick.

"Tell me everything," the Vice President urged, gesturing for them to sit.

They recounted the details of their mission, from the rescue operations to the final confrontation that dismantled the Ortiz Cartel's stronghold. Simon spoke with measured confidence, while Lori's narrative was laced with the perspective of a mother who had fought for her daughter's safety.

Simon stood with casual ease, his muscular frame relaxed despite the Vice President's keen gaze.

"Mr. Vice President, Ted," Simon began, "the operation is complete. The Ortiz Cartel has been dismantled, the threat to Hart County—and indeed, to American soil—has been neutralized."

The Vice President nodded. "Your confidence speaks volumes, Mr. Wilson. We are all indebted to your courage and your unyielding commitment to this cause. Your dedication to duty is truly commendable."

"Thank you, sir," Simon replied, his blue eyes scrutinizing.

"Remarkable," the Vice President commented once they finished. "The administration wants to ensure Hart County receives the support it needs to continue rebuilding."

"Appreciate that, sir," Jack said with a nod.

"Your acknowledgment means a lot to us," Lori added softly.

"Indeed," Simon agreed. "Our town has shown its resilience."

"Resilience that won't be forgotten," the Vice President assured, rising. "Now, let's join the celebration. You folks are the heroes today."

As they emerged, the townspeople erupted into cheers, their applause washing over the group. For a moment, Simon allowed himself to bask in the glow of their achievement, the politics momentarily eclipsed by pride in their shared victory.

Simon found Lori standing alone for a moment in the burgeoning twilight after he had been ambushed again by Sandy Kurry. She was leaning slightly against the wall, her blond hair catching the rays of the moonlight, and her once tentative movements now more certain as her physical wounds healed.

"Hey," Simon greeted her, his voice losing the edge it held in front of the Vice President.

"Hi," Lori responded, her smile genuine, her blue eyes reflecting a similar sense of relief and introspection.

They stood together in silence, Simon moved behind Lori and wrapped his arms around her waist, resting them on her stomach, the distant sounds of the townspeople's celebrations a soft backdrop to their private reverie. It was a welcome reprieve from the intensity of the past weeks, a moment to breathe and simply be.

"Simon," Lori started hesitantly, her gaze fixed on him with an earnestness that spoke volumes. "What happened in Reynosa... it changed everything. For me, for Jennifer. For us."

He nodded, understanding implicitly the depth of what she meant. "I know, Lori. And I've been thinking—about us. We've been through hell and back, but we came out the other side. Together."

She leaned in closer, her presence a warmth he hadn't realized he'd needed. "Do we dare try again?" she asked softly, the vulnerability in her voice mirroring the uncertainty that flickered in her gaze.

"Nothing worth having comes without risk," Simon said, turning her to face him and gently cupping her cheek with his hand. "I want to reestablish what we had before... before all this madness and our priorities had to be switched. I want to see where this connection can take us."

Lori leaned into his touch, her eyes closing briefly as if savoring the contact. "Yes," she whispered, the single word carrying the weight of a promise, a hope for the future they could build together.

"Then let's start now," Simon said firmly, resolute in his decision. A slow smile spread across Lori's face, one that matched the determination in Simon's eyes.

Simon and Lori walked back toward the celebration, their hands intertwined, their steps light with the anticipation of a new beginning.

As night fell over Hart County, Simon's cabin became an enclave of soft shadows and whispered promises. The flicker of the fireplace cast an amber glow across Lori's face, illuminating her features as she moved towards him. There was a quiet strength in her stride, a silent testimony to the battles they had endured.

"Are you sure you're okay?" Simon's voice was low, tinged with concern as he watched her approach.

"Never better," Lori replied, her Kentucky accent wrapping around the words like a comforting blanket. "The pain's just a memory now."

Their eyes locked, a myriad of unspoken thoughts passing between them. In that gaze, there was an understanding that transcended words—the acknowledgment of shared trauma, the recognition of mutual desire.

Simon reached out, his fingers tracing the line of her jaw before slipping behind her neck to draw her closer. Their lips met, softly at first—a tentative exploration that soon deepened into urgency. Clothes were shed in a quiet symphony of rustling fabrics, each piece discarded symbolizing the shedding of fears and insecurities they both carried.

In the glow of the fire, their bodies came together, a tangle of limbs and whispered endearments. Lori arched beneath him, her blond hair fanning out across the pillow as Simon worshipped her with his mouth and hands. Every touch was a reassurance, every kiss a promise to heal the wounds of the past.

"Simon..." Lori gasped his name as he moved within her, her nails digging into his back, urging him on. He responded with a low growl, his movements becoming more insistent, driven by a primal need to claim and be claimed.

They found their release in each other's arms, a crescendo of passion that left them breathless and entwined. As the fire crackled its approval, they lay there, basking in the afterglow, finding solace in the warmth of their joined bodies.

Weeks passed like this, a tender dance of rediscovery and rebuilding. Simon and Lori took long walks, hand in hand, through the verdant timbers surrounding his cabin or Lori's much bigger home. They laughed together, cooked meals, and shared quiet evenings filled with meaningful glances and soft touches.

Jennifer would join them on weekends, her vibrant laughter filling the spaces of Simon's once solitary home. The trio would venture out into the town, attending community events, or simply enjoying the joy of being together. Jennifer's presence was a constant reminder of what they fought for—family, love, and a future unmarred by fear.

Outings often ended at Lori's house, where the comfort of routine wrapped around them like a well-loved quilt. They'd gather in the living room, the television playing some movie no one really watched, content in their own companionship.

As days flowed into nights, and nights back into days, the trio wove a new tapestry of life—one filled with hope and the kind of peace that comes from enduring the storm and emerging stronger on the other side. Simon, once a loner, found himself part of a family, and the knowledge settled in his chest like a missing piece finally slotted into place.

The chapter of their lives marked by gunfire and desperation slowly closed, giving way to softer moments and the kind of love that heals all wounds. In Hart County, among the rolling hills and under the vast Kentucky sky, Simon, Lori, and Jennifer discovered what it meant to live fully—not just to survive, but to thrive.

Simon's line cast a perfect arc over the placid surface of Green River, the lure breaking the water with a gentle plop. Beside him on the sun-warmed bank, Jennifer watched with keen eyes, her rod in hand. They had fallen into a comfortable rhythm, one that came not just from countless casts and retrievals but from the growing bond between them.

"Think you'll out-fish me today?" Simon teased, his blue eyes crinkling at the corners as he glanced at the young woman who reminded him so much of Lori.

"Wouldn't be the first time," Jennifer shot back, her green eyes sparkling with the challenge. She was vibrant, and full of life—a stark contrast to the somber memories that often clouded Simon's thoughts. But here, in these shared moments, the shadows seemed to recede.

"True enough," he admitted with a chuckle. The river flowed by, oblivious to the significant shifts happening on its banks. As their lines drifted with the current, so did the conversation—meandering through topics light and heavy, building a bridge across the gap that danger and trauma had carved between them.

The sun dipped lower, casting a golden hue over the landscape. It was during times like these, when the world slowed down and let them breathe, that Simon found himself grateful for this unexpected family.

Back at the house, Lori settled on the couch, her legs tucked beneath her. She watched Simon and Jennifer return, their laughter seeping in through the open windows before they even crossed the threshold. There was an ease between them now, a closeness that filled Lori with a mingled sense of relief and affection.

"Caught dinner!" Jennifer announced triumphantly, holding up a stringer of fish with pride.

"Only because she cheats," Simon grumbled playfully, ruffling Jennifer's hair as she dodged away with a laugh.

"Mom, can you believe him?" Jennifer appealed, seeking an alliance in their ongoing friendly feud.

"Of course, I can," Lori replied, her Kentucky drawl wrapping around her words like warm honey. "You're my daughter. We Hawkins women are known for our fishing prowess."

As the evening unfolded, the trio found themselves immersed in the glow of the television screen. A movie played some action flick that none of them followed, serving more as a backdrop to their quiet camaraderie. Simon sat in the middle, an arm draped over Jennifer's shoulders, her head resting against his chest. On his other side, Lori leaned into him, her body fitting against his like two pieces of a puzzle long separated.

Lori caught Simon's eye, sharing a silent conversation. In his gaze, she saw appreciation—a thankfulness for the simple act of being together. He pulled Lori closer, placing a tender kiss on her forehead before turning to drop a similar affection on Jennifer's crown.

"Love you, kiddo," he murmured, the words carrying the weight of unspoken promises—to protect, to cherish, to be present.

"Love you too, Simon," Jennifer responded, her voice soft and sure. She then snuggled deeper into the cocoon they'd created, safe in the knowledge that here, with these people, she was home.

Lori's heart swelled as she watched the interaction, the love between Simon and her daughter clear and unguarded. It was a balm to the wounds of the past, a sign that they were moving forward, healing together. And in those quiet moments, Lori knew that no matter what uncertainties lay ahead, they would face them as a family—one forged not by blood but by the fierce, enduring bonds of love and survival.

Jennifer's laughter echoed across the field, a jubilant sound that mingled with the thud of soccer balls and the encouraging shouts from the young players. Lori, standing at the sidelines, watched her daughter move with effortless grace, directing the drill with a confidence that belied her years. The afternoon sun cast a warm glow over the scene, and for a moment, Lori allowed herself the luxury of simply basking in the normalcy of it all.

"Mom?" Jennifer jogged over, her green eyes bright with excitement. "Can we talk?"

"Of course, honey." Lori smiled, gesturing toward the nearby bench. They sat, the cadence of life continuing around them—children chasing after goals, parents chatting idly on the grassy outskirts.

"Simon's been amazing," Jennifer started, twisting a blade of grass between her fingers. "I mean, after everything... He's been there, you know?"

Lori nodded, her heart swelling. "I know. He's been our rock."

"I love him, Mom." Jennifer's voice was earnest, her gaze steady. "Not just like a hero or something, but like... like he could be Dad. Is it weird to say that?"

Tears welled up in Lori's eyes as she pulled Jennifer into an embrace. "No, baby, it's not weird. It's beautiful. I love him too. So much."

They held each other, the future unspoken but deeply understood—a mosaic of hope pieced together by shared affection and resilience.

"Look, there's Loran!" Jennifer pointed across the field where Loran Smith stood alone, her indigo-tinged skin making her distinct from the crowd. Her slight frame seemed even smaller against the expanse of the pitch, but her presence was undeniable.

The late afternoon sun cast long shadows across the soccer field as the girls of Hart County's youth team chased the ball with tireless energy. Loran stood to the side, her hands tucked into the pockets of her faded jeans, eyes tracking the game with quiet interest. Her indigo-tinged skin, a mark of her lineage from Troublesome Creek, glowed subtly in the golden light.

"Momma, look," Addie tugged at her mother's sleeve, her gaze fixed on the solitary figure by the sidelines. "Miss Loran looks sad all by herself. Can we go talk to her?"

Her mother hesitated, her eyes flicking towards the other parents who chatted amongst themselves. Addie's insistence was undeniable; it was one of those demands only a six-year-old could make with such conviction. With a sigh, she nodded and took Addie's hand, approaching Loran with tentative steps.

"Hey there, Loran, isn't it?" she ventured, offering a warm smile that seemed to ease the invisible barrier between them.

Loran's response was a slow nod, her deep mountain drawl rolling softly off her tongue. "Yes'm, that's me. How can I help y'all?"

"Addie just wanted to say hello," her mother said, gesturing to the little girl whose beaming face mirrored none of the adults' initial apprehension.

"Hello, Miss Loran! I know you. You are one of the heroes at the party," Addie chirped, untroubled by the difference in their appearances.

"I guess I am," Loran squatted down and addressed the little girl.

As they conversed, Loran's insightful comments and gentle humor charmed Addie's mother. It wasn't long before the other mothers, drawn by the sound of laughter, drifted over. One by one, their preconceptions melted away, replaced by genuine admiration for Loran's intelligence and easygoing nature.

From that day onward, Loran was no longer an outsider but an accepted member of the community—a transformation that unfolded as naturally as the changing seasons around them. That transformation extended to the rest of her family as well.

Meanwhile, Simon kept his distance from the field, observing the interactions with an unreadable expression. His muscular frame leaned against the fence, arms crossed, his sharp blue eyes scanning the surroundings with an alertness that never quite faded.

Despite his outward appearance of relaxed vigilance, his mind was always racing—processing every new face, every car that drove by a little too slowly. He couldn't shake the instincts honed by years in the CIA, nor did he want to. The safety of Lori, Jennifer, and this small town they were part of depended on it.

Over time, however, with each passing week of undisturbed peace, Simon's guarded posture softened. He began to join Lori on walks through the town, his hand finding hers with a natural ease that spoke volumes of their growing bond. They'd stop to chat with locals, and share laughs with shopkeepers, and even though Simon's responses remained terse, they were tinged with a warmth that had been absent before.

In the evenings, he would sit on the porch of his cabin with Lori nestled beside him, watching the stars emerge in the twilight sky. They spoke little during these moments, content in the silent assurance of each other's presence.

It was in these quiet times that Simon allowed himself to truly relax, letting the barriers around his heart crumble bit by bit. With Lori, he found a love that was fierce and tender, a balm for the scars left by a life spent in the shadows. And in the laughter of Jennifer, echoing through the house as she played video or board games with Loran, Simon heard the sweet promise of a future he once thought unattainable.

And so, life went on, with soccer practices and shared meals, with new friendships and deepening love, all under the watchful eye of a man who had finally found something worth protecting beyond duty or country—his newfound family.

The bell above the door to Framwald's restaurant chimed as Simon and Lori made their weekly pilgrimage to the corner table that had become their own. The aroma of strong coffee and sizzling bacon wrapped around them like a comforting embrace from an old friend.

"Your usual, Simon?" Laura, the waitress with a smile as warm as the pie on display, called out before they'd even slid into their seats.

"Make it two," Simon replied, his gaze sweeping the familiar faces in the diner, always alert despite the casual setting.

As they settled in, the low hum of conversation from neighboring tables invariably turned their way, and one by one, patrons approached. An elderly man with hands gnarled by years of farm work patted Simon's shoulder with reverence. "Can't say thank you enough for bringin' our girls home," he said, his voice thick with emotion.

"Wasn't just me," Simon said, nodding toward Lori with a proud tilt of his head. "Lori here, she took a bullet but never stopped fighting."

Lori blushed a deep scarlet, ducking her head to hide her embarrassment. She was a hero in these folks' eyes, but she felt more like a mother who'd simply done what was necessary to protect her child.

"Still," the old farmer insisted, "we're mighty grateful."

The interruptions were frequent, each one a testament to the town's gratitude, but also a reminder of the violence that had brought them all together. Lori and Simon exchanged knowing looks, their private connection an unspoken conversation.

As the last of the well-wishers returned to their meals, Simon reached across the table, his calloused hand covering Lori's. "You okay?" he asked, his blue eyes searching hers.

"Always," she replied, her voice steady despite the flutter in her chest. They might have been talking about the interruptions, or the shared past that still haunted their dreams, but either way, the answer was true. Together, they were always okay.

Time passed like the gentle flow of the Green River, smoothing the jagged edges of painful memories and leaving behind a landscape reshaped but still familiar. Simon, Lori, and

Jennifer found a rhythm to their days, a new normal in the afterglow of chaos.

In the evenings, as the sun dipped below the horizon, painting the sky in shades of fiery orange and calming purple, Simon, Lori, and Jennifer would sit on the porch of Simon's cabin. The day's end brought a coolness that whispered promises of tomorrow, and they would talk about everything and nothing until the stars claimed the heavens.

This was their life now—simple, full of love, and fiercely protected by a man who had learned that the greatest adventure wasn't in the adrenaline-fueled battles of his past, but in the quiet, everyday acts of courage that defined their present.

"Here's to new beginnings," Lori would say, raising her glass in a silent toast to the future.

"And to peace," Simon would add, his gaze lingering on the faces of the two people who had become his world.

"May it be long and sweet," Jennifer would chime in, her green eyes sparkling with hope.

And in that moment, as they clinked glasses and let the serenity of Hart County wash over them, they knew that no matter what lay ahead, they had already won the greatest victory—they had each other, and they were home.

One evening as the three sat on Lori's porch watching as the sun set and the lightning bugs began to fill the light with flickers of green-tinted sparks, Simon's phone rang. Worry thick in the voice at the other end.

"Simon, the boys are missing. They were in North Dakota sightseeing, and they have called home every day. We ain't heard from them in a week. They are not answering, and we are scared. We need to go find them," Loran pleaded.

ABOUT THE AUTHOR

Larry Burks, a retired USAF Security Forces Technical Sergeant and former Operations Manager at Texas Tech University's Museum, brings a lifetime of diverse experiences to his debut novel.

Born in Lubbock, Texas in 1961, Larry joined the United States Air Force shortly after graduating high school. His 20-year military career took him across the Southern United States and around the world, including tours in South Korea and

Northern Italy. He also served in Kuwait between the two Gulf Wars. These diverse experiences and global perspectives inform his storytelling, bringing authenticity and depth to his fiction. Larry currently resides in Lubbock with his wife of over 40 years, where he continues to draw inspiration from his rich life experiences.

If you have a moment, please consider rating this book on Amazon. Your feedback will provide valuable insight into my performance and help potential readers determine if this book aligns with their interests.

My father used to say when I would doodle, "Boy, the only thing you could ever draw is flies." If you're familiar with country expressions, you'll understand his meaning. I never showed him my writings; perhaps I should have – he could have critiqued them with another colorful country colloquialism. With your support, maybe he'll look down on me and say, "Boy, you done good."

Please feel free to reach out to me at lburks.writer@gmail.com with your thoughts on the book or simply to introduce yourself. I'll respond to as many emails as possible. You can also follow me on Facebook by searching for "@larry.b.writer," where I'll keep fans updated on my life and upcoming works.

Currently, I'm working on the follow-up to "Lightning Strikes Twice." I hope you enjoy "Lightning Strikes Twice" enough to continue following our team's adventures as they work together to make the world a better place, while also introducing you to locations like Hart County, Kentucky.